THE LAST FLEET

THE LAST FLEET
BOOK 2

JOSHUA T. CALVERT

PROLOGUE

"The Grad Forest is cursed, Ma!"

Masha gave her eldest son, Artiom, a scowl across the breakfast table and nodded as discreetly as she could in the direction of his little sister, who was busy eyeing her tiny protein bar and then sullenly biting into it. Seeing her little disappointed face in the process broke Masha's heart anew, as it did every morning.

"A new job," she tried to change the subject. "Now that's something. Double pay, I can even buy us some vitamin injections and mineral tabs with that."

"The best thing would be a ticket away from this suka mudball," her son sighed, getting up to tighten the rubber band that held her small, splintered kitchen window in its frame. It had come loose and the metal frame rattled in the wind.

I know, she replied in thought, gulping down the rest of her own protein bar. *If there were any ships flying to us at all, we could certainly never pay for the few seats - no matter what kind of job.*

"We'll do what we can," she said aloud, pushing

No, she decided. For these very reasons, she hadn't hesitated for a moment when the governor's recruiter had knocked on her container.

"Here we go," she said aloud, snapping herself out of her thoughts. One last time, she checked the brittle rubber band that held the kitchen window in its rusty frame, then grabbed her rain cape from the coat rack and threw it over herself.

"Ma!" protested Artiom scornfully, as only a pubescent teenager could, as she checked the fit of his jacket and his sister's.

"Do you want to show up at Uncle Zvarev's with a rash?" She pulled their hoods over both of their heads and then shooed them out.

The wind howled like a whole chorus of wolves as soon as she opened the door, and a swarm of dark brown sleet flakes blew into the living room. Quickly, she squeezed through the crack behind her children and pulled the door shut behind her. The magnetic lock had not been working for a long time, and even if it had, the few hours of electricity during the day would not be enough to feed the battery with any significant amount of energy. If the many gangs and mobs of the industrial levels wanted to break in, they would do so anyway and would not be stopped by a locked door. The best protection against burglars on Arcturus was to own nothing of value - something that was probably the only simple thing on this godforsaken world.

With her hood up, she walked to her rickety electric cart, which she had bought from one of the nomadic junk dealers only two years ago and which miraculously still worked. It was parked right next to the rusty charging station, which was once again flashing red and begging for power.

Oleana's plate in her direction until it touched her small chest. "Eat up, dear, we've got to get going soon."

"But Ma, we have to get to the mine. If we don't, Overseer Gorn will beat the crap out of us!" protested Artiom, and the very idea made Masha angry and sad at the same time because she felt so helpless.

"No. You're coming with me to Arcturusgrad. I'll drop you off at Uncle Zvarev's place while I have the new job." She raised a finger. "Don't argue with me. I won't let you be enslaved by that pig Gorn in the mines even one day longer, you understand?"

"But..."

"No buts. You will not end up as thieves or slaves!"

"Ma, everyone on Arcturus is a thief or a slave. That's what you always say yourself."

"You're not everyone, though, honey. You're something special. You just need a chance to prove it."

Artiom crossed his much too thin arms in front of his chest, but finally nodded.

"Uncle Zvarev smells like old feet," Oleana muttered sullenly, eyeing her last bit of protein bar with a deep contempt that a six-year-old shouldn't even be capable of yet. At least, in a better world than this godforsaken one.

"If you help him at home, I'm sure he'll have more time for personal hygiene." Masha got up and put away her plastic plates, which had been in use for so long that the many scratches and stains on them formed intricate patterns. She put everything in the sink unit and set the automatic start that would initiate the wash cycle as soon as her container was supplied with water. Maybe today, maybe tomorrow.

"Do we have to take the road through Grad Forest?" asked Artiom, looking genuinely glum.

Masha gave her son a *not-in-front-of-Oleana* look, and he covered his little sister's ears.

"The forest is cursed, Ma. Everybody knows it. There's hardly any traffic on the road anymore because people are disappearing there."

"You shouldn't listen so much to the break talk at the mine." She waved it off and pointed to the narrow bag next to his chair. "Now get that in the car, we're about to leave."

While her fifteen-year-old son rolled his eyes in resignation and followed her request, she looked out through the small kitchen window at the settlement. Clunky former spaceship containers piled on top of each other as if giants had broken off an ill-fated game of Jenga. Rusty and stained, they gleamed in the first morning light looking dirty as ash from all the sleet in the air. That there really had been ash mixed in with the snow, which couldn't decide whether it preferred to be rain after al was not at all unlikely; after all, the iron mines of Stolbov were only a few miles away and their chimneys smoke day and night.

Double pay, one year, Masha thought, thanking Go for the opportunity. If she did well, at least it would gi her two children a chance to get out of here. Anywhere. third of her salary would then go for the right bribes a the rest she would spend just for the passage of her cl dren to the nearest system, but it was all worth it to l After all, the worries about them couldn't be greater tl here, in the hell called Arcturus. What could they exp here? If they were lucky, they would not die of tube losis or heavy metal poisoning, and they would surpass average age of forty years of life. But for what? For longer servitude in the mines or the 'chance' to work way up to overseer and sell their own souls by maltrea others for more rations and money?

The last Fleet

Artiom took a seat in the passenger seat, the only other seat in the car, and put his sister on his lap as usual. There were no seat belts, nor was there a heater or anything else that promised comfort but consumed energy. There was a steering wheel, a brake, and the accelerator pedal. Windshield wipers were also a luxury that the junk dealer had eliminated when he assembled the car, but she wasn't about to complain. If she drove fast enough, the drips and melting flakes disappeared quickly enough that she could see reasonably well.

"I don't want to go to Uncle Zverev's," Oleana complained, sniffling.

"It's all right, Oleanskaya," she coaxed the little girl and started the engine, which began to hum softly. "It's not for long."

That was a lie, because the work order was for a year, and since she was to go to the spaceport of Arcturusgrad, it might be a matter of removing the vegetation barriers - which, given their decrepit condition, could mean a very, very long repair process.

The Grad Forest lay like a dark patch in the landscape between their container settlement and the planet's capital, which they could often see in the evening as a red glow in the sky through the kitchen window, if soot or rain wasn't too heavy. A single road with two lanes in each direction ran through it, dating back to the early days of colonization when massive amounts of money had flowed into Arcturus from the Solar Union to build up the infrastructure. At that time, it had connected the spaceport on the other side of the forest with the solar farms on this side, of which not much remained these days except the weathered steel pillars on which the pivoting panel clusters had been mounted. Since then, the road had become less important, with little funding available to maintain the road network after the complete blockade of planet in 2205 in the wake of the antimatter attack on the hostile Kerhal. Now it consisted of potholes, overgrown weeds, and dangerous cracks where tires could disappear.

The space port was the reason that Augustgrad had come into being exactly where it was now: in a wide plain with two rivers and fertile soil, but sealed off to the forest after several gang raids and secured with high walls. This was finally the final nail in the coffin for the road, where gangs were still roaming. At night, they could be heard shooting and partying there. The fact that people often disappeared in that area did not surprise Masha, especially since those who strayed there could only be described as stupid or naive.

Now, however, things would be different. The recruiting officer had handed her a simple key card, along with one thousand rjubels - one thousand! - and assured her that the gate in the wall to the spaceport would be open as long as she identified herself with the key card. So all she had to do was drive - fast enough, because of the gangs - and not stop. Then they would be in the shelter of the spaceport, from which they saw shuttles rising every few days like distant fireflies in the night. Zverev would pick up her children at the West Gate, as arranged. The fact that the recruiting officer had told her to come alone didn't matter to her at all. The children couldn't stay alone, so her new employer would have to live with her driving them to the West Gate before she took her job. The only liberties on Arcturus were those taken. Asking permission here was about as promising as seeking basic human rights or social security.

Masha steered her car rumbling along the gravel road between the containers of her settlement, which were crisscrossed and seemed to follow no pattern, until they reached the edge and the entrance to the ring road. On the large traffic circle, in addition to a few horse-drawn carts, there were a few other cars and buses taking miners north. One road went north around the forest, one south, and the third turnoff went straight through. This early in the morning, the Grad looked like a black hole in the dark blue landscape. Even the flickering of fires or the flashes of fired guns were not visible today.

"Ma," Artiom said accusingly.

"Superstition is for Kalklingers," she said with feigned lightheartedness, turning onto the forest road. "The drive won't even take an hour, and then we'll be there. You'll see the spaceport, from the inside. Isn't that great?"

Artiom merely grumbled sullenly, but said nothing more. Masha missed him already, and her little Oleana, who had fallen asleep on his chest. It would break their hearts when they learned from Zverev that they would never see her again - and it was already breaking her heart. But only the love between a mother and her children could ensure that what was painful had to be done to spare them suffering in the future.

She rounded a few potholes that looked more like craters, and then passed the wreck of the *ASS Volgograd*, the colony's only warship, which at the time was trying to oppose the blockading forces of the Solar Union and had been lying broken apart at the edge of the forest for two hundred years. In the twilight of dawn it looked like the skeleton of a dead primeval monster, from which young trees already grew and whose skin was covered by creepers. Everything that had been movable in any way had long since been stolen by the gangs, despite the radioactive contamination of the wreckage, and so today it took a lot of imagination to recognize in it the remains of a spaceship.

As soon as she drove into the Grad Forest, it became abruptly darker. The trees here were dense and the forest floor was an impenetrable thicket of bushes and shrubs, many species of which came from Terra and had displaced the native ones. The local ecosystem had never recovered from this, which seemed to fit in a sad way with the development of the entire colony.

After ten minutes of driving as fast as Masha dared with all the road damage, she saw red taillights ahead that didn't seem to be moving. Then more and more appeared, extending to the other lanes as well.

"Is that a traffic jam?" asked Artiom incredulously.

"Looks like it," she muttered in reply, squinting her eyes. In fact, the entire street was jammed.

"Do they all have the same job as you, Mommy?" asked Oleana, rubbing her eyes sleepily as they came to a stop at the end of the far right queue. Artiom was silent and looked tensely into the dark forest.

They should not be stopping here.

"Sit tight, lock up behind me," Masha said, pulling her hood over her head and getting out. The driver of the car in front of her was standing in the sleet, talking to the one in the neighboring car. She walked up to them both and raised a hand. "Dobroye utro."

"Privet," one of them said, the other merely nodded at her.

Masha pointed to the blocked flow of hundreds of vehicles. They had to be from all over the solar plane, there were so many of them. "Are you here for a job, too?"

"Da, but from the front it says the gate to the spaceport is closed and no one can get in," said the more talkative one, an unshaven man whose age was hard to judge from his face in the shadow of his hood.

"We shouldn't be standing here," she opined.

The last Fleet

"We've been standing here for half an hour and nothing has happened. Probably the gangs partied too hard tonight. It's going to start soon enough. They paid so much dough, I doubt they'll let us get away with it without callused hands and bulged discs." The two laughed mirthlessly and then ignored her again.

Masha returned to her car and was about to signal Artiom to unlock the door again when she heard a loud whistle above her and leaned her head back. Along with all the others waiting outside, she stared up into the dark sky, from where a small blue dot was approaching, rapidly growing larger. Then it disappeared as suddenly as it had appeared, and there was a single, deafening clap of thunder. The air seemed to shimmer for a moment and then it became dead silent.

And dark.

All vehicle lights had disappeared and the many cars stood there in absolute darkness like corpses of steel and plastic. Masha could barely see her hand in front of her eyes, except for a shimmering haze caused by her own breath.

"MA!" she heard Artiom call out, noting that he had apparently been calling for her for some time. His voice sounded muffled through the door of the wagon, the outline of which she could not make out.

"Stay in the car!" she called back, walking cautiously in the direction of his voice, on the basis of which she tried to distinguish the silhouette of her vehicle from that of the others.

"What's wrong, Ma?"

Artiom's voice was barely intelligible.

"STAY IN THE CAR!" she yelled back, as more and more people had now gotten out. Their voices filled the night like a chorus of fearful whispers and murmurs.

Then came the eyes.

The first she saw in the darkness of the forest, a single pair of red eyes, like those of a demon. At first it was pitch black, then suddenly they were there. And more followed. A few dozen at first, then hundreds, as if someone had flipped a switch. Masha felt like she was in a horror sequence and bumped her knee on something cold that turned out to be her car - at least Artiom's voice was much louder, sounding very close.

"Ma! What is it?"

"Stay in the car," she breathed, her voice vibrating with fear. Louder, she shouted, "Don't come out!"

She groped her way along the brittle bodywork until she reached the door and braced herself so that her children wouldn't cross her after all, praying that they wouldn't get out on the other side.

The pairs of red eyes approached and were accompanied by the rustling of undergrowth and bushes, like a wave approaching slowly but inexorably.

Masha was frozen, unable to move. Her eyes, however, darted back and forth in a panicked attempt to understand what was going on. Was it the gangs? But then why that red glow? The criminals were usually loud and rowdy.

"Who's there?" someone shouted into the darkness from the invisible crowd beside her.

More voices rose.

"What does that mean?"

"Was that an EMP?"

"The damn government!"

"My car won't open!"

"Who is that?"

Whether it was the familiar sounds of other people or her rational thoughts taking over again; Masha shook the rigidity from herself and frantically groped for the door handle. She yanked it open and called out in a clenched voice, "Come out, quick! Artiom! Oleana!"

"Mommy!" Her daughter sobbed.

"It's okay, my dear, you have to climb out with your brother to me now."

Masha looked over the roof to the red eyes that had almost reached the embankment beside the road. The silhouettes of those to whom they belonged were still merged with the darkness. Her only chance now was to flee in the opposite direction.

She glanced over her shoulder and her heart sank. The red eyes were also on the other side of the street, where apparently other men and women were seeking their salvation. They certainly didn't get far, because all at once a multiple clicking started, continued a hundred times in all directions, followed by the sound of falling bodies. She didn't hear any screams, just the dull clap of people falling onto asphalt.

Only now was the silence broken by loud shouts and screams as the rest of the vehicle drivers panicked and let their cerebellum propel them into unsubstantiated flight. The clicking increased, as did the clapping and rumbling. Mixed in between was the hollow whine of metal on metal as the projectiles they were being shot at slammed into the cars where they missed their targets.

"Stay inside!" she yelled over the din to her children, shoving the tangle of arms back into her car.

A movement out of the corner of her eye made her look up and stare directly into a pair of red eyes. They belonged to a figure whose outline was more of a hunch, a soft glimmer, invisible almost.

She didn't even notice the barrel of the gun before it clicked.

1
GUNTER

Gunter's first two days after the arrival of Captain Akwa Marquandt were anything but pleasant. He had to take care of his 'host', whom he had to feed and wash, for the man had done nothing wrong and was a poor pig himself. If there was any truth to his forged story, he was from Kerrhain and had been involved in a robbery there that did not go as planned. Afterwards, his prisoner transport was attacked (miraculously, there were no casualties among the policemen) and he was dragged here. Well, *abducted* was the term Gunter chose, but his host had called it a liberation, after all he had a job here and a reasonably tolerable income.

From Gunter's point of view, the technician had merely traded one prison for another; after all, he had no chance of ever escaping from Cerberus. The low salaries and the lack of a passport made sure of that - after all, there was no issuing authority for miles around. Not that he doubted the Broker could forge one, but why should he? His flock worked and died here, living just well enough not to complain and always staying below the fear threshold. They guarded his secrets and cooperated in their protection - for their own safety. A perfect web of mutual benefit, like insects that multiplied and thrived around feces and rotting dirt.

A disgusting, despicable place, in Gunter's opinion. It reeked of fear and dishonor.

To familiarize himself with his new surroundings, he spent an hour at a time alternating between the tiny quarters, which by now reeked of human exhalations because the air conditioners were calibrated for only one occupant, and forays into the immediate station area. The corridors were mostly narrow and unlined, so the walls were made of cold rock that reeked of moisture and mold as water from the air conditioners dripped from countless leaks. Entire squads of maintenance technicians were busy crawling through the narrow tubes in the wall, patching what could be patched - but it was a battle against windmills, chasing a fake rabbit. Impossible to win, yet just enough to keep from perishing, and just enough to maintain motivation. After all, no one wanted to suffocate or fall ill from the many mold spores.

The 'residents' of Cerberus, whom he considered more like serfs of the Broker, hardly talked to each other when they were outside their quarters or the bars, and their gazes remained lowered. Not attracting attention and avoiding contact with others, lest by chance they overheard something that might tempt someone else to want to eliminate witnesses.

On his third evening on station, Docking Bay B-2 once again crouched on a truck, pretending to take a break and sip his coffee. The traitor's daughter still hadn't cast off - unless she'd taken a different route off this unholy rock. Her *Ferret* frigate, at any rate, still lay on its ledge as before.

Gunter still had no idea whatsoever how he was going to comply with High Lord Andal's order and find the Orb body, let alone *steal* it. After all, he couldn't question anyone unless he wanted to take the risk of once again overpowering and taking someone hostage in a corner of the station where a camera had just gone down and maintenance crews were running late. If there was one thing he had learned as a Marine, it was not to push his luck. Once something unlikely had gone well, you took your winnings and didn't gamble them away on the next opportunity hoping for a streak.

His hostage had informed him (in exchange for a sandwich) that most of the outer station bars were exempt from 'security surveillance'. Not because the Broker had had a weak moment of patronage, but because of sabotage. There had probably been repeated acts of sabotage against cameras and microphones in the workers' meeting places, so that at some point repairs had become too time-consuming and costly. Since then, the administrator probably accepted that there were some black holes in the station where the ordinary workers could blow off steam. A smart move, when Gunter thought back to his basic training. Long after that deprivation-filled time, he had learned that the instructors had always known when they had stolen away from the barracks area to go have a go in the nearby town. They just hadn't said anything because they had been aware that young soldiers needed an outlet for the pressure and frustration they inevitably faced during training.

The administrator had probably had a similar thought and so accepted an unsolvable problem, at the very welcome price of boosting morale.

So, after two hours of work - his cover had to be maintained, after all - he walked out of docking bay B-2 and left it in the direction of the *Double X*, his hostage's regular bar, where mostly 'cavers' bustled about, as he had them explain to him. These were the longest-serving technicians on Cerberus, who had the dubious honor of serving in the planetoid's equalization caverns and keeping the life-support lines there in good working order.

In front of the run-down establishment, which had taken up residence in the rooms of a former food counter from the early days of the station, stood two goons with tattooed faces, trying hard to look as if they were merely talking. It couldn't be more obvious that they were the bouncers here.

"Evenin'," he mumbled to them, and they eyed him with a mixture of irritation and disdain. They didn't seem to want to stop him, however, and so he walked through the double doors of scratched steel into the interior. What met him first was the drone of the completely overloaded life support system. Somewhere in the blowers, loose parts were flying around, making for an unpleasant rattling that mingled like a disturbance with the muted beats of some old synth song.

The fifty or so patrons stood on the crumbling tiles of the floor between a long wooden-looking bar that had seen better days. A lone bartender, who looked like he could grind rocks into dust with his meaty hands, poured beers with surprising calm for the crowd at his counter.

Gunter fought his way through the small groups of sweaty workers, some still wearing their stained coveralls and helmets here and there, getting the day's experiences off their chests. At the bar, he drew attention to himself with a raised hand that was concealed in a work glove to hide its synthetic origin.

"Haven't seen you here before," the bartender greeted

him, setting down a pint glass, a whole gush of which spilled over the rim.

"New shift, B-2," Gunter explained. "Just in from Kerrhain."

"Ah. Convicted?"

"Escaped from my wife."

"Not mutually exclusive, after all." The bartender laughed like an out-of-control bass and turned back to other patrons.

Gunter picked up his beer and walked to the center of the room, tuning out the many conversations and adjusting his acoustic filters that were in his ear canal via neural computer. The software blocked out all the constant background noise for him - the rattling of loose parts in the air conditioning, the roar of the fans, the drone in the pipes and the two-four time of the music. What remained were the voices of the guests, lumps on a carpet of artificial silence.

It took him twenty minutes to find a conversation that seemed relevant enough for the little time he had. He walked over to the two workers standing a little off to the side, who were visibly older than the rest and from whom others seemed to keep a respectful distance.

"Evening," he mumbled, as he had at the entrance, trying to imitate the somewhat leering Kerrhain accent. "You're the silverbacks around here, huh?"

"Uh, what?" asked the older of the two, whose upper lip was adorned with a powerful mustache. The other, lanky and with drooping bags under his eyes, eyed him up and down.

"The old timers. I'm new here and heard that only the oldest workers are allowed down into the equalization caverns. Cavers, huh?"

The looks on their faces turned somber.

"Oh, all's well, mates," Gunter said, raising his beer glass defensively. "I'm one of you."

"Oh?" Mustache made no effort to hide his disbelief and seemed to already have a "fuck off!" on his lips.

"Yeah, technician with A-10 clearance on Gastral-II. I spent two years unscrewing, cleaning and screwing on gas pressure valves. If I hadn't seen my damn bonus on the credstick every first of the month, I wouldn't have believed the dirty job was a promotion," he lied, hoping what little knowledge he had of a total of three days of punishment work at the Andalian Fleet asteroid station was enough.

"You were in the fleet?" asked Eyebag incredulously.

"Not enlisted, conscripted. Worked on a Light Hauler before that."

"A smuggler, then." Mustache barked a laugh and toasted him.

A smuggler, then.

"Free shipmaster," Gunter objected, trying for a grin. He would have loved to extend his forearm sockets and slice this scum with his monofilament blades.

They clinked glasses and took a few sips.

"Should be off in a minute, though, kid," Eyebag said in a voice wet with beer. Ironically, he was at least a head shorter than Gunter and half as wide. "We've worked hard to keep the peace here. If the rest of the morons around here are under the impression that any nitwit can slobber on us..."

"All right, I'll be gone in a minute. You guys can pretend to chase me off then," he suggested. "I just want to know what it's like down there with you guys. You hear all kinds of stuff. Secrecy and all that."

"It's a shit job. The gas pressure lines keep clogging up and then there's the howling," Mustache explained.

"The howling?"

"Yep. Sounds like there's a choir of girls sobbing their heads off."

"In the equalization chambers?" wanted Gunter to know.

"Yep, some resonance effect or the jefe is trying to scare us into working faster. There are rumors that he doesn't like us having the peace and quiet down there and wants us to stay on our toes."

"Well, it works, anyway," Eyebag interjected. "I hate it. Every morning at the hustler's dock, the same yowling. Gets to you."

"Does that shit even work anymore? With the low pressure on the air streams and in the water lines, I can't imagine you guys are doing a good job down there." Gunter already feared he had gone too far with his gruff manner, but Mustache merely scowled and leaned forward a bit.

"They don't give a shit. They just want us to do what's on the work schedule. It doesn't make any sense at all, but we've spent over ten years here learning not to ask questions. You should get in the habit, too, Kepal."

"The plans don't make sense? Oh, come on. That's what I used to say to my foreman. In the end, though, it turned out that everything would have blown up in my face if I'd done it differently."

"Nah, seriously," Eyebag returned. "Two-thirds of the areas we're not even allowed to walk. We have to ignore leak reports and instead worry about shit we've already gone over three times. We polish one side of the diamond while the other rots away under our eyes."

"Don't you guys get your plans from the administrator himself?" Gunter inquired.

"Every morning before he goes on duty. He can't help

himself, the fucking eunuch." Mustache's anger seemed to fade abruptly, as if he were waking up from a dream. "Now you'd better get out of here, we've got a couple of retards staring at us already, and I'm sure they'll want to bug us next."

"If you want me to beat someone's brains in for you guys, just give me a sign. Cavers have to stick together, after all." Gunter toasted them and they actually returned the gesture before he turned and headed back toward the counter to get another beer. His Toxoplasma filters cleared up with the alcohol faster than he could feel warmth in his fingers, but he still kept up appearances. He calmly finished the second beer as well, paid with his hostage's credstick, and then disappeared again.

The trip had been more fruitful than expected. He now knew that the administrator personally briefed the most senior workers before they went on duty in the equalization caverns. Every morning, presumably at this hustler dock, wherever that was supposed to be. He didn't think he'd find that designation anywhere on any of the station's official plans, analog or AR variants. But he still had a host who had been here a few years and was familiar with colloquial place names.

Back in the cramped quarters, he wrinkled his nose at the stench of sweat and unwashed hair. His hostage (Gunter had not asked his name, because a name generated sympathy, and he could not afford that right now) was still sitting on the small cot that called itself a bed. His hands and feet were bound and tied together behind his back. Apparently he hadn't even tried to attempt an escape in this condition.

"What's the hustler's dock?" asked Gunter as he untied

The last Fleet

the bonds so his host could move. Conveniently, it had occurred to him early on that there was no point whatsoever in fighting.

"The hustler's dock?"

"Yeah, that's what I just said."

"Uh, that's over on the other side of Beta Bay, the last dock above B-8. Doesn't have an official name because it was never completed," his hostage explained, rubbing his wrists. "It's where hookers and stuff hang out. Men, women, mutants. So it's called the hustler's dock."

"And why would the cavers meet there?" echoed Gunter.

"I don't know. Maybe there's an entrance to the equalization caverns. Would make sense because they're between bays B and K on this side of the station."

"Is it possible there's no surveillance there?"

"Sure. Like I said, never finished it, and all the fuckbees don't like it when they're being watched. Same as their clientele," his hostage said, walking over to the sink, which basically just required him to stand up. He poured himself a glass of water and drank it down in one go. "What makes you think that anyway? Are you gonna go clown around?"

"No," Gunter growled. Once again he wondered if all those brutish workers on the Cerberus were such uneducated bumpkins as this guy was. The two cavers, at any rate, had not given the impression that their status as veterans was a sign of better behavior.

"Can you even do that?"

"Excuse me?"

"Well, you're pretty augmented, aren't you?"

"I'm not an augment zombie," the words escaped Gunter, and he felt anger welling up inside him, which, thanks to years of experience, he ground between his jaws and swallowed before it could manifest on his face. Maybe he had been too nice to the guy so far. "But I can show you what a cyberfist feels like to the face."

"No need." His hostage waved it off and took a half step back until his heels bumped against the bed frame and he swore in pain.

"I talked to two technicians who work in the equalization caverns. They were kind of angry about their jobs. Didn't seem like privileged employees, more like they got the short end of the stick."

"I don't understand that. They get double pay and work independently in small teams, while we get work schedules so tight we can't breathe," his counterpart grumbled, sitting dutifully back on the bed at Gunter's signal.

"They apparently find it creepy in the caverns, if I understood correctly, and they're only allowed to do certain things. That didn't sound very self-determined and free to me," he objected thoughtfully. "Besides, they are personally instructed by the administrator."

"That can't be, they were just bragging." The hostage waved it off and shook his head decisively. "The administrator doesn't bump toes with the pedestrians, he's got more important things to do than meddle in the day-to-day business of maintenance. Nah."

Gunter thought back to his conversation with the two technicians, trying to remember their facial expressions and the way they spoke.

"You're wrong. They were really pissed off and them telling me about it sounded more accusatory and angry than them showing me what great guys they are. They also knew I was new and their boasting probably wouldn't have told me anything."

"Why would old Goosens go into the hustler's dock to

give orders to a couple of vacuum rats? He's got his people for that and certainly better things to do," his hostage insisted. "They're screwing with you, dude."

"I don't think so. But there's only one way to find out."

"If you don't do my shifts, someone will notice."

"That's why you're going to do your shift."

"What?"

"You're going to do your shift and you're not going to tell anyone about me," Gunter ordered with a stern look that had caused many a recruit to piss their pants. Judging from his hostage's widened eyes, he wasn't far behind either.

"I'll take care of my business and you take care of yours, and when I'm done, I'll let you go back to your ways. No one will know about this, and you won't get in trouble with your bosses or me. How does that sound?"

"Uh. Good?"

"Right."

"So what are you going to do now?" his hostage asked, pulling his hands back when Gunter looked him in the eye.

I'm going to grab the administrator when he's not expecting it, and then I'm going to give him a good shake until a few apples fall from the branches that I can use to get ahead. I'm sure the smug son of a bitch won't expect anyone to be stupid enough to grab him on his turf. But I know where no one can go now, he thought, looking at his chronometer, which projected the current time into his field of vision. He could still spend the night getting ready and dealing with the station control system, which he still hadn't quite figured out. As soon as the night drew to a close, he would head out, spending as little time as possible outside his work area so as not to attract attention.

And then it would be Goosens' turn, the son of a bitch. If anyone knew where the Orb body was, it was the Broker's right-hand man, that much was certain. If all went well, he might even be able to do the universe another service and send him to the afterlife. That would be a relief for the whole Star Empire.

2

GAVIN

Gavin realized he had dozed off when his wrist terminal chirped. Sleepily, he rubbed his eyes and brought his forearm to his face.

"Yeah?" he muttered in an occupied voice.

"Hey, it's Bambam."

"What time is it?"

"I don't know, I don't keep track," the mechanic replied laconically.

Gavin flashed the chronometer into his field of vision. It was three a.m. Terran Standard Time, which was also their shipboard time.

"Were you going to tell me why you called me?" he asked.

"Ah, yep. I fixed the leak in the oxygen lines and hooked up the new supplies from the Demeter. Life support shouldn't shit out now."

"Good work. How far along is Dodger?"

"I don't know, she's not answering and I don't feel like going over to her..." Bambam said.

"She's still sleeping," Gavin answered his crewmate's unspoken question.

"What does Sphinx say?"

"That she's stable. Our transfusions have been sufficient, but she's also lost most of her smartnites with the major blood loss. She is no longer in a coma, so it's currently normal sleep. We will have to wait for her to wake up."

"Ke, ke." Bambam disconnected and silence fell again in the infirmary.

Gavin lowered his hand and looked at the sleeping Hellcat lying next to him on the hospital couch. Her face was completely relaxed in sleep, a sight he was unfamiliar with but enjoyed despite his concern for her. Her features appeared so even and finely drawn that he imagined how she might have turned out had she not been socialized in poor circumstances and later trained as a terrorist. She might have become a model for a New California or Yokatami fashion line and made a lot of money. She would have also been taken on in the Marine Guard Corps with a kiss on the hand, just like in the recruiting offices.

But that had not been meant to be. Instead, she lay there with her blonde hair combed to one side, looking stringy and tangled, while the other side of her skull was shaved to a few millimeters. Her body, which was merely in an undershirt and surgical pants, was well-toned and her breasts bulged stately under the polyamide silk. Normally, with so much attractiveness, he would have felt some desire, at least mild arousal, but nothing about his life was normal anymore. Instead, he merely saw the old-fashioned needles in her arm and the IV bag. The digitattoos, which covered her well-trained arms as if they were made of classic ink, reminded him that this woman was

PROLOGUE

"The Grad Forest is cursed, Ma!"

Masha gave her eldest son, Artiom, a scowl across the breakfast table and nodded as discreetly as she could in the direction of his little sister, who was busy eyeing her tiny protein bar and then sullenly biting into it. Seeing her little disappointed face in the process broke Masha's heart anew, as it did every morning.

"A new job," she tried to change the subject. "Now that's something. Double pay, I can even buy us some vitamin injections and mineral tabs with that."

"The best thing would be a ticket away from this suka mudball," her son sighed, getting up to tighten the rubber band that held her small, splintered kitchen window in its frame. It had come loose and the metal frame rattled in the wind.

I know, she replied in thought, gulping down the rest of her own protein bar. *If there were any ships flying to us at all, we could certainly never pay for the few seats - no matter what kind of job.*

"We'll do what we can," she said aloud, pushing

Oleana's plate in her direction until it touched her small chest. "Eat up, dear, we've got to get going soon."

"But Ma, we have to get to the mine. If we don't, Overseer Gorn will beat the crap out of us!" protested Artiom, and the very idea made Masha angry and sad at the same time because she felt so helpless.

"No. You're coming with me to Arcturusgrad. I'll drop you off at Uncle Zvarev's place while I have the new job." She raised a finger. "Don't argue with me. I won't let you be enslaved by that pig Gorn in the mines even one day longer, you understand?"

"But..."

"No buts. You will not end up as thieves or slaves!"

"Ma, everyone on Arcturus is a thief or a slave. That's what you always say yourself."

"You're not everyone, though, honey. You're something special. You just need a chance to prove it."

Artiom crossed his much too thin arms in front of his chest, but finally nodded.

"Uncle Zvarev smells like old feet," Oleana muttered sullenly, eyeing her last bit of protein bar with a deep contempt that a six-year-old shouldn't even be capable of yet. At least, in a better world than this godforsaken one.

"If you help him at home, I'm sure he'll have more time for personal hygiene." Masha got up and put away her plastic plates, which had been in use for so long that the many scratches and stains on them formed intricate patterns. She put everything in the sink unit and set the automatic start that would initiate the wash cycle as soon as her container was supplied with water. Maybe today, maybe tomorrow.

"Do we have to take the road through Grad Forest?" asked Artiom, looking genuinely glum.

Masha gave her son a *not-in-front-of-Oleana* look, and

he covered his little sister's ears.

"The forest is cursed, Ma. Everybody knows it. There's hardly any traffic on the road anymore because people are disappearing there."

"You shouldn't listen so much to the break talk at the mine." She waved it off and pointed to the narrow bag next to his chair. "Now get that in the car, we're about to leave."

While her fifteen-year-old son rolled his eyes in resignation and followed her request, she looked out through the small kitchen window at the settlement. Clunky former spaceship containers piled on top of each other as if giants had broken off an ill-fated game of Jenga. Rusty and stained, they gleamed in the first morning light, looking dirty as ash from all the sleet in the air. That there really had been ash mixed in with the snow, which couldn't decide whether it preferred to be rain after all, was not at all unlikely; after all, the iron mines of Stolbova were only a few miles away and their chimneys smoked day and night.

Double pay, one year, Masha thought, thanking God for the opportunity. If she did well, at least it would give her two children a chance to get out of here. Anywhere. A third of her salary would then go for the right bribes and the rest she would spend just for the passage of her children to the nearest system, but it was all worth it to her. After all, the worries about them couldn't be greater than here, in the hell called Arcturus. What could they expect here? If they were lucky, they would not die of tuberculosis or heavy metal poisoning, and they would surpass the average age of forty years of life. But for what? For even longer servitude in the mines or the 'chance' to work their way up to overseer and sell their own souls by maltreating others for more rations and money?

No, she decided. For these very reasons, she hadn't hesitated for a moment when the governor's recruiter had knocked on her container.

"Here we go," she said aloud, snapping herself out of her thoughts. One last time, she checked the brittle rubber band that held the kitchen window in its rusty frame, then grabbed her rain cape from the coat rack and threw it over herself.

"Ma!" protested Artiom scornfully, as only a pubescent teenager could, as she checked the fit of his jacket and his sister's.

"Do you want to show up at Uncle Zvarev's with a rash?" She pulled their hoods over both of their heads and then shooed them out.

The wind howled like a whole chorus of wolves as soon as she opened the door, and a swarm of dark brown sleet flakes blew into the living room. Quickly, she squeezed through the crack behind her children and pulled the door shut behind her. The magnetic lock had not been working for a long time, and even if it had, the few hours of electricity during the day would not be enough to feed the battery with any significant amount of energy. If the many gangs and mobs of the industrial levels wanted to break in, they would do so anyway and would not be stopped by a locked door. The best protection against burglars on Arcturus was to own nothing of value - something that was probably the only simple thing on this godforsaken world.

With her hood up, she walked to her rickety electric cart, which she had bought from one of the nomadic junk dealers only two years ago and which miraculously still worked. It was parked right next to the rusty charging station, which was once again flashing red and begging for power.

from a completely different breed of people and had come from a different class that he had never had access to. Granted, Lizzy had been a commoner, too, but her parents were respected doctors who had worked at the Skaland Naval Hospital. Both women were as different as they could be, and yet they were fighters - each in their own way teachers to him, from whom he had learned more about perseverance and self-reflection in a few hours than he had in all of his previous training.

Which was certainly not due to his instructors, but to his unwavering determination to get into every skirt he came across. How ashamed he was today of his superficiality, how all the trivialities paled before the fate that had reached his family and him.

"Good morning," he heard a raspy voice and his gaze flew to her face.

Hellcat's eyes were only half open and her features remained relaxed, as if she wasn't really awake yet.

"More like good night," he said with a smile, trying to reach for her hand. She couldn't see it, yet he paused in mid-motion and pretended to check the fit of her cannula.

"Have you been sitting here long?" she asked.

"No," he lied. "I guess I got lucky."

"Can I..." Hellcat closed her eyes and pursed her mouth as if something was causing her pain.

"Something to drink?" he asked, grabbing the drinking tube of water and electrolyte solution he had prepared.

She nodded, barely noticeably, and he brought the mouthpiece to her lips, which were surprisingly full when she was relaxed. Greedily, she drank half the tube and then sighed with a mixture of exhaustion and satisfaction.

"Didn't think I'd wake up at all again."

"Well, in any case, we're all a part of you now."

"What?"

"In the last twenty-four hours, you've gotten two pints of blood from Dodger and just under one each from me and Bambam," Gavin explained, trying not to let his relief show. Instead, he tried for casual cheerfulness, even though he would have preferred to sigh aloud. "When you start talking like a stuck-up lord, don't talk at all, or you talk as uncouth as a space miner, you know why."

Hellcat managed a tired smile. "Thank you."

"I... thank you," he said, rubbing his nose, though it didn't itch at all.

"For what?"

"Things got pretty messed up when the Demeter went down, but I haven't forgotten that you saved me from suffocating in the vacuum."

"You would have frozen to death before you suffocated, I think."

"I wouldn't have been comfortable with that either," Gavin replied.

"I can imagine."

"I mean it. Thank you."

"Forget it," she said, raising a hand in an attempt to make a dismissive gesture with it.

"I don't forget things like that."

"If we make a scene out of it every time we save each other's asses, we won't get anywhere."

Gavin couldn't help but laugh. "Your first curse! You must be feeling much better by now."

Hellcat began to chuckle now too, but contorted her face as if it caused her pain.

"You should laugh more often, it suits you," he found, standing up a little too quickly. A slight dizziness came over him.

"Are you all right?"

"Yes. I think my body is still busy replenishing its blood supply."

"Where are we, anyway?" she wanted to know. "Looks like those fuckers didn't blow us to kingdom come with their stealth ship after all."

"Looks like it. We jumped into the Yokatami Seed System."

"S2. But that's restricted territory."

"Was the next best jump location since we didn't want to go back to Andal."

"And why haven't they intercepted us yet?" asked Hellcat. "Not that I'm complaining."

"That's the funny thing. We've ended up somewhere else. Neither in the vacuum as planned, nor in the S2-Yokatami system. Maybe we're not in the Seed Traverse at all." Gavin shrugged.

"Huh?"

"We are on a planet. More specifically, inside a planet. Dodger is cutting us an exit right now. The good news is that the atmosphere is breathable, the bad news is that the *Lady* is in the middle of a mountain or something and we're experiencing massive system failures. It's going to take us a while to fix that. *If* we can even fix everything, we don't have access to spare parts and materials." Gavin saw the deepening lines on her forehead and waved tersely with his right hand. "We'll figure it out. Anything's better than getting blown apart by missiles. At least we'll have our peace and quiet here."

"Hmm."

"Get some rest first, and I'll see how far Dodger's gotten."

"No objections here," she said, and gave a long, drawn-out yawn before closing her eyes. As he turned to leave, he heard her voice again, "If you don't mind, Captain, it's a nice break to not be hunted or fight for our lives for a few hours."

"You called me *Captain* again!" He grinned, though she couldn't see it because she didn't bother to open her eyes.

"Haven't found an adequate replacement yet."

"It's going to stay that way because there isn't one."

"I'm starting to feel nauseous."

"Really? Sphinx..."

"I'm over ninety percent sure the patient was joking, which falls into the category of sarcasm," the AI replied in her pleasant mezzo-soprano, and Gavin merely grumbled.

He left the infirmary and headed down the central corridor toward the stern. The gravity of the world they were stranded on was noticeably less than Andal's 1.1 g, so each of his steps was springier and more expansive than he was used to. He had to be careful not to trip or hit his head against the already low ceiling. Since his home was considered a heavy world, his bone structure and musculature were somewhat coarser and stronger than most inhabitants of the Star Empire, and he felt like a ruffian with ataxic disorder under the conditions here.

At least until he ran into Bambam in the engine bay. The squat mechanic was lying under one of the tubular covers of the total of six bundles of energy pattern cells that surrounded their primary fusion reactor.

"Fucking piece of shit!" he raged in an unfamiliar raspy voice. "Oh, thank you very much, GOD, for letting me pinch my thumb. That's very helpful because it's swelled now and I'm in fucking pain. Oh no, *of course* it didn't go without bad luck. After all, everything has to stay the same. Oh, Winston has to fix something, the stupid *Kepal*? Then we'll just jerk him off with fucking

The last Fleet

pitch until he's knocked up just from breathing. We can do it with him, he's probably used to it by now anyway."

Gavin paused in the doorway, blinking in disbelief. Only the mechanic's surprisingly small feet peeked out from under the tube, from whose direction the angry babble came. There was a bang of metal on metal, followed by a series of angry curses.

"TO HELL WITH THIS!" Bambam roared.

"Your name is *Winston*?" asked Gavin with a smirk, and silence fell for a moment before the former Navy technician emerged from under the tube on his wheeled board, his face glowing with anger. When he noticed Gavin, his features smoothed a little.

"Oh, Captain. Didn't notice you at all."

"Winston?" he repeated.

"Yeah. Winston Kowalski, to be exact. My great-great-great-great-great-great grandparents were from Polish-speaking Ukraine. Probably forgot a few 'greats'."

"Ah, a European. My ancestors came from the Scandinavian Confederation. From Norway, to be exact."

"I know," Bambam replied. "Everybody knows that."

"Sure. Nice performance you had there."

"Huh?"

"Your tantrum. Did they teach you that on the Mjöllnir?", Gavin inquired, and his counterpart suddenly looked guilty and made a dismissive gesture.

"Did a lot of time in vice for that on the Mjöllnir."

"I can imagine."

"Those obdurate blue-blooded bums and their manners," grunted the mechanic with anger flaring again. "Sorry. You're one of them yourself."

"All good." Gavin realized he hadn't even noticed. "How are we doing?"

"I'm figuring out the energy pattern cells right now. A

lot of relays are blown on the transducers, but I can probably save about half by re-soldering or replacing them. We'll need a dock for the rest, but a launch wouldn't fail because of that."

"But?"

"The matrix cells are so fucked up that they're going to turn to shit at any moment. We can completely forget about it. Either we get new ones in a timely manner, or we don't get enough flow pushed into the superconductor bundles. We're not going to get the atmospheric number, that's for sure."

"At least we survived it," Gavin found. "Just do your best, we'll get out of here somehow."

"Honestly have no idea how, unless you open up a space shipyard. Wouldn't know what planet they're crafting spaceship components on, after all."

"We'll figure it out," he lied, unable to think of anything better to do than spread optimism, even if he had to fake it. He was about to turn to leave when he paused once more. "Hellcat woke up, by the way."

"Really?" Bambam's features visibly brightened.

"Yes. She's clearly feeling better. She was smiling."

"No!"

"Yes!"

"Oooh! Better not get too excited. Good moods are usually just made up for with even worse ones." The mechanic laughed as if he had made a fabulous joke and slapped his thigh. He looked like a chunky little Buddha as he did so.

"I'm going to go check on Dodger."

"Yep. I'll finish up here."

"Don't you want to go see Hellcat?" asked Gavin, not sure why himself.

"Nah, I'm good."

The last Fleet

He shrugged and returned to the central corridor, where he walked with well-measured steps toward the forward airlock. There he found Dodger again with the communications laser in her hands, normally intended as a replacement for one of the hull-mounted twins. At nearly six feet long, it was a clunky device, but she seemed to hold them quite effortlessly. Only the glistening sweat on the arms and neck of the hunky mutant gave any hint of how strenuous the work was for her. The upper part of her flight suit was knotted around her waist as usual, and she wore only her white undershirt around her upper body, which was soaked in several places.

She steered the laser as if in slow motion in a large circle that would hopefully one day become her passage to the unknown world out there. The heat emanating from the red glowing, tightly focused beam of light was oppressive and made all the pores in Gavin's skin pop open like buds in spring.

"Dodger?" he asked just loud enough for her to hear and hopefully not startle him. The mutant turned off the laser and lowered the barrel to the ground. She took off her privacy goggles and slid them over her sweaty forehead before turning to him and eyeing him calmly.

"Hey."

"How is it going?"

"It's going. Got the prism adjusted so the photon beam is as narrow as possible and just enough for the density of the rock," she explained.

"Very good. Unless we're alone here, we don't want to start a beacon right away." Since she didn't answer that, but merely looked at him neutrally, he continued, "How much longer do you think it will take?"

"Ten hours without a break. I'll need one though, I have to go to the bathroom soon and that will take time."

"Uh, yeah. Take your time. Hellcat woke up, by the way."

"Cool."

"She needs a lot of Smartnites. She lost most of them trying to keep the pressure up in her body," he explained.

"Do you think we'll find any out there?"

"Yes." He once again practiced optimism, but no better alternative came to mind.

"Good."

"Get back to me as soon as you're through."

"Yep." Dodger slid the goggles back on her nose and pulled the communications laser back up into both hands as if it were a light toy.

INTERLUDE: WALL SECTOR DELTA, TRAFALGAR SYSTEM

Commander Dalio Stevenson stood with his arms folded behind his back behind the three rows of men and women working at the central space control consoles to process and correctly interpret the data from the total of thirty deep space listening stations. The tracking stations, scattered throughout the outer system, were crude spheres with large gold-coated mirrors and a central sensor array, shielded in the direction of the central star at their backs by large sunshade sails. With their telescopes, they monitored almost the entire spectrum of electromagnetic radiation in the direction of Orb territory. Their eyes and ears never slept, just like Commander Dalio Stevenson and the space control staff rotating in shifts.

Their job was simple because it involved the same monitoring tasks over and over again, namely detecting possible faults in hardware or software and looking for signal anomalies that might indicate movement in Orb territory. Since there was little data from the first two run-ins with the mysterious aliens, Dalio didn't even know what exactly they were looking for. No one here knew, and his job was to provide focus and discipline, because where nothing happened for decades, soldiers tended to lose their faith in the threat. Meanwhile, there were surveys that proved that more and more recruits believed that the Orb did not exist and that it was fear-mongering on the part of the imperial authorities to justify the maintenance of martial law.

For Dalio, of course, this was utter nonsense, because he knew all too well that the Emperor could decide anything he wanted anyway. The Senate would nod it off in any case. Why should he go to so much trouble to maintain a conspiracy when he could have the result so much easier? The principle of simple probability still applied to him: when something seems complicated, the simplest explanation is usually the right one.

"Deviation," reported one of his Specialists from the interferometer monitor on the far left. Her voice was calm and professional.

Deviations occurred regularly, sometimes due to erroneous measurements, sometimes due to the failure of individual components that were disconnected from the automatic heuristics, or due to bugs in the software that resulted in shifted decimal places in the absolute data.

Nevertheless, Dalio treated the message with the same priority as always and went to his soldier. As soon as he stood with her, the curved display wall in front of her came to life, reflecting the augmented reality data she saw in her field of view.

"What do we have, Specialist?" he asked.

"The interferometer at listening station thirteen has registered an anomaly. Fourteen and fifteen are confirming the anomaly right now."

The interferometers were extremely sensitive miniature lasers located in a fifteen-yard tube mounted behind the mirrors that responded to minute changes in cosmic gravity waves.

"Is there an unannounced transit of one of our ships?" he wanted to know, going through his internal checklist as directed.

"Negative, Commander. The pattern does resemble a subspace event horizon, but the spikes are much stronger and shorter wavelength," the Specialist replied. Her fingers were in constant motion, moving invisible sliders, rearranging windows or making entries on virtual input fields. "Another deviation and a third. There's more coming."

"Database reconciliation!" ordered Dalio. "Release the data into the pool."

"Roger that, sir."

"Focus radar and lidar, pings and scanners on areas marked by interferometry. Confirm anomalies." He called the system data into his field of view and received the Specialist's raw data, which his neural computer automatically translated into what were by now six points located at the far edge of the system, even farther out than the deep space listening stations. He sent a medium-priority warning message to inner-system space control, where the eight space forts and their nearly two hundred defensive platforms were located, so they could confirm the signals and look for similar patterns between their respective positions.

"No contacts," the radar reported.

"I've got something here," said the specialist from the lidar.

"Report!"

"The signal propagation time of the photon sweep is within the expected range considering the distance to the sources of the gravitational waves, but the beam is unusually refracted," the soldier explained. Although he was seated at the far front right, Dalio heard his voice in his ears as if he were standing right next to him.

"Express yourself clearly."

"The returning photon message is more than ninety-five percent below the expected value."

"What could that mean?"

"I don't know, Commander. Maybe it's a simple measurement error, but the same data is coming back from all five signal sources."

Dalio didn't think twice, "System-wide red alert. Stand by."

"Sir?" the Specialist in front of him asked, not pausing in her gestures.

"Go ahead."

"Could that be the Orb, sir?"

"If something is out of the ordinary, we should be prepared for it," he replied, returning to his seat. The huge display wall at the front of the control center came to life, showing an overview of the Trafalgar system. The space fortresses were represented by green stars, and the weaponized defense platforms that formed a tight ring around the central star were shown as green squares. Under normal circumstances, two hundred more green triangles would have indicated the garrison fleet that was now, of all places, at the far end of the Star Empire, fighting a Never infestation. The six deviations were just outside the orbits of the deep space listening stations that formed the edge of the outer system. Even at first glance, it was obvious that this could not be a natural phenomenon, as the distance between them was exactly the same.

Dalio sent a liaison request to Admiral Rosinski, Trafalgar's commander-in-chief, which was routed through one of the quantcoms.

"Dalio," Rosinski immediately answered. "I was just awakened by the system alarm. What's going on?"

"Potential Orb incursion, sir," he said freely, even though his own words struck him as completely crazy. "The interferometers have picked up, and the lidar scan is spitting out unclear results. It's not one of ours, in any case."

"Then it must be them," the admiral concluded. "Right call, commander. Stay in close contact with systems intelligence and stream your data through the quantcoms directly to us."

"I've already arranged that, Admiral."

"Well done."

"Commander!" he heard the duty officer from systems heuristics call out excitedly. "Failure of listening posts fourteen, fifteen, seventeen, and eighteen."

"Sir, I think we're under attack right now." Dalio gulped. "Request permission to fire, Admiral."

"Granted!" came the immediate reply.

"Target signal deviations, fire clearance for all launch bays. Forward x-ray and maser guns: Fire at will!" he ordered loudly. The outer control center was not a space fortress, because its armor was considerably thinner and its hull was not magnetizable, but it had a not insignificant amount of the most advanced weaponry the Star Empire had to offer. The entire asteroid was crisscrossed with superconductors that connected their battery packs to offensive systems.

"Launch pads one through thirty activated. Fire," the fire control officer reported. Next came the X-ray and microwave lasers. Invisible to the human eye, they cooked space with their hard radiation, licking over the points that had been marked by the interferometers and had not moved so far.

If there was an effect, it was undetectable to their sensors, as the guns expended masses of energy without anything being seen or even one of the signals disappearing.

"Listening posts thirteen and sixteen down!"

"Commander, I'm getting no interferometry data," shouted the Specialist he had been standing by earlier.

"Then get me new data!" he insisted.

"To do that, I would have to reprogram the listening posts that are currently out of range, sir. To do that, I need your authorization, and even then it will take fifteen minutes for the closest ones to be properly aligned."

We don't have fifteen minutes, he translated her words in his mind and licked his lips.

"Contact!" The specialist from the radar almost shouted. "Ten thousand clicks from us."

Dalio frowned and compared the newly displayed red dots with the signal sources from the interferometers several million miles away. Nothing could cover that distance in a few seconds.

Unless it jumped. But if the first signals had been event horizons, for which the gravitational waves could speak, then there would have been only a few minutes between the jumps.

Impossible. His mind automatically formed the word to 'Orb' and his mouth abruptly went dry as dust.

"Take aim! Fire at will!" he ordered redundantly, as all weapons, including the previously silent railguns fired at maximum cadence.

Dalio turned on the optical sensors that littered his station like dark shells. The six alien starships were huge, seemingly resting motionless in the darkness of space. Their hulls were mighty cones with tentacle-like appendages waving at their terminal edge. Tiny rosettes

The last Fleet

blossomed on the shapeless, pearly shell, opening in rapid succession. Light, as hot as the insides of stars, connected them to the space station in the next instant, and where it hit, it cut through regolith and the yard-thick Carbin armor like butter.

The very first hit bisected the hollowed asteroid at whose heart Dalio stood, cutting through the control center from top to bottom. Before soldiers and equipment were torn into vacuum by the sudden drop in pressure, they had long since vaporized in a cloud of highly excited particles.

3
JANUS

Janus stood on the observation deck of the Star Empire's largest helium-3 refinery, gazing at the garish gray landscape of Luna. Over the centuries, the monotonous regolith wasteland had been transformed into a rather varied one: Craters as deep as lakes alternated with mighty hills where the churning debris had been piled up. The greed for helium-3 had ensured that companies like the Luna Mining Corporation had long ago extracted all the supplies of the satellite from its surface. What remained was this new topography of Luna, a sign of efficiency and coordinated plunder. Janus was always impressed to see how humans, as a cooperative collective, could accomplish such great things. He stood here on a station the size of a small city on Terra, with an artificial atmosphere, staring out at a vast landscape littered with inactive derricks and launch pads for cargo drones. They just stood there, colorless and complicated like optical industrial puzzles.

"Hard to believe we managed to extract all of Luna's resources in just two hundred years, huh?" a familiar voice asked, and Janus eyed the woman clad in an elegant evening gown who had stepped up beside him at the panoramic window. Her dress betrayed wealth, probably woven of cashmere wool, without synthetic fibers with smart features and changing colors.

"Hard to believe we have managed to keep Luna alive since then," he replied, taking a sip of his *Antibes* champagne. Even though he despised any kind of lavish luxury - and he definitely counted drinks that cost five hundred crowns per bottle among them - he had to admit that after five years in his job, he had gotten used to the taste. That was probably how it always started with waste.

"We've done quite a bit to that end, I'd like to think." The woman motioned for him to follow her, and he walked with her along the broad plateau that ran around the entire atrium like the battlements of a castle. Except instead of a wall and battlements, there was a glass panel that formed a ring. The dome above them was made of programmable silicon and was currently heavily darkened to block out the glaring sunlight that fed life-giving radiation to the small park where hundreds of imperial officials and employees of the Luna Mining Corporation now bustled. The jumble of their voices blended into a single rising and falling sound, like a poorly conducted choir.

After about a hundred yards, the Kashmir lady stopped and gestured elegantly out the window. The view was now so completely different that one could have thought they were on another celestial body. There was hardly anything left to see of the lunar surface, since it was almost completely built over. Between multi-story cuboids made of composite, on the surfaces of which ran any number of pipes and cable trays wrapped in thick, hardened foam, freight trains moved around like snakes in a labyrinth. Huge radiators grew hundreds of feet high

The last Fleet

from the pellet refineries, glowing cherry-red like stretched sails. On the horizon beyond, the steady comings and goings of pot-bellied cargo shuttles could be seen, their plasma tails cutting through the darkness of space like torches. At a distance, it could already be guessed how large the spherical spacecraft were, capable of swallowing even smaller asteroids.

"To me, First Secretary, this is the genius of capitalist spirit," the woman declared. "Luna may have reached its production limit, but it is far from dead. In the last five decades alone, we've been able to increase the capacity of our pellet refineries sixfold. Helium-3 is gone, and yet there has never been as much of it here as there is today."

"Thanks to the Emperor's investments," he replied, and the lady turned to him with a business-like smile.

"Of course." She extended a hand to him. "I am Tatyana Shaparova, First Executive of this institution."

"I thought as much." He shook her hand and smiled kindly. "It is a pleasure to meet you."

"On behalf of Luna Mining Corporation, I would like to thank you for honoring us with your visit, First Secretary."

"You don't have to use my title every time," Janus countered, gesturing toward the noisy crowd below them in the park. "Otherwise, my brief grace period before speech and banquet is about to end."

"I understand, Mister Darishma."

"So, you are the new girl."

"Arrived yesterday."

"Transit via Callisto?"

"Correct," she confirmed, nodding. "My first trip away from Sokhol, believe it or not."

"You must have had a stellar career," he noted, adding, "Or pissed off someone who couldn't quite get rid of her."

A shadow flitted briefly across her graceful face. He had probably hit the mark.

"Something like that. Still, I'm glad to be here. May I speak frankly with you, Mister Darishma?" She turned to face him fully now and lowered her champagne glass. Only now did he notice that her eyes were cyber-substitutes. The whites were a little too white, the irises too uniform and too blue. Still, they didn't seem as cold as the ones he'd seen in the Marines. Whenever he dealt with the high management of corporations, it irritated him how different they were compared to the leadership of the Star Empire. No noble would ever have an organ replaced with augments. It was considered unseemly at best and, behind closed doors, a sign of low status and a kind of sacrilege against the human body. Of course, Janus did not overlook the double standard, as no highborn would forgo the blessings of nanorevolution, genetic modification, or rejuvination treatments, and had at least one neural computer installed.

"Please," he replied, well aware that no one ever really spoke openly to him - except perhaps the Emperor. Every word addressed to him as the ruler's right-hand man was necessarily borne of politics and angles. He didn't blame her for that any more than he blamed anyone else. Indeed, it was equally impossible for him to speak to the Emperor with complete impartiality because, after all, the Emperor always remained the Emperor, even in private.

"When I accepted the new assignment, I wasn't particularly happy about it. For us, working outside the corporate protectorate is like putting a leash on us," Shaparova explained, touching with her free hand the diamond-studded chain that lay glittering around her neck.

"You mean because of the forced participation of Terran companies."

"Of course. To us, it feels like we're doing all the innovating and then getting a leash put on us that you can tighten at will."

"That is the way 21st century China did it quite successfully."

"Except in this case, you're the China and we're the innovative Western companies."

"Yes," he admitted. "But at the time, both benefited greatly. One had innovation, the other had the largest consumer market in the world."

"I see your point," Shaparova said. "Because that's exactly my point, too. We wouldn't be doing it if it didn't benefit us. Today, we're both thriving, and standing here on Luna and seeing what we've put together shows me that fact extremely vividly."

"I thought you were going to be frank with me, First Executive," Janus remarked. "Am I supposed to be flattered by your extremely politically correct words now?" Before she could answer - he didn't want to embarrass her - he added, "I appreciate your lie, but we both know it is still just that: a lie. The Corporate Protectorate may be thriving, but only because it can draw its profits from the huge market that is the Star Empire. Our economy, on the other hand, is down, stagnant at best due to decades of a war economy and restrictions on free trade. We're fighting on fronts you've only seen in the news, in locales far removed from corporate protectorates and your balance sheets."

"It's a shame you see it that way, Mister Darishma. According to our calculations, nearly fifty percent of the Star Empire's tax revenues come directly or indirectly from our corporations and businesses."

"If you add our fifty percent holdings, then that calculation is correct," he countered, sighing. "Now we are in a discussion I did not really want to have. Please excuse my behavior, Miss Shaparova. I'm afraid I've been a bit overworked lately."

That was a blatant understatement. All he had to do was listen to himself for a breath and he was filled with worries, forebodings, and ideas for his next dodge over the Marquandt problem and the Mirage matter.

"That's all right. I understand, and I apologize for my clumsy attempt at flattering small talk. My assistants warned me that you had no use for it. I guess I should have listened to them," returned the First Executive of Luna Mining Corporation. "You are a man who has seen a Saphyra tree and knows about things that would keep some of us up at night. I can only imagine how it must feel to be burdened with so much information."

Janus gallantly passed over the suggestion and merely nodded. "I'm actually more comfortable getting straight to the point of a concern rather than spending time working my way through the shells of political platitudes. If I may ask you a question: What has surprised you the most since you left the corporate protectorate?"

"Parity," came the immediate answer. It escaped the attractive lady rather than having been formulated, and thus probably corresponded to the truth.

"If you would elaborate?"

"Our joint ventures finance half of the state budget. Employees of companies based in the Corporate Protectorate make up about half of the Star Empire's workforce. The Protectorate's budget is about half of what the Emperor has available each year, and patent applications to the Jupiter Bank are also remarkably evenly divided between you and us. I'm a mathematician by training and I like to see equations that work out, Mister Darishma, but I also know that mathematical parity in the universe is

The last Fleet

an absolute outlier, and I don't believe in statistical accumulations of outliers."

Janus stiffened inwardly, and only his many years as a politician, during which he had had to deal with the shrewdest tacticians and power-hungry potentates, left him smiling with unchanged indifference.

"Don't you think you're reading too much into coincidences?" he asked, ashamed of the lie. Of course he knew what she meant, and as one of the few living people he was also aware of what this unnatural division between the power blocs of humanity was based on. If he had told her, she would not survive the next hour.

And neither would he.

"Maybe," she said, sighing before a neutral smile graced her face again. "I've probably been working in cryptography too long, and I rack my brain too often because I see puzzles where there are none."

"What do you think about the state of the Star Empire? And please remember: you gain my respect through honesty rather than the next diplomatic phrase," he noted amiably.

"I think you're up against a wall. The war economy doesn't merely have negative fiscal consequences. It also fatigues the working population, stifles innovation and investment alike through excessive tax burdens, and shifts power away from Congress to Admiralty."

"Okay, that was very honest," Janus agreed. "Thank you for your candor. I agree with you in your analysis."

"Does the emperor?"

"Ah, there it is again, politics." He did not reproach her. "The Emperor is always concerned about the Star Empire and its inhabitants. But especially for the Seed Traverse."

"The Seed Traverse?" repeated Shaparova, looking

confused. He saw nothing but confusion in her gaze. A dead end for him.

"Well, we wonder when we can expect the first results," he answered evasively. Thus, his participation in this reception had turned out to be a waste of time. He knew that Tatyana Shaparova had worked on the planning staff of the Seed World S-4 LMC until her transfer to Luna. She would have been in the picture had Yokatami shared anything about his particular ownership structure of his own Seed World S2-Yokatami with the other veto power of the corporate protectorate.

"Sir?"

Janus turned to the deep bass voice. Two of his Imperial Guard bodyguards stood there, men like trees with chrome eyeballs and hairless heads. They were hard to tell apart, but he recognized them as Jericho and Charlie.

"Yes. Is there a problem?"

"I'm afraid so," Jericho returned. "We've prepared a secured room for you."

"Please excuse me, First Executive. It was a pleasure to meet you," Janus turned to the hostess of the reception and followed his bodyguards before she could reply.

With quick steps, they left the atrium - obviously in enough of a hurry that he could feel most of the stares from down in the park on him. That his men risked chatter among the guests could only mean that there was a real problem.

They had prepared a conference room, outside of which two more guardsmen in black suits were waiting and respectfully bowed their heads when he arrived. Inside, white-noise generators were set up, one at each end of the table. They made his ears feel like they were occupied, and the silence inside their invisible spheres of interference was oppressive and strangely voluminous.

The last Fleet

Between them, a holodisplay came to life, showing a still image of an admiral with four yellow eagles on his shoulder, identifying him as a fleet admiral. Janus recognized him at second glance as High Lord Samuel Taggert, the commander-in-chief of the Wall forces in the Gamma Sector. His face looked sallow, his eyes surrounded by deep shadows.

Involuntarily, Janus tensed. He waited until Jericho had closed the door behind him and a green light on his wrist terminal indicated a secure Quantcom connection to the *Rubov* Halo's central computer. Then he checked the transmission data. It had arrived at the IIA's Neptune listening station ten minutes ago with the highest level of encryption and had been forwarded directly to the central office in the orbital ring, from where it had been sent with the highest level of secrecy to the Emperor, Janus, and Grand Admiral Albius as Chief of Staff.

With an uneasy feeling in his stomach, he started the video transmission, which according to the log file had been recorded nine hours ago.

"Your Majesty," Taggert began to speak. "I bring bad news: It appears that an Orb fleet has attacked Trafalgar in the Delta Sector. Our reconnaissance was able to confirm the destruction of all military installations in the system. Preliminary data indicate that there were six cloaked ships, which could only be located by interferometry using their gravitational waves. It's a total military loss. Currently, there are indications that the civilian population on Trafalgar I was spared. At this point, we must assume that the current defense strategy has failed and the Beta Quadrant systems are now defenseless. It is also disturbing that the enemy apparently knew exactly where our defenses were and at what time. The bombardment of the inner system was by long-range weapons of unknown type, which had no obvious guidance properties, but could disable the most sensitive systems. We must therefore assume that the enemy has sensitive intelligence information ..."

The video was broken by a priority link showing the Emperor's seal rotating around its long axis.

Janus accepted it and moments later saw the face of Haeron II on the screen in front of him.

"Janus," said the. "Have you seen Admiral Taggert's message yet?"

"The most important part, yes."

"This is a disaster! I should never have allowed Marquandt to withdraw his fleets just because it's been quiet for a few decades!" the Emperor grumbled, and the anger in his voice was only overshadowed by the concern in his gaze. "So many dead! How could it happen that the damned aliens strike just now?"

"I am afraid their long-range reconnaissance is clearly superior to ours, Your Majesty. All they had to do was to wait for the right moment."

"So what do we do now? We can't just leave this unanswered."

"I don't know, your majesty. The Chief of Staff ..."

"Albius? He wants me to wait until we have more intelligence," the Emperor rumbled. "WAIT? We just lost tens of thousands of soldiers! If we do nothing now, it will be construed as weakness on my part, and rightly so."

"The advice is justified," Janus said cautiously, surprised himself that Albius should have reacted so prudently and tactically. He just could not figure this man out. "The danger is too great that we will run into the nearest blade. Besides, who should you send? You just appointed Taggert as the new commander of the home fleet yesterday, and with him three of his fleets. If you send

The last Fleet

him to Trafalgar now, Terra will continue to be unprotected."

"I know, but Taggert is one of our best."

"And one of the most loyal," Janus noted. "We need him here. Better send Admiral Ramone from the Epsilon Sector."

"She only took her post two weeks ago. We would just be sending her to a meat grinder," objected the Star Empire ruler. "We have no choice but to send Taggert there. After all, he is already pulling his three fleets together, so he has a head start. He can get there much faster."

He wanted to contradict the Emperor, but could not. Everything he had said was true, after all. At the same time, he didn't need to be an officer to understand that when you had only one choice, it was always the worst.

"Your Majesty, you must not allow yourself to be backed into a corner. I know it is difficult to delay a decision in this case, but ..."

"Not difficult, Janus, impossible!" the emperor interrupted him, and his brusque words surprised him. The death of his eldest son had undoubtedly changed Haeron II, and Janus did not believe it was for the better. At the same time, he felt sorry for the man. His entire being seemed overshadowed by pain.

Grand Admiral Albius' face appeared next to the Emperor's.

"Your Majesty, First Secretary of State," the old officer greeted them politely.

"Marius, I have made up my mind. Send Admiral Taggert. Tell him to leave for Trafalgar and drive out the invaders if they are still there. The priority is to protect the civilian population on Trafalgar I and the asteroid settlements," the Emperor ordered.

"Your Majesty, may I..."

"No. I have made up my mind."

Albius obediently bowed his head. His expression showed well-controlled reluctance. Once again, Janus wished he could see behind the old admiral's gnarled facade. Whenever he expected the Chief of Staff to lay his cards on the table to reveal a strategy, he did exactly the opposite of what he had assumed. The guy hadn't even taken Janus' hint about using Marquandt and his fleet as the new home fleet. Instead, he had made the very suggestion to the Emperor that Janus himself had wanted to make: To choose Taggert, one of the Navy's most loyal and battle-hardened fleet admirals.

"I will prepare the appropriate orders and send them via Quantcom within the next twenty minutes," Albius assured their master.

"Janus?" asked Haeron II, looking him straight in the eye through the hologram.

"I'm coming back to the palace."

"No. Stay on Luna and finish the reception. We cannot seem upset. Besides, I want you to use the press crush to distract them. I do not want those damn vultures to start circling until we know how the battle has turned out."

"Of course." Janus also inclined his head. *We already know how the battle will turn out, don't we?*

INTERLUDE: PLANET RUHR, CORPORATE PROTECTORATE

Ludwig Sorg, chairman of the supervisory board of Ruhr Heavy Industries, went over for a second time the data from the Hermes probe that had flown into the system a few minutes ago. First Executive Nurheim's report was tersely written: The Demeter was attacked by an alien ship that possessed unknown technologies that made it invisible to the ship's sensors. It was also capable of recharging its jump nodes within minutes. Andal was infested by the Never and destroyed. The only survivors were the youngest son of the High Lord Cornelius Andal and his crew, who had previously posed as the crew of a pellet freighter out of concern for their lives. Nurheim's sobriety in the face of his approaching death contrasted sharply with Gavin Andal's message, recorded with video and sound. His facial expressions were embattled with conflicting emotions, oscillating somewhere between divine anger and crushing pain as he spoke: *This is Lord Captain Gavin Andal, last survivor of House Andal, High Lord of the Karpshyn Sector. During the defensive battle of my home system, Fleet Admiral Dain Marquandt abandoned his designated positions and retreated when he should have attacked the Never. He also had three suspected Orb-manufactured drones with which he was able to direct the Never swarms in unknown ways. He was responsible for the destruction of the Home Fleets under the command of Crown Prince Magnus and the Border World Fleets under the command of my brother Artas, as well as the extermination of Andal with over a billion women, children and men. To get rid of witnesses, he disabled all jump engines in the system by imperial priority code. We must assume that the ship that killed the ice freighter* Alabama *and the passenger liner* Morning Star, *and is now attacking the Seed Vessel Demeter, is acting on Marquandt's orders to prevent anyone from carrying this information to the Emperor. I vouch for my words with the honor of my House and that of an officer in the Imperial Navy.*

Ludwig also opened the log file of the on-board computer of the *Glory*, the corvette that had been under young Andal's command. The telescope images, flanked by more telemetry data, showed the three strange spherical objects - thousands of vector lines showing directions of movement of the Never swarms, along with AI calculations suggesting a correlation between swarms, their course changes, and the courses of the spherical objects. Interferometry data followed, indicating how Marquandt's fleet was jumping out of the system in rapid succession instead of joining the flank attack according to battle planning. All of this excited him greatly, it was so unbelievable, but none of it as much as the image of the alien emerging from behind a figure in a Reaper suit in the airlock of a shot-up Light Hauler and being hit by a tungsten bolt.

The last Fleet

For minutes he stared at the still image, eyeing the oval face with pitch-black eyes so large and alien that his hair stood on end. Ludwig counted the six breathing holes between the eyes and the mouth, which was narrow and blood-red. The skin shimmered pearly.

"Supervisor?" his assistant called to his attention. He had already cleared his throat several times, but Ludwig had not turned away.

"It must be an Orb, Jonathan," he said, clicking his tongue as he leaned back and turned his chair so that he could look down on the city, much of which lay hidden under a thick blanket of cloud. Only the mightiest starry skyscrapers rose out into the stratosphere, where it was already getting extremely dark. "An Orb. In the Andal system."

"That's possible. Even if we can't know, since..."

"... no Orb has ever been seen. I guess the process of elimination will have to do. It's not a Never, that much is certain, and we know of only one other species besides our own: the Orb."

"It is also apparently certain that the Never did not come from the Tartarus Void after all. Or was on the way for quite a long time. What do you intend to do about the other matter?", Jonathan wanted to know.

Ludwig turned back to the young man with the many data jacks at his temples, almost all of which were occupied by memory sticks. Before answering, he scratched his short-cropped beard for a long time and thought.

"We'll have to take the matter to the Corporate Council," he finally decided.

"Does the explosive nature of the data allow a delay in forwarding it to the throne?" his assistant asked. "That could be construed as a political move on our part."

"If Congress or the Emperor want to pull a fast one on us, they can, and it will be painful. But the alternative would be to override the council. We can still flounder on a rope and hope our friends will come and cut us loose. But if our friends pull at our feet out of hurt vanity, things won't look good for us." Ludwig leaned forward and rested his hands on the Gagantua oak table. "Call a meeting on my behalf. Supervisors only, no assistants, and veto members only." He glanced at his old-fashioned wristwatch. "Let's say five minutes."

"Already done," Jonathan said a few seconds later, during which his gaze had become transparent.

"Good, I'll talk to you after." He waved his assistant out and started the electronic sealing of his office until only the analog line to the rooftop transceiver was powered. The 360-degree encrypted Quantcom signals were streaming directly through subspace, and it wasn't the first time Ludwig was glad to have brought the appropriate prototypes to the council. In doing so, his corporation effectively lost the patent, but in his experience, such cutting-edge technology could rarely be truly protected or even concealed. So why not build some credit with his valued partners?

The holograms of the other supervisors appeared almost lifelike in front of his desk a few minutes later, forming a semicircle: Sato Ran of Yokatami, Elisabeth Detton of Alpha Corporation, Min Sok Hyun of Dong Rae, and Jennifer Orlan of Luna Mining Corporation.

"We have a problem," Ludwig got straight to the point. If his refraining from any pleasantries worried the other veto chairmen, they certainly didn't let on. In short, forceful words he described to them truthfully what he had learned from the data of the Hermes probe - apart

The last Fleet

from the existence of the Orb or its corpse. If they should learn through their informers that it existed, he could still pretend that he had not been able to identify the alien as an Orb. Which was the truth. Ludwig believed in the corporate protectorate and the need for close cooperation at the top, but he wasn't ready to give up every ace up his sleeve.

Not yet, at least.

"This is troubling," Sato Ran noted tersely.

"What could Marquandt gain from this?" asked Elisabeth Detton. "He is far too low in the Star Empire hierarchy for a coup d'état."

"The emperor no longer has an heir. Unless he appoints his daughter Elayne and breaks with tradition," Ludwig thought aloud.

Jennifer Orlan's likeness swayed her head from left to right, as if trying to expel a stubborn tension from her shoulders. "Let's not forget that it is not uncommon in high nobility to pass the scepter to female descendants."

"Elayne Hartholm-Harrow did not serve in the Navy, which is the reason she should not be appointed. And if the Emperor does, he will have the Council of Nobility against him. Service in the space forces is mandatory for any dignitary of rank," Detton explained nasally, as if threatened with a bout of allergic sniffles at the thought of the monarchists' ridiculous traditions.

"No matter what Marquandt plans, it is not in the best interests of the Star Empire or humanity. Sacrificing an entire system to Never and delivering the Crown Prince to the hangman is not only treasonous and immoral, but economically damaging to boot. The entire Karpshyn Sector and its neighboring systems will suffer for decades from the disappearance of Andal." Ludwig thought of the loss of the Demeter when he used the word economically damaging and felt an unpleasant tugging in his stomach area. He had not informed the other supervisors about this either. They knew about the stealth ship even as they did from the sensor data from Gavin Andal's ship. They must not get the impression that he was trying to distract from an investment disaster of his corporation.

"The Emperor must be informed," Min Sok Hyun spoke up for the first time. "This board is certainly aware of that."

Everyone nodded. Only Sato Ran did not stir, and all eyes turned to the Yokatami supervisor.

He inhaled in his typically deliberate manner and nodded as if in slow motion. "The data is too explosive to keep to ourselves. One way or another, it will come to light that something is going to happen. The truth always finds a way. It's just a question of when, and we can control that."

"What do you suggest?" asked Orlan.

"Let's just send the pure data. Not Gavin Andal's accusations."

"His accusations sound extremely plausible in light of the data," Ludwig stated. "Moreover, as the new High Lord, Cornelius Andal's son occupies a not inconsiderable position in the Council of Nobles. This makes him one of the one hundred most powerful men and women in the Star Empire."

"Well, not factually, because he commands a diminished and - as you mentioned - economically weakened fiefdom for decades to come," Ran indicated.

"What you're saying is that we could be betting on a sick horse," Orlan offset.

The Yokatami supervisor did not reply, and there was a brief pause in which no one said anything.

The last Fleet

"The way I see the options, the following applies," Detton finally spoke up. "Marquandt could be a traitor and have it in for the throne, as young Andal said. We have to ask ourselves what the likelihood of that is. According to the dossiers I have, the boy is a shallow womanizer, a daredevil who wanted to be a fighter pilot. His Navy record is replete with reprimands: disorderly conduct, violation of cadet regulations, leaving the training area without permission, and theft of a spacecraft are just a few. Marquandt is a respected fleet admiral, but is relatively new to the Admiral's Council. He is unlikely to have many allies, unlike heavyweights such as Takahashi, Taggert or Albius, and even they would have a hard time toppling the emperor. The Navy has been so indoctrinated for decades that loyalty ratings for Haeron II could hardly be higher. I don't currently see anyone as having a chance of overthrowing the leader of this Punch and Judy show."

The others chuckled cautiously at this remark. Ludwig pretended to be amused as well. In his head, however, several calculations were running through the obstructed talent lines of his brain, running simulations and comparing scenarios. All of this was happening while he listened to Detton.

"But maybe there's a reason for Marquandt's actions," the Alpha Corporation supervisor continued. "What if he saw something we don't yet know about the Never? What if he judged the battle to be unwinnable?"

"Then why would he have used imperial priority codes to shut down all jump engines?" wanted Hyun to know.

"I don't know, and we can't tell if that was even the case. We have no evidence of that because Gavin Andal rebooted his on-board computer."

"However, the fact that no one in Andal survived underscores his credibility," Hyun opined.

"I agree with that," Ludwig rejoined.

"We would be breaking our principle of not interfering in imperial affairs," Sato Ran said.

"I can only take that as a bad joke, my friend. We interfere all the time because we are closely intertwined. We should not make the mistake of forgetting that we are rich and advanced because we control a lean, easily managed political entity that relies on the billions and billions of consumers from the Star Empire," Ludwig replied. The mood was now at a tipping point, and he had to do something. "Elisabeth. You weren't finished a moment ago."

"Thank you. The other option besides a betrayal by Marquandt and a pending coup would be that he wasn't after the throne, but Andal, and the crown prince's presence was a problem he didn't factor in."

"Why Andal of all places?" wanted Hyun to know. "Not insignificant economically, yes, but a Border World and ..."

"... And within shortest jumping distance to the Seed Traverse." Detton opened her hands clasped in front of her stomach. "The stealth ship attacked Ludwig's seed ship. Normally, by treaty, that would be followed by a Navy detachment from Andal coming to the rescue and securing the system."

"What are you getting at?" asked Orlan.

"Just the fact that there are always connections, even if we don't see them yet. Something is being played out that we have no information about, and that should worry all of us. We're dealing with a system lost to the Never, accusations of treason, possible Orb technology, and a stealth ship that, to our knowledge, shouldn't even exist. If our investments have not yet provided a breakthrough in

The last Fleet

stealth ships, none have," Detton summarized. "So we are in the dark."

"That's why I suggest we inform the Emperor of our findings," Ludwig chimed in. "With that, we'll scare up the entire dovecote, and all we'll have to do is keep our eyes open for anything that stirs."

"That could put us in the line of fire," he said.

"We're already in the line of fire," he countered. "The Demeter was attacked, and I don't even know if it still exists. Accordingly, under current treaties, the Imperial Navy will enter the scene anyway. I say we keep the initiative, then we won't have to justify ourselves later if it comes out that we knew."

"I agree with that," Hyun said, and Orlan nodded as well. Detton still hesitated.

"We would have to send a high-ranking courier to get the urgency of the message across."

"I can take care of that." They wanted the bearer of bad news to be him, to pull himself out of sight. He had counted on that.

"Good, then I'm all for it."

All eyes turned to Sato Ran. The eldest supervisor in their circle considered with a motionless expression and finally nodded as well.

"I also agree," he said thoughtfully. "We must act quickly. I'll provide my personal yacht, it's the fastest ship, and space flight controls won't ask too long questions."

Now Ludwig was very much surprised, and an infinite number of gears began to turn in his head.

"With that, our course of action is unanimous," he summarized and ended the meeting. Pressing a button, he called Jonathan back in.

"Well?" his assistant asked.

"Something's not right."

"Can you specify?"

"Yes. The Demeter was attacked by a ship equipped with unknown technology - one we've been searching for for a long time without success. It must have been clear to everyone in the meeting that our Seed Vessel was doomed. Even the old fish should have been worried because his Seed World is only three light years away from ours. I would have expected him to ask for all the data I had so he could protect his corporate property. Even for Yokatami, the investment volumes in the Seed Traverse are enormous," Ludwig explained as his wrist terminal chirped.

"Mr. Sorg," one of his AI secretaries answered. "I have a request from Supervisor Sato Ran. His office is asking for specific data that only you can release."

Ludwig looked up at Jonathan, who merely shrugged.

"Mister Ran is not the youngest anymore," his assistant pointed out.

"Perhaps," he said absently. "Prepare a courier ship. The Council wants to send a joint message to the Emperor, I'll send one of my own."

"Is that wise?"

"No, but I stand alone in the dark forest and hear voices. I need to know who they belong to and what they are talking about. Call Admiral Giorgidis. I want to see all our available spy ships in S2."

"What about our fleet?"

"No corporate fleet, no guardsmen," Ludwig decided. "We can't look like we're panicking. But have Giorgidis put together a mercenary fleet, and I'll provide ten billion for the mission."

"What is the mission?" asked Jonathan.

"Officially: securing our seed system. Unofficially: the spy ships report directly to Giorgidis, who is in overall command, but officially acts only as a representative of the corporation. The goal is to find out what happened." Ludwig leaned forward. "And I want to know where young Andal is, if he's still alive."

"That should be doable for ten billion, even if we have to take a lot of write-offs after this disaster."

"If we don't shed light on this soon, we can write ourselves off."

4

GUNTER

The hustler's dock certainly lived up to its name. After just a few minutes in the never-finished dock, Gunter felt as if he had to wash himself to avoid catching some disease that he would never be rid of.

There was a dense crowd, in which he saw more faces than he had seen since his arrival. Although the Cerberus was well-stocked with staff everywhere, unlike in the supervised areas, the local characters did not shy away from eye contact. They even sought it, much to Gunter's chagrin. Prostitutes made eyes at him, touting their skills with words and descriptions that his imagination had apparently not been able to come up with. Some touched him on the arm to get his attention, others shouted their salacious offers to him from the second row or unceremoniously presented their 'assets' to him. Most were women, but some were men who looked like they were at a theme party for dominatrixes.

Gunter fended off all advances with muttered "No" or "Maybe later", avoided any eye contact so as not to encourage anyone, and looked for what looked like an entrance to the maintenance tunnels. For that, he kept to the walls, but it wasn't exactly easy, as many corners were already being used to exchange bodily fluids. In one, someone was being stabbed by a hooded figure. Gunter broke his neck with a short, precise passing blow without slowing down. By the time the killer's body fell to the ground, Gunter had long since disappeared back into the crowd.

He was not supposed to interfere or make a fuss, and had to concentrate on what he had come here to do. But he was still a Marine of the Guard Regiment of House Andal. Either he finished his mission as such, or he died as such. He would not allow himself to act like one of those criminals. At least not more than was absolutely necessary.

The walls of the dock were roughly hewn, as if the drills had just come off. In some places the bare rock was as sharp-edged as blades, in others it had been sanded away where there were indentations, some of which were hidden from prying eyes with curtains. The sounds from the other side, however, were clear enough to know that these were not maintenance access points.

Gunter had to turn on his olfactory filters to keep from being distracted by the multiple smells: sweat, cheap perfume, soy, and the cloying scent of things people should rather leave at home, if it were up to him. His noise filters were doing a good job, too, blocking out most of the conversation and searching incessantly for the voice pattern of Adam Goosens that he had recorded. But the administrator either wasn't here yet, or the acoustic onslaught on his ears was too much even for his augments.

So he spent several hours searching and listening and listening and searching. He did find several smaller tunnels where no one was hanging around because they

The last Fleet

were apparently off-limits, but no cavers and certainly no administrator Goosens. Whatever the reason for their absence, he could not shake the impression that he would not encounter anyone on this night shift. Since wasting time was something of the sixth circle of hell for a Marine, he tried to mingle as best he could and create an interior map of the dock. His Battlenet computer wasn't working on the Cerberus, was disrupted by some kind of jamming, so he wasn't able to make any mappings of his surroundings. Instead he memorized the tunnels and the few sealed bulkheads the old-fashioned way. At some point, at a very late hour, he encountered three figures in an apparently abandoned bore tunnel that went only two yards into the rock face, two of whom were beating up the third, a petite woman.

Gunter stood behind the two men and cleared his throat until they turned around. Both were hooded, with only their eyes uncovered, and moving quickly.

"Push off," one of them hissed.

Gunter remained silent and stayed where he was.

His counterparts cast brief glances at each other and then gave him their undivided attention. Blades suddenly flashed in their hands, quickly enough that he wondered if they were wired.

"You may go," he said. "While you are still able."

Again the hooded men exchanged glances, then made the mistake of attacking him. They were smart about it, he had to hand it to them: Simultaneously, they attacked him with a stab, moving away from each other to make the best use of the little space in the tunnel approach. Their movements were quick and slightly choppy, leading him to conclude they had either neural accelerators or neuroburn.

Gunter's reflex boosters automatically kicked in as the

first surge of adrenaline shot out of his adrenal cortexes, slowing his world down. Strictly speaking, it wasn't the figures and their shiny knives that were moving slower, but his artificial synapses that were working at twice the signal speed, making him move significantly faster.

He grabbed the wrist of the first attacker, jerked it aside, and slashed at the second with it. Bones broke and tendons snapped under the servo-enhanced grip of his cyberhands, which the sensors relayed as vibrations to his brain stem.

The second dodged at the last second and rolled backward. Gunter dropped, knocking the first off him in the process. Before he caught himself on the ground, he took the second off his feet with a foot sweep. His significantly increased speed made it easy for him to anticipate his opponents' every move, and his trained reflexes did the rest - he was simply too fast to think clearly and act consciously. His upgraded body at that moment was nothing more than a machine programmed by endless training to follow its sequences.

The second collapsed to the floor with a strangled cry. Gunter was already with him and spun around to face the knife, which the hooded man deftly pulled from under his belly and stabbed upward where Gunter's chest had been a moment ago.

He extended the right monofilament blade and, with a fluid motion from below, sank it through the man's chin and into his head. When a good ten inches of the ultra-thin weapon exited the top of his head and his eyes bulged before him, he hadn't even felt any resistance. Out of the corner of his eye, he perceived the first bending over his destroyed hand and fleeing.

Gunter stretched out an arm, got hold of his ankle and yanked it back. A moment later he was clutching the

The last Fleet

hooded man's neck with his right and pushing him up the rough rock face until his legs dangled in the air.

With all the willpower he could muster in his hormone and artificial reflex driven frenzy, he turned off his reflex booster and the normal world gradually returned. Sounds were again more than categorizable individual sounds, smells settled into his nose, and the light moisture of the environment on his skin. He felt like a human being again. Slow and somehow inadequate, but familiar and fully in command of his senses.

"Are you all right?" he asked without turning to the woman.

"Uh, I don't know," croaked a frighteningly fragile-sounding voice.

Gunter looked the hooded man in the eye, spun him in the air, and then sat him down next to the injured woman, rather pulling the veil from his face. Underneath, the features of a young man with digitattoos on his face were revealed, showing skulls, weapons and snakes in many colors, entwined in constant motion.

A Vault, he thought. Damn gangsters. That answered the question of whether Bone Eaters and Vaults got together.

"You sit there and don't move," he ordered the guy, looking to the knife between them that the gangsterer had lost when Gunter had broken his wrist. "If you're thinking about grabbing that blade and doing something stupid, there's nothing in your way. But you should ask yourself if I can't get it in my hand faster. If I win, I'll give you thirty new orifices in less than two seconds. Your call."

He didn't wait for the answer and turned to the woman. Her face was badly battered with split skin and lips. One eye was already completely swollen shut and the other was marred by green-red discoloration. Her auburn hair was shining with blood and the way she was bent to the side, at least two ribs were broken.

"Everything's fine," he told her, ordering his auto-injector to eject a vial of painkillers and one of Smartnites. Before doing so, he pulled his jacket up over his right hipbone and held out a hand. The small flap under the synth skin opened and two finger-sized glass containers fell into his hand like bullets ejected from a gun. Since they were normally injected automatically into his circulation, he had to improvise, exposing a wound on her shoulder that was bleeding profusely.

He opened the plastic cover of the analgesic and pressed the open end into the flesh wound, whereupon the woman groaned in pain and stared at him reproachfully with widened eyes.

"Sorry, can't be helped. The pain should be over in a moment," he said. The Vault still didn't budge.

Gunter waited sixty seconds and then repeated the procedure with the next vial to get the nanites into their bloodstream.

"Smartnites," he explained. "It's not much, but it's better than nothing."

The woman merely nodded and whispered a faint "Thank you" in his direction. Now Gunter turned to the boy.

"Now to you." The boy seemed to want to retreat into the wall, to melt into the rock and dissolve. His panicked gaze kept wandering to Gunter's right arm. The thirty-inch monofilament blade had retracted by now, but they both apparently knew how quickly it could reappear.

Good thing.

"First, your name."

"Ron," the gangster stammered in obvious pain, squinting at his ruined wrist lying uselessly at his side.

Gunter nodded, and Ron, with his uninjured hand, took the other to press it to his chest like a ravenous animal that had pulled its leg from a trap. A senseless but natural reflex. He wondered if "Ron" was the young man's real name, but for all intents and purposes it didn't even matter.

"You're a Vault."

A nod.

"You work for the Broker."

Ron's eyes got big. A size too big.

"For the administrator. Adam Goosens."

This time, only the gangsters' lips quivered. Score. Gunter knew he had taken a risk with his intervention, perhaps only because he hadn't gotten his desired result here tonight and was desperate to make progress. It was unprofessional and not particularly wise, but he was no closer to fulfilling his orders and needed to make a change accordingly. His instincts told him that there were clearly more important things going on here in the hustler's dock than could be guessed. When the sun shines everywhere, evil tends to linger in the only spot with shade. That's the way it always was, and that's the way it always would be.

"Why did you attack that woman?"

"We wanted her fucking credstick," Ron lied, and Gunter extended his monofilament blade. Just a few inches of the shiny, mono-bonded steel was enough to make the gangster's eyes bulge.

"Okay, okay," he gasped and swallowed. "We've been looking for her all fucking night. Jefe said she didn't have a residency permit, sou prende?"

"Your mission?"

"To find out what she knows and who brought her here."

"Brought her here from where?" echoed Gunter.

"I don't know, man!"

Tilting his head slightly to the side, Ron pleaded, "Really, I don't know!"

"Well?"

"Huh? What?"

"What did you find out?" wanted Gunter to know.

"S-she's got a technician helping her. She's been out here for days. Just in the hustler's dock. Hasn't come out with who the fucker is, though."

"What were you supposed to do with her once you get your information?"

"Well, what do you think?" asked Ron.

"Then you've done your job, do we understand each other?" Gunter pointed to the other gangster's body. "She was armed and surprised your buddy, but you disposed of her. Unfortunately, as hard as you tried, she didn't talk."

"Uh ..." The young man's face worked, then he understood he'd just been offered a way out.

"Sure, man. That's the way it went."

"Buzz off."

Ron didn't need to be told twice, got to his feet and disappeared outside into the crowd, which was pretending not to be interested in anything that was going on in the darker corners of the dock.

Of course, he could have questioned the gangster further, but only at the price of fearing for his life when the administrator scanned him with chemical-optical analysis programs. This way he could credibly assure that he had told no one and keep his secret to himself. In any case, Gunter didn't believe that these kind of foot soldiers who did the dirty work in the shadows of the station knew anything of value.

This woman, on the other hand, radiated a sublime calm that he knew only from civilians who had lost everything. He had been in the field long ago when the Republican underground had blown up a tritium plant on Bragge and they had hunted down the fleeing terrorists. Later, it had been his unit's job to secure the living quarters of the relatives. He had seen the same calm in the eyes of the children who had lost their parents and were now all alone in the universe. After the shock and the tears, when only hopelessness remained and they began to take the next steps with amazing clarity.

The woman across from him had that exact look in her eyes.

"Thank you," she whispered with obvious effort, then sighed with relief.

"Is the painkiller working?"

She nodded.

"It is a military emergency stimulant. The analgesic is mixed with amphetamine as well as arginine and is optimized for my circulation. Don't worry if you get dizzy and nauseous. It will pass," he assured her. His gaze went over his shoulder to the passersby pushing through the dark hustler dock. Their conversations wafted heavily through the aisles as an acoustic melange. No one was looking in at them yet, but he wondered when the first freelancers would claim this place for themselves and their 'clients'. And then there was still the body. He turned back to the woman. The Smartnites seemed to have already begun their work, for her left eye was visibly swelling. "I'm sorry, but I need to ask you a few questions."

"That's all right. It's the least I can do, I guess," she replied, and there was a strange accent in her voice that he couldn't place. He had once attended a meeting as part of High Lord Cornelius Andal's bodyguard, to which a diplomatic representative from the Core World of Poznan had been invited. That one had sounded similar with its rolled R and long drawn I. In any case, she was not from one of the Border Worlds or Sol, that much was certain. "Who are you?"

"It's best if you don't know," he returned.

"What did those guys really want from you?"

She eyed him long and hard. If his chrome eyes frightened her, she certainly did not let on.

"I can't prove it to you, but I'm one of the good guys."

"I got away and tried to escape," she explained, as if he had not said anything. She still seemed uncomfortable speaking, as she had to clear her throat and restart several times. "I thought I was on a spaceship, but then I realized this was an underground facility."

"A space station," he corrected her.

Her eyes widened, and her courage visibly sank. He gave her time to continue.

"I was in a tunnel where crates and containers were being handled. Nothing special. When someone saw me behind a stack of barrels, he got all excited and pointed at me. I ran away and hid here. Then these two ..." She groaned and pursed her mouth. "Well, they did this to me and kept asking me who let me out."

"Do you remember what the dock was called?" When she merely frowned, he added, "Were there markings on the wall?"

"Some places were taped over."

Gunter grunted in frustration.

"But in one place," the woman continued, "I could see parts of a letter that was either a C or an O."

"And a number?"

She shook her head.

C would mean it was one of the cargo docks, he thought, remembering the rosters of his hostage, who had no clearance there and was urged to give it a wide berth.

So Gunter didn't know much about it, only that the place handled large quantities of goods destined for transport out of the system - so it could only be Assai.

"You witnessed their drugs being loaded," he sighed. "Freighters with fake logs bring it here, and smugglers then get it out of the system to half the star empire."

To his surprise, she shook her head. "These weren't drugs. I could see a lot of it because there were whole crews with AR goggles on their heads packing."

"What are you talking about?"

"It was mostly cots, protein packs, and batteries for recyclers. Some containers were filled with biofilters and others with neural cables," she explained, and the more time passed, the clearer her eyes became, even appearing slightly feverish now under the influence of the stimulant cocktail.

"How were you able to see all this?"

"It's been boxed up, and I've spent a lot of time looking for usable junk in junkyards." A tear escaped her suddenly red eyes and rolled down her soiled cheek. Her gaze was all at once riddled with a deep-seated pain.

"What else did you see?" he pressed her more brusquely than he had intended. Beds? Neural cables? Recycler batteries? He had expected something special, but apparently she had merely come across a normal handling of goods, or the booty of a pirate who wanted to get rid of them because of their low value on the Cerberus.

Apparently, the stranger seemed to relate his request to the same experience: "There was a woman, she didn't fit in there somehow. Looked like one of the governor's daughters back home: stiff, stuck-up, and cold."

"What did she look like?"

"Had a narrow face, dark-skinned, plus a thin ponytail. And she was almost as tall as you."

Gunter froze. The description more or less matched the masked appearance of Akwa Marquandt, whom he had observed two days ago when she arrived. Now his interest was rekindled. What did the fleet admiral's daughter have to do with loading everyday goods on the Cerberus?

"Did you see anything else? Anything at all? This woman, did she speak?" he asked.

"No." The stranger indicated a shake of her head. "I think she was just there for a minute."

Gunter thought, but couldn't figure out what he had heard. At the same time, he could see no sign that the woman was lying to him.

"You're not from around here," he noted. "They didn't even know we were on a space station."

She shook her head, but didn't reply.

"How did you get here? The gangster said someone helped you escape. Escaped from where? And who helped you?" he pressed her as he sensed someone approaching. His gaze jerked left to a lanky guy in skin-tight latex who was wiping off strange lipstick.

"Hey, I work here, man!" the hustler leered.

Gunter gave him a definite look and the troublemaker retreated with his hands up. Their time had apparently run out.

Since the woman made no effort to answer his questions, he decided not to probe further. He would not threaten violence against an innocent civilian anyway.

"Thank you for saving me," she said with honest gratitude in her eyes. He stood up and helped her to her feet. "What's your name?"

The last Fleet

"Marine," he replied, and she nodded in understanding. "And you?"

"Masha." Then, as if she had to convince herself that was still the case, she repeated with a rapt look: "My name is Masha."

INTERLUDE: WALL SECTOR DELTA, TRAFALGAR SYSTEM

Admiral Samuel Taggert, high lord of his house, senior member of the Council of Nobility and ruler of Gamma Sector, fleet admiral of the Imperial Navy and member of the Council of Admiralty, shook off the brief sense of disorientation that each jump brought.

"Status." he ordered calmly, opening his eyes. Before him were the two semicircles of consoles in the dim yellow light of the readiness alert. At them sat a total of forty specialists in a wide variety of ship systems that controlled everything aboard his flagship. The *Invincible* was a last-generation battlecruiser, squat as a pit bull and at least as dangerous. What the latest models offered in speed and lower manpower, his *Invincible* more than made up for in his eyes with its yard-thick Carbin armor and sheer number of launch ramps.

"Transit successful," Salisbury reported from navigation. "Receiving pings from the fleet. No casualties so far."

"Extend sensors, full battle alert!"

An alarm of seven short tones, deafening and piercing, followed by a long drone, echoed across the bridge and through all the corridors. Red alert sirens sent their glow through the battleship, sending every soldier to the nearest acceleration couch and emergency seats.

"Fleet complete," Salisbury reported. "Eight hundred and forty valid transponder pings."

"Initiate battle plan alpha. Issue formation order," Samuel ordered. "Prepare jump thrusters."

"Energy matrix cells building potential, energy nodes charging at full efficiency," replied Anastasiou from Energy Management. "Time to T: twenty-nine minutes."

"Recon? Give me something!"

"Six drive flares, seven hundred million clicks away. No known signatures."

Samuel did a quick calculation in his head. "Then the recordings are just under twenty minutes old. We'll stay put for now. Report as soon as the *Alexandria* transmits data."

The *Alexandria* was the only civilian ship in his fleet and one of the most powerful research vessels in the Science Corps when it came to gravitational waves. Four highly sensitive interferometers jammed like giant spears on her slender back, several miles long and barely thicker than a tree trunk. It had dropped out of subspace one hundred thousand clicks ahead of their formation to avoid being 'blinded' by the gravitational bursts of its fleet.

On the main screen, Samuel watched the countdown to full charge tick down. Half an hour could pass agonizingly slowly. Every combat commander knew that time was the most relative force in the universe. The 'bloody tyrant', as Shakespeare had so aptly put it centuries ago in the land of his ancestors.

His battle plan was daring and risky. After half a century, he knew that great victories could only be accomplished with great risk, and they needed nothing less here

The last Fleet

if the Wall Sectors were to keep from collapsing completely.

Six ships. Six enemy ships had been enough to destroy the entire defenses of a Wall System. So the Science Corps' theories that the Orb had only a few ships - due to the expected massive energy consumption of their advanced systems and their previous appearance in small numbers - did not exactly reassure him. But it was also a fact that static defenses caught off guard were quite different from a fleet of mobile, weaponized ships equipped with the best munitions in the Star Empire and having the Navy's most experienced and best-trained spacefarers. It was about the difference between a rook and a queen on a chessboard, nothing less. However, a queen was only as good as she was used, and so it all came down to Samuel's battle plan, for which he had determined maximum element of surprise and the exploitation of her mobility in the compound as the prime maxim.

And he had an advantage that the defenders of the Trafalgar system had not had: he knew that the enemy's ships were invisible to all sensors except interferometers. Also, that signal interference from the lidar was not really interference but contacts - albeit difficult to pinpoint precisely - was a trump card that no commander had yet held against the Orb. Data from the few survivors of the Trafalgar raid had also revealed that the enemy ships had highly effective energy weapons, visible as light in a vacuum. So they were probably dealing with some form of extremely hot plasma, and that meant that their origin had to be visible - and thus the enemy weapons that were usually on the ship. Damned if those weren't good targets for his fire control officers.

The only catch was that he had to be close to the enemy to do this, so that there was virtually no time between the launch and impact of torpedoes, beam weapons and railguns. Metaphorically speaking, as a boxer, he had to catch a shooter's bullet and then somehow sprint to him and knock him out. Not a situation any commander wanted to find himself in, but that was how the dice fell.

Gravity waves moved through space at the speed of light, and that meant that distances away from planetary surfaces, incomprehensible to the human mind, again turned honest battles into mathematical moves, with hours often passing between them, or at least minutes. His ancestors had still fired cannons at the French in the historic Battle of Trafalgar. Shoot, impact. Very simple. At that time, distances were still measured in yards and miles, today in units of time, because they reflected distances more precisely and comprehensibly for humans in space.

Here and now, nothing was simple anymore.

After ten minutes, the *Alexandria* finally reported.

"Interferometer showing six deflections. Position marked," Anastasiou from reconnaissance translated the incoming data stream. "Ten minutes away."

So the bastards covered twenty minutes, he glanced at the countdown, *in six minutes*.

"Transit pattern?"

"Deflections equal," the officer confirmed.

"Then they've jumped." Ten minutes away meant ten light minutes and about four hundred million miles. Too far, even for the fastest long-range weapons in his arsenal. Questions automatically arose in his mind: why had they not jumped directly into his formation and opened fire? Was their range reduced? Was their navigation disrupted by the significant gravitational waves of his fleet? Or did they jump twice because they were in no hurry and could do as they pleased anyway? At least they could do their

The last Fleet

scans at their leisure without the data being half an hour old. The question of all questions, however, was: How had the enemy been able to react so quickly when it was barely twenty light minutes away? Neither the gravitational waves of his fleet nor their radar signatures could have made the trip in a few minutes. Yet the enemy had located them - not with 'old' light, like them, but with some technology that Star Empire scientists still believed to be physically impossible.

"Pull formation together," he ordered. For with all the questions burning on his commander's soul, he did know one answer: what he would do to take out such a large mass of opponents. The wolf snatched the most sheep if he managed to get into the middle of their flock, and the wolves that were lying in wait for them were invisible. He hated his own command, knowing how costly it might be to them in precious human lives. A game. Everything was a game in the face of the enemy. The only question was whether they could see his cards. With their overwhelming technological superiority, he had to assume that they could. And that was why the next command followed immediately.

"Fleet-wide order: Abort jump engine power-up. Full power to weapons systems. Open all launch bays, magnetize railguns, charge laser capacitors! Turn all ships one hundred and eighty degrees!" he shouted with measured urgency.

Less than five seconds later, as his bridge crew worked frantically to implement his orders and coordinate the fleet of over eight hundred ships, the enemy appeared.

The alarm rang out, triggered by six event horizons whose concentric gravitational waves made even the cruder interferometers of the Navy ships cry out and appear in close proximity behind their formation. His ships, in the midst of a turning maneuver, executed their orders and turned toward the enemy's new position.

Now, according to the data of the lost defenders of Trafalgar, they had about two minutes before the enemy could jump again. A tiny time span for a space battle and at the same time possibly longer than they would survive.

The Orbs did not even think of waiting for the full turn of the assembled fleet and already started firing. Six projectiles, their propulsion flares appearing for only a fraction of a second, sped toward them. They appeared on the radar as ultra-fast objects and immediately disappeared. In accordance with his orders, the ships under his command fired at the suspected source, but there were no explosions to indicate hits.

Instead, the *Invincible*'s gamma ray detectors began screeching shortly thereafter, and half of its sensors jumped to red, signaling total failures. The remaining ones had shut down quickly enough and were only starting up again.

"What happened?" he asked.

"Unclear!" shouted Recon.

"Initial telemetry data coming in, Admiral."

He could already see it. In the tactical holofield that provided him with real-time data, six huge, spherical holes gaped in his fleet. They had been there a moment ago; now they were annihilated. There was not much left of them but spreading clouds of high-energy elemental particles.

Two hundred ships. In one fell swoop.

"All railguns open fire! Barrage!" he ordered, and thousands of magnetic sled cannons spat their tungsten rounds into empty space, hunters firing indiscriminately into the forest in hopes of a lucky hit.

"Reuters, prepare the four Mark II Phantoms!" came

The last Fleet

his next order, and silence fell abruptly on the bridge. Not the professional silence of well-trained soldiers, but a heavy, weighing silence spread.

"Mark II Phantoms one through four in the launch bays and ready," reported Reuters from fire control.

"Stand by. Fire only on my command. Prepare launch pattern Epsilon."

The next six invisible torpedoes, or whatever the aliens' infernal work might be, appeared. This time five thousand clicks away from another location. Three explosions lit up the room, glaring white and followed by a burst of hard radiation that lit up all the warning displays. Then the next three pnched holes in his formation, which was far too narrow for such kind of bombardment and allowed the enemy to reap a bloody harvest. Still - and it pained Samuel - he kept to his plan.

He waited, clenching his jaws until it hurt, enduring the sight of red flashing and disappearing symbols on his battlefield hologram. Because he had to. Because behind each of them were dozens, sometimes hundreds, of soldiers' lives. Erased and torn from the pattern of the universe, from one second to the next.

Shortly after, the terrible energy lances appeared, with which the aliens cut through his formation like through butter. The sight of them horrified and relieved him at the same time, as they finally had a targeting solution. The remaining sixty percent of his ships fired everything they had at the Orb's starships, their alien squid shapes appearing briefly each time the glaring beams came to life, always destroying ten or more of his men and women's ships.

And they hit. Hundreds, thousands of projectiles as well as X-rays and laser beams. They had no appreciable effect. True, the enemy's cloaking seemed to fail at times to repel the kinetic and energy onslaught, and the ships kept flickering. But they did not explode.

" Fire Phantoms!" he gave the order he wished he never had to give.

The four special torpedoes, which had been in the best-secured underground bunker in his Queensferry home just the day before, left their launch bays and sought their way to the enemy. The latter did not even bother to intercept them - why should they? The previous weapons had no effect whatsoever on their fighting ability.

That's what Samuel was counting on.

It took thirty seconds to reach the predicted detonation points, which had been carefully selected. Thirty seconds in which more and more of his ships were destroyed. They dissolved in volatile gas clouds under the extreme heat of the alien beam weapons. Larger ones, like the two remaining carriers and cruisers, were sliced open and then vaporized or went into such a spin that they turned into expanding zones of debris.

Then the first Orb ship jumped and disappeared, followed by another before the Phantoms ignited. Four warheads, each containing fifty grams of antimatter, cut off the power supply to their magnetic coils. The containment chambers dissolved into pure energy in the instant annihilation reaction, which manifested as white flashes of light that boiled the universe. Whatever was within the radius of action of the merciless physical processes simply dissolved. Two alien ships disappeared, two more stopped flickering, lost their cloaking fields, and began to light up in several places when the heat inside could no longer be dissipated.

Many of Samuel's remaining ships were swept to their deaths with them, either melted by the extremely high

The last Fleet

temperatures, or the crews killed by radiation racing up and down the entire electromagnetic spectrum.

Those that still had a serviceable crew and a handful of sensors that had not fallen victim to the particle storm concentrated their fire on the damaged enemy, shredding it to pieces.

The feeling of triumph was short-lived and soon gave way to the stale taste of loss and guilt that worked its way into the pit of his stomach like acid. They were the first to ever successfully fight the Orb. The first to destroy not just one of their ships, but four. And yet, with the thousands dead, it felt like defeat. Not to mention that he had had to achieve the 'success' with the use of outlawed weapons, which brought with them two problems at once: First, there was a terrible debt on the technology, namely the lives of millions of people who had been destroyed by its existence during the time of the Solar Union. Second, there would be no denying hereafter that the Navy had secretly stockpiled what should have been forbidden weapons, the possession of which officially carried the death penalty and the prohibition of which was enforced with an iron hand by the fleet.

But political problems were now the last thing Admiral Samuel Taggert had to deal with.

"Admiral!" shouted Anastasiou, and the excitement in the reconnaissance officer's voice did not bode well. He expected the two remaining alien ships to show up, and they did, five hundred thousand clicks away - to finish them off, he supposed. They didn't have more than the four phantoms at their disposal, after all, and he doubted the enemy would let themselves be taken by surprise like that again. But there was something else, the reason why the usually controlled Lieutenant Commander sounded so shrill: massive gravitational waves, which the Alexandria identified as a total of five hundred event horizons, three hundred thousand clicks away.

"Oh, damn," was all he could say. No more than a hundred ships remained of his fleet and no more than smoke and mirrors of the Science Corps' theories about the numerically small strength of the Orb forces.

5

GAVIN

Gavin's last spinal cord treatment was the most pleasant of all. The injection needle for the pluripotent stem cells that Sphinx had extracted and multiplied from his thymus gland reminded him more of a dagger than a needle, but it was only a quick prick. Without a subsequent headache that turned the top of his skull into fire or the feeling of having shards of glass in his spine.

Significantly more unpleasant was the conversation with Hellcat when he tried to tell her about Dodger and him going out to explore the area - without her.

"Out of the question!" she echoed, shooting up from her bunk like a rocket.

"You're not ready yet," he countered, trying for a soothing tone. "Even though you seem to be back to your old self in some areas..."

"My treatment is complete. I've had another six bloody hours of sleep now. I'm certainly not going to sit here and listen to Bambam's bleating booming through the plumbing!"

"You barely have any Smartnites left in your body, and I'm guessing half your implants aren't working."

"I don't have many anyway, so it doesn't make a damn bit of difference." She swung her legs, long and toned, out of bed. As if automatically, his gaze traveled along them before he cleared his throat and quickly looked back up into her face. Hellcat didn't even seem to have noticed, her expression a mask of righteous anger. "Give me a fucking gun and let's get on with it."

"I'd like to order you, as captain..."

"You're welcome to do so, but I don't give a shit."

"A functioning chain of command..."

"...is essential for survival on a starship. I can see that. But right now we're not a spaceship, we're a wreck in a mountain. So it's more like a house."

"Ah..."

"Gun," she reminded him, and he sighed in surrender.

"I don't have a chance to change your mind, do I?"

"Nope."

"Great." He groaned in resignation.

"Are you worried about your favorite terrorist?" she asked, smiling amusedly before eyeing him with a provocative smile.

Gavin grumbled and gave her a wave. "You can just stand in front if a bloody alien dinosaur comes to eat us."

"Spoken like a Republican underground fighter," she cooed wryly. "Topped off with a curse. There you go."

He kept his next curse to himself, swallowing his genuine concern for her. Watching her put her life on the line for him and then bleed out in a vacuum had stirred something inside him. What exactly it was he couldn't even say, only that he never wanted to experience it again.

They met Dodger in the armory. The mutant had already equipped herself with a *Thunderbolt* pistol and an

Avenger assault rifle. A belt with spare magazines hung around her chest.

"Those are Army weapons," Gavin noted with surprise - and some relief, since zero-G weapons didn't do well inside gravity wells.

"Yep."

"Where did you get them?"

"From Andal."

"You don't say," he snorted.

"We got the stuff from an abandoned Army depot in Skaland," Hellcat replied.

"By abandoned depot, surely you mean you drove off or killed the soldiers and then took it all?" speculated Gavin.

She looked him in the eye, seemed to want to say something, then apparently changed her mind. "Do you really want to know?"

"No. I'd rather not." He had Dodger give him a rifle and pistol of his own, loaded them through, then put a holster around his right thigh. He swung a magazine belt over his hip. He familiarized himself with the Avenger by raising the shock pad to his shoulder a few times and looking through the targeting optics. As a fleet officer, he didn't have a target link like the ground forces or Marines, which used induction pads in the palm of his hand to allow direct targeting through the retina, so he had to fight with it the old-fashioned way. Training on the *Avenger* had been rudimentary at best and long ago, had to have been sometime in the first few weeks after he enrolled.

"What about body armor? Did you guys take those too? Right now, I wouldn't judge you for that..."

"Already took a step out," Dodger said, shaking his head. "Roaring hot and humid. That's where we're going in. With the battery packs we've got, the power might last a couple of hours."

"Then we'd better save it," he agreed with her. "First, we should explore the surrounding area."

"Fit again?", Dodger inquired, addressing Hellcat. When she gave a thumbs up, the mutant merely nodded.

Gavin wished his life were that simple.

As soon as they were finished arming themselves, he radioed Bambam to let him know they were leaving and would return in an hour.

"Did you bring the signal booster I gave you?" the mechanic wanted to know.

"I did." Gavin tapped against his pants pocket, which held the finger-sized cylinder that appeared to be Bambam's own design. "We'll check in every fifteen minutes."

They made their way to the airlock. The outer door was closed, and it was nowhere near as hot as the last time he had seen Dodger handle the laser.

"Wherever we are, we stay together and don't do anything rash, understand?" he said with a commander's manner, which the other two seemed to find kind of funny. Hellcat chuckled and shook her head, while Dodger merely snorted once, which sounded like the labored beginnings of a laugh that died out immediately.

"Sure thing, *boss*," Hellcat said, slamming a fist on the button next to the outer airlock door, which then slid upward into its socket.

Immediately, Gavin was met with a wall of heat and humidity that had him breaking out in a sweat in short order. He grabbed his rifle and angled it in front of his chest as he had been trained to do. While he was still bracing himself, Hellcat led the way. A few steps only, then she stopped.

The last Fleet

Gavin followed her through the tunnel cut into the rock, where they all had to stoop. At its end, it was almost as bright as inside the ship. He had to squeeze next to the underground fighter to see anything.

What he saw then took his breath away.

They were above a gently sloping rock slope on which a tongue of molten and re-solidified rock had formed, and they could look out over a vast land. As far as the eye could see, forests stretched out between the individual woods rising from them. The trees were large and magnificent, their leaves seeming to glow from within, forming a sea of fluorescent greens and blues. As the son of a High Lord, Gavin had visited many worlds of the Star Empire - even at his young age. Most of them had somehow disappointed him, as nature looked mostly like on Andal: mixed forests in the temperate zones, mighty and diverse palm analogs and trees with countless creepers along the equator, and tough conifers in the cold polar regions. Wherever he had traveled with his family, hardly anything had really impressed him or seemed strange to him. Of course, the wide-reaching branches of the Laprachen on Indirium rightly attracted millions of visitors from all over the Star Empire every year. The tree species, in which individual specimens spread for miles and formed dense structures that covered entire valleys, were unique. Similarly, the floating radendron flowers on New Eden, as large as houses and beautiful habitats for countless life forms, have not unjustly been chosen as backdrops in many romance films. But even these two examples, still very present in his memory, were features in a largely familiar environment.

In the valley before him, however, *everything* was foreign.

The colors seemed fake, almost artificial, the leaves more fleshy than anything he knew, and even the smell did not evoke anything familiar in his brain. He didn't even know what to compare it to. Perhaps with the scent of burnt steak and a hint of lavender - but even that was only a false approximation that did no justice to the strangeness. Then there was the soundscape. It reminded him distantly of the world-spanning jungles on Lagastia, but only distantly. Hollow-sounding calls resounded through the valley, mingling with the sounds of birds - or what he interpreted as birds.

"Shit!" breathed Hellcat. "Where did we end up?"

"I don't know," Gavin felt compelled to reply without taking his eyes off the scenery below them. "Looks like something out of a fantasy movie."

"We're not on Yokatami, anyway," Dodger agreed.

"S2-Yokatami," he corrected her absent-mindedly.

"At least you're still the same," Hellcat sighed. "A smartass."

The mutant made a sound that was possibly meant to be a chuckle.

"Seriously?" he asked in her direction. "You're laughing at *that*?"

She shrugged and he rolled his eyes.

"Well, let's take a look around." Gavin pushed past Hellcat, intent on removing their motivation for renewed jokes at his expense, and jumped down onto the slope. As soon as he left the tongue of dried rock behind him, the scree became coarser and interspersed with pebbles. He had to concentrate to avoid losing his balance and sliding uncontrollably down the slope. The way back would be strenuous, that much was certain.

At the end of the descent, he reached the first bushes and shrubs. Fascinated by the sight of them, he reached out a hand for the leaves. They were as large as saucers and the edges were serrated. Unlike anything he had known so far, they possessed a uniform structure, not the apparent jumble of different cells. They were also fleshy, thick like his fingers, and bluish veins shimmered beneath their green surface. The intensity of their coloring increased and then decreased, like a pulse beating.

"Fascinating," he murmured, but paused with his fingers before touching the strange plant. Only now did he notice that Hellcat and Dodger had arrived beside him and seemed equally captivated by the mystical beauty of their surroundings.

"Don't touch it," he advised them. "It was pretty stupid of us to go out without breathing apparatus and gloves."

"It's way too warm," the mutant opined, as if that answered all their questions and fears.

"Well, I got my annual inoculation cocktail already," Hellcat said with a shrug. "Two thousand pathogens or so."

"More than four thousand. But it's not a vaccine cocktail, it's an immune booster that's tailored to you based on your own stem cells. It doesn't vaccinate you in that sense, but it gets your immune system working as efficiently and quickly as possible, so it doesn't matter what it's fighting."

"Well then, we're safe."

"This isn't flora that we're familiar with, and if the flora is different, the fauna is inevitably different because the two are in symbiosis with each other - in any ecosystem," Gavin explained. Being able to explain something felt good, *normal*, in this anything-but-normal environment.

Hellcat and Dodger gave each other questioning looks, and he sighed once more.

"Plants and animals here are unlike anything I've ever seen, and that's saying something."

"Surely you don't know all the systems in the Star Empire," Hellcat said, shaking her head.

"No, but I certainly would have heard about them in biology class if there had been plants with blue veins and their own pulse beats," he replied.

"In my experience, teachers don't know jack about the real world outside the classroom."

Gavin thought about saying something more to that, but then shrugged and watched the two of them paw at the leaves like children seeing lily pads for the first time. Instead of following suit, he looked up at the blue sky and saw a large moon with its surface scarred by craters a few handbreadths from the central star, burning a yellowish hue down on them. But there was something else, a black spot just above the horizon like a bat that had spread its wings to cover as much of the sky as possible and plunge into darkness.

Where have we landed? he asked himself once more.

"Let's move on." Without waiting for their response, he walked deeper into the forest. The bark of the trees was dark, almost like anthracite, and streaked with the same blue veins as their leaves and those of the bushes and shrubs. Creeping plants made it difficult to progress, and he had to keep circling particularly dense sections. Every single plant had the blue pulse - but why? To his knowledge, ecosystems consisted of species in competition and symbiosis with one another, which formed a cohesive whole by occupying a wide variety of niches. Here, the individual plants looked different in size and shape, but they were all united by the blue pulse. Distantly, it reminded Gavin of the blue glow of the Saphyra tree on the forbidden planet, which he had seen in photographs. But only very distantly.

"I know I missed a lot, what with all the near-death

stuff," Hellcat commented as they wandered in wonder through the alien biosphere - except for Dodger, who seemed focused and bored at the same time, as always. "But I'd like to know where you jumped, Gav."

He winced when he heard her say his nickname. She emphasized it almost as much as Lizzy had.

"I swear to you, I entered the neighboring seed system. But we jumped into the atmosphere of a gravity well during a fall, about the riskiest kind of jump there is in the pilot's manual. We could have come out anywhere."

"Well, we certainly didn't come out on S2-Yokatami," she noted.

"No," he agreed with her. "In fact, I'm sure we're not on any world ever mapped by the Star Empire."

"Amazing that we can still breathe normally," Dodger observed.

Gavin hadn't thought about it at all, blaming his mental absence on the fact that twenty-four hours ago he had been paralyzed from having his spine shattered by a treacherous Marine. Only now did he call up the data from his environmental sensor, which was in the form of tiny probes on his septum.

But no data was displayed to him.

"Can you get in touch with your neural computers?" he asked, frozen to the spot. "I can access it, but not the secondary systems data."

"Nope," Dodger said, and Hellcat also shook her head.

"It was working a minute ago. Weird."

"Maybe a jamming field."

"Maybe," he repeated with a furrowed brow, reaching again to his wrist terminal, which had its own unit of environmental sensors, even if it wasn't a wickedly expensive Deltaware like the one in his nose. The atmospheric composition was almost like that on Andal, with a little over seventy-two percent nitrogen and twenty-three percent oxygen. The rest was carbon dioxide - somewhat elevated - and a number of noble gases, of which only argon was too high to be considered healthy. But there was nothing to cause them problems in the short term - which, on such an alien world, was tantamount to a miracle.

"Photosynthesis seems to be something universal,"

"You know what photosynthesis is?" asked Gavin in Hellcat's direction, and she merely gave him the finger in reply. He grinned to make it look like he was joking.

"If photosynthesis is universal, so is oxygen as the basis for more highly evolved life," he continued in an attempt to rationalize what he was experiencing. "Or carbon. So everything here looks strange, but it's made up of carbon as the main element. Carbon atoms can form many bonds, making them extremely stable. That's probably why all the terra-compatible worlds in the Star Empire have had comparable biospheres, even if the animal kingdom differs greatly."

"Let's move on before he writes another book," Hellcat suggested, and Dodger nodded.

Gavin shook his head and followed them. Rational or not, he didn't want to stay behind in this place alone, despite all its fascinating beauty. For this beauty was uncanny to him. As a teenager, he had once seen at a friend's house one of those forbidden sex robots that his parents kept hidden in the basement. The perfection of the intelligent doll had frightened him, and he didn't dare touch it. He had felt like a fish being held out a tempting bait, which nevertheless contained a sharp hook.

He had exactly the same feeling again now.

"Have you ever been to the jungles of Andal? In the southern plains?" he asked after a few minutes, during which they had circled man-sized tree trunks and touched far too many things for him to feel sane. Now he could only hope that after centuries of human colonization of exoplanets, their upgraded immune systems could withstand whatever alien bacteria and viruses this world had in store. Had he not discharged a large portion of his Smartnites with the patching together of his neural stratum in his spinal cord and only a hull supply left in his intestinal lacunae, he would have been considerably less nervous.

He looked at his chronometer and winced. Quickly, he took the signal booster from Bambam and held it close over his wrist terminal before opening a connection.

"Gavin?" he heard the mechanic ask through a storm of white noise.

"Yes. I'm running late, sorry. But we're fine! We'll check in every hour from now on."

"Got ... up. As of ...ow ...ill ...orsecode. Sta... interf..."

"The connectiong is gone," he said loudly, turning the signal booster once in his hand. There was a single button on the bottom. He pressed it long three times, paused, and then pressed it long once, short once, and long again. *O-K*.

"A signal jammer nearby?" asked Hellcat. "Don't see how a forest would jam radio signals. No matter how strange it comes across."

"Possibly. I suggest we keep moving. He should be picking up Morse code, because that can also be represented as noise, or gaps in the noise."

"Yep," Dodger said, and walked on, undeterred. For a while they plodded along in silence, accompanied only by the manifold sounds of the alien jungle and the rhythm of the steady pulse that passed through the forest as a blue flicker, as if through a single organism. It happened every five seconds, he had counted.

After fifteen minutes, he transmitted *OK* again in Morse code. Ten minutes later, Dodger suddenly stopped and raised a hand which was clenched into a fist. Gavin and Hellcat stopped and looked around uneasily.

"What?" he hissed to the front.

"Voices," the mutant replied in a whisper. "Ten o'clock."

Gavin listened as best he could, and after what felt like an eternity, he heard them. Voices, laboriously suppressed and wildly jumbled. They were getting closer.

Clearly they were not alone.

6

JANUS

"Admiral," Janus greeted the Chief of Staff as they met outside the door to the Emperor's office.

"First Secretary of State," Marius Albius said.

None of them made any move to place their hand on any of the DNA scanners that would identify them as permitted for the upcoming meeting and open the door.

And disable the many active and passive weapons, Janus thought. He had never liked this place. It looked ostentatious and heavy in a baroque sort of way, but not like a weapons-rigged airlock that could blast to dust and poison anything that approached.

"I trust you had a good journey?" he asked the admiral.

"A little faster than expected," Albius returned. They both stared at the door. They were a minute early.

"Ah, but you like to be ahead of your schedules, I suppose?"

"At the right time. I make sure to always be there at the right time."

"I'm sure that's why you've made it this far up the

ladder," Janus commented. "Only a man who is tightly organized and can plan, as you do, is destined for greater things."

"Quite so," Albius countered in his rumbling way, which of course was only a facade. "But I'll tell you something, Lord Darishma: I only got to the top because I don't play games like you do."

"Is that so?"

The Chief of Staff turned his head toward him and eyed him with narrowed brows. "Excuse me?"

"At the top."

The corners of Albius' mouth twitched, but before he could retort, Janus beat him to it, putting on a carefree smile, "Ah! Look at the time."

He pressed his hand to the scanner pad and had his palm print and DNA matched. The door opened. Behind it, ten Imperial Guard soldiers stood to the right and left of the next door that led to the office itself. Their pitch-black powered armor with gold trim hummed menacingly as they took posture. Two palace servants stood ready to open the two heavy wings.

Janus walked with Albius across the marble of the short hallway where they were again screened, and then they were finally let through to the Emperor. He was standing in front of his window and was just kissing his daughter, Princess Elayne, on the forehead after noticing her, as if surprised by her arrival.

"Ah, Janus, Marius. Come," he greeted them, gesturing to the ornate genuine leather sitting area that sprawled in front of a stone fireplace on one side and the window front on the other.

"Think about it, Dad," Elayne asked, then retreated. As she passed, she nodded to Janus and ignored the admiral. Both bowed according to protocol and waited until

The last Fleet

she had departed and the door was closed again. Hearing the emperor addressed as 'Dad' seemed so absurd to Janus that it felt surreal every time.

They sat down on the sofa some distance away and waited until Haeron II put glasses of whiskey down for them, as he always used to do at the small meetings. The death message from Magnus and the affair with Paris had visibly affected his master. Deep crow's feet had formed in the corners of his eyes, as if the next rejuvination was overdue, his hair looked brittle and thinning, his eyes puffy. His modified genes were still undeniable, giving him a fundamentally impressive vitality and ageless youthfulness, but all radiance of power and wisdom was now covered by a shadow. It made the room seem colder and the fire in the fireplace like an unfulfilled promise of homeliness.

"Samuel has fallen," the Emperor began the conversation as soon as the glasses were set down on the top of the low teak table in front of them with a hollow *clunk*. He sighed heavily and settled into the wing chair across from them. As he did so, he seemed to slump, as if his bones had suddenly liquefied.

"The loss of Admiral Taggert is a tragedy, Your Majesty," Albius took the floor. "But he died a hero and accomplished something that no one before him had ever done: He showed that the Orb can be beaten."

"He didn't beat the damn aliens, though!" roared Haeron II. "He destroyed four ships. FOUR! And he lost the fleets of an entire Wall Sector for that. Not to mention the fact that we now have to justify our possession of antimatter weapons."

"The monopoly on force in the Star Empire rests with you and the Navy. Everyone knows that. In the old days, nukes were outlawed - for those nation-states that did not possess them. I don't see why it should be any different today. People associated trauma with nuclear weapons for a long time, too; Hiroshima and Nagasaki," the Chief of Staff said.

"Do you really think that the general population will display such historically based foresight as you do, Admiral?" the Emperor wanted to know, snorting to leave no doubt that it was a rhetorical question.

"We still have the option - and I'm not saying I like it - to reprimand Admiral Taggert post mortem for this."

"There's no way we're going to throw High Lord Taggert out the airlock!" said Janus firmly, and was relieved when his master nodded.

"Janus is right. Samuel laid down his life for the Star Empire, and no one could have accomplished more under the circumstances. He died a hero and will be honored as such!"

"Of course, your majesty. That is the right thing to do." Albius obediently bowed his head. "However, we still have the problem with the Orb fleet, and with the passing of my honored comrade and his entire fleet, a problem here on the ground as well. Especially in light of the increased threat level, Sol must be our absolute priority. We cannot afford to put the heart and head of humanity at risk."

"The Wall Sectors are a long way from here," Janus pointed out.

"Even for the Orb?" Albius gave him a questioning look. "They can jump within two minutes and are almost invisible to us. Why should we assume that they are not at least as fast as our couriers, who take only a few days to travel the distance?"

"That danger is undeniable," the Emperor agreed with his Chief of Staff.

The last Fleet

"Nevertheless, we should not rush things. The choice of Taggert as the new commander of the Home Fleet and the recall of his Wall Fleet was an easy decision because his loyalty and abilities were beyond doubt," said Janus, who was the only one who had not yet touched his whiskey. "Besides, there is no evidence that the Orb even know that Sol is our center or that we have a centralized form of government. They probably don't even know our language, and the Science Corps has no evidence that the aliens ..."

"The Science Corps!", Haeron II broke him off, snorting like a bull that's hoofing it's way to the attack. "You mean the same Science Corps that thought the Orb had only a few ships?"

"His Majesty is right," Albius spoke up again. "In addition, we have no way of knowing how often and in how much detail the enemy has spied on us so far. With their cloaked ships, they could have mapped all the systems of our star empire in the last few decades and learned everything they need to know."

The Emperor pointed an outstretched index finger at the Grand Admiral to indicate his agreement.

"I do not think so. Our system defenses all have dense networks of interferometers to record even the smallest transits of unauthorized drones or the like. If there had been corresponding border violations, we would have noticed," Janus countered.

"I would not pin my hopes on that, First Secretary. With all due respect, I think that attitude is naive," Albius said.

Janus gritted his teeth and looked to his master, but he seemed to be elsewhere in thought and scowled.

"We have no clue, if I may put it so casually, what the murderous Orb can and cannot do. The fact is, however, that they are so far ahead of us that we must expect anything. Even getting to Sol in one jump, knowing full well that it is our home system and seat of the most important man," the Chief of Staff continued, displaying an almost grandiose self-conviction, fueled by the apparent free ride.

"Sol *must* be protected," he said.

"We can't pull out any more Wall Fleets," Haeron II decided, "No matter what. The border is far too thinly defended. We'll give as many antimatter weapons from the depots as we can - but only to the Wall Sector defenders. Taggert's sacrifice will be celebrated as a victory, and our stockpiling of outlawed weapons will be portrayed as wise foresight. The people must know that only by this could we accomplish anything, and then they will not reproach us."

"What fleets should we withdraw then?" asked Janus. "The Border Worlds have run out of capacity due to the loss of most of their fleets and will not be able to make up for the losses for decades. The Core Worlds? Those are fat, lush colonies from the first wave of expansion. They are loyal because they are doing well and the economy is humming. If we ask them to put down ships, they'll see that as a loss of resources that they won't be compensated for. And the Frontier Worlds need everything they have in terms of warships, even to disrupt rampant smuggling routes and defend against piracy and border disputes."

"I agree with this - rather rough - assessment," Albius said graciously, as if he had just patted his son on the head for dutifully reciting something he had learned.

"Then let's focus on the Wall Systems," Janus suggested, ignoring the Chief of Staff. He looked directly at the Emperor, seeking his gaze. "Your Majesty, the Orb have never approached any systems other than

The last Fleet

those in the Wall. Wherever we withdraw forces, they are lacking elsewhere. If we continue to decimate them in the Border Worlds, your most loyal supporters may revolt."

"With what? They have no fleets left," Albius interjected.

"The Frontier Worlds have at best third-rate ships at their disposal, mostly discarded cruisers and frigates from the Core Worlds," Janus continued, as if the aged admiral had said nothing. "The Core Worlds, however, will not be pleased, but they are the economic engine of your Star Empire. If we anger them, we create a whole new set of problems for ourselves. Besides, they share an inadequacy with the next solution, which seems logical: hire mercenaries. If we hire all the mercenary companies in the corporate protectorate, they might be able to provide a thousand or more ships. All of them converted former Navy ships or home-built. Effective and pragmatic, but also chaotic and created not for system defense but for variable combat missions. They lack loyalty, however. How long will they fight if they find themselves in a situation like Admiral Taggert? Their loyalty is to the money, not the throne."

"But Sol *must* be protected," the Emperor insisted.

"What about *your* fleet?" asked Janus in the direction of the Chief of Staff.

"If you mean my House's fleet, I have dispatched it to the Gamma Wall Sector by order of His Majesty."

Surprised, he looked to Haeron II, who, however, did not return his gaze. "To Taggert's sector?"

"Yes. Since, as you know, my sector is directly adjacent to Gamma and Delta, it was only logical that I personally see to the swift compensation of losses," Albius replied graciously in place of the Emperor. The slight mockery in his voice was barely noticeable, but impossible for Janus to miss.

"Of course," he played the game. "A pragmatic solution, though it surprises me, given your insistence that Sol was the most important place in need of protection now."

"That's true, but we still have a fleet left - one of the most powerful currently."

"Marquandt," Janus said, a knot forming in his stomach. *Of course.*

"Yes."

"This is not a good idea, Your Majesty. The circumstances of the Battle of Andal are still unclear."

"In this regard, I have news to announce," Albius said, tapping his wrist terminal. "The fleet admiral has prepared and sent his full battle report. It has been sworn and verified by all officers on his staff."

Janus blinked in surprise. He had the unmistakable feeling he had fallen into a trap. Now lying there with his legs broken while the Chief of Staff walked around him with bared teeth, wondering where to bite first to get the best piece, did not appeal to him at all. He received the file, just as the emperor did, and skimmed the report. Basically, it said that the Never had been directed by unknown alien technology - presumably from the Orb - and had behaved unpredictably. There had been a lack of opportunity for the planned flank attack, and there had been indications that individual ships had been captured and taken over by the aliens, such as the *Ushuaia*. Marquandt had therefore decided to completely isolate the system and escape with this new knowledge, which he considered possibly vital to the survival of the Star Empire, to report.

Everything in it sounded logical, except for one thing.

"There's not a word about why the fleet admiral didn't do everything he could to save the crown prince," he

The last Fleet

stated, looking again at the emperor. The corners of his mouth twitched, but otherwise he said nothing, although his gaze briefly brushed Janus'.

"There will, of course, be a detailed, personal follow-up briefing that High Lord Marquandt will have to face," Albius replied. "But we need his fleet."

"And what if that's exactly what he wants?"

"Fleet Admiral Marquandt is one of the objectively best commanders in the Star Empire. Any member of the Admiral's Council will attest to that. His fleet is well equipped and highly trained. We need him here - by the way, apparently this has escaped your network - he is currently en route from Omaha to Wall Sector Delta. We would need to divert him from his current course to his homeland."

This nail also struck painfully, Janus had to admit to himself. Too many things were happening without his knowledge, and no matter how or why, this was nothing less than a disaster for him in his capacity as First Secretary of State. All the strings slipped from his fingers because they were stuck to his shoulders and now he had to dance to Albius' tune.

"Make it so, Marius," Haeron II decided abruptly. "High Lord Marquandt and his fleet are ordered to Sol to strengthen the defenses."

"Of course, your majesty. A wise decision." The Chief of Staff bowed his head and rose when the Emperor did. "May I assume, then, that he will be integrated into the Home Fleet and lead it?"

"You will tell him exactly what I have said. This meeting is over."

Albius bowed deeply and headed for the door. Janus moved to follow him, but the Emperor stopped him, "Not you, Janus."

The Grand Admiral slowed for a moment and gave him a look - unseen by their master - that dripped with satisfaction. They had never been friends, and Albius had never made any secret of the fact that he felt it was wrong for someone of lesser nobility - raised to it, moreover, and not born into it - to hold the most important office in the Star Empire. Now, however, Janus realized that it was pure hostility that he was facing. And he had not even seen it before.

"I have failed you, Your Majesty," he said, forcing himself to give a sincere look of remorse, straight into the eyes of the leader of humanity. He would have liked to smash something out of anger at himself and that he had been so blind. Something of value.

"Albius took you by surprise. Those are the moves of shrewd politicians," Haeron II said with disdain. "My idea was actually to put Samuel at the head of the Council of Admiralty. Marius would have abdicated with full honors, and no one would have doubted the suitability and authority of Samuel Taggert."

"That would have been a good decision indeed."

"But now he is dead, and he would have been the only one whose connections and reputation would have equaled that of the acting Grand Admiral. It's a disaster, Janus."

"Yes." He didn't know what else to say. Then something occurred to him, "Your Majesty. I don't want to doubt your decisions, but I don't trust Marquandt. He is involved in some financial dealings with Albius and Yokatami that I don't yet see clearly. I still need time."

"He let my son die!" roared Haeron II abruptly, his mouth twisting with frightening bitterness. "That is why I want to speak with you. I want you to do something for me that you will not like."

The last Fleet

"I am your right hand, your majesty. Anything you wish," Janus replied, relieved at the Emperor's apparent remaining confidence, which he had already feared had been squandered.

"We need Admiral Marquandt's fleet here in the Sol system. I know it sounds selfish, like the words of an autocrat, but my daughter must be protected. As a father, I could not bear to see my last remaining child killed."

Janus thought of his own children. "I understand that."

"But Marquandt will never be able to make up for the guilt of leaving my son behind, that is also something I will not forget as a father." Haeron II took a deep breath, as if trying to swallow something that was too big. "I want you to find proof after he arrives."

"Evidence of what, sir?"

"I don't care. Find his vulnerabilities, a suspicion of corruption - every admiral is guilty of corruption in some sense. He may have been disloyal at one time, he may have embezzled funds or let maintenance intervals slip on his fleet - like any pragmatist. Bring me something I can use to bring him down without it looking too much like imperial despotism. He will pay for his failure in Andal. He didn't just give up my son, he gave up hundreds of millions of people."

"In doing so, he has complied with the doctrine in the fight against the Never," Janus indicated. "At least he could invoke it."

"I am aware of that. Nevertheless, it is *wrong*. We fight to the last man to protect our subjects. If we cease to do so, our reign will end just as the McMaster dynasty did, and we might not even mourn it, because we ourselves are to blame. Our power is only as strong as our willingness to protect those who surrender it to us - willingly or not."

The emperor paused briefly and rubbed his reddened eyes. "The common people may think I am a dictator. They accept me because I rule the powers and they live a good life. They have no reason to revolt. I am perfectly clear what I am and also that I can be so only as long as I am convinced that it is for the good of mankind that I hold the reins firmly. I know of no better alternative for holding together one hundred sectors and over five hundred inhabited systems. The day may come when we are far enough along as a species not to get lost in division and petty politics instead of pulling together. That will be the day when there is no need for me and my kind."

"Yes," Janus said with warmth in his chest, "that is why I serve you."

"Good, I appreciate that. Prepare yourself and give me something to sideline Marquandt and have him imprisoned. Then I'll have a new Home Fleet and be rid of him at the same time. You can take care of his succession afterwards."

"As you wish, your majesty."

"Good, and bring my personal physician to me."

Janus dismissed the idea of asking why he was visiting, and bowed after he stood up. He hoped Mirage would give him results soon, for then he would do nothing more eagerly than to follow his master's orders and remove Marquandt while putting Albius in his place.

INTERLUDE: MIRAGE

"B-B-Bronja," the dominatrix stuttered. "My name is Bronja."

"*Mistress* Bronja, I presume," Mirage remarked dryly. The small room on the east side of town was on the third floor. The single window - taped shut from the inside - was open just far enough to hear the roaring and chanting of Grand Admiral Albius' bondsmen. They weren't real bondsmen, of course, but paid thugs who kept order here and protected those who were friends of the Chief of Staff. Mirage had not found it difficult to see through the spectacle. A Chemsniffer in her index finger, held inconspicuously in the drink of one of the sailors she had glamoured with a standard repertoire of flirtations: no alcohol in the supposed cocktail. A stealth drone in the air, recording their movement patterns for thirty-six hours: They always patrolled the same areas, always made stops at the same places. Scans of their faces, cross-checks with fleet databases: each one with file notes. Presumably they were in debt to their superiors, who had turned a blind eye to certain quid pro quos.

So now Dimitri Rogoshin's secret, which humans would call 'dirty'. Of course, it was not really a secret, otherwise Albius and his lackeys would not be so obviously privy to it, and the existence of his ineptly covered-up private pleasure would not be so easy to see through.

This allowed only one conclusion, from which a second one followed: this place was used by Warfield's manager to meet business partners or to get rid of shadows. Every other evening. Riding in a robot cab from the Hofzacher Plaza Hotel, without a transponder. White-noise generator.

"I'm not police," Mirage said, releasing a discreet dose of calming pheromones from her left index finger to keep the woman from panic. She then made sure the door was locked securely and looked at the only piece of furniture in the black-shrouded room: a chair in the middle with two handcuffed chains hanging over it.

"When is he coming?" she asked, though of course she knew. It would take another two minutes for the robo taxi to arrive. Two minutes and thirty seconds for the stairwell, ten seconds for straightening his suit and a brief stretching of the chin. So between two minutes and forty seconds and two minutes and fifty seconds.

Mirage set her timer for two minutes and forty seconds.

"He should be here any minute," Bronja replied, eyeing her with widened fear. Mirage wondered if the dominatrix was playing her role as a punishing prostitute better than that of an intimidated woman with bad makeup. She was aware that in her present form she did not radiate any threat, unless her counterpart was smart enough to perceive that very fact as a threat.

Mirage doubted that. She also doubted that she was dealing with a victim. She had seen the subliminal trem-

The last Fleet

bling of her hands even as she entered. A high probability for reflex enhancements. Also, her implanted environmental sensor on her septum registered greatly diminished body odors and the soles of her patent leather shoes depressed a millimeter more with each step than they should with an estimated weight of sixty kilograms.

She looked around the room, scanning the floor with her cyber eyes, zooming in and activating her laser distance meters. It didn't take her long to find four bottle-cap-sized prints in one corner. She took the chair, went to the corner and placed the four legs on the prints. They fit perfectly. Then she took a seat and looked to the right and left. The bloodstains had been removed well enough to show no discoloration or clear outline - even with her vision enhancements, which were unparalleled in the Star Empire. But the underlying smell of solvents, coupled with slightly lighter areas blended together quite effortlessly to form a clear picture.

"Stand by the window," she instructed the dominatrix. She continued to act out her frightened mask and nodded her obedience. Her vision was a bit fogged by the pheromones, as if she had taken drugs.

Mirage crossed her legs when she heard footsteps through the soundproof door. They roughly matched Rogoshin's weight from the sound of it. Her shoes on the doormat didn't seem to surprise him, as expected, and he entered without hesitation.

She measured him at six feet and five inches. Dressed in a tailored suit that was probably meant to advantageously highlight his well-toned and undoubtedly cosmetically enhanced body. Lightly armored, she could tell by the slightly too rigid shape and how the fabric fell. He pulled a Reface mask from his face and set it aside along with the cloak he wore over his arm. His features were ageless and smooth, as if shortly after a rejuvination, and only his eyes and deliberately gray temples betrayed some age.

"Bronja," he greeted the dominatrix, who dropped her acted fear and cooed at him with half-closed eyes. His gaze wandered to Mirage, insinuatingly eyeing her from top to bottom. "And you are?"

"Close the window, please, Bronja," she instructed the dominatrix. A brief expression of surprise flitted across Rogoshin's face, then he nodded, and the next moment the window was closed.

"I don't think the admiral's men would come to my rescue," she explained succinctly. "And I don't think you need their help, either."

"You're sitting in my seat."

"Is that so?" Mirage leaned back. "Would you like to switch?"

Rogoshin's expression flickered. The corners of his mouth twitched as he tried to reassess her with his eyes and what lay behind them.

"Who are you?"

"No one. I've never existed, and I never will. The fact that you don't know tells me you're probably uncomfortable. I have a few questions for you."

"I'm afraid I'm indisposed." He pointed at the dominatrix who had begun to dance around him. She gave him a punch in the pit of the stomach that didn't even make him flinch. His gaze remained fixed on Mirage and became smug. "It is time for my punishment, for I have been very naughty and will be again, I fear."

"I understand," she said, making an impatient wave. "Go ahead, then."

"Not me." Rogoshin pointed with a diabolical grin at the dominatrix who had stopped dancing around him.

The last Fleet

She had crouched beside him like a predator when Mirage's firewall registered the ECM attack. Sophisticated signal jammers and software attacks on all frequencies. She hadn't fought something this powerful in a long time. Rather than allocate further processing power to her nanocephalon, she unceremoniously shut it down.

Rogoshin's grin widened, triumphant and lustful in anticipation of violence.

His dominatrix, who as expected was not one at all, *changed*. Her hands became razor-sharp claws that pushed through the retreating synth skin, and her muscles swelled like snakes filling with blood. The lower jaw hinged open, exposing extended fangs of gleaming metal.

The killer robot jumped, and Mirage activated her EMP launcher, which sat as a sphere the size of a tennis ball where others had their gall bladders.

"Lights out," she said calmly, and let her left fist shoot forward. The reinforced Carbin prosthesis crashed into the robotic head hurtling toward her, shattering it into a crackling piece of scrap metal.

With a loud crash, the scrap metal fell to the ground, and the artificial limbs jerked about uncontrollably.

Rogoshin stood frozen like a pillar, looking at her like she was a ghost.

"Now there are two options," Mirage said calmly. "The first is, you sit in this chair and answer all the questions I ask you. The second option, I'm going to break your legs and arms and put you in this chair, and then you're still going to answer all the questions I ask you."

She took a step to the side and he lunged for the seat as if there was a prize to be won.

"A good decision." After powering up her nanocephalon again, she estimated the time she had left before Rogoshin's reinforcements arrived, almost certainly alerted with the failure of the room's security systems. Taking the path up the stairs and her prepared directional mines as a guide, she decided to hurry. "Here are the rules: I only ask each question once. I have scanner-based psychophysiognomic software. If you lie, I notice it. If you lie, I kill you - before your people arrive."

Muffled by the soundproof door, the deep boom of an explosion could be heard, and Rogoshin winced. But he nodded eagerly.

"You killed Agent Walker."

"Yes."

"How did you track her?" she asked. Walker had been an extremely competent agent, according to all available files.

"I have a contact in a high position at IIA," the former colonel replied.

"Name?"

"Afrin Makuba."

She filed the name away in one of her memory clusters.

"Who gave you the contact? The Grand Admiral?"

Rogoshin nodded.

"What is the connection between Fleet Admiral Dain Marquandt and Yokatami?"

"There are regular meetings between Marquandt and one of Yokatami's execs."

"Name?"

"Yoshi Ketambe."

"Do the two work together?"

"I assume so, yes. He has a stake in their Seed World, and the forces in their system are from his private units. There's some deal there," Rogoshin explained, biting his lower lip as another explosion was heard from the stairwell, followed by the muffled screams of dying people.

The last Fleet

"What else do you know, about this collaboration?"

"Nothing."

Mirage activated her implanted forearm shotgun and raised her hand.

"WAIT!" pleaded Rogoshin. "I really don't know much. I only overheard one thing: During a pretty wild evening with Makuba, the IIA contact, the son of a bitch once bragged that he'd screwed Marquandt over. He'd scammed him out of so much money just for deleting a few files in the fleet archives."

"You can't delete anything in the fleet archive. Only archive," she noted. "When was that?"

"A couple of weeks ago."

"More precisely."

"Three?"

A third explosion sounded. Her time was up.

"You believe in sin, don't you? Otherwise you wouldn't be here."

Rogoshin blinked in irritation.

"Yes."

"That's a lie," she stated, giving him a look. "And rules are rules, after all."

Mirage walked to the window, activated her ruthenium polymer suit, then opened it. From her jacket pocket, she pulled out the finger-sized white phosphorus grenade and tossed it into the room behind her before jumping down the three stories and disappearing into the night.

7
GUNTER

Gunter could easily follow Masha - if that was her real name. The crowd was no longer as dense as before in the corridors of the hustler dock, and the main tunnel with its unfinished windows, recognizable as square markings, was also less busy. That didn't mean it wasn't crowded, but he clearly found it easier to spot individual figures than merely a faceless crowd.

Masha moved purposefully toward the far end of the abandoned dock, where an entrance to the Vaktram system was probably originally intended.

Her head kept popping up among scantily clad prostitutes and loudly shouting hustlers trying to lure the last customers of the evening to join them. The stench had become noticeably worse, for over the sweet and sour note of human excrement now lay the heaviness of burnt skin. There must have been a fire somewhere further ahead - not so big that the official extinguishing bots would have come on the scene, but extreme enough that the place smelled even more inhospitable and dangerous than it already did.

As she rounded a small shed, Masha suddenly disappeared.

Gunter switched sides to increase the angle of view, and after a few yards saw that she must have gone into a narrow crevice that looked like a crack in the rock. Just wide enough for a human.

He went there by a circuitous route and stood beside it, pretending to count his crowns on the wrist terminal and checking that no one showed any particular interest in him. Only then did he follow her, pressing his way between the damp and cold rock walls. The gap was just wide enough for him to reach with bated breath, and deep enough that it took a few seconds before he noticed a faint glow.

Something bit into his leg until his military neural computer reported an electrical attack and channeled the considerable amperage into the ground via his metallic clawed feet. When he felt a slight protrusion with his leg, he raised his knee and kicked it.

After that, he was free and found himself in a cavern - along with a startled looking Masha and Mustache, the caver from the night before who had been talking to Eyebag as a 'VIP' in the Double X. Here and now, he didn't look at all like the cocky veteran technician. More like a teenager caught chewing assai grass.

"You!" the older man blurted out with a mixture of indignation and horror.

"But ..." stammered Masha.

"Don't worry, I won't hurt you," he promised, coming toward them with his hands up.

The cave measured about ten yards in diameter and was apparently something like the preliminary stage of a planned camp, since recesses for magnetic rails already adorned the floor. The ceiling was apparently not very far,

The last Fleet

because the top of Gunter's head almost touched the roughly hewn rock. On the other side - Masha and Mustache stood as if they had just walked through - was a door with a control panel.

"Who are you? And how did you find us?"

"It doesn't matter. I'm looking for someone, and I think you can help me find him."

"No, no, no, you can't be here. I could only turned off the Somawatcher for a short time. If they..."

"I think he's looking for me," Gunter heard a familiar voice behind him and wheeled around. Administrator Adam Goosens stood in front of the crevice and took a step toward them. Behind him, two more figures came in, muscle-bound mutants, hairless and with cortical disruptors in their hands as long as a leg. Why hadn't he heard them coming? A distortion field in the crevice, perhaps? If there really was a Somawatcher buried in there, it could be quite possible.

"That's right," Gunter said, appraising the two mutants, who towered over him by more than a head and had to walk stooped accordingly, giving them the appearance of gorillas.

"Well, you found me. So before I float that traitor there and bring back the runaway goods, I'd like to know with whom I have the pleasure of speaking?" asked Goosens, tapping his temple. "You don't exist in our system, and that happens rarely enough. So, out with it."

"Where is the Orb body?"

Behind him, Gunter heard gasps for air. The administrator blinked twice, and the mutants gave each other irritated looks.

"Ah. Last try, who are you?"

"What is Akwa Marquandt doing here on Cerberus?"

"Wrong answer." Goosens gave the two mutants a wave, and they immediately attacked.

Simultaneously, and with practiced motions, they swung at his torso and legs, the whirring cortical disruptors as extensions of their powerful arms. Gunter's reflex boosters threw him forward and to the ground. Rolling, he extended the monofilament blades of his two forearm sockets and activated his foot anchors. The diamond-coated steel rammed into the rock beneath his feet. The cortical disruptors whizzed through the air, one narrowly missing his head, and he turned left too late. Hit in the shoulder, the effect set in immediately, and a violent dizziness overcame him before his neural stratum blocked the appropriate signaling pathways. Then the sudden nausea also disappeared.

He blocked the other weapon with one of his blades, which cut through as if it were paper.

But the brief moment of disruption of consciousness was enough for his opponents to get ahead of him, even though they were a bit slower than he was. The armed man dropped his apparently useless electric club and wrapped his tree-trunk-sized arms around Gunter's torso, the one with the suddenly shortened mind amplifier punching him first in the stomach and then in the face. A mistake he paid for with a shattered fist, a shrill yelp, and a second punch that was nothing more than soft pudding on bone.

"Cybertorso," Gunter grumbled with a grin, taking advantage of the fleeting confusion of the one clutching him to headbutt him. He used the brief moment of freedom to release the foot anchors and kick his left foot, followed by a twist of his body and both monofilament blades.

While three of the mutant broke away from each

The last Fleet

other and went to the ground, he rammed his shoulder into the remaining one's chest and drove one of the blades through his chin and the top of his skull from below.

Adam Goosens stared wide-eyed at the carnage and seemed to calculate his chances of escaping through the gap. Gunter gave him no time to find an answer and went straight for him. With one hand he grabbed him by the collar, with the other he ripped the wrist terminal from his arm and crushed it.

"That door there," he pointed to the metal door next to which Masha and Mustache were standing, holding each other in their arms. "Open it."

"That's not a good idea," the administrator said, but hurried to comply as Gunter effortlessly lifted him up and set him down in front of it. He pressed his hand on the control panel, which immediately changed from red to green. A hydraulic hiss sounded from the wall, followed by the smell of mold and ozone.

"Where does this go?" he wanted to know. "To the equalization caverns?"

"Close by," Goosens replied, giving Mustache a withering look, who then seemed to collapse as if his life was over.

"Then we'll take a little trip now, because I have a few questions for you that I'd rather have answered now than right away," Gunter said, and with a nod he motioned Mustache to open the door.

They walked through a short tunnel lined with spray plastic. It rushed as if they were under a waterfall. He pushed Goosens ahead of him, paying no further attention to Mustache and Masha after realizing they were following him anyway.

"This is not going to end well for you, soldier," the administrator said. "Who sent you? You can still do the right thing. For yourself, I mean. The Broker always finds uses for veterans like you. Money, assai, women - you name it."

"I'm not for sale."

"But yes, you are. Even if you're working for some blue-blooded no-good, you're doing it for a paycheck. Recognition, social status, whatever. Everyone can be bought, it's just a question of what currency."

"Save the stupid talk."

"Here you are who you are because you accomplished something. Everyone on Cerberus contributes their talents and rises through the work of their hands, not because of the favor of someone who shit in gold diapers," Goosens continued, as if Gunter had said nothing.

"You're criminals."

"We take care of our own, there's a big difference. Isn't that what the aristocratic nutcases do with their whole boondoggle? Everyone lives safely and reasonably contentedly as long as they play by the rules and don't challenge the power of the elite. If they do, there are dead people."

"One more unsolicited sentence and I'll break something important to you," Gunter warned the bald man with all the data jacks on his skull.

Mustache's workplace did indeed look like a cave. They reached a rock ledge, in front of which stretched a large cavern that tapered left and right along the curvature of the asteroid. Scattered lights clung to the ceiling and floor, both dozens of yards in height and depth. Their brightness was barely worth mentioning, just enough for him to make out the large balloon tanks that occupied most of the space. Each of them was as large as a house and connected by man-sized pipes. Tens of pipes led to the tanks from inside the station, bundled into dense walkways with metal grooves running across them, presumably

The last Fleet

for technicians to walk back and forth on. Gunter recognized two of them in the distance by their headlamps, which reflected off one of the tanks and moved in time with footsteps.

He switched his eyes to residual light amplification and saw much more clearly. Even the maintenance consoles between each unit peeled out of the darkness, and the joints of the welded-together steel containers for the pressure chambers' gas cartridges formed a complex pattern.

"Now what?" asked Goosens. "Do you want to get a job as a caver? If so, the interview isn't going very well."

"Shh!" Mustache quipped from behind them, and Gunter gave him a disapproving look.

"Not so loud!" the technician hissed, and the whites of his wide-open eyes stood out clearly in the half-shadow. "You'll wake the Whisper!"

"Superstition," the administrator grumbled, shaking his head. "And that on the Cerberus."

"Masha!" shouted Mustache so abruptly and so loudly that Gunter's reflex booster kicked in and the subsequent adrenaline rush caused his blades to extend.

The woman he had saved from the knives of the two gangsters just ten minutes ago ran away across the ledge to a passage carved into the rock and disappeared into the shadows.

"And away she goes!" laughed Goosens, and Gunter would have liked to push him off the ledge into the depths. "Go ahead and run after her, Reese, you know what you're in for anyway."

"Sir, I ..." stammered Mustache.

"Quiet now," growled Gunter, grabbing the administrator by the collar and giving him a shove so that he would have fallen had he not held him back at the last moment. Now he dangled over the precipice, emitting a strangled croak.

"Stop!"

The extended foot anchors and his claws gave Gunter a firm footing, and his augmented arms, thanks to the installed servo motors and artificial muscle strands, had no trouble holding the administrator's exactly one-hundred and seventy-two pound body weight for quite a while. Should his solid-state batteries run low, they would switch to ATP synthesis.

"I can do this all day," he assured the bureaucrat, when suddenly he heard a rising noise. It began as a kind of hiss, hollow and with an eerie echo that reverberated off the walls of the cavern. At first he thought it was gas flowing through the line in the balancing valves, but then it sounded more like many-voiced howling or wailing, the singing of ghosts.

What was it? It had been a long time since anything had spooked him. For a Marine raised to relish harsh conditions and depriving maneuvers, nothing frightened him that quickly, as life seemed to consist of extremely down-to-earth situations. But this one sent a shiver down his spine.

Especially as it got worse; what at first seemed to come from one of the tanks in front of him continued to the right and left like a contagious disease. Shouts without words and screams without voices multiplied and gained depth in the darkness.

"What in the bloody heavens is that?" he blurted out.

"The Whisper," yowled Mustache behind him. From the sound of his voice, he was on the verge of a panic attack. "You woke the Whisper!"

Goosens had gone quiet and was no longer fidgeting. Gunter considered asking him again and forcing him to answer, but instead he decided to use the administrator's obvious fear to elicit more important information.

"The Orb," he said. "Where is it?"

"If I tell you, it won't do you any good anyway ..."

Gunter lowered him a foot. A shriek mingled with the eerie Whisper before he lifted the man back up.

"Shit! In a cooler in the garrison!"

"How do I get there?"

"You don't" Goosens squeaked. "It's guarded by fifty Ultras from the Vaults. They don't mess around, and they'll make mincemeat of anyone who comes within five yards of them."

It did not escape Gunter's notice that the man's manner of speaking had changed. He now possessed the leering accent of the Kerrhainians and expressed himself in a manner far less chosen. Apparently, his facade lasted only until he wet his pants and forgot that he had never actually belonged to better classes than the one from which he had crawled up.

"I'll take my chances on that."

"You don't know where the body is. It's in an unlabeled zero-humidity capsule. Only the Broker knows which one it is."

Gunter believed the son of a bitch. So it was going to be difficult. But he hadn't expected anything else. At least now he knew where to look and what was in his way. However, first he would have to find out more about these Ultras of the Vaults. He didn't believe that they were normal gangsters, former garbage brats who had been given a few digittattoos and knives in their hands. They were possibly mutants like the two who were currently lying in well-portioned slices in the small anteroom.

"Akwa Marquandt," he changed the subject. "Why is she here?"

"Business," Goosens groaned.

Gunter lowered him again, farther this time.

"FUCKING SHIT!"

"I want to know everything. Last warning."

"Okay, okay, okay," the administrator pleaded. "She made contracts with us, way back in the last standard year. Out in the belt, she's leased eight of our storage asteroids for twenty months. We use them as temporary storage for the Assai trade."

"Has she also leased your smuggling ships?"

"Yes. Eighteen of them, and they've been taking goods there ever since. Leave me alone already!"

"Maybe in a minute." Gunter thought of what Masha had told him. Akwa Marquandt at the cargo dock, supervising the loading of standard goods. "What kind of goods and how much? Where are they going?"

"Nowhere. It's already several hundred thousand tons. They just started moving them off the asteroids three days ago. By then it was getting more and more and they were just hoarding it there. That's all I know, though, man!"

"I thought the Broker knew everything."

"Yeah, but am I the bloody Broker?"

Gunter pondered the criminal's words. Why would Marquandt's daughter hoard goods for months, then start hauling them away three days ago? Sure, Kerrhain was probably the best place to hide stuff - but cots, recycler batteries, and neural cables? Those were all things you could buy in 24h malls. Neither illegal nor particularly valuable. Unless, of course, the packaging Masha had seen was just camouflage.

"What was being stockpiled? And don't tell me you don't know because you would have signed contracts," he warned the administrator.

"Cots, recycler batteries and neural cables, mostly.

Standard things to connect data jacks to universal connectors, like those used in any network terminal. Food was there too, long shelf life packs of soy protein. Crappy marine food," Goosens replied.

Gunter suddenly had to think of his escape from Andal, when Gavin Andal had saved them all by escaping the stealth ship - at the cost of the Morning Star and the ice freighter, whose name he couldn't remember.

"They're smuggling with passenger liners. Through Andal," he noted.

"Yes."

Son of a bitch, Gunter thought. Marquandt had had Andal cleared through the Never to set up a smuggling route for himself. But to where? Beyond lay only uninhabited territory, systems without terra-compatible worlds or resources to speak of. Or the Seed Traverse, but that was restricted military territory, except for the Ruhr system; not even a member of House Marquandt would be able to smuggle there unnoticed or with impunity.

The Whisper had died down by now, fading into a wailing chorus of sounds that still made his hair stand on end.

"What is it?" he demanded.

"You'll soon find out, I'm afraid," he heard an extremely accented voice say behind him.

Once again his reflex boosters took over as he was startled, so Gunter wheeled around, involuntarily hoisting the administrator back onto the ledge. Behind him stood a figure that he recognized as a hologram only at a second glance: an average-sized man in a black and white suit with sunglasses on his head and short-cropped hair. He knew immediately that it had to be the Broker - and that the five mutants behind him had to be Ultras of the Vaults. This time they didn't have cortical disruptors in their hands, but electric rifles, the barrels of which were all pointed at him.

"Did you think you could do anything on my station without me knowing?" The Broker sounded almost disappointed.

Gunter was silent, assessing his chances. They were virtually nonexistent.

"I've been watching you. You must be a Marine. Andalian, I guess. With special training, but just a sword and not a scalpel." The Broker sounded as if he pitied him. A pet peeve that hadn't done his trick right. "Now I know you. I'm disappointed in your master, we had a deal."

"Fuck you," said Gunter.

"We should kill him," suggested the administrator, who scrambled to his feet and gave him a withering look.

"No. We're not wasting anything. After all, we have a quota to meet and we get paid by number of survivors. He meets the criteria." The Broker raised a hand. "Go with dignity. Like a Marine."

Gunter heard the shots before he felt them.

8

GAVIN

Five, Dodger indicated with one hand. Gavin crawled through the strange, blue-glowing creepers to her. Hellcat had disappeared behind a tree and out of sight.

When he arrived next to the mutant, he once again felt like a toddler with his mother because she was so much taller and stronger than he was.

The five people whose voices they had heard were huddled in a small hollow in the middle of the forest, lined by slightly younger trees with slightly lighter bark. In their midst they had lit a small fire that was emitting a lot of smoke, which they seemed to be arguing about right now.

"I told you not to take fresh leaves!" one of them hissed. His accent sounded strange, with a terse rolled R. Like the others - three men and a woman, he wore a dirty gray jumpsuit torn open in several places. Two of them had their sleeves rolled up and their pant legs folded, so he guessed one-size-fits-all off the rack. As if the presence of humans in this environment wasn't strange enough, glowing blue buttons jammed at their temples where data jacks normally were.

"I did not!" protested a younger one with the same accent.

"Forgot to clear the floor, though!"

"Now the shit's smoking like a pig," the woman complained. "Might as well have yelled: *Hey, here we are! Come and get us!*"

"All you can do is bitch, bitch, bitch," grumbled another.

Their lowered voices made them sound like they were shouting in whispers, which ironically made them easier to understand.

"If I don't scold you rust buckets, you won't get anything done! You want them to take us back to the damn pen?"

"Hey, calm down!" intervened the elder who had spoken at the beginning. He made a placating gesture, perhaps also to urge them to speak more quietly.

"If we don't roast the damn thing, we're going to get some plague or something. So we need a fire, and fires smoke!" another growled, turning something on the ground that Gavin couldn't see from his position.

"How would you know?" the woman caughed. "You're a damn junk collector and you've never seen more than three trees in a pile."

"Or one with leaves bigger than your brain," the older man remarked, chuckling. But the gloating sound was quickly stifled.

"We're lucky to have escaped. So pull yourselves the hell together and don't act like stupid solar settlers! We'll eat up, hide what's left of the fire, and then get the hell out of here before they discover us."

"Where are we supposed to go, anyway?" The speaker

The last Fleet

had his back turned to Gavin, looking lanky and hunched from a distance.

"I don't know. Anything's better than the pen!"

Murmurs of agreement.

Gavin felt Dodger's elbow in his side and looked to her. She held two fingers in front of her eyes and then pointed to the right and left of the small hollow. At first he didn't understand what she wanted him to do, but then he saw it: four figures on each side slinking through the dense foliage, well camouflaged and coordinated. They were clad in light body armor with full helmets, with patch camouflage patterns in green and anthracite. Synchronized with the blue pulse of the local flora, what appeared to be erratic blue stripes shone across the pattern. What on any other planet would have made them visible for miles like beacons in the night, here made them blend with the alien nature. If they hadn't moved, Gavin wouldn't have recognized them even if he had been standing a few feet in front of them.

One of the figures silently raised a hand and took a submachine gun in front of his chest, painted with the same camouflage pattern. The others followed his example and stopped, aiming at the unaware people by the fire, eight hyenas leering at a family of unsuspecting meerkats. Gavin felt reminded of a corresponding scene from his children's book, *Erdmann Family*, an old book from Terra that his father had read to him a lot. It had given him nightmares for years.

"Leave some for me, too!" the woman hissed just then, far too loudly. Seeing the group so ignorant stung Gavin. Any moment now, fire would be opened on them. A death on an alien planet, in fear and loneliness.

"This thing is still completely tough!" the older man

grumbled. "Be glad I'm pre-cooking the grub for you. Tastes awful, too."

"What is it anyway?"

"'A rat!"

"Nah, can't be. It's a lizard."

"Have you ever seen a lizard with a curly tail?"

"No, but then again, I haven't seen one with two incisors either."

"What's a curly tail?"

"The thing you can see on Gregor when he pisses."

Four of them giggled, except for one, who must have been Gregor.

Gavin nudged Dodger and nodded to the left. She merely frowned. He tapped his assault rifle and she shook her head.

Then he crept away from her to the left, pausing again and again to watch the soldiers tighten the circle. They were now only a few feet from the fugitives. Between two bushes connected by a small moss bed and glowing with a steady pulse, he lay down and slid the Avenger in front of him, with the shock pad at his shoulder. Through the targeting optics, he took aim at one of the cloaked, a faceless warrior whose colors looked as otherworldly as an alien, even if his body shape identified him beyond doubt as human.

Only for a brief moment, two voices argued in his head: *are you sure you know who is good and who is evil? Are you not being deceived? The obvious is not always as obvious as you think. But they are unarmed and afraid.*

He made his decision and opened fire. The *Avenger* spat out ten rounds per volley, pressing marginally against his shoulder. He hit the first one in the shoulder and neck, piercing the light armor. Familiar red blood splattered into the unfamiliar surroundings, glowing like signal paint

The last Fleet

on the foliage. He missed the second soldier, who was surprisingly quick to throw himself into cover - just like the others, who suddenly disappeared.

Not good, he thought. Whoever they were, they were certainly better trained for this situation than a captain of the Imperial Navy.

But his goal had been to flush out the fugitives anyway. He succeeded, too, as they wheeled up from their little circle of seats, their gazes darting in all directions. The attackers knew how to take advantage of the moment of confusion, for all at once there was a click all over the clearing, as if a dozen old-fashioned cameras were being triggered, and the five in the tattered overalls went down like puppets with their strings cut.

"Not good," Gavin whispered, scrambling to his feet to change positions. He turned left and circled the bush on his elbows, only to face a pair of armored legs. "Not good at all."

He looked up and down the barrel of a submachine gun as a loud rattle sounded and the warrior's torso seemed to disintegrate in a twitch. Blood splattered Gavin's face and stung his eyes. Unable to see anything, he crawled backward, trying to regain clear vision. He felt like he was on display, uncamouflaged and splattered with blood, so he made the best decision he was capable of: with wet fingers, he fumbled for the signal booster Bambam had given him and took a deep breath before sliding it with his hand into his pants from behind. What came next was not fun.

After waking up, Gavin's skull buzzed as if he had exchanged its contents for a swarm of bees. The metallic taste of blood was on his tongue. Somewhere a bird chirped long-drawn-out and plaintively. Louder and more unpleasant, however, was a hydraulic hiss that hurt his ears at regular intervals.

Cautiously, he opened his eyes and looked directly into a large face. It was Dodger, looking at him expressionlessly. She appeared to be sitting down, for her knees were drawn up and her arms rested on them like massive punching bags.

Gavin's gaze fell on the magnetic cuffs that forced her wrists together in opposite directions so she couldn't grab anything.

"Dodger?" he muttered dazedly, wanting to feel his forehead, which felt like it was no longer in one piece. Unfortunately, he found that his hands were as bound as hers and he could barely scratch his forearms.

"Great work," Hellcat growled. She sat next to him on the bench seat, which was so hard it hurt Gavin's tailbone. Past her angry face, he saw other figures, four men and a woman, in tattered gray coveralls. Their heads hung despondently on their chests and their stares were blank. He was pretty sure that the unpleasant smell of old sweat and urine came from them. He didn't feel disgust because of it, rather compassion and the feeling of having failed because he hadn't been able to help them.

I know those looks, he thought with a thick lump in his throat as he realized what kind of situation they were in. He knew that look of absolute hopelessness and lack of any resistance from the footage of Turan-II. The destruction of the colony by the Never. On Andal he had seen hardly any civilians, only soldiers who had had no time for defeatism as they fought for their lives and the lives of others.

"Where are we?" he asked, squinting his eyes. They were sitting in a cage on a truck bed. There was a barred hatch to the rear and what looked like a cab in the front. But they were almost certainly not in a vehicle, because they were rocking to the right and left and sometimes to the front and back. In addition, the alien jungle around them was extremely dense. It almost seemed as if they were climbing over the undergrowth.

"Up my ass," Hellcat replied.

"Yep," Dodger agreed with her.

"What happened?"

"You got us in the shit, that's what happened." It was hard to recall Hellcat's graceful appearance when she was glaring at him as angrily as she was now. A stapled laceration was emblazoned on her forehead and a palm-sized bruise on her neck.

"I was trying to help those people," he justified himself, but it sounded weak. "What happened?"

"You were the first one they got. Dodger took three of them before they knocked her out," she explained, her lips thinning.

"Why are we ..."

"Stun guns with neural shockers." Dodger shrugged his rounded shoulders. "Make a nasty headache."

"You can say that again." Gavin looked at Hellcat. "What about you?"

"They just busted my face," she replied sourly. "Stuck my guns out voluntarily."

"Good call."

"No. A good decision would have been to damn well not play bloody hero and get us all in deep shit! Then we would have followed the bastards and maybe found out what kind of sick shit was going on and where the hell we were."

"He's just a pilot," Dodger said calmly.

Hellcat seemed to want to say something more, but

merely bared her teeth and leaned her head against the bars behind her.

"What's with this cage?" asked Gavin after a few minutes. Outside, a mighty tree passed the bars, its trunk as thick as a concrete column. Either it was already getting dark, or they were bumping through a part of the jungle that was under a dense canopy of leaves. In any case, he couldn't make out that much anymore, and the sounds of the local fauna had dimmed considerably as well.

"Looks like a fucking beetle. Has six legs instead of wheels and is extremely slow."

"If they didn't knock you out with neural shockers, what did you see? And why did they beat you up like that?" he huffed, reflexively raising his cuffed hands in her direction before lowering them again. At first he thought she would ignore him in her rage, but then she forced herself to answer.

"I thought they were going to knock me out anyway," she said with her eyes closed. "When they tied me up, I made a little Skaland-style small talk with them."

Dodger chuckled, which sounded something like the whump of a fusion reactor in slow motion.

"I can imagine."

"Then carted your useless bodies together and waited until this bug vehicle came waddling through the underbrush. Didn't talk to any of them, I'm guessing suit-internal comlinks or transducers or something," Hellcat continued. "Then you all got put here on the truck bed and tied up. Something they injected us with, I don't know what, didn't talk, the bastards. Well, after thirty minutes Dodger was awake, you after about two hours. Since then, we've just been driving through the same old crappy forest."

"Lumbering," the mutant corrected her, "that's what this thing does."

"Agonizingly slow."

"Mhm."

"I saw some animals on the way. Real weird," Hellcat said. "Glowed blue in the same pulse, too."

"What kind of animals?"

"I don't know, never seen them before. Mostly bug things, don't know anything about them."

"Mhm," he merely went silent for a while, trying to ignore his headache, which was becoming increasingly difficult.

After a while, during which an oppressive silence had spread, they came to a wide clearing. The forest had been cleared here, which he could tell from dark burn scars on the ground. They broke through a clearly drawn line of vegetation, beyond which it became level and scattered sods of grass grew from the earth.

Gavin abruptly struggled up from his seated position and was surprised not to be tethered to the vehicle bed. A glow in the dusk had caught his attention. If he stood and pressed his arms against the lattice roof above him, he could stand reasonably safely and look over the driver's cab - or wheelhouse - despite the constant rocking.

In front of them was a huge clearing that he would have thought was a plain had it not been circular. The exact shape bore the unmistakable signature of an intervention in nature. A ring - at least that's what he assumed from the receding appearance of the open area - of about two hundred yards lay around a single building that nestled close to the ground like an oversized, upturned plate. Faintly glowing lights sent a diffuse glow from small windows that covered the structure like fireflies. Gavin estimated that it measured a quarter mile or more across.

It looked different from anything he had seen so far, possibly because the structure was covered in what appeared to be an erratic pattern of joints. Despite the darkness, he recognized them by the way they glowed blue in time with the pulse beat of the jungle, as if jolts of electricity were passing through.

The sight was so mesmerizing that he realized his mouth was open. His mind wanted to identify a system in the luminous spectacle. The pulse beat was the same, but how were the joints arranged? Why did they form the confusing pattern he saw in them? He felt he had to look at it only once on a slowed-down recording to understand the bigger picture that would reveal some alien mystery to him.

"See anything?" Dodger inquired, bringing her arms forward to catch him as he stumbled because their spider-legged vehicle took an unexpected lunge to the left. Some fast vehicle whizzed past them and disappeared into the jungle behind them.

"There's a building, flat and very wide. From a distance I would have thought it was the landing pad of a spaceport," he replied as a fire appeared in the sky, bathing the dark landscape in bright light as if the sun had risen from one second to the next. The edge of the forest seemed to be on fire, it was so brightly illuminated, and Gavin's nictitating membrane protected his retinas from the glare. Still, the photon onslaught wasn't helping his headache.

He craned his neck and squinted his eyelids to see what was coming at them from the darkness.

"Bloody heavens!" he snapped. "It's a spaceship!"

Now Dodger and Hellcat also stood up and stared up through the bars of their cage. Only the five fugitives remained seated with their heads bowed. What made

Gavin stiffen in awe seemed to them a familiar sight. Or they had given themselves up so much that even the demise of the universe could not awaken them.

The spaceship had to be huge, for its engine flares split the starry sky in half. With each passing second, they drew closer until finally their alien craft stopped and a bluish glow settled over the grid. The loud roar and hiss disappeared.

The miles-long tails of the alien vehicle touched the building complex in front of them and split as a firestorm in all directions, while a gigantic shadow descended. The flames grew shorter and licked across the charred grasslands. Like a storm, they also swept over their vehicle, causing the force field around them to flicker and glow red.

Then, suddenly, it was over. The engines were no longer spewing plasma, and atop what he had only thought was a single-story building sat a silhouette of sooty composite and hundreds of portholes from which light shimmered like a field of stars.

Gavin's confusion only worsened as he realized what he was looking at. True, he had never seen a *Mammoth* freighter on a planet, and didn't even know that the largest spaceships ever designed by humans were capable of landing on one. But there was no mistaking the outline, a long cylinder with eight circular drive nacelles at the stern, now pointing downward, and the massive retaining brackets, each of which would have dwarfed a skyscraper.

The glimmer around their cage disappeared with the fire.

"What was that?" asked Hellcat. "A force field?"

"I think so," he said, without taking his eyes off the impressive monstrosity of a starship that stood before them like the throne of God himself, jutting miles into the midnight blue sky.

"But there's no technology like that," he said.

"I don't know what's going on, but there seems to be some stuff here that shouldn't exist. For example, a *Mammoth* on a planet." His gaze wandered to the house-sized mark on the upper hull. They hadn't even bothered to remove the markings of the House of Andal. His house. "At least now I know where they disappeared to."

INTERLUDE: MIRAGE

"The fleet archive?" the Voice asked.

"Yes," Mirage said.

"Then you have to go to New York."

"I know. The risk is considerable."

"It always is. I'm going to activate our sleepers. This is too important."

Mirage nodded. The shuttle's 1st class cabin was empty except for a businessman sitting on the other side of the twelve-seat cabin who seemed engrossed in a VR sim. Still, she spoke softly.

"All right. I can be there in two hours."

"It'll take longer," the Voice objected. "There's been a development."

"A development."

"A courier ship from Alpha Prime left Yokatami headquarters twenty hours ago. According to the network, it is the private yacht of Supervisor Sato Ran himself."

Mirage raised her right eyebrow. A few millimeters only. "Unusual."

"The yacht exploded at its exit point from subspace when it arrived in Sol." The voice paused.

"An attack?"

"Unclear. According to a preliminary analysis report from Vacuum Forensics, a reactor malfunction is likely."

"A very expensive ship."

"Yes," the voice confirmed. "But also supposedly the fastest in the Star Empire. Latest generation Raptor engines operate at the highest specifications with overclocking."

"That increases the risk of malfunction," Mirage concluded.

"Yes."

"Do you believe it's an accident?"

"No. If I believed in coincidences, we'd all be dead by now."

"Right. What does that imply for the network?"

"Unclear. But another ship reached Sol. Four hours ago. You'll have to make a slight detour before accessing the fleet archives," the Voice commanded, and Mirage would obey. As always. "You have to meet Zenith."

"He's hard to reach these days."

"Not for you."

9
JANUS

"Mister Darishma," he heard Nancy's voice say from his desk and turned to face the intercom.

"What's up, Nancy?"

"I've updated the schedule for today and revised and added to the schedule for the rest of the week. Want me to send the file over to you?"

Janus looked at the glass of botcha in his hand, from which a downright beguiling aroma wafted. Ground to a fine powder, the yellowish herb contained a caffeine analog found exclusively on Grassia that had catapulted the colony to Core World status in no time after its founding during the second wave of expansion. The entire star empire was addicted to botcha and its indescribable taste of sweet and bitter notes. He himself was no exception and usually didn't start work until the cup was empty.

It wasn't even five in the morning. Outside his window, the North American continent lay shrouded in shadow. Only the bright dots of the arcologies shone like festering pustules in the darkness.

"Send it over," he finally said, emptying the contents of his cup in one go.

Yawning as he tried to shake off the last remnants of fatigue after what had been, as usual, far too short a night, he opened his schedule and skimmed over the day's planning. Not much had changed. Except in the requests for the waiting list.

"Nancy?"

"Yes, Mister Darishma?"

"Yokatami has asked to reschedule?"

"Right, the ambassador said he wants to wait for the report from their own vacuum forensics people before attending the police briefing," she explained.

"Doesn't he trust our people's data?" he asked, shaking his head.

"I think Sato Ran still needs time to explain why his private yacht might have been destroyed."

"And he doesn't want to negligently distribute blame or make insinuations in our direction because he knows Sol is currently suffering from the loss of eighty percent of its defense force," he thought aloud. "He could make it seem at a press conference that Sol is no longer safe or that there is political tension between the Star Empire and the Corporate Protectorate. Even if that's not what he wants."

"That's entirely possible," Nancy agreed with him. "Should I tell the ambassador to keep the appointment as scheduled?"

"No," Janus decided, shaking his head, and looked at the waiting list. On the last spot was a single name with no title, designation of his position, or photo: Jonathan Haifer. The name sounded familiar somehow, but it didn't immediately come to mind. "Who is that? And why isn't there any data on the name?"

The last Fleet

Normally, access to his office's mailbox for appointment requests was subject to extremely high hurdles - his network address was owned by the families of the high nobility, fleet admirals of the Admiral's Council and members of the Saturn Congress, in addition to the supervisors of the permanent members of the Corporate Council in the Corporate Protectorate. But this name belonged to no one on that exclusive list, he was sure.

"I don't know," Nancy admitted, sounding as if she had confessed to him a grave offense in doing so. "But I put the name on the list because it wasn't clear to me how he could even have access to the network address. If it's an unauthorized transfer of authority using criminal methods, I'm sure the police would be interested."

"Hmm," Janus said and thought about it. It was common among politicians - and that included everyone who had direct or indirect access to him, whether they wanted to or not - to always keep an eye on the activities of competitors. His appointments were not publicly announced, but the mailbox for network requests was intentionally not secured with the highest levels of security. He knew all too well that it gave him an easy tool to send messages without opening his mouth by controlling the appointments. This was possibly also aware of this Jonathan Haifer, who didn't want to show up on anyone's radar in case someone used net crawlers to search for names, positions and photos.

But why? The person was obviously worried about discovery, that much was sure. But then why did the name sound so familiar? *Haifer* sounded like a German name, or at least from the former German-speaking area, which had not existed for more than two centuries, except for a few isolated communities on New Berlin.

Janus had a net crawler look for corresponding name bearers on New Berlin or Ruhr in the corporate protectorate and got answers pretty quickly: the chief surgeon of Governor Lars Janssen, high lord of the Janssen dynasty, was named Jonathan Haifer, as was the personal assistant of Ruhr's current supervisor Ludwig Sorg. He had only been in the position for two years, according to the results. Janus recalled shaking his hand once at a Jupiter Bank reception a year ago and making some small talk. Still, the appointment request didn't make sense. He could have used Sorg's direct channel and been assigned, if not the highest, at least a very high priority in the mailbox. So it was an impostor, or Ludwig Sorg wanted to get to him without attracting anyone's attention.

Thoughtfully, he considered his first appointment: preparations for the Emperor's trip to Saturn, where he would attend the funeral services for Varilla Usatami in three days. To do so, he had to fly to the Emperor's system travel planning staff, which operated in a bunker in Newark, cut off from any network access, secured by the IIA service. There was little in the Star Empire as secret as Haeron II's travel routes.

"Nancy, send Jonathan Haifer an invitation outside official channels. His terminal number seems to belong to a one-time terminal. He will accompany me to New York."

"My lord, I have certain security concerns about that..."

"I'm being escorted by four Imperial Guard Marines, I don't see who could be dangerous to me," he interrupted and turned off the intercom.

Janus stood up, wishing for another cup of steaming botcha, and sighed. As he slipped into his civilian clothes, which were tucked into a sight-proof garment bag, he activated the messages by voice command. The holodisplay followed him back and forth between the small bathroom and his office.

Terra One was running a report on increased terrorist activity around New York.

Great, he thought.

"Police Chief Zara Vance and Chief of Staff Marius Albius have gathered for talks on *Rubov* Orbital about this," news anchor Monica Ferrini was just saying. She was standing in the middle of New York's Arcology, with Madison Square Garden behind her, where crowds of passersby were pushing their way across the streets. A play-by-play showed the grand admiral with the burly police chief for North America shaking hands in front of the press before retreating to a conference room.

"The terrorists from the Republican underground seem to be intent on attacking the Emperor's private travel planning staff. The latter is expected to attend Saturday's funeral services for Senate President Varilla Usatami, who was assassinated by the underground in Paris. Since then, raids near the notorious military installation have skyrocketed. Police Chief Vance, who like all heads of security agencies has had special powers to maintain law and order since Paris, was forced twice yesterday alone to use orbital defense platforms to target terrorist elements," Ferrini continued, and the next clip showed a rainy wooded area in upstate New York, shot from an airplane. The flicker of muzzle flashes could be seen in the darkness. Blue lights in the distance. Then a single bright yellow beam lit up the night, vaporizing clouds and burning its way into the middle of the forest. The infernal violence was extremely brief, but when the laser beam disappeared, a large area of the trees lit up in blazing fires. Muzzle flashes were no longer visible.

"So far, there have only been a dozen arrests, which Vance attributed to a rigorous crackdown. The days of understanding and seeking compromise are over, the police chief said." Ferrini, the face of Terra One, reappeared in the frame, his nose as red as a cherry in the winter cold. "Contrary to expectations, the Saturn Congress has not yet filed an official note of protest over the use of orbital weapons against ground targets. Observers expect this will not change, as even the Republican wing in the Senate was appalled by Usatami's assassination. Vance would not answer whether this unprecedented use of force against non-military targets will continue for much longer in a late-night statement. Homeland security experts, however, believe that no change in the resolve with which security agencies are cracking down on terrorist elements can be expected until the end of the Emperor's journey."

Janus turned off the holodisplay with a swipe, and it disappeared like a fleeting hallucination.

"The whole Star Empire has gone mad," he grumbled, checking the fit of his clothes in the mirror. Simple business suit with no digicolors. No moving patterns, no smart fibers that widen or contract according to their environmental sensors. Good old cotton from the 3-D printer. Unobtrusive and commonplace for the business world on Terra, where modern bells and whistles have always been regarded with wrinkled noses. People pretended to be purists because every citizen knew that they lived in the center of humanity, even though the standard of living in many Core Worlds had long been higher. The last thing he did was put on a Reface mask, which

The last Fleet

altered his features just slightly enough that optical sensors could not identify him, but those who knew him well would. Not at first glance, but at second glance.

Janus left his office through the secret exit behind his bookshelf. A small tunnel of composite, narrow because of the many hoses and cables on the walls, led to a ladder. Via that ladder he reached the office complexes of the orbital control for the *Rubov* ring three levels below, where several thousand imperial officials were on duty. They all looked just like him. Their suits were standardized and, according to regulations, free of electronic fibers. Their hairstyles boring, just like his. No one paid any attention to him as he walked past lots and small kitchens where groups chatted before going on duty, botchas in hand.

Janus' Imperial Guard bodyguards joined him one by one. One on the first level, the next in the elevator two decks below. They wore the same suits as he did, looked a little taller and sturdier, but played the boring officials surprisingly well.

As soon as they reached the shuttle bays, he went to the bay 3 check-in, where a normal passenger shuttle was waiting - and the last two bodyguards. They stood there in technician coveralls, as if they were talking through the next steps between maintenance jobs. But he knew they had to be special forces Marines, saw it in the fleeting sideways glances they gave him.

Navy personnel shuttles all conformed to a standardized dimension so that they fit into the appropriate docking pedestals of each station and ship. So the entrance to the small craft was also the tailgate, and when it flew off it was simply ejected from a mundane skid. Janus went inside and sat all the way back in the last row of seats. In front, the two pilots were busy with the preflight check. His bodyguards sat forward and in the row next to him. There were only twelve seats in all.

Through the front windshield, Janus could see the Terminator line shifting, bathing the east coast of North America in the first rays of the sun.

"Ready to depart," the pilot called out.

"We'll wait five more minutes," Janus decided.

"No need," someone said breathlessly. The man had two pistols under his chin before he even entered the shuttle. The bodyguards held him in a forced grip.

"Haier, I presume?"

"Uh, yes," croaked Ludwig Sorg's assistant, rubbing his chin sullenly as the two guardsmen with stony expressions released him at a wave from Janus. He was a youthful-looking man with short-cropped dark hair and the handsome face of a yuppie who spent a lot of time polishing up his appearance. The look from his eyes was smart and composed, despite the disapproving expression in them.

"Please." Janus gestured beside him. In his field of vision, he had Haier's resume pop up. Degree in process logistics with advanced MBAs in change management and financial transaction trading. A steep climb through the ranks of Ruhr Heavy Industries and early office assistant to Ludwig Sorg when he had been a simple board member. Jonathan Haifer was definitely older than he looked, that much was certain.

"Thank you, my lord. I wasn't sure you'd even get to see my appointment request."

"Call me Mister Darishma, or First Secretary of State, if you must," Janus countered. "I know you don't care for our titles in the corporate protectorate."

The last Fleet

Haifer frowned in surprise and seemed to reassess him.

"Thank you, First Secretary."

Janus sighed. "So, to what do I owe the honor of such an unusual visit from Ludwig Sorg?" He waved forward for them to cast off as the pilot turned to him questioningly. The tailgate closed with a hiss.

Why is the supervisor contacting me through you and with such secrecy as well? That would have his real question, and Haifer was smart enough to understand it. But instead of answering, he pointedly looked around at the bodyguards.

"These men," Janus explained, "would rather suffer all the torments of all the circles of hell than break their loyalty to the Emperor, and thus to me. With them every secret is safe."

Sometimes he even believed that the Marines had special augments to be able to tune out conversations, so stoic and motionless did they remain even during the most delicate conversations.

"I see." Haifer faltered as the shuttle lurched forward and was thrown into orbit, where two seconds later it ignited its engines and plummeted like a meteor toward New York on Terra.

"The flight only takes ten minutes," Janus reminded his visitor.

"Our Seed Vessel in the Seed Traverse has been attacked. The *Demeter* is to be counted as a total loss."

Janus blinked in surprise. "By whom?"

"Unknown. A Hermes got away and had some sensor data loaded, most of it from a corvette in the Andalian fleet: the *Glory*." Haifer eyed him carefully, presumably to gauge his reaction.

"That's Gavin Andal's ship," he read off the data from his cerebral memory lacunae. "How is that possible?"

"Captain Gavin Andal was on board. Our on-site project manager was able to verify his identity."

"Then someone from House Andal is alive after all." Janus breathed a sigh of relief. "That's good news."

"Whether he is still alive is uncertain, but at least unlikely. The attacker was a Triumph-class frigate, apparently modified to be invisible to all *Demeter* and *Glory* sensors. Only the gravitational waves of its transit bow wave could be registered. In addition, the unknown ship was able to jump again within a few minutes."

Janus felt a chill run down his spine.

"You're not surprised," Haifer stated thoughtfully, looking alarmed, although he had his expression almost masterfully under control. But Janus had been dealing exclusively with grandmasters of political intrigue and false facades for five years.

"The Orb have attacked Trafalgar. The reports from there sounded frighteningly similar," he said truthfully.

"The Wall Worlds were attacked?" The assistant took a moment to catch himself. "I'm afraid I've heard very little in the last ten hours that hasn't happened on my ship."

"I don't suppose the only reason you took this trip, or are concerned for your welfare, is because you wanted to tell me about the loss of your Seed Vessel? A normal courier would have done just as well."

"Actually, another ship was supposed to deliver the message," Haifer said somewhat nebulously, his lips hardening for a moment.

"Sato Ran's private yacht."

A nod.

"Now you have my attention."

"Gavin Andal has brought disturbing news from

Andal. He spoke in a video message that was in the memory of the Hermes drone that made it back to our headquarters." Haifer tapped his wrist. "I have it here with me."

Janus licked his lips, then nodded. A moment later, his wrist terminal received a nameless video file. In it was the face of an attractive young man with golden curls. His eyes radiated something arrogant hidden behind the shadow of pain. But his expression betrayed only painfully restrained sorrow. Behind him was the tidy command center of a Seed Vessel, dark and minimalist. When Gavin Andal began to speak, he sounded a little rushed - the attack had probably already begun, for shouts could be heard in the background - but above all he sounded angry. His voice quivered, " *This is Lord Captain Gavin Andal, last survivor of House Andal, High Lord of the Karpshyn Sector. During the defensive battle of my home system, Fleet Admiral Dain Marquandt abandoned his designated positions and retreated when he should have attacked the Never. He also had three suspected Orb-manufactured drones with which he was able to direct the Never swarms in unknown ways. He was responsible for the destruction of the Home Fleets under the command of Crown Prince Magnus and the Border World Fleets under the command of my brother Artas, as well as the extermination of Andal with over a billion women, children and men. To get rid of witnesses, he disabled all jump engines in the system by imperial priority code. We must assume that the ship that killed the ice freighter* Alabama *and the passenger liner* Morning Star, *and is now attacking the Seed Vessel Demeter, is acting on Marquandt's orders to prevent anyone from carrying this information to the Emperor. I vouch for my words with the honor of my House and that of an officer in the Imperial Navy.*

When the recording ended with a freeze frame, Janus did not move and stared into space for a moment.

"I knew it," he finally said bitterly. Marquandt.

Haifer possessed enough subtlety to remain silent.

"I take it that the Corporate Council met before deciding to break this news to the Emperor?" Janus let his question be followed by a look that better made it clear to the younger man that he was to answer truthfully.

"Yes. Only the permanent veto members."

"And Sato Ran provided his private yacht?"

"She is the fastest."

"But Sorg didn't trust him enough."

"He trusts no one," Haifer said, as if it were the most natural thing in the world. "Otherwise he wouldn't have become supervisor."

Janus had his cerebral booster's security software isolate the file and check for malware and electronic data threads. But it was apparently clean.

"Who else knows about this?"

"No one so far."

In his mind, the names Yokatami, Marquandt and Albius swirled around each other like a whirlwind. The connections existed, but while some of them seemed unusual on paper, they were far from frivolous or even illegal. Now he heard that the Seed System between Andal and that of Yokatami had been attacked by a stealth ship - of all places, where the only so far known survivor from the battle for Andal appeared. Who accused Marquandt of treason and thus painted a clear picture.

"Do you also have the evidence data?"

"Yes."

Janus lowered his head and looked at Haifer like a bull about to paw its hooves.

The manager bit his lower lip and then sent him the

The last Fleet

relevant file. It came from the *Glory*'s on-board computer and showed that a priority code from Marquandt's flagship, the *Mammoth*, wanted to write the jump engine shutdown into the base code. Only with a cold reboot of all systems had Gavin Andal apparently managed to prevent this. Of course he knew about it; after all, the admiral had admitted just that in his report.

"You are not surprised this time."

"No. Marquandt already commented," he said.

"He certainly paints a different picture." Haifer did not let it be known where he stood on this.

Janus had to remind himself once again that the Corporate Protectorate was another nation, closely intertwined with the Star Empire but by no means equal to it. If he or Sorg cared at all about what political upheavals were going on outside their small sphere of influence, it was at most because of anticipated threats to their markets.

"Yes. But the accusation of a high lord of the Council of Nobility weighs heavily," Janus said. "Very heavy."

"Then hadn't we better turn back to inform the Emperor? After all, this is related to the death of his son."

"No. If we turn back now, the wrong people will know something is wrong. Any deviation from the norm is a risk of drawing attention to yourself."

"The wrong people? So it's not just Marquandt who could be playing a false game?" asked Haifer, looking around uneasily as if they might be stalked by ghosts that materialized at any moment.

"You're in Sol, young man," Janus reminded him. "Everyone who has made it here is interested in everything, and no one works without allies. If Marquandt dared to commit such treachery, it's because he has backing."

"Backing that can take out a private yacht after it transits and make it look like an accident?"

"Yes. If that was even necessary." He was glad Haifer didn't ask him about what exactly he meant by that, because his suspicion of Yokatami was almost entirely theoretical. So far. "We'll land normally, and I'll get my appointment over with quickly. Tonight I'll meet the Emperor, then I'll show him everything. Until then, everything must go as planned. You'd better get some acting talent, because you're going to be one of my bodyguards for the next three hours."

In front of the windshield, the sea of clouds that enveloped the entire east coast of North America was already growing, dense cotton balls that seemed almost massive. Less than five seconds later, they punched through at insane speed and it grew darker in the cabin.

"Landing in two!" the pilot shouted.

Janus saw out of the corner of his eye one of his bodyguards twitch the corner of his mouth. Perhaps the closest thing to a smile the man had.

"Why so chipper?" he asked in a conversational tone.

"Admiral Marquandt has just arrived in the Jupiter transit zone, sir," the Marine replied.

"Ah," Janus merely said and sighed inwardly. He should have expected that the troops, and probably large segments of the public, would look at Marquandt very differently than he did. The admiral who had fought the Never and survived. The admiral with real combat experience, who did not throw his sailors away lightly, who did not care about their lives. The admiral who would abandon his home system in favor of protecting Sol and Terra. He didn't even have to look around to know that this would be the narrative. And apparently it caught on. How could he blame them either? They didn't know what

The last Fleet

he knew; that Marquandt had nefariously left them all to die. But Sol had always been interested only in Sol and not in the distant Border Worlds somewhere on the edge of the Sigma Quadrant. Only one thing counted here: that finally enough fleets were present again to feel safe and superior.

INTERLUDE: MIRAGE

Mirage stood on the edge of Landing Pad C of the Ridgewood private spaceport in upstate New York. Although it was a fringe area of the third-largest arcology on Earth, the houses here also rose hundreds of feet tall. Vast swaths of Ridgewood were dominated by public housing, providing homes for those struggling to make ends meet through basic imperial services and petty odd jobs. Their only hope for a fresh start lay in a new wave of Star Empire expansion and accompanying forced deportations. As with the previous colonization pushes.

The spaceport was something of a slap in the face to these people, serving the well-paid employees of Jupiter Bank, which had a branch in adjacent Oakland and provided a landing pad for private shuttles north of the city to managers of other corporations. In Ridgewood, it should not have been difficult to obtain a building permit and demolish some apartment blocks to secure the area with electric fences and security drones. The landing pads had been built on the flat level, the 'surface' of the arcology, below which was the undercity, a dozen or so sublevels stretching down to the ground. There, far from sunlight and fresh air, dwelled the *truly* sinister characters who traded assai, weapons and illegal VR stims.

Mirage didn't miss the irony that the landing pads of the rich and important were right on the roof of this criminal microcosm, sealing the surface with their monobonded composite.

She sat clad in an airport security uniform on a Grid bike next to the gate that led onto Interstate 2, which bisected New York from south to north. Two shuttles descended simultaneously between the weathered giant buildings after their sonic booms announced them. Both times, the clanking of windows all around had sounded like cold applause.

"Which one is it?" she asked in her helmet.

"The one on the left with civilian ID 2022-CC," the Voice replied.

"It would be easier if you gave me direct access to the signal."

"Yes, it would."

Mirage did not respond. The Voice certainly had their reasons. They always did.

"Be careful, Mirage. I'm picking up a second signal from the shuttle, and it's not from one of our transmitters."

"Understood. Should I initiate contact with Zenith immediately, as planned?"

"Negative. Hold off and try to figure out what the second signal is all about. Something is not developing as expected," the Voice commanded.

"Understood." Mirage wondered when the last time something of interest to the Voice had escaped the network, but came to no conclusion. It didn't matter either; the instructions were clear.

The last Fleet

Her eyes zoomed in on both shuttles in turn, squat cuboids with four pivoting thrusters on their undersides. Roaring, they ejected blue plasma as they went into final braking thrust, kicking up dust and ubiquitous plastic debris. Shortly thereafter, she had identified her target shuttle by its painted visual identifier. Its outline stood out against the sick-looking sky, whose clouds gave the appearance of pus that told of the sickness of the Terran biosphere.

It extended its landing struts and, after a sharp turn, landed on the pad to its right. With a sigh, the thrusters shut down and the tail ramp slid open.

Zenit exited with four Imperial Guardsmen who looked like aides-de-camp, busy bureaucrats, and one who instead seemed to be a bureaucrat, even if he seemed a little too smart for that. But the techaura scanners in her eyes told her, despite noteworthy shielding, that unlike the four, he had no military augments.

Her memory clusters spat out the result immediately after: Jonathan Haifer, personal assistant to Ruhr Heavy Industries CEO Supervisor Ludwig Sorg. She sent a quick message to the Network's distribution list and flipped down the visor of her helmet.

Three vehicles came racing from the small terminal and gathered Zenith and his bodyguards. Two of them each boarded the front and rear cars, Zenith and Haifer taking the middle one. The models were heavily armored, although their surely high price might be mainly due to the fact that they hid this fact well. She pulled up next to the first car and knocked on the driver's door with the flat of her hand.

The window rolled down and one of the guardsmen looked at her with the near-perfect imitation of an impatient Imperial Service bureaucrat.

"What is it?"

"I need your authorization, standard procedure," she said, flipping up her visor. His companion in the passenger seat pressed something on his wrist terminal. "Thank you, have a safe trip."

Without a retort, the driver closed the window.

As the small column of nondescript civilian cars rolled up to the gate, the two security guards in the puny little house opened and nodded toward the tinted windows.

Mirage steered her motorcycle behind them and turned right as Zenith headed north. Knowing where he was headed, she would catch up with him at the next block. But she didn't want to catch the eye of the well-trained Marines. Once out of sight, she changed the pattern of her chameleon suit by loading the logo of a local food delivery company into the programmable silicon layer. The bike was a basic model and didn't have such upgrades, but it was black, so at least it was of a standard color.

Traffic in the poorer Ridgewood was also controlled by the traffic management system, which took control of all vehicles and moved them back and forth with the help of the Gridlink AI. But in places like these, there were plenty of bikes and scooters that were unplugged and meandered through the frugally moving columns. She was one of them now and soon caught up with Zenith. She had to hand it to them that the cars actually blended in well with the tangle of poorly maintained vehicles. Had she not marked the window of the front car with a radioactive isotope, even she would have had a hard time finding them again. But as it was, the marker substance glowed in her field of vision like digital confetti.

Mirage made sure to keep a few cars between them at all times, constantly switching the three lanes that led

The last Fleet

north. The interstate was quite wide here, although it didn't appear to be. The one- to two-hundred-yard-high apartment buildings with their myriad balconies created a sense of confinement just through the dark concrete covered with mold and grime from age. Just above their rooftops, the numerous Copters zoomed along on their invisible airways, creating an uneasy play of shadows on the asphalt in front of her. Here she could well imagine what might be behind the concept of desolation.

When the first shots rang out, she was not surprised, except by their intensity. From one moment to the next, muzzle flashes burst from numerous balconies and windows, bathing the interstate in an artificial thunderstorm. Bullets pelted the cars, creating an erratic chaos of sparks. Gridlink slowed them all down simultaneously, according to its safety protocols. Mirage had to brake hard to avoid colliding with the van in front of her, jumped off the seat, and slid under the van's bumper for cover with the rest of her energy directed forward. Her ears analyzed the rattle of fully automatic weapons and counted at least fifty shooters.

She crept forward so that she had visual contact with Zenith's vehicles. Unlike some civilians who had gotten out and tried to run for safety, they remained seated, maintaining their cover. Since the Gridlink locked up all occupants until Arc Police arrived when crimes were committed nearby, those who had overridden the system now found their freedom a death trap. No one made it to the edge of the interstate, where the littered boulevards of small businesses began and promised salvation.

A movement demanded Mirage's attention: from far ahead, a monstrous semi-truck roared in, plowing through the stationary vehicles as if through dry grass. Smashed and bent bodies were hurled to the right and left. Somewhere in the distance, the wail of sirens could be heard. The network sent her a countdown to the arrival of security: five minutes. A long time in New York, but an extremely short one in this part of New York, where Arc Police rarely showed up. Why sacrifice lives and valuable time for criminals and the less productive? But this was too big to ignore, and likely from a terrorist background. Since Paris, that meant maximum hardship by maximum powers of the authorities.

Her attempt to contact Zenith undetected had just become significantly more complicated. The semi would reach Zenith's vehicles in less than a minute, at which point the guardsmen would be forced to abandon them to try on foot - a death sentence in the crossfire of the attackers. One minute.

Mirage made a decision and rolled out from under the van. The inferno of impacting projectiles around her sounded like hail on sheet metal. She grabbed the driver's door and effortlessly ripped it off its hinges, holding it over her like a shield. Then she ran forward. Several impacts in the door forced her to make compensatory movements to keep from falling.

Then suddenly all hell broke loose around her. A laser beam was simply there from one moment to the next, a glistening column of light the diameter of a house. It seemed to have been sent from heaven by God himself and vaporized the semi within a breath. Lightning compensators settled over her sensitive eyes, somewhat dampening the onslaught of free photons. Those who did not have the appropriate hardware and were currently looking through one of the thousands of windows around them lost their eyesight in an instant.

But the bombardment of the orbital defense platform did not let up. With no regard for civilian casualties, the beam streaked across the street, giving the roadway a hole that undoubtedly ate its way to the ground, destroying everything that 'lived' in the undercity. It sank the front of the houses on the right, leaving an open skeleton where balconies had been a moment ago. Instead of muzzle flashes, there was only molten steel there, dripping like lava into the depths.

The guardsmen saw their chance coming and got out on the left side, where the attackers had been volatilized into their atoms. Mirage's neural computer warned her that the ambient temperature had reached a hostile level and would soon denature body proteins. Not a problem she had to deal with.

She sprinted to the column, grabbed a guardsman's service weapon and pointed it to the side as he fired at her. The shot whirred a hair's breadth past her right ear.

"Your team," she murmured, but the Marine was not the trusting sort. He slipped from her grasp, lightning fast and powerful. She was faster, minimally so, but it was enough to kick him between the legs and get to Zenith, who, just like Jonathan Haifer, seemed to move as if in slow motion. Downright agonizingly slow.

"Extraction!" she shouted to him over the din of evaporating buildings, and he raised a hand as the two other guardsmen - just about to grab him and drag him along - attempted to shoot her.

"We're staying here until it's over!" he yelled.

"Negative. It's not over." She gestured to the side with a nod. The orbital laser should have stopped firing, readjusted, and then melted away the other front of the house. But instead, the beam came at them, taking the shortcut in whose path the column 'happened' to be. Their noise filters sorted out the sounds of the approaching death sentence: screams of occupants being cooked in their vehicles just a few yards from the laser, vaporizing tires and bodies, bubbles of sensor dust hitting the asphalt.

"Ten seconds." She yanked him to his feet and started running. South, where she had come from. The guardsmen caught up with her, as they were faster without weight, and formed a cocoon around their charge, weapons drawn. Where a door was opened, they mercilessly gunned down anyone who dared make their way out.

She realized how close it was getting when Jonathan Haifer, unable to keep up with them, barely escaped the beam that swept across the interstate behind him, disintegrating the entire section. The assistant shrieked in pain as skin dripped from his flesh and he tumbled forward. Two seconds later, he was nothing more than a smoking corpse.

10

GUNTER

Gunter was awakened by a headache. Something he had not felt since his youth. Thanks to his neural computer, which was connected to an auto-injector in his flank, most pain stimuli above the threshold of a mild pulling sensation were suppressed by analgesic blocks. Just enough that he was aware when he had been shot or a body part was no longer functioning as it should. A physical stimulus to the flashing warning icons in his field of vision.

Only this time it wasn't just a tug, but a feeling as if someone had placed an activated vibrohammer between his temples. There were no warning symbols either, there was just nothing at all. His wrists felt as if he had placed them on a poisonous hedgehog, and there was a metallic taste on his tongue.

Blood.

When he opened his eyes, he was looking into the dirty face of a woman.

"Masha," he noted. His eyelids were so heavy that he would have preferred to close them again.

Masha withdrew her hand, which held a damp rag.

"You're awake at last."

"Where am I?"

"In the shit," someone else answered in her place. A gaunt fellow with sunken cheeks, whose bones were clearly visibly under his stained clothes. He spoke with the same, oddly rolling accent as Masha.

"Shut up, Sergei," she said, and sighed. Looking back to Gunter, she shrugged and dabbed at his forehead. It felt cool and gave him at least a hint of relief. "But unfortunately, he's right. You really are in the poop."

"In the poop?" asked Sergei. "Who in the bloody heavens talks like that?"

"Someone who hasn't lost all manners like you, simply because he thinks poor wretches like us have to talk like that!"

"My goodness." Sergei raised his arms defensively and left.

Where is he going, anyway? Gunter peeked past Masha and saw a huge cave whose walls he couldn't make out because it was too dark. There were cots and water fountains everywhere. The floor was littered with soyfood bags, the leftovers of cheap meals. It smelled of feces, sweat and unwashed clothes. For once, it didn't bother him so much that it was too dark to see much, except for hundreds of human silhouettes. No one moved quickly, most not at all, others wandered seemingly aimlessly like lost ghosts.

He tried another question. "What happened?"

"I don't know," Masha said. "I woke up here the same way you did. You just came to a little later, I was told. And with these things."

She gestured down at his wrists. Gunter followed her gesture heavily and saw two black rings resting on his skin at the base of his forearms, reddened all around as if trying to repel the metal.

"Augment blockers," he growled in frustration. The administrator must have put them on him after the Broker's Ultras had taken him down with their shock rifles. At least that explained why he had no access to his implants and felt naked, slow and inadequate. The small devices each had a dozen hypodermic needles that gave the magnetic tape and computing unit in the bracelet access to his nanite circulation and circuitry, paralyzing anything electronic in origin. They fueled his augments with continuous signals that overloaded the system. What he would have given now to be a mutant or bionic and not have to rely on electronics.

I never thought I'd be thinking that way, he thought, shaking his head, which immediately turned out to be a bad idea.

Masha nodded. "Guess you're just like us now."

"No," the word escaped him without thought.

If she was offended by that, she didn't let on. Instead, she dabbed at his forehead again, which he shrugged off.

"It helps."

"I'm fine," he lied. His refusal to be helped was childish at best, he realized, but a Marine was always a Marine.

She shrugged and handed him the damp rag. It smelled like his underwear after a week of maneuvers, but the coolness helped enough that he willingly placed it on his forehead.

"What is this place?" he asked as he heard a loud rumble followed by booming static. Whatever Masha answered him was lost in a sudden swelling of shouts from people who were in the cave. They were not words they were formulating, but rather a wail, as if they had a swarm consciousness. Distantly, he thought they were shouting a long-drawn-out "Heeere!" He had heard it before, and its sound sent a shiver down his spine-not only because it was so loud and insistent, borne of desperation and pleading.

The Whisper!

"What are they doing?" he asked aloud.

"When noises are heard from outside, they hope food and medicine will be brought," she explained. "This happens at irregular intervals. Once two workers came and tried to free us, but they were shot. Their bodies are still lying further back." She gestured over her shoulder with a thumb. "Probably as a reminder or something."

"So they're hoping to get somebody's attention."

"Yes." Her gaze grew heavy, pained. "I'm to blame for this. I managed to sneak out when the workers came here and I told them what was out there."

"Then Mustache found you," Gunter said.

"Mustache?" She frowned at first, then nodded. "Peter. His name is Peter."

"Is he something like ..."

"He took pity on us. Just like everyone else in this ward," she still seemed to be struggling to come to terms with the idea, "he didn't know about us."

"It's probably going to stay that way." Gunter looked around again and thought he saw walls bulging in the distance to the right and left. It was hard to tell for sure because of the poor lighting conditions. But a somber thought still came to him instinctively, "We're in the equalization caverns."

"Yes."

His courage sank.

Masha eyed him anxiously. "You know something."

"I know that the equalization caverns have access points for incoming and outgoing gas that can be capped

The last Fleet

at any time," he said, and as if to punctuate his words, two loud clanging noises sounded, as if someone were banging a huge hammer against the shell of the tank in which they were trapped like flakes in a snow globe. "And then it's sealed."

"Why would we be sealed?" asked Masha, her eyes wide. "Why would they bring us all the way from Arcturus just to suffocate us?"

"I don't know, but the traitor's daughter is smuggling cots and rations through Andal into the Seed Traverse," he explained quietly, more to himself. The ground beneath their feet began to vibrate and the wailing of the many hundreds or thousands of men and women all around swelled into a surge of panic.

"The Seed Traverse? Why would they kidnap us to ..."

"I don't know." He shook his head. "Are there children here, too?"

"No. Just adults."

"And you're all from Arcturus?"

Masha nodded weakly, pride shining in her eyes. "I bet our disappearance didn't even make the news on Terra One. No one cares about us because our ancestors made a terrible mistake two hundred years ago."

"The extermination of Kerhal with antimatter bombs," he said.

"None of us were alive then. Not even our parents. Yet, since the end of the blockade one hundred years ago, no development aid money has been coming to us."

"I guess they disappear into Black Haven in orbit." Gunter grunted. He had never had anything but contempt for Arcturus and its inhabitants until now, he had to admit to himself. It was easy to see only the historical debt and not the lives of the individuals who came after it, striving for happiness as much as anyone else.

"Yes. The damned black market," she countered, clenching her fists in frustration. A tear trickled down her cheek. "I wanted nothing more than for my children to be able to leave that damned planet. Artiom and Oleana deserved better. And now it's me who's far away, trapped in this horror I don't understand. Everyone here has experienced something like this."

"Have many of you... you know?"

"No!" Masha sounded indignant. "We're Arcturians. We never look for the easy way out."

"Fighters." He nodded appreciatively.

"Those who live on Arcturus are either hard as steel or dead as ashes. Unfortunately, we are also hard on eachother. If one of us sees something valuable, he takes it. Always."

"I guess that's why you guys are known for the Black Haven," Gunter remarked.

"We're only good at two things: stealing and survival. With us, you have to be careful not to tell anyone you've discovered something interesting. You steal it right away. I wanted my children to have something better to look forward to in their future." Masha's eye expression turned sad.

Again the ground shook, this time longer. It jolted so hard that his teeth chattered. Then, all at once, weightlessness set in, and they disengaged from the ground.

"What's happening?" asked Masha in alarm.

"I think we're leaving the Cerberus."

"Where to?"

"We'll soon find out," he said with a somber expression, thinking of the neural cables Akwa Marquandt had overseen the loading of. A sick feeling formed in the pit of his stomach.

11

GAVIN

No one spoke to them during the clearance, but Gavin didn't feel like talking anyway. Their strange crawling vehicle climbed down a dark ramp into an area that looked like a large concrete funnel. Floodlights of cold white light turned on, blinding him so much that his eyes hurt. Then the tailgate was opened and under stun guns held at the ready, they had to line up.

Dodger looked indifferent at this, as if none of this was new to her, while Hellcat struggled to hold back her anger. Gavin knew that her anger was fed by the fear of the unknown, which also had a firm grip on him. Everyone dealt with fear in their own personal way. For him, the looks of the refugees were the worst: empty and devoid of hope. Nothing reminded him of the five men and women who had fought over an animal and planned their escape. They were broken, no more than empty shells that breathed but did not live. In their condition, the soldiers didn't even need their weapons, and the fact that they had broken so quickly after being captured also made Gavin's courage sink. What scared them so much?

After standing in a line, they were led in front of a door located at the end of the funnel. Cold gray concrete on all sides. There were no control panels, no DNA scanners, nothing. Not even cameras, but Gavin tapped sensor dust all over the walls.

The door opened and they were led into a short hallway. The walls were white and smooth, there were no visible joints at all, but there were glands in the floor and ceiling. Panels on the sides flipped open, and their guards disappeared behind them before slamming shut again.

"Remove clothing," a voice commanded from invisible speakers, and their shackles came loose with a loud click. They fell uselessly to the floor. The five fugitives immediately complied with the request, though they moved slowly and lethargically. Gavin watched them undress and turned. Dodger was already undressed. She was indeed a woman.

She didn't seem to mind.

Hellcat, on the other hand, did not move.

After what felt like an eternity, the voice from the speakers sounded again, cool and businesslike. "Strip, final warning."

"Better do it," Dodger advised them from behind. "Better a bare bottom than a whipped one."

"I'm not getting naked in front of these fuckers!" hissed Hellcat.

"We can switch places," Gavin suggested, moving past her so she was behind him. She said nothing, but he briefly heard the rustle of her clothes. After a gulp, he undressed as well.

The next thing he knew, white steam was coming out of the glands, enveloping the hallway in a dense fog like the airlock of a high-security lab. It smelled of disinfectants and ozone, reminiscent of nanites that had finished their short life cycle and were ready for recycling.

"I'm going to fuck these motherfuckers up," Hellcat growled behind him.

The wall panels flipped open again and men and women with cortical disruptors emerged from them. They wore white chemical suits that almost blended into the surroundings, along with rubber boots and breathing masks. Only their eyes were visible, and there was nothing but cool professionalism in them. Not the sort of guards with whom it was possible to negotiate or even elicit sympathy, that much was certain.

Fresh gray coveralls fell out of flaps in the ceiling and they had to hurriedly put them on before moving on.

Next they came to a long hallway that was just as white and seemed to glow out of the walls. Gavin's headache grew a little stronger as he had to constantly squint his eyes to keep from being blinded. Single file, the guards led them along several turns past a curved wall that seemed to be hundreds of feet long, like the outer wall of a stadium. At one point, Gavin heard screams as they passed and shuddered. Another time, in a wide corridor, windowless like the rest, another column approached them. The prisoners wore gray coveralls with a letter and long numbers on the chest. Their gazes were lowered; no one sought contact.

"Shit, who are all these people?" whispered Hellcat behind him as the exactly fifty men and women passed them in silence. The silence in which it all happened was eerie. Except for the rustling of coveralls, nothing could be heard, almost as if the walls were swallowing every sound. Gavin even forgot for a moment that he was stark naked as well as the feeling of humiliation that this fact caused in him.

"Quiet!" one of the guards snapped at them, and the sudden loudness made their entire column flinch like a single organism. Gavin expected Hellcat to forget herself and throw a tantrum, but even she remained silent the rest of their way.

That led them past a large area, a cavern a hundred or more yards across. There, hundreds of people in a wide variety of torn clothing were herded like cattle down a ramp by guards. Armed men directed them to a wide gate where they disappeared. The faces of the men and women looked haggard and dirty, of such fatigue that they offered no resistance. They must have been brought in by the *Mammoth* freighter, as many as they were. Their flow did not slacken as he left the cavern with his fellow prisoners.

Down a wider corridor they went. At one point he could see a grisly scene through a door that closed behind a guard: A prisoner lay fixed on a raised cot while figures in white plugged neural cables into his data jack. They ignored the poor guy's cries of pain as if they were robots following their programming.

Then they reached a large cell block, the end of their long march. The ceiling was low, the floor ice cold, consisting of gray slabs of some metal. Each cell was open, but had a sliding door for privacy. There were about twenty on either side, relaxing music sounded from loudspeakers, mixed with birdsong and the sound of wind brushing over a forest.

They had to line up in front of the cells they were assigned, prisoners came out of the others to see what was going on. As soon as they saw the guards, they lined up as well, as if they were controlled by a single brain.

A guard put eye blockers around the wrists of him, Hellcat, and Dodger and explained to them in terse sentences what to expect: you each get a cell, there will be food, enough to drink. By nine in the morning, you're dressed and ready for your daily exercise. There are entertainment programs from 8 to 10 pm. 10:30 p.m. Lights out. Those who become violent are put in solitary confinement. Those who behave aggressively towards their fellow inmates will have the taste of food removed and the entertainment programs will be cut off.

Gavin looked with a furrowed brow at Hellcat, who was glaring at the guard as if she wanted to tear him to pieces with her gaze. For the first time, he really understood why she had her call sign. She really looked like a predatory cat from hell, despite her undeniable beauty.

The guards disappeared and the door closed behind them with a hydraulic sigh.

The other prisoners - what else could they be? - eyed them for a few more moments, then retreated to their cells. Apparently they had been disturbed while sleeping.

"Hey, you must be the new guys, huh?" asked a middle-aged woman who came to them in a stooped posture like a dog awaiting a blow from its master. Her hair was neat and unlike the five fugitives, she looked healthy and kind of ... *happy*, which irritated Gavin.

"Guess so," he replied. He noticed that her accent was the same as that of the five who had been picked up with them. "I guess you can tell."

"Yeah." She chortled. "I'm Yaisha. Been here for two weeks."

"Sounds like you should get a medal, the way you're saying it," Hellcat grumbled, turning away to inspect her cell.

"Oh, I'm just glad it's over." Yaisha waved it off. "It was a lot worse where I came from than here."

"Where would that be? Deep in the ass of a Never

entity?" asked Hellcat. Her voice sounded muffled, as she had already disappeared into her cell.

"Not that important. Anyway, it was awful there. Unlike a lot of people here, I didn't leave any kids behind." The woman's expression changed briefly, then her eyes lit up again. She nudged Gavin in the side as if they'd known each other forever and bounced past him into the section that was obviously meant for him. On the left side, there was a cot with pad, pillow and blanket. A multispectral lamp provided warm light that matched the relaxing sounds of nature that reached his ears. Yaisha pulled a lever on the wall opposite and a toilet flipped open.

"Loo," she said, flipping it shut again and walking over to two hoses next to a small mirror and a change of clothes rack. "One for water and one for food. This stuff tastes really good and there's as much as you want. Fortified with vitamins, minerals and trace elements."

"How do you know all that?" asked Gavin.

Yaisha held out her hand to him as if that would answer any question. When he didn't respond, she pointed her index finger at her nails. "I had more than four deficiency diseases. Cracked nails, bleeding gums, chronic bowel inflammation, and bad eyes. All gone after a week here." Her grin grew wide. "Plus sports programs every day, and they even have the latest episodes of Terranator streaming." She tapped the display slide on the ceiling above the cot. "I didn't have any of that at home. I probably wouldn't have even survived this year."

"How did you get here?"

"I don't know. I got stuck in traffic at home and then I was locked in a dark room with a couple hundred others for a few days. Maybe a couple thousand, too. It wasn't pretty. But then we were here!" Yaisha's expression brightened again. "It's all good now!"

"You're a prisoner," he stated, eyeing her uncomprehendingly.

"So what? Better than poor and sick."

"Where are you from?"

"Arcturus," Dodger replied, leaning behind him at the entrance to his cell, her powerful arms folded under her chest. "Nowhere else can you make people disappear in large numbers."

"Make them disappear?" he asked.

"Somebody kidnapped them, after all. You can buy anything in the Black Haven since time immemorial. Guns and stuff, sure. But also slaves, forced prostitutes, and children."

Gavin swallowed, mostly because of the calmness and matter-of-factness with which the mutant said it.

"Your world is wholesome and idealistic," Dodger opined. "The real world is harsh and ruthless. You may think it's terrorists and pirates who frequent the Black Haven. You're wrong. Enough of them are blue bloods like you."

His comrade unfolded her arms, shrugged, and walked to her cell, where she lay down on her cot with the door open.

"Well," Yaisha made as if nothing had happened. "Now we should sleep. We want to be fit for our exercise tomorrow, after all."

With that, she left Gavin alone, and that was how he felt. Ever since they had left the *Lady Vengeance*, everything had seemed like a bad drug trip to him. Clearly as alien a planet as could be, with alien plants and animals, a huge secret facility, the stolen *Mammoth* freighter landing on it. The imprisonment and the dejected new arrivals. And now this cell tract that he couldn't make sense of. This was so irrational it couldn't be real. The guards carried weapons and were clearly not in a joking mood. They were locked up, no question - but with entertainment displays, food as much as they wanted, and their own space with privacy? Sports programs and relaxation music?

If he had been afraid before, it now slowly expanded into panic.

"Gavin?" It was Hellcat who came in to him after the lights went out and a soft passive lighting on the floor bathed his cell in a pleasant glow. She pulled the door closed behind her.

"Are you all right?" he asked, wishing he could have bitten his tongue, his own words sounded so stupid. Fortunately, she didn't seem to register them at all.

"We need to get out of here."

"I realize that."

"No, I mean we need to get out of here now," she repeated firmly.

"I wasn't planning on staying any longer than necessary."

"Did you see the people in here? They looked happy."

Gavin nodded. "I know, really weird."

"You can say that again. They seem like a different species than the five from the forest. But they were absolutely scared to death when they were in that crawling thing with us. So much so that they lost all hope in one fell swoop. Have you ever seen that happen to anyone who just managed to break out?" she asked, stroking her hair over the top of her head as she always did when she got nervous.

"I haven't had to deal with that many prisoners on the run."

"If you've made it once, you believe you can make it again, no matter how high security is," Hellcat explained, as if he hadn't said anything. "But these don't. They kind of know it's over. All over."

Gavin understood what she meant. He had felt the same way. In some ways, the sight of the five fugitives had scared him more than the guards with their guns and cold professionalism.

"That's not what scares you the most. To die," he stated, looking her in the eye. At first she seemed to want to look away, but then she held her ground. There was no aggression in her gaze, but something that struck him far more: a touch of vulnerability.

"I can't be locked up," she whispered so softly he could barely hear her. Images of her expertly, and with almost robotic calm, freeing him from the cables they'd been thrown into during their escape from *Demeter* ran through his mind. How blood had shot out of her pores into space as a fine mist and she had simply gone on to save him. At that moment she had been a superhuman apparition to him, a symbol of what a human being could be capable of through sheer will and perseverance. Now he saw her limit and at the same time so much more; the core of her and what drove her - perhaps even made her a rebel, fighting against the system that he, of all people, stood for by birth.

Instead of saying anything, he wrapped her in his arms and hugged her tightly. He expected a slap or a beating - he had no illusions that she could beat the living daylights out of him despite her physical disadvantage - but she surprised him by moving straight for him.

They stood there for a few moments before she hardened again like a gargoyle and broke away from him.

"We need to sleep," she decided, and disappeared from his cell as if she had never been there.

12

JANUS

J anus felt like he was trapped in a nightmare. Everything happened so rapidly that he could hardly keep up. His neural computer was trying hard to make the best possible use of the cerebral booster to sort out his sensory impressions superhumanly fast and to provide capacities for conscious decisions. But the Guardsmen and Mirage were moving at a completely different level with their artificial reflex lines, forcing him to become a spectator of events.

Behind them, the orbital laser raged, palpable by the enormous heat that felt as if they were rushing through the most hostile desert on Terra. The steam of cooked paint and metal was heavy in his nose and lungs, but worse were the screams of burning people. They could be heard even over the roar of annihilation, reminding him of the hurricanes on his homeworld of Hadron.

They reached the edge of the interstate after his guardsmen had shot several passersby - at least that's what Janus thought he saw. Or maybe it was his adrenaline-addled brain. Regardless, he felt nauseous.

Two of his men jumped the five or more feet down, landed lightly, and turned around. Before Janus could let out a sound of protest, Mirage threw him down like a doll, and he was caught by strong hands. Suddenly he was on his feet again, trying to find his way along the wide pedestrian boulevard. Everything was burned, black where the laser had lingered only briefly. It smelled of charred flesh and chemicals from the melted asphalt. Farther to the left, a huge gap gaped in the ground and the interstate, with darkness descending deep.

Once again he was grabbed and shortly found himself in one of the high-rises, which they passed through a maze of corridors. Again, frightened faces appeared, peering through gaps in doors.

"NO!" he ordered loudly as the guardsmen raised their weapons, and to his relief they did not fire.

Stairs. He saw stairs. Only briefly, because it was pitch black as soon as the door behind them slammed into the maglock. What to him was impenetrable blackness that not even his natural residual light amplification in his eyes could penetrate seemed to bother neither his bodyguards nor Mirage. Shortly, they were in a parking garage.

"Three vehicles," barked one of the guardsmen. "I'll take Obsidian."

Obsidian, that's my code name, he reminded himself. Suddenly Mirage's face was in front of him. A false face, sure, but he knew it was her. Her cold eyes could not be forgotten by any man who had really looked.

"You're in shock," she said, but her words made no sense to him. They were just sounds made by air pressure that escaped her lips. It would pass in a moment. He felt a twinge somewhere on his neck. "There is information. I've been talking to Rogoshin."

"Rogoshin," he repeated lamely. Then his mind

The last Fleet

suddenly cleared, and an unnatural inner calm set in. "You found out something?"

Mirage looked at the guardsmen who were busy canvassing vehicles. Then she said quietly, "Yes. He revealed two of Marquandt's contacts. A bribed IIA employee who moved files for him in the fleet archive, his name is Afrin Makumba. And a high-ranking Exec from Yokatami, Yoshi Ketambe, with whom there were regular meetings. He didn't know anything about the contents."

Janus stored the names in his memory clusters. Mirage's gaze became demanding. He nodded and sent her the award for her service.

"The ship's name is *Virginia*, *Thethis*-class as promised. It is located in Section U in the civilian sector at *Rubov*, Hangar U-87. The priority codes are secured, and the authorizations for the restricted area of the Seed Traverse are in the ship's computer." After transmitting all the authorizations to her wrist terminal, he grabbed her arm. "Don't make me regret this, Mirage."

She looked down at his hand and then gazed unblinkingly into his eyes.

"I'll get the data from the archives," she said. "There's a cost for me to extract it."

"As always."

"The price is to be paid immediately: What information did Ludwig Sorg's assistant share?"

"Gavin Andal is alive. He was on *Demeter*," Janus replied, without hesitation. That knowledge would be available to the Network soon anyway, if it wasn't already and this was a test. "The *Demeter* was destroyed by a cloaked ship that has novel jump engines. Gavin Andal accuses Dain Marquandt of treason and indirect murder of Crown Prince Magnus and the people of Andal."

Mirage nodded with an expressionless face. "I will make contact as soon as I have the data in my possession."

A short time later, she was gone and Janus' wrist terminal chirped. The imperial seal spun on his display.

"First Secretary of State, the Emperor for you," announced Felicity, one of his master's secretaries. A moment later, the line clicked.

"Janus?"

"Your Majesty."

"Damn it, Janus, are you all right?" asked Haeron II, upset.

"I'm alive," he replied.

"Those damn terrorists. I was lucky that Albius was just with me and got the news about the attack in Ridgewood. I was already afraid you might get caught in the crossfire and ordered the deployment of a defensive platform."

Janus thought of the destroyed house fronts, the civilians cooked in their vehicles, and all those who had been vaporized by the laser along with the terrorists. His nausea worsened abruptly. The relief with which the Emperor spoke was in direct contrast to his own feelings of guilt. How alienated could one be from the effects of one's own orders? How easy was it to make tactically correct decisions without being in touch with the suffering they were causing?

"Come back," Haeron II ordered, and Janus had the type of signal the Emperor was using to contact him superimposed on his field of view. 360-degree encrypted radio. He should have called through Quantcom, but his master was getting far too careless and erratic since his son's death.

After a brief risk assessment, he said anyway, "I believe the attack was on me."

The last Fleet

"On you?"

"Yes, your majesty. The terrorists attacked the very section of the interstate I was on. That can't be a coincidence."

"But how would they have known it was you?" the emperor asked doubtfully.

"I don't know. Someone in the chain must have passed on the information."

"They're all loyal people, Janus. And these bloody rebels are not as well connected as you think."

Janus would have said the same thing until the attack. Now, however, the image of the laser that had streaked across the road, right where his motorcade had been, was burned into his mind. Deployments of orbital weapons against targets on Terra's surface had been legal solely because of the emergency decrees since Paris, and the hurdle for them was still extremely high. For a commander to fire them indiscriminately through a neighborhood was unthinkable until today.

"Your Majesty," he said, as calmly as he could so as not to sound hysterical. "Please review the footage of the orbital defense platform deployment."

"I'll do that, Janus. But now come back to the *Rubov*. Meanwhile, I have sent your second-in-command, Jorge, to Newark."

"As you wish. It may take some time, though, sir. There is only chaos here."

"Of course. Be as careful as you have to. I can also give you a whole fleet of ..."

"No, your majesty, thank you. I'll find another way. More inconspicuous."

"All right."

When the connection was severed, he looked to the guardsmen who were preparing the three cars in the darkness. The fourth stood at the gate of the underground garage and opened it using his imperial priority code.

Janus weighed the risk that one of them was working for those who wanted him dead. Or whether it had been one of the shuttle's pilots. Against that was the fact that they could have effortlessly eliminated him in the chaos of the orbital bombardment. Unless only one of them was bought and still hanging on for dear life. In addition, the laser would also have vaporized them without consideration. But did he really want to take a risk, however small? Only the most loyal and best of the Marines even got into the Guard selection program; betrayal from their ranks was virtually impossible - but only ever until it happened. How unlikely was it that the other side had been preparing one of their agents for many years to slip him through all the Guard's instances and then activate him at the right moment?

Janus made a decision and retreated into the shadows of the pillar he had been leaning against. His old routines took over, routines he had long thought buried and forgotten. Yet they still functioned as if he had never turned his back on all that. He slipped back and forth between the parked vehicles. On tiptoe and as quietly as a cat. Again and again he ducked and paused silently until he arrived at an exit.

"Where is he?" he heard one of the men call.

"He was just..."

He didn't catch any more because he squeezed through the crack in the door and very quietly pushed the door into the maglock. He was lucky that the power had been turned off for the entire block, so no magnetic locks were working.

He rushed up through the stairwell and out into the open after checking the fit of his Reface mask and tightening up. Onlookers had already gathered on the boulevards. Police vehicles stood to the right with their blue lights on, setting up holobarriers. From the interstate above them, the noise of sirens reflected off the wall of buildings. The sky was full of Copters from police and emergency services, and firefighters' drones were extinguishing smoldering fires that kept flaring up.

Horrified, he watched as the first victims were pulled from the destroyed facade to his right. Emergency workers in exoskeletons jumped out of Copters, clawed and picked up injured people to fly them out. Some of them were missing their legs, others were half-burned like coal. Most of them emitted bloodcurdling screams of pain until they were sedated. All this chaos, along with the barely describable swath of destruction before his eyes, painted an apocalyptic picture. There would have to be a news blackout to keep this from the wider public.

He had to find out who was responsible for this. Who had managed to find out his whereabouts? Who had the commander of a defense platform so deep in his pocket that he threw away his career? Who was so fanatical that he would accept the deaths of hundreds for the chance to kill the First Secretary of State?

It was related to his digging, that much was obvious. So only Albius or Marquandt came into question - both of whom were currently in the system. If they went so far as to do this, whatever they were trying to hide must be momentous.

INTERLUDE: MIRAGE

The first hurdle was the entrance to the Fleet Archives. The building looked like an ancient castle, only much larger. Its base was a cuboid with five hundred yards of edges and twenty floors, built of composite, like everything else since the beginning of asteroid mining. But the facade looked as if it were made of sandstone, which gave it a prehistoric and stately look. At the corners, skyscrapers of glass grew into the sky like towers, modern and conical.

With her fake database entry into the officer directory and the DNA reservoir in her Second Skin glove, the automated security systems gave her no trouble. She breezed through the doors and scanner area of the west reception with the many other fleet bureaucrats. From there, she connected to the house system and had directions to the maintenance department projected into her field of view.

Once again, it amazed her how easy it was to infiltrate organizations as long as you acted like everyone else. Bored, preoccupied with themselves, and relaxed at the same time. All things that were not difficult for her. She had never understood why people tended to get nervous just because they succumbed to their thoughts of doing something illegal. With other thoughts in their minds, they would seem quite normal, unremarkable. But they were not capable of that.

Unlike Mirage. Of course, she had her augments and virtually infinite resources when it came to money, computing power and information. But when it came down to it, a nervous mind could outweigh even these advantages.

When she reached the fifth floor, where data maintenance was located, her path ended at a glass door. Behind it, she saw hundreds of office cubicles where Fleet Archives employees went about their work with AR glasses on their noses. The only thing she hadn't been able to prepare in advance was access authorization for internal departments. And so there was no way in, even though data maintenance was one of the most boring and unfamiliar areas of the agency.

So it was a matter of waiting. Waiting until the first soldier came out, an older officer with the insignia of a captain, curly gray hair and a slight belly.

"Good afternoon, sir," she said dashingly, taking her stance to salute.

"Lieutenant?" He tried to walk past her without giving her a glance.

But Mirage was prepared. From the little finger of her right hand she emitted a fine cloud of tailored pheromones.

"You're the head of data maintenance, aren't you?" she asked in a sugary voice.

"Yes, and ...?" The captain turned to her, first with a critical furrowed brow, then with a suggestive gaze that

The last Fleet

slid over her body from feet to crown. Lust flared in his eyes.

A victim of his hormones. Mirage was disgusted by all this. But she didn't let it show.

"I want to be transferred to you," she lied, pretending to be sad.

"To us?" he asked, surprised. Nothing suggested that he had wanted to go anywhere else a moment ago. Suddenly he smiled winningly. "Well, everyone says we're real bores who do the same thing all day."

"It's not like that at all!"

"No!" the captain agreed, winking at her as if they had known each other for a long time. Several times his gaze wandered toward her cleavage. "In fact, in some ways, we do the most important job of all."

"Without data maintenance, the integrity of files cannot be assured. They could be corrupted or damaged, and if someone is looking for them fifty years from now..." said Mirage, shaking her head.

"Exactly! Then there'll be trouble. Finally, someone who gets the big picture. What's your name then, my friend?"

Lieutenant is already disappearing from your vocabulary, she thought.

"Monica," she said with a shy twinkle in her eyes. "Captain..."

"Why don't you call me Erni?"

Erni? Of course you're an Erni...

"Thank you, Erni. I know it's too much to ask, and I've been avoiding it for weeks, but ..."

"Well out with it. Don't be shy!" The older officer's face seemed distressed at the thought that she might have worried her pretty head, especially when it was in charge of such lovely breasts. Would the blood on the wall look like a butterfly if she shot him in the face?

"Maybe you could put in a good word for me with the admiral. I'd love to be transferred to you guys."

"That's difficult," he admitted, making a desperate face. His hormone-addled brain was visibly working. "They only take people with experience, and then there's a recruitment test in data analysis."

"But in the test, surely they don't do anything other than set up a virtual work environment that's basically exactly what you have in there, right?" she asked, gesturing vaguely through the glass door.

"Pretty much exactly that, yes."

"So if I knew how it worked...", Mirage prompted him, and finally he put two and two together. She could practically see the thought fighting its way through his reptilian brain and becoming a gleam of realization in his eyes.

"Aaah." He looked to his office level and back to her. "Well, this isn't really allowed, but..." He made a dismissive hand gesture, as if this was all a big joke. "Well, we can say you're my intern, right?"

Mirage chuckled, batting her eyelashes innocently.

"Come on." The captain gestured for her to follow him and opened the door using the DNA scanner at his side.

As they walked to his workstation, a cubicle like all the others except that it was placed at one of the tinted windows, no one paid any attention to them. They sat there in their unadorned uniforms, AR glasses on their heads and engrossed in their virtual work environments.

"So, I'll show you..." Erni began, about to settle into his immersion chair.

"Oh, I can do that." She placed a hand on his forearm

The last Fleet

in a gesture of trust, eliciting a boyish smile of rapture. "Maybe I can just try it out and get familiar with it."

"Hmm." The captain looked a touch too thoughtful for her.

"After that, you can evaluate me in private," she suggested, giving him a smile that was just salacious enough.

"Oh," he said, shrugging his shoulders. "It's not like it's a high-security system. Just archival data, most of which isn't even classified."

He walked over to a small console in the semi-circular desk and typed on the built-in keyboard.

"Go ahead. Give it a try."

"I'm getting excited." Mirage left it unclear whether she meant her little foray into the data maintenance desktop, or something else. Then she accepted his AR glasses. Not that she needed the aid; after all, she owned latest-generation Datamotes. But such access might have caused any lights to go on at Internal Affairs. So she entered the internal dataverse the old-fashioned way. In front of her, she saw endless lists and blocks of data, sorted by directories. They loomed before her like green 16-bit skyscrapers, slightly tilted as three-dimensional entities. If she reached out, she could pull each one closer or push it away from her. The closer it got, the finer the records became. Each record was a tiny box with a label that had factors for subject, date, file format, size, and specific tab number. A search box allowed her to enter search terms by voice command or virtual keyboard.

"So, are you finding your way around okay?" the captain inquired in a fatherly tone.

"It's a bit much," she lied as her fingers flew over keys only she could see. "It's impressive that you can master it all and keep track of it all."

"It's not an easy job," he said with childlike pride. "But somebody's got to do it."

Mirage knew she had won, and once again it had been far too easy. The 'hard part' had been getting in. Not finding the data, because Rogoshin and Marquandt's bribed IIA officials had made a smart decision: to hide what he was doing quite openly. Imperial Intelligence had free access to the archives, probably even had its own office in the building. No one would look twice if one of their employees copied, moved or compressed data. The latter was a standard procedure to cope with the flood of data that five hundred worlds and an overflowing bureaucracy accumulated. Compressed records were generated from the directly accessible files, which first had to be decompressed and were only accessible to a limited extent via the search function. Normal processes that did not set off any red lights.

"I think I've started my first successful search," Mirage said, acting cheerful as she prompted the system to show her the latest records processed by Afrin Makuba. They were six - as expected - compressed packets. She commanded decompression and skimmed the result. Making copies was risky, even with her sophisticated data crawlers feeding into the system in disguise, covering their tracks as they worked. The risk, however, was worth it.

Once everything was filed in her memory lacunae, she exited the system and beamed a broad smile at the captain. "That was fantastic!"

Erni's chest swelled a little. "Like I said, not an easy job, but..."

"I have to get back to my seat quickly now, or I'll be in trouble."

"Oh." He looked disappointed as his more immediate fantasies burst.

The last Fleet

"But I'll come back on my break and give you my terminal number," she promised.

With that, she left him standing and walked out of the department and then out of the building. Briskly, but measuredly, one of the many busy female bureaucrats.

As soon as she got rid of her fake uniform, she also removed the SecondSkin glove and threw both into a public recycler.

She then used her transducer to make contact with the Network's spy satellite, which was orbiting above her. Using Quantcom, she was connected to the Voice within seconds.

"Mirage."

"Mission successful," she said, and climbed into a robotic cab that leisurely merged into the arcology traffic and headed for the spaceport. "Afrin Makuba has disguised fleet movements. Standard operations that no one would notice unless they were explicitly looking for a pattern."

"What's the pattern?"

"Akwa Marquandt has changed operational areas with conspicuous frequency. Over the past two years, she has repeatedly traveled to the Seed Traverse and remained there for weeks at a time. Within those periods was an official visit to Kushiro by Senate President Varilla Usatami - to Yokatami headquarters. The main appointment was a meeting with Supervisor Sato Ran. Also coinciding with Akwa Marquandt's trip to the Seed Traverse - supposedly to review the fleets that will provide enforcement for the restricted military area - was a tour of the Seed projects by Usatami."

"Which Seed Worlds?" the Voice asked.

"Doesn't show from the data. But there are more. Akwa Marquandt has been personally assigned by Chief of Staff Albius as a special agent to investigate the theft of two Mammoth freighters from Andal. The incident caused a great stir in the Border Worlds a year ago, as a pirate attack had to be assumed."

"Not feasible for pirates. Unless they had help."

"Yes. Two weeks later, a patrol ship in the Arcturus system reported that two *Mammoth* freighters were docked at Black Haven," Mirage continued. "The report was relayed to Fleet Headquarters, where the Office of the Chief of Staff personally took over the matter."

"And nothing happened after that."

"Correct. Forces were also diverted from known smuggling routes leading from Dain Marquandt's Wall Sector Delta to Kerrhain - mostly under the pretext of fleet restructuring. Albius has had all such requests approved by the Fleet Admiral. He has also waved through Marquandt's higher-than-average resupply requests for cots, rations, and neural cables, which have been several hundred percent above average for the past two years. There is evidence that about one hundred Ultras from the Vaults were hired from the Kerrhain system and moved to Dust for training. The intelligence report to that effect was immediately archived and is unlikely to have crossed a desk. Whatever the reason, they are being prepared for some kind of commando action."

"All of this has escaped us," the Voice noted. "Except for the abductions on Arcturus. But no connection has been made."

"Until now."

"Yes. So Marquandt has been smuggling cots, rations, neural cables, and people no one misses through Black Haven to Kerrhain for years." The Voice spoke quickly and raptly now, as if in a trance. Mirage waited. "The Broker is in on it. Marquandt wipes out Andal and then

The last Fleet

the *Demeter*. So the way is clear from Kerrhain through Andal and S1-Ruhr to S2-Yokatami. Restricted area, maximum secrecy, even for the fleet."

"So we've come full circle," Mirage agreed with the Voice. "The investments in the Seed World, the meetings with Yokatami. There's just the one thorn left in their side."

"Gavin Andal."

"Yes. I think it's likely that he's right in the black spot of all of this: Yokatami's Seed World."

"Varilla Usatami is still a question mark. And the fleet admiral."

"Marquandt."

"He has arrived in Sol. His secret game relates to Yokatami's Seed World in an unknown way. So why is he coming to Sol to request the Home Fleet? A coup does not make sense. Then he could have waited with his activities in the Seed Traverse until he had the power. He would have saved a lot of effort, money and risk," the Voice said.

"Maybe a distraction. Possibly his project in the Traverse is not yet complete and he is intent on distracting from it and making sure the Emperor listens to him and not Gavin Andal, if he somehow makes it to Terra," Mirage opined.

"Possibly. The Network will have to confer. Make your way to the *Rubov*. Offer Janus the information, including Gavin Andal's probable whereabouts."

"What's the price?"

"We want Zenith back. He may soon be of no use to us if he remains in his current position."

"What about the *Thetis* ship?" the Voice reminded her of the price Janus had paid for Rogoshin's information. Mirage was once again impressed by the network's foresight. When the Voice had demanded from Janus a *Thetis*-class research vessel and special permits for the seed traverse in return for the research, none of the recent data had been known. But even the tiniest inconsistencies in the complex data system that constituted humanity was enough for the network to take the first steps in any direction.

"It's already waiting for you. Get to it as fast as you can."

"Roger that. I'm getting a call in from Zenith right now."

13

JANUS

"Zenith," Mirage said.

"I need an extraction."

"You can't request an extraction. You don't work for us anymore."

"Did you find out anything?" Janus ignored her remark. Thanks to his transducer, he walked seemingly silently through the passersby shuffling along Clifton's boulevards. One of many. Nothing here suggested that a few miles to the north, half a block had been reduced to rubble.

"Yes."

"Then you'll want to sell me on your findings," he concluded, knowing he was also speaking directly to the Voice, as usual. "I'm currently staying in Clifton."

"That's not a good idea."

"I'm alone."

Mirage was silent for a moment. Then she hung up.

"Mirage," he grumbled as his wrist terminal beeped, displaying a message from an unknown sender. Coordinates and a timer that counted down from thirty minutes.

Ridgewood spaceport, really? he thought, and summoned one of the numerous robotaxis by neural computer. With the countdown running in his field of vision, he toyed several times with the idea of uploading his priority code to the on-board computer, freeing it from its Gridlink shackles. But he decided against it. He must not cause a stir of any kind, no matter how small. He did not even answer the calls from the Emperor's office. Surely the guardsmen were going crazy right now, and their superiors even more so. He felt sorry for them, but something was going on that was bigger and more important than them, and he wasn't willing to take another chance and have the blood of hundreds on his hands.

Not your hands, he reminded himself. Albius and Marquandt.

When he arrived at the spaceport, he had one minute left. He sent his authorization code to the automated security system at the gate and nodded to the waving guard in his cottage. Mirage stood on the ramp of an unadorned civilian shuttle, like the thousands that frequented the port every day from Terra to orbit and vice versa.

She glanced pointedly at her wrist terminal as he walked to her. Janus had no doubt that if time had run out, she would have ditched before his very eyes.

"Sit down," she said, closing the stern ramp as he dropped into one of the seats, struggling for breath.

"What's the hurry?" he gasped.

"Extraction window." Mirage shrugged. "The Network assumes you appreciate the service here."

"Aren't you allowed to fly with old friends who have the same road ahead of them anyway?"

"Do we?"

"You tell me, Mirage."

The last Fleet

"We should. I've been to the fleet archives and have the data you're looking for. One thing's for sure: it's exactly what you wanted. Solid. And it paints a clear picture."

"Now we're probably getting to the price part," he said. Her eyes had turned the color of polished amber and were systematically eyeing him. "What exactly are you offering me?"

"The data," the Voice answered from Mirage's mouth. It would have disturbed him if he had not experienced this irritating process many times before.

"I already knew that."

"And a way to use it in the spirit of your beliefs."

So it's about protecting the emperor, he thought.

"What do you want?"

"The Network wants you to return to us."

"Out of the question!" he roared. The shuttle jerkily detached from its pad and accelerated toward orbit. The pull of gravity felt more uncomfortable than usual.

"I was afraid you would say that. However, I must insist. The data are extremely valuable and give the Network a decisive advantage. Giving it up for a lesser price would not be in our best interest," the Voice stated unemotionally.

"No."

"I'm sure I don't need to remind you that letting you move five years ago was a major concession on our part."

"I'm not stupid," Janus said. "I know for a fact that the only reason I was able to leave the Network was because I was put in a high position that you thought would benefit you in the long run."

And as usual, your damned predictions were right, he added in his mind with some frustration, "

"A benefit to humanity."

"For the Network."

209

"They are one and the same."

"From your point of view," he corrected them.

"Our price is set." Mirage's voice was her own again. "The decision is yours now, Zenith."

"There is no decision for me to make." He gave her a grim look, which she returned impassively.

"Then it is decided. I will drop you off on the *Rubov* before I begin my journey."

"Into the Seed Traverse," he said.

"Careful, Zenith."

"Is the emperor in danger? I must know."

"The price has been named," she insisted coolly. "It always has been, and it always will be. We keep our agreements."

"Mirage," he said almost pleadingly. "After our past, you should know who I am and what I stand for. I took an oath of conviction that I must fulfill. It forbids me to return. You know I cannot return for many reasons."

"The same reasons you can't return to the A-League in baseball?"

"That's not funny."

"Take care of your emperor, Zenith," Mirage replied, pausing as their gazes locked on each other. Her words sounded dismissive, but along with the expression in her amber eyes, they seemed to express more.

Finally, he merely nodded and remained silent for the rest of the flight. Now he sat there with no evidence, but with the knowledge that the Emperor was in danger. An unthinkable circumstance, although he'd had a queasy feeling since his initial research. But he had believed that Marquandt and Albius were involved in corruption and their own projects, which they kept secret from the Empire in order to expand their power. Not that they could have it in for the Emperor - that was

The last Fleet

exactly what Mirage had been trying to tell him, wasn't it?

When they docked at the *Rubov* orbital ring, she disappeared before he could unbuckle himself. Part of him longed, for the first time in a very long time, for his old abilities back, which he had given up along with the Network.

Since they were at the civilian docks - Mirage was probably heading directly for the *Thetis*-class research ship - it would take him a long time to get to the Imperial offices, which were on the other side of the ring. He didn't dare request an official shuttle. Not after what had happened in New York. They wanted him dead, and he had no doubt that they were feverishly searching for him right now. If they were prepared for an éclat like the use of the defense platform, then surely they were prepared for the unauthorized firing of the First Secretary of State.

So he took the Vactram, which took fifteen hours to cover the fifty-thousand-mile route, including thirty stops.

Nevertheless, he did not think of remaining idle and contacted the Emperor via a Quantcom satellite. By means of his authentication, his request received the highest priority. Not surprisingly, Haeron II answered immediately.

"Janus! Where have you been? I was about to have my guardsmen whipped!"

"I'm fine. I had to make sure no one knew where I was."

"I requested a mission report from Orbital Defense. The commander in charge has been arrested. He wiped out an entire city block."

"I saw it. He must have been after me," Janus opined.

"Treason."

"Yes. I believe Marquandt is behind it, possibly Albius himself."

The emperor was silent for a moment. When he continued, he sounded thoughtful and his voice quiet. "Those are harsh accusations."

"I am aware of that, and I would not have made them if I did not have reasonable suspicion."

"Do you have proof? If so, I'll have them arrested or liquidated immediately."

"Not yet," Janus admitted, and the frustration of Mirage having it at her disposal nearly drove him mad. "I need more time. In the meantime, surround yourself with your most loyal guardsmen and don't take any more appointments. Don't trust anyone. If they've managed to win over an Orbital Defense commander, their network will be significantly more powerful than I thought."

"If you're sure, Janus, that's good enough for me. I'll have them both arrested now." Once again he was startled by the Emperor's renewed impulsiveness.

"No, your majesty. That would only play into their hands. Since your son's death, there have been too many rumors about your condition. If you strike out against them now, we won't have gained anything because we don't know who is in cahoots with them and what their goal is. We need to work with a scalpel, not an axe," he explained. "I just need some more time. If we act hastily and they count on it, we might get rid of Albius and Marquandt, but not the treacherous network they've built."

"When will you be back?"

"In fifteen hours, a little more. Can you wait that long and cancel all your appointments?"

"Yes. But come quickly. There can be only one answer to treason."

"Yes, Your Majesty."

Janus broke the connection and called the news feed into view. Marquandt and his five fleets had long since reached Sol, and the news channels were abuzz with special broadcasts and speculation about what had happened at Andal. Most hailed him - as was the custom in the media landscape monitored by the authorities - as a hero of the Navy, the shining example that would flush new recruits into the recruiting offices. The consensus was that he was the first admiral in history to win a battle against the Never and survive. Unlike McMaster in the century before last, who had won the battle but met his death in the process.

On the spur of the moment, he called Nancy, also via Quantcom.

"Mister Darishma! I was afraid that..."

"I'm fine, Nancy."

"Thank God. Everyone's talking about the orbital laser deployment. The commanding officer has already been taken into custody by the MP and is expected to be hanged as early as tomorrow."

"That's good," he said without any sympathy for the traitor. "I need your help."

"Of course."

"How soon can you be on Romulus?"

"Fleet headquarters? With jump clearance in three hours."

Janus looked up the message that Marquandt was to dock there at 1:45 p.m. standard time, for the official presentation of badges as commander of the home fleets, including his special swearing-in ceremony.

"That's fine. I want you to set up a meeting with him. He won't turn you down," he instructed her.

"With the fleet admiral? Me?"

"Yes. Tell him I know about everything. And the Network, too."

"The Network?" she asked, confused.

"Yes. Those words are not meant for him, but you must speak them."

Janus cringed at the thought of what his plan might unleash, but a Marquandt putting out feelers to find out what it was about this Network that the First Secretary's secretary and his enemy warned him about was potentially a trump card. The best and fastest way to get rid of him. At the same time, trying to back the Voice into a corner was tantamount to playing with fire.

But he had to do something, even if it meant startling the wolf.

"I don't understand, Mister Darishma, but I'll be on my way shortly."

"Thank you. After that, return to the office immediately."

"Of course."

In his mind, the plan was gaining structure. Marquandt and Albius had to know they were under suspicion, and they should let their agents ask the wrong questions. Then the Voice would have to respond. But that was just the beginning.

He had himself put through to the head of the IIA, Director Enrique Fuao. As First Secretary of State, it was within his power to deploy the entire network of agents. For this request, Fuao would consult with the Emperor, but that was not a problem. All he needed was all the agents in the Sol system to jump on any unusual communications following Nancy's visit to Marquandt. Then he would already expose his Network, and once that happened, he would feel Janus's wrath. The images of the murdered Ridgewood residents were something he would have to live with forever, but the traitor would die for it. Without the data from the fleet archives, he had no proof, but Mirage's hints had been enough to remove the last doubts he had about Marquandt's character. He considered going to the Fleet Archives himself to look for files that had been processed by Agent Afrin Makuba, but Mirage would count on that. He didn't think she would give him the chance. She had probably made sure that no one else got into the relevant department, or even snuck a cacodemon into the system.

So all that was left for him to do was the old-fashioned way, and that's what he was best at. So far, Marquandt had played by his rules and who knew how long he had had to prepare. But now the bastard was playing on Janus' playing field.

14

GAVIN

The first day in their strange prison passed as if in a strange dream. When a soft ringing echoed through their tract, he had already been awake for over an hour. He had slept for a long time, but like every night since his escape from Andal, he was haunted by horrible nightmares. Sometimes it was the faces of his family, bloodied or grotesquely disfigured, sometimes memories of better days or confusing scenes that were a mixture of both. And so he woke up with tears in his eyes and an indescribable emptiness in his stomach that no food in the galaxy could fill. Even the amazingly tasty food mush from the hub on the wall did nothing to change that.

At some point, another signal sounded. The hundred or so inmates of their wing gathered good-humoredly in front of the front door in neat rows of two, as if they were remote-controlled.

Hellcat had remained in her cell until then. Gavin had considered going to her, but then let it go out of concern that it would be an awkward moment. Either he didn't talk about last night, in which case it would be odd, or he did and possibly caught more than one bashful look.

"Comfy beds," Dodger commented as she stepped out of her cell next to him.

"That's what makes me uneasy," he replied quietly. Up ahead, the door opened and several guards stepped aside to let the two columns through. "I feel like a pig being fattened up before slaughter," he said.

"All the more reason we should enjoy it."

Gavin looked at her obliquely from the side, searching for irony in the mutant's gaze, but she merely stretched and cracked her fingers like a boxer before his upcoming fight.

Hellcat remained silent behind them. Looking to her once, he noticed deep circles under her eyes and imagined she had not slept at all.

The gym was a huge cavern, similar to the one where the demolished figures from the *Mammoth* freighter had arrived. Gavin estimated that five hundred to a thousand men and women were exercising at the many machines and VR stations. He noticed that they all looked similar, probably also from Arcturus, just like their cellmates. No one was underage, but they also were not elderly.

As they walked again with trembling muscles, newcomers were already approaching the hundreds. If there were always five to ten tracts training at the same time on a shift, then there had to be many tens of thousands of prisoners housed here. The building he had seen from the outside had been admittedly huge, but to house so many, the complex had to extend many floors underground.

But for what? Why all of this?

He asked himself the same question as he lounged back in his cell, eating and drinking something and listening to the soothing sound of leaves in the wind and chattering birds. The rest of the day he watched a little TV, talked to Dodger now and then, but she remained as taciturn as ever, and pondered around how he could talk to Hellcat. He felt sorry for her, as her horror the day before had shaken him. For a moment, her mask of toughness and imperturbability had fallen, and he had seen a helpless person desperate for a way out.

Sometime in the afternoon, when most of the population was watching entertainment programs on their displays, or sitting together in small groups talking, he went to see her. She was lying on her bed, staring at her own display, except it wasn't on.

"Hey," he said.

"Hey." She didn't look at him.

"You okay?" Gavin pursed his mouth. What a stupid question.

"Nope. But I'm trying not to freak out."

"When I was a kid, I always wondered who those people were in the VR movies who were afraid of the vacuum because they'd never left their biosphere. Or aquarists who get trepidation as soon as they don't have water around them. Dust desert dwellers who get nightmares when they get to see rivers or even oceans in VR. I never had anything like that - at least I thought I didn't," he explained, sitting down on the floor next to her bed. "It's only since... since Andal that I know that's not true. I had a panic that I never wanted to admit to myself."

"What's this going to be? Fucking psychotherapy?" growled Hellcat, her eyes fixed upward.

"I was afraid not to become like my brother," Gavin continued, as if she hadn't said anything. "The one our house needed, the one who wouldn't live up to our reputation. For years, I did a lot to affirm just that. To be different, a rebel in a way. I liked the role of swashbuckling pilot and womanizer, but in truth I was driven by the idea of being so different from Artas that no one would compare us. I probably thought that I couldn't lose if we weren't on the same playing field. After everything that happened, I could have been ashamed of it, but I'm not. I didn't know any better at the time. It's not that I think my fear was unwarranted. It was what it was and at the time I felt it that way, which is fine, I guess. It's like irony that I'm alone now. They're all dead, and there's nothing left to compare mywself to except memories."

"My mother was locked in an escape pod for two weeks and suffocated there when she was pregnant with me," Hellcat said. "Two weeks in a fucking escape pod with four other clones."

"Your mother was a mu... an Invitro?" he asked, surprised.

"Yes. My father was a Norm, she was a clone worker on Ceus-III."

When Gavin heard the name of arguably the most famous asteroid in human history, he tensed involuntarily. It was where Lizzy's parents had perished. How merciless could the universe be?

"They fell in love on Ceus-III, and she got pregnant. Most of the clones' modified genes are recessive by design and can't be passed on." Hellcat spread her arms. "And then you look like this."

"Sorry about your mother."

"Happened before I was born. I never got a chance to miss her. The rescue forces of your shitty Star Empire solved the mutant problem by picking up the escape pods but never opening them. She was in the hangar of a Navy ship and my mother and her comrades just suffocated or died of thirst. They later cut me out of her stomach and resuscitated me in a Medicasket. But I guess you don't know about that."

"No," he admitted.

"Because in the Star Empire, you only get to hear what the Emperor wants you to hear. I never met my father, either, by the way. He didn't know I survived and threw himself into a bore pit on Grassov, at least that's what I was told," Hellcat continued. "Every night since I can remember, I've dreamed of suffocating in an escape pod with the bloody Emperor's hands on my throat."

Gavin didn't know what to say to that and swallowed. After a few minutes of silence, he said, "That's terrible. How did you even survive?"

"The authorities put me in a crap family on Andal as an adopted child. I always knew they couldn't be my parents, but they played their fucking lie well. Until later when they had a child of their own and I was just a glitch. I ran away and dug deep. Eventually every truth comes out. If the Republican underground hadn't given me a new home, I probably would have killed myself, just like my fucking coward of a father." Her fist shot up so fast Gavin winced. The display film, paper-thin, warped slightly, and blood ran down her knuckles.

"Leave me alone," she growled. When he didn't move immediately, she hissed, "Go on, fuck off!"

He swallowed and left her alone. In his cell, diagonally across the hall, Dodger sat on his bed, forearms propped on his knees.

"The last one who made a pass at her is no longer alive today," the mutant said quietly. Her voice sounded like a bass drum smeared with honey.

"I didn't..."

"Yep." She shrugged her shoulders leisurely. "I'm just telling you. She's got a good heart, but fate's got it wrapped in barbed wire. If you touch it... well, you know. You're a smart guy with an education and all."

Gavin was too taken aback by the sudden depth that lay in Dodger's words to reply. So he merely nodded as she stood up, patted him on the shoulder like a giant to a dwarf, and then left his cell.

With every minute that passed after that, he worried more about Bambam and his anger at Marquandt grew - though he had not thought it was possible. Time locked up in here was time the traitor could use to pursue his plans with impunity. And what they entailed, he experienced on his own body.

For about an hour he lay on his bed and stared at the ceiling. Again and again the faces of his family passed him by. His father Cornelius, as he gave him a reproving look that was nevertheless full of affection - a mixture that only parents were capable of. His mother Sophie and her kind expression on one of the many Sundays when the family had gathered late for breakfast. He saw Artas in front of him, thoughtfulness incarnate, Mariella's eyes gleaming excitedly, and Elisa's grumpy expression. What he would have given right now to hear her nagging just one more time.

He desperately needed to get out of here, otherwise his chance would soon be lost to put a stop to the culprit of the mass murder and bring him to justice. Because if he was no longer able to do so, what was he still living for? What was the point of living with the demons that plagued him every waking minute, which he was only able to keep at bay because he was constantly busy trying to get closer to justice?

Later, after he had had far too long to contemplate the emptiness inside him with what felt like a swarm of sinis-

The last Fleet

ter, evil butterflies fluttering in his stomach, the bell rang again.

The inmates of their wing appeared agitated as he looked out of his cell. Again they lined up in rows of two, but this time not in joyful anticipation, but tense. Some whispered quietly among themselves.

"What's wrong?" he asked Yaisha as she walked straight past him to stand at the front. She reluctantly stopped, glanced at the door, then joined him.

"It's all good. I've heard about this before. Others have told me about it at the gym. It's just a few flickering lights." She waved it off. "Nothing special."

"What do you mean?" whispered Gavin as she motioned for him to lower his voice after several fellow inmates looked over at them.

"Other groups have had unscheduled ringing, too."

"Do you remember who told you that?"

"No, they haven't been to the gym since." Yaisha looked at the door again and seemed to weigh what was more important to her: Her urge to talk and help others along, or being first in whatever was waiting for her. "They probably hurt themselves or something."

"Sure," he said wryly, but she didn't seem to notice and ran forward as the hydraulics of the heavy doors hissed out.

"Should we be worried?" asked Dodger, who joined him at the same time.

"Yes. She said she'd heard about it before. The ones who experienced it didn't show up the day after, though."

"Oh," said the mutant. That was all she could say, because the doors were already open and several guards came in.

"Line up!" one of them barked with voice amplifiers

that made his voice go through marrow. "Unscheduled training exercise!"

"We need to find out what's going on," he whispered.

"You want to try something," Dodger observed.

"Yes. It's very obvious they need us alive. Otherwise, they most certainly would have shot the five fugitives or hanged them as a reminder to the others, instead of just corralling them again."

"They were talking about a pen, too. Remember?"

"Yeah. They said anything was better than the pen. I guess they meant their cells."

"Nope. For Arcturians, this is better than ninety-nine percent of their everyday life. They meant something else. For sure."

Gavin felt a chill run down his spine. "We'll split up."

"When?"

"I don't know. After whatever they do to us. If the others could still tell about it the next day at the gym, it won't kill us. And we might find out what all this is leading up to."

"Okay," Dodger replied, as it was also their turn to follow their front men. He didn't find Hellcat at a cursory glance over his shoulder, but it was probably better that she didn't follow. She was already struggling enough with all this, and he feared her anger would become a problem.

The guards led them through the hallway in front of their wing and to the left at the intersection instead of to the right, as if for sport. Again, the walls were white as snow and lit in such a way that the gaps between the panels disappeared. It took at least ten minutes, if not longer, before they finally stopped and were taken one by one into a long room where there were exactly one hundred seats for them to spread out on. Nothing indicated what it was. Two rows faced each other, staggered.

The last Fleet

The angry butterflies in Gavin's stomach began to flutter more vigorously.

"SIT DOWN!" yelled one of the guards in his chemical protection suit, and his ten companions raised their short-barreled weapons to lend emphasis to his demand.

The prisoners complied and made their way to their seats. He could see that most of them were flustered, though not frightened. He wasn't surprised, if they were even half as enthusiastic about this place and its monotonous security of supply as Yaisha was. Only now did he notice that they were not at full count. He spotted Hellcat behind him, her eyes downcast and her hands clenched into fists. But the five fugitives they had spotted in the forest were not among them.

"We're not all here," he said to a young man who dutifully took a seat beside him.

"The Penners," his neighbor hissed, looking around at the guards who were about to go through the ranks in teams of two, threatening cortical disruptors to anyone who didn't sit down quickly enough.

Penners, Gavin repeated in his mind.

"Why are they called that?"

"They weren't from our wing. Came to it at some point and were totally out of it. Babbled something about a pen and cried at night. Unbearable, I tell you. Then they disappeared and came back with you..."

"SHUT UP you two or I'll fry you!" snarled one of the guards who had reached them.

The tone has become harsher, Gavin noticed and put his arms on the armrests, as he was ordered. As it quieted down in the long room, he tried not to think about what the 'pen' might be. That the refugees had cried themselves to sleep because of it was one thing, but that they seemed to have no will to live since their forced return, even though they had voluntarily fought their way through an alien jungle before, seriously worried him.

As soon as they were all seated, a metallic click spread like a wave from one end to the other. As it swept toward Gavin, he saw from the side what it was: previously hidden metal cuffs that closed with a snap around his forearms and lower legs, pinning him to the seat.

A tense murmur went through the inmates, which turned to silence as a dozen figures in white coats and breathing masks entered. They carried suitcases in their hands and spread out on one side of the room, where tables and cabinets rose from the floor.

"The treatment is short and relatively painless," one of the guards announced from somewhere. Gavin stretched his neck in an attempt to see what was going on at the other end. "We can't sedate you, but you'll hardly feel a thing. We'll give each of you a prototype of an advanced data jack implanted free of charge."

Free of charge? repeated Gavin in his head. The bastard's words were a mockery.

"In two days," the guard promised in an amplified voice, "your time here will be up and you can go home knowing that you have done a great service to humanity. Thanks to you, our future will be golden."

"Cut the bullshit and get it over with," Dodger said, sitting diagonally across from him. Gavin already feared the guard would hit her or grill her with the cortical disrupter, but they did nothing of the sort and instead left the room with the others. Now only the doctors were there - at least he thought they were. They went around and put small objects in their ears that blocked all sound.

It became dead silent, except for the murmur of his own blood.

With growing unease, he watched as the figures in

The last Fleet

white began their procedures. They worked on six prisoners at a time. As far as he could tell from the corner of his eye, they were being fitted with helmets that were open at the sides, where the temples were.

Gavin checked the fit of his shackles, but instead of being able to break free, only his wrists and ankles hurt in response. The prospect of a second data jack being fitted to him without anesthesia was not something he was keen on. So he continued to jiggle and pull until his arms and legs were exhausted.

Then the doctors were with him. They proceeded with the uncanny precision of professionals who saw him as work, not a fellow human being. Gavin yelled at them, screaming that they should leave him alone, that he already had a data jack - but he couldn't even hear his own voice. He swam in a lake of silence, unable to fight back.

As they slipped the helmet over him, darkness fell before a display came on. It smelled of blood and sweat. Like old-fashioned VR goggles, he saw an artificial environment in front of him that looked lifelike. A large room with a domed roof, in the center of which was a throne. Far in front of it, lower down, was a console with transparent cables.

A figure appeared before him that every citizen of the Star Empire knew: Varilla Usatami, the Senate president. She stood there in her tailored pantsuit, her hands folded in front of her lap, her gaze fixed on him from her proud eyes. She was quite the upright and energetic figure he knew from the feeds, full of engaging charisma and a shirt-sleeved manner that had already won her her third term.

"I salute you," Usatami said in Gavin's direction. "Your journey here was arduous and you were afraid. For that I apologize. However, I hope your days here with us have been pleasant. We want you to be healthy, balanced and alert, because humanity needs you. Your cooperation on the way to a safe future, which is not marked by deprivation and war, but democracy and peace, will bring the light of this dream into our midst. Be sure that you will have the gratitude of all of us. What you will do for us is a great gift for you and for all people. We are deeply in your debt."

Even as Gavin wondered why, despite her lofty, uplifting words, he felt he was listening to a eulogy, the procedure began. An indescribable pain exploded in his right temple and the thud and grind of a bone drill vibrated through his skull. He screamed until his throat dried up, yelling unheard against the sensation of someone sucking his brain through a small hole. He wanted to lash out, fueled by adrenaline that boiled in his veins and overtook him with his instinct to fight.

Until the lights came on. Where a moment ago there had been the strange domed hall with the digital Senate president, now myriads of lights flashed across the color spectrum. Unable to close his eyes, he let the lightning storm flood his retinas. It washed away the pain and numbed him in a strange way, as he could still think clearly but feel nothing except the presence of his body, without the pull of gravity. Something similar to being in zero gravity.

Eventually it was all over and he sank back, deeply exhausted. They took his helmet off and by the time he realized it, they were already torturing the next in line. His head felt like a vessel into which too much liquid had been poured, now pressing against his skull. Dazed, he looked around, gazing into faces with open mouths from which long threads of saliva hung.

Dodger's eyes were half-closed, as if she were drugged.

Blood ran from her left temple. He sought her gaze, but she merely stared at the ground and he could not muster enough concentration to look at her for more than a few seconds.

After a while - time was barely noticeable to him - he was roughly washed and his bonds retracted into the seats. Slowly, with muscles like lead, he groped for his temple. His fingers encountered cold metal.

15

GUNTER

Gunter walked onto the ramp with his arms hanging, squinting his eyes against the sudden light that assaulted his retinas like a hurricane of tiny needles. Hundreds crowded in front of him and hundreds more waited behind him to leave the *Mammoth* freighter.

Even as they had been sucked out of the equalization tank and distributed like parcels by figures in white spacesuits, he had been struck by the size of the spaceship into which they had been loaded. Seemingly endless, tube-like sections with at least a thousand or more acceleration seats built into the wall. Nothing in the Star Empire had such capacity, except *Mammoth* freighters. This, in turn, told him that they must be the stolen ships from Andal, whose disappearance had puzzled the Border World fleets for so long. During their passage, they had jumped a total of five times and had spent little time under acceleration. Masha, who had sat next to him in the tightly packed compartment, had not been particularly talkative, and he himself had largely indulged his dark thoughts as well.

He had failed. He had not carried out his orders. He

had not been able to bring back the orb body, nor stop Akwa Marquandt. As if fate wanted to mock him, she had even once appeared with them and had spoken to one of the soldiers who had shooed their flock of torn sheep into their kennel.

The cold, hawk-like features of her face burned into his mind, igniting a deep-seated anger. She was in one a symbol of betrayal and of his failure.

That they would actually land on a planet - which a *Mammoth* freighter should not even be able to do - had dawned on him a few hours ago, when everything had begun to shake and the walls creaked protestingly. The pull of gravity had kicked in again and dragged them down.

At some point, silence had fallen after the engines had hissed one last time and then shut down. Since then, unloading had been underway, which he had gathered from the muffled noise that had carried through the walls. When it had been their turn, a new sort of guard in white chemical suits and breathing masks had come and shooed them, cortical disruptors drawn, into the central corridor, which was so large that whole columns of tanks could drive through it.

The gunmen reminded him more of high-security lab employees than soldiers, but with augment blockers around his wrists, it didn't matter what they were. As long as they had cortical disruptors in their hands and he didn't, he was no match for them. Not to mention that trying to break out at this point was tactically stupid, since he didn't even know where they were.

As his eyes adjusted to the sudden brightness, he saw the many figures in smelly old clothes crowding in front of him and Masha. Single file, they descended into a huge cavern with walls and floors of unadorned gray concrete.

The last Fleet

More guards formed a kind of funnel leading toward a wide door behind which gleamed brilliant white walls, as if they were the gates of heaven.

"Where are we?" whispered Masha beside him.

"I don't know," he answered, without taking his eyes off the foot of the ramp, where the crowd was jammed and allowed to proceed only in rows of two. "But we jumped five times, so we probably went through two systems."

"This place smells like death."

To this he did not reply, for he could only agree with her, which did not help them either. There was something oppressive about the atmosphere here that made the hairs on the back of his neck stand on end.

It took an hour or more - without access to his augments, he had no way of knowing for sure - for them to even reach the foot of the ramp. The line of two in front of them moved only in single file, and had to wait again and again in the white tunnel, at equal intervals, until it went on.

Half an hour later, they themselves were standing in the tunnel, surrounded by white walls so contourless that they seemed spherical, as if they were far away or only imagined. At first, there was no moving forward. There was silence after the doors closed behind them. Then there was a loud hiss, and bright steam that barely stood out against the walls, floor and ceiling billowed around them. It smelled of disinfectant, cleaning bacteria, and a trace of ozone.

"Remove your clothes!" a disembodied voice commanded over loudspeakers. At first no one stirred, but then the first ones began to undress, and gradually the others followed, as apparently no one was eager to spend more time than necessary in the suddenly cramped-looking corridor.

Once they were all naked, they had to go into a new corridor. He noticed that there were no smells at all. His nose perceived absolutely nothing, which should not have been the case even without the olfactory filters. They were disinfected, and after that, flaps in the walls slid open and out of them fell packets of gray coveralls that they were made to put on. When that was done, the door at the front opened and they were ordered on.

He tried to remember how many times they turned and in which direction. Twice right, once left, twice right, twice left and a long bend.

There he stopped jerkily and was almost knocked over by those behind him. The two guards in front of them also stopped and turned so they could see their menacingly raised cortical disruptors.

From a door behind them came shuffling men and women wearing the same gray coveralls as they, except that their heads were lowered and their footsteps resembled those of zombies. Among them he recognized his master, the new High Lord of Andal.

"My lord!" it escaped him before he could think about it, but Gavin Andal stared blankly through him. In any case, there was no emotion in his exhaustion-stricken features, and he plodded on down the corridor in single file. The tall mutant was also with him and he saw the angry beauty from the *Lady Vengeance* as well. Only the bearded little mechanic was missing.

"SILENCE BACK THERE!" one of the guards admonished him, but Gunter paid no attention. His thoughts flashed over each other in rapid succession.

Gavin Andal is here. How is that possible? Where are we? And why didn't he recognize me? Didn't hear me?

What were they doing to him? Anger rose in him, fueled by crippling helplessness. The augment blockers began to itch and send pain to his wrists, as if to remind him that he had no chance to fulfill his oath and protect his High Lord.

16

GAVIN

"I saw the master sergeant," Gavin said in a lowered voice to Dodger as they sat in their cell later. Hellcat was there, too, but she had not spoken since her return. Most of the other inmates were asleep, some crying quietly in their beds.

"The augment zombie?" the mutant asked incredulously.

"Yeah. Didn't you hear him calling?"

"Nope. Did you maybe imagine it?"

"No!" he snapped.

"Okay."

"Last time he was on the Cerberus. I told him to get the Orb back."

"I remember, it was only two days ago or so," she reminded him.

"How did he get here?"

"I don't know. We'll have to ask him."

Gavin tried to run his hand through his hair and accidentally touched his temple. The sharp pain that ran through him made him flinch.

"Bambam should have found us by now," Hellcat muttered under her breath.

"Not in here." Dodger shook her head.

"She's right. The facility is almost certainly shielded in some way, and it's deep underground. Even with his signal booster, it won't work," Gavin agreed with her.

"Where is it, anyway? Still up your ass?"

"If you could get me some fiber, maybe my bowel movements would be more regular," he hissed, then sighed. "Even if I had it here now, it wouldn't do us any good. We'd have to get outside for Bambam to locate us, and even then, what could he possibly do?"

"He always thinks of something. He's a smart little guy," Dodger said optimistically.

"Not this time." Gavin watched her eyes fall shut, and he, too, found it hard to stay awake anymore. "We should be asleep."

"Why did they do that?" asked Hellcat without looking up. "The bloody data jacks, I mean."

"I don't know. I'm mostly wondering what Usatami had to do with it." He shook his head. "It's all like a bad nightmare, a drug trip or something. But we'll figure it out."

"Will we?"

"Yes."

"And what makes you so sure?"

"We have no choice, and I refuse to give these bloody traitors even a foot of ground."

He could tell from both Dodger's and Hellcat's expressions that they didn't believe him. However, while the mutant exuded a calm indifference, his words seemed to infuriate Hellcat.

"There's always a way," he tried to convince himself and stood up. His legs almost gave way. He was at the end of his rope, but not at the end of his revenge, and that kept him from falling over on the spot and falling asleep.

Before they could infect him with their defeatism, he returned to his cell and lay down in bed. With one hand he pulled the water hose from the wall and mustered the last of his strength to drink a good amount. He tried hard not to think about Yaisha's words that tomorrow would probably be their last day here.

More and more he came to think that Varilla Usatami had thanked him and everyone else for some kind of sacrifice that was imminent. Was it related to the pen? He could have asked the five fugitives, but there was no trace of them. Before he fell asleep, he again saw the faces of his family before him. Never before had they felt so far away and he so lonely.

17

GAVIN

Gavin was awakened the next morning by the soft sound of ringing, mingling with the sounds of nature, just noticeable enough to rouse him from sleep.

He had slept so deeply that he hadn't even dreamed - or couldn't remember. His headache was not gone, but it was considerably less severe, and the feeling that his skull was going to burst under the pressure in it had subsided as well. He took another sip of water and then used the restroom.

It took him a while to fish out the signal booster and meticulously clean it. To his own surprise, his anger at the conspirators around Usatami and last night's torture made him not even feel disgusted or anything like shame. There was no room next to his righteous anger anymore.

He then opened his jumpsuit and tugged at the seams on the inside near the hip area until he had loosened a few threads. He used those to attach the signal booster when there was also a knock on his door.

"Captain, are you ready?" he heard Dodger's bass voice.

"Yes, small moment." Gavin pulled the zipper up, then stepped out to join her.

"Gym," the mutant said. He eyed his fellow inmates, who seemed reassured by the sudden return to routine, though the looks on most of them had changed. Whereas before they had been dogs on leashes, resigned to their fate because food and exercise were available, now there was an expression of resignation in their eyes, as if they had been beaten too many times to still enjoy the relative comforts of the time before the intervention.

So, as usual, they lined up in their rows of two until the door opened and the guards once again escorted them to exercise.

Once there, they traded places with the previous five tracts that had the shift before them and began their programs. Since they were at least unobserved by guards here, he didn't bother or exert himself. Instead, he searched the faces of all the other inmates until, at one point, a load fell off his mind when he spotted the Master Sergeant. He was working out on a cable pulley with a grim expression on his face. Gavin told Dodger he'd be right back and headed for the Marine. Not directly - he stopped at one balance station and did some stretches at another until he arrived almost by accident at Gunter Marshall's cable pull.

"Just pretend I'm a stranger," he said quietly, pulling on one of the weights.

"My lord!" The Marine's expression remained blank as he increased his resistance.

"I'll have to make this short because I don't have much time. Something is going to happen tonight or tomorrow, and then there will be no turning back," Gavin explained quietly, performing his exercises. "I have a signal booster in my coveralls. If anyone can do anything for us, it's

Bambam, the mechanic. He's still out there on the ship and doesn't know where we are."

"There's no signal here."

"Yes. You've got to try to get the amplifier up there, somewhere where it can get a signal. Today, before it's too late." Gavin casually reached into his coveralls and thrust the device the size of his pinky finger into his hand as they pretended to high-five.

"My lord, regarding my assignment..." the Master Sergeant continued.

"Forget about that. Something is going on here."

"Marquandt's daughter is involved. She's smuggling the cots and rations in. She stole the *Mammoth* freighters from Andal." The Marine sounded as if he was trying to use his findings to apologize for not doing his job.

"I figured as much. They put data jacks in us. I've never seen models like this. The connectors don't conform to any Star Empire standards either," Gavin whispered, tugging on his handle another ten times. The cable gave a droning sigh as he did so.

"There were also neural cables in the supplies, my lord."

"I'm afraid I'll soon find out what those are for," he replied somberly, turning to leave. "Do your best, sergeant. And thank you."

"I'll see you on the other side, my lord. You can count on me."

Gavin eyed the augment blockers on the Marine's wrists, then glanced at the metal feet with their claws peeking out of the hems of his pants. He very much hoped that even without his many augments, the Master Sergeant was the deadly weapon that members of Andal's Guard Regiment, the Ice Guard, always referred to themselves as.

When it was time to leave, he knew something was wrong. Their tract was called by one of the guards to line up in their usual rows of two. Just as they had the day before. But this time, not in front of the same door, but in front of another one that was a little smaller and that he had never seen open.

"It's happening," he whispered to Hellcat, who was standing next to him this time.

"The pen." She nodded somberly. "Whatever they're going to do to me, I'm not going to let them do it to me. Not after..." Her fingers wandered to the data socket that had been brutally inserted into them. The skin around the edges was still heavily reddened, evidence of lingering inflammation.

INTERLUDE: MIRAGE

The *Thetis*-class ship, which had been assigned the internal name 42-UQLUE by the Network, proved adequate. Mirage's own ship, the *Destiny*, was more advanced, assembled entirely from high technology with prototype status, but of all the Navy's mass-produced ships, the *Thetis*-class was the best for her purposes. Lightweight, exceedingly fast, and maneuverable with ample space aboard, having used recyclers to convert all laboratory equipment into resources for internal 3-D printers. As usual for Science Corps ships, there was armament even on the light class of research reconnaissance craft: a railgun mounted under the bow and two communications lasers that could be overloaded for up to two minutes to convert them into potent weapons.

First, she had jumped toward the Corporate Protectorate, upgraded her equipment for the upcoming mission at a Network node on Alpha Prime, and then continued toward the Seed Traverse.

She spent the first six hours doing maintenance on the appropriate machine, which hooded members of the

Network had pushed down the ramp into the converted cargo bay. It looked like an erect spider, dark with many tubes protruding from its torso and its connectors fluttering in the air current of life support. She killed time after that in a virtual environment while the modified onboard computer took over navigation and jumps and transmitted her transponder code to the respective space controls of the fly-through systems.

She went over and over the information from Gavin Andal, then read the official battle report from Fleet Admiral Dain Marquandt and the relocated records from the fleet archives. She cross-referenced all of this with what Rogoshin had reported to her before his death, as well as with the financial flows of the Albius and Marquandt dynasties and Senate President Usatami. The three were somehow connected, their convoluted investment activities suggested, as did the fake assassination of Usatami, which they could never have staged so perfectly without the Chief of Staff and bribed people in the police.

Well, close to perfect. It had not escaped the Network's notice, of course. They were all the more interested in what exactly the admirals and the Senate President had been concocting with Yokatami for years. Whatever it was; it was obviously approaching its longplanned climax, and the fact that the Network had no data on what exactly it was could only mean one thing: that they were dealing with an equal opponent, which should not be possible at all. The Network saw everything, the Network knew everything, and the Network intervened wherever it pleased. Nothing remained hidden from it.

Until now.

Just before her last jump, when she was in the Lugano system, she was contacted by the Voice.

The last Fleet

"Mirage. Our crawlers in the dataverse have been able to obtain the signature specifications of Gavin Andal's ship. It is a *Sphinx*-class medium attack frigate, approximately forty years old," the Voice said.

"I have received the data. The on-board computer has already been upgraded."

"Good, I also recommend you activate Deus."

"She is in memory?" asked Mirage in surprise.

"Yes. I'll authorize her deployment if you deem it necessary. You have operational decision-making authority, my recommendation is to activate it."

"I understand."

"I await your report." The Voice disappeared from her system, and she was alone again.

Well, not entirely alone. The thought of Deus being part of the ship did something to her she didn't like: it created unease in her mind.

Nevertheless, she did the only thing she could think of: she followed the Voice's recommendation. Before doing so, she took all the necessary measures that went along with an activation. She manually jammed all of the ship's transmitters that exceeded a certain minimum bandwidth, which also meant that her communications lasers could only send tiny packets of data and would no longer be suitable as weapons. She then started the data sealing of the ship's computer and all memory clusters, which were now programmed to shut down immediately if they exceeded a certain level of activity. Also, any intervention - even by her as the ship's commander - in the appropriate code resulted in the immediate destruction of the clusters by means of physical shutdown devices in the data lines.

Shortly before her jump to S2-Yokatami, into the restricted military area, she finally activated Deus after

Lugano Space Flight Control accepted her transponder code and special permission.

"Hello, Deus," Mirage said.

"Hello," the AI replied. "This ship is interesting."

"I need your help."

"Of course you do. S2-Yokatami, Seed Traverse, restricted area. The special permits are not fake, come from the highest level. The First Secretary of State?"

"Yes."

"We are looking for a ship, the *Lady Vengeance* of High Lord Gavin Andal," Deus summarized. "Also, this is a fact-finding mission to uncover the background of a probable collusion between Chief of Staff Albius, Fleet Admiral Marquandt, and Senate President Usatami."

"Correct." Mirage almost found the next words difficult. But only almost. "I can't make any mistakes in what's coming. I cannot divide my attention and I need your support."

"Of course. I'm taking control of the *42-QLUE*. An exhilarating name, by the way."

"Yes."

"Transit in ten seconds, jump alert," Deus announced, and the cockpit was bathed in red light.

The brief feeling of depersonalization came and went, like the reverberation of a distant memory, and they were already at their destination. Navigation was perfect, their exit point was directly over the second moon of Yokatami's Seed World.

"Extending sensors and scanning. Completed." The first data appeared on the virtual displays in Mirage's field of view. "Apparently, this Seed World is no longer a Seed World at all."

Mirage saw it, too. The planet below them was not the barren rocky desert with a thin atmosphere that it officially was, the first to be colonizable in more than a hundred years. While the Seed Vessel still hovered in orbit like a giant kaiju moth, it was clearly not working. Low heat radiation, no biomass. And the planet itself was anything but barren. On the contrary, green sprouted on the continents between the blue oceans. Lush and vibrant, it alternated with dark browns where mountains dotted the landscape. White bands of clouds, which also would not have been expected, testified to an already functioning water cycle of the world. At first glance, nothing distinguished it from other terra-compatible planets in the Star Empire, had it not been for a strange glow that appeared every 5.1 seconds. Like a photic pulse, it traveled from all directions on the planet to a point on the equator, died out, and then reappeared, only in the other direction.

"What is it?" she asked aloud, reflexively leaning forward.

"It seems to be a local effect affecting the entire flora of the planet," Deus explained in an androgynous voice not unlike that of the Voice, though slightly more accented and less urgent. "It seems to be coupled to a central location, the location of which I have been able to pinpoint to within two centimeters. The bow telescope is finishing up high-resolution images right now."

"How is that possible? The world is already completely terraformed from the looks of it."

"It's not possible."

"That doesn't help me much. When are the last verified images of the fleet from?" wanted Mirage to know.

"From 2397, so they're four years old. There's no doubt about their authenticity."

"So all this is supposed to have happened since the last change of defense fleets?"

"Yes. Since Fleet Admiral Dain Marquandt provided

the bulk of the units from his house fleet, to be exact," Deus opined. "Also, we're being intercepted and attacked with jamming signals right now."

The way the AI delivered this bad news reminded them of the monotony of newscasters. Mirage saw a total of eight corvettes on intercept radar shortly thereafter, setting a direct course for them. In addition, two dozen missiles from defenses on the moon below were accelerating toward them at triple-digit g's.

"Didn't you send our transponder codes? We have clearance!"

"Of course I did. Apparently that clearance isn't worth anything here anymore." Deus was already initiating evasive maneuvers while Mirage activated the restraints on her acceleration seat.

The *Thetis* accelerated at 15 g and burned rapidly through its fuel, causing the readings to climb ever higher.

"I have the images of the structure where the photic effect is coming from," the AI casually explained over the transducer network as she sped the *42-QLUE* toward the planet, firing the railgun at the missiles pursuing her. Each shot was eerily accurate and hit its target, but the cadence would not be enough.

Mirage had the image projected into his field of view and saw a cleared area on a vast plain densely forested all around. In its center was a megastructure reminiscent of an upturned plate, and on it sat the mile-long, barrel-shaped hulk of a Mammoth freighter, as if it had crashed and broken through the plate with its snout.

"Can you get me down there?" asked Mirage. At 35 g, she was still able to steer the ship using virtual controls, but they were subject to a lag of a few milliseconds - and they would matter one way or another from now on. The intercepting ships were falling behind, but their missiles were still rapidly catching up.

And more were coming. She counted on the radar a total of two hundred ships in the nearer system and a dozen orbital defenses, which should not exist either, on top of that a second *Mammoth* freighter circled the world in a parking orbit.

"I could try a fly-by through the stratosphere. In doing so, I would get rid of the missiles right away," Deus opined. "However, that would be very close, and there are atmospheric fighters coming up from a base near the North Pole."

"Apparently they want to shoot us down at any cost before we tell anyone about this," Mirage stated the obvious. Yet she didn't know how they would have done that. Once they diverted all power to the jump engine power pattern cells, they would be nothing but flotsam in the water for several minutes.

"Do it," she finally commanded the AI, and the acceleration levels increased another 5 g. Movement was long out of the question, so she watched as Deus insanely flew the limits of the *42-QLUE*, stretching it to levels Mirage would not have dared to explore. Just before entering the atmosphere and under the steady whump of the railgun, the ship braked and then burst through the uppermost layers of air with the elemental force of a meteor. Behind them, six missiles exploded as they slammed into the air particles with too much kinetic energy and were consumed by the resulting plasma. More and more of the warheads pursuing them followed in dense staccato.

The hard acceleration levels were now replaced by a violent wobble and vibration that continued all the way to the top of Mirage's head.

"Calculate my probability of survival in a jump in a

Reaper suit with an evac bubble," Mirage shouted over the groans and roars of her ship, unbuckling her seatbelt and ripping open one of the wall flaps to press one of the suits to her chest. The nanite mass spread over her body, quickly enveloping her except for her helmet, which she pulled over her head just in time.

"Fifty-five percent. But the data base for this calculation is weakened by too many variables."

"Sufficient," she found, and with a thought command, opened the tailgate. Immediately, there was a deafening roar. Behind her, it was still dark.

"Attention, evasive maneuvers!" said Deus, and Mirage grabbed one of the grab rails and jammed her left foot into a joint. The ship rolled to the side so fast it flipped several times, then went into a mad dive before climbing again. "Commencing engagement with interceptors," she said.

"Disembarking." Mirage grabbed one of the evac bubbles, which resembled small backpacks, and strapped it to her back. On her chest she clamped a vacuum control unit with four gas jets. "Are we above the facility?"

"Yes. Jump is best now!"

Mirage didn't need to be told twice and ran to the ramp, where she jumped off with her arms outstretched. She immediately went into freefall position with arms splayed, back arched and hips thrust forward, legs slightly bent so they pressed on the relative air.

Once she was lying stable, she turned, bending her left leg slightly until she could see the *42-QLUE*. She used her railgun to destroy one of the interceptors, of which Mirage saw only an explosion and debris, and dodged a second, whose rapid-fire cannons narrowly missed the ship.

Some of the debris came dangerously close to her, but

The last Fleet

she dodged them by putting her arms at her sides and shifting into a head-down position that once again accelerated her sharply. There was very little resistance due to the extremely thin air at twenty thousand yards, and her neural computer indicated a falling speed of five hundred miles an hour. She could no longer reach supersonic, however, because the frictional resistance was increasing rapidly.

The terrain below her was a two-dimensional green-brown carpet with mountains to the north and south and canyons to the west that looked as if the landscape had been furrowed with a giant ridge. Even in the glaring light of the central star, the blue pulsation was visible.

A shot-up interceptor, resembling an arrowhead carved from a piece of metal, sped heavily tumbling past her into the depths. After two minutes, during which she covered half the distance, a cover of the wreckage detached itself from an area of several square yards. Mirage slowed down by going back into her free-fall stance. Her head was noticeably less jolted now and she found it easier to maneuver. With fine movements of her hands, she headed for the piece of debris, which had considerably more air resistance due to its high surface area and was therefore slower. At the last moment, she moved into a sitting position and crashed into the metal. To avoid bouncing off, she extended her foot anchors and hardened Carbotanium spikes. With them, she clawed into the material and got just deep enough to avoid being hurled away.

One minute to impact.

With a concentrated expression, she worked to align the piece of metal beneath her against the relative wind, significantly slowing her rate of fall, which was a constant effort.

"Deus," she radioed to the AI over her encrypted channel.

"I'm still here, but will have to hide soon."

"Do it and wait for my messages, keeping only passive systems activated."

"I'm trying hard. There's something else."

"What?"

"If you survive this: I registered a minimal heat deviation from the environment near the megastructure. The reading wasn't much more than a brief spike in ambient amplitude, nothing a geological satellite system would consider a deviation."

"But you're not a normal satellite system," Mirage opined.

"Right."

"Send me the location."

"Good luck."

"Stand by for an extraction under combat conditions." Mirage looked at the data on her internal variometer. Only one thousand yards to go. In her memory lacunae, she had preloaded the topographic readings and started an environmental simulation with her data collected during the fall. Then she activated the evac bubble.

Within a second, the nano-reinforced polymer fabric formed into a sphere that completely enveloped her and locked out the chaos of a world in free fall.

If she was lucky, the interceptor's shroud was still beneath her, slowing her down, but since her variometer had calculated a fall speed of fifty miles an hour, she didn't assume that. Moreover, she was picking up speed again.

When she was still two hundred yards from the surface - at least that's what the simulation that continued to run in her memory lacunae on the brain stem claimed -

The last Fleet

she swung the jetpack from her chest to her back and immediately ignited without checking for proper fit.

The hot gas shot hissing from the jets when she was fifty yards above the ground, melting a growing hole in the evac bubble that was being torn upward by the relative wind.

Mirage had a split second to make a correction and intuitively swerved to the right after nearly being impaled by a pointed treetop. So she crashed through branches and twigs with still considerable speed until she came to a stop just before the ground and the jetpack's gas supply was exhausted. She fell the last yard and landed with a spring on her feet.

She nodded in acknowledgement and pulled the empty jetpack off to hide it under a bush with dense leaves, then marked the spot in her field of view where Deus had fished out the heat signature from her sensor records. Her Reapersuit had lost thirty percent of its integrity, warning her that massive vacuum damage could occur.

Mirage brushed the warnings aside and began walking toward the marker. She effortlessly blanked out her fascination with the obviously alien nature all around. Deftly, and with reflex boosters activated, she made the five miles to the finish line in under thirty minutes, even through the undergrowth. The fact that gravity was only about 0.8 g here helped, even if it wasn't exactly inconspicuous. Here and now it was a matter of speed, because her landing site would soon be swarming with emergency forces, she had no illusions about that.

When she reached the edge of the forest under a scree slope, she immediately saw the circular hole in the rock. Her vantage point was not ideal, but with the exact marker, she could not miss it.

She climbed up and used her implanted ECM launcher to turn off the motion detector on the hole, which hid its electronic signature well. But not well enough for her sensor system.

Through the hole, she entered an airlock that she tried to open with Zenith's priority code, only to find that it didn't work. She raised an eyebrow and loaded the specifications of the *Sphinx* frigate from her memory lacunae. After three well-placed shots from her implanted smartgun, the mechanical bolt system was history, and she was able to push the bulkhead aside with her hands. Fortunately for her, Gavin Andal had apparently shut down the secondary systems to give off a lower signature, even though he had apparently jumped his ship into a mountain.

"Fucking hell though, what kind of fucking..." she heard someone grumbling, just coming up from a hole in the central corridor, his face filled with anger, a thick bump on his forehead. "Oh."

"Gavin Andal," she said, "where is he?"

"Uh." The man climbed out of his hole. He was short and squat, without a neck, his head round and surrounded by a cloud of thinning hair. "And you are?"

"Don't do that," Mirage prompted him as he leaned against the wall, seemingly casually.

"Do what?"

"I will kill you."

Her counterpart visibly swallowed and wrestled a smile from himself. "Well, the captain's not here."

"Then where is he?"

"That's what I'd like to know," he grumbled with a somber look. "Could you possibly tell me who you are?"

"No."

"Then could you tell me if you're planning to kill us?"

The last Fleet

"No."

"No, you can't tell me that, or no, you don't want to kill me?" he asked with a furrowed brow.

"You're still alive," Mirage noted. Her psycho-physiognomics program showed no sign of him lying. "Where is Gavin Andal?"

"I don't know. They took off two days ago to look around. I tracked their signal for a while, but then they didn't get back to me, and it disappeared. Poof, just gone!"

Mirage pondered. "There's a big structure to the east, probably made of plastic concrete. There shouldn't be a signal going out of there."

"You know more about that than I do. Thought about going after them, but somebody's got to watch the damn *Lady* and get her back in shape."

"Is she?" she asked curtly.

"What?"

"The ship. Fit."

"Oh, yes, yes, it is. We could even jump if we could calculate proper coordinates."

"We can." Mirage sent him appropriate coordinates in the outer system and had her neural computer extrapolate their current position to the central star to derive as accurate a starting position as possible. Then she relayed the data to his wrist terminal.

The mechanic looked down at the device on his forearm, aghast, and back up at her. "Who the hell are you?"

"Nobody," she said, "Stand by."

"For what?" he called after her, but she was already in the airlock and on her way out.

She had to head east.

18

GAVIN

They were led through two corridors and an unadorned bulkhead of armored steel, visually no different from any other Gavin had seen so far in this facility. That was not true, however, of the room into which they were taken. It was large enough to hold two corvettes like his *Glory* that had been destroyed on Andal, with a high ceiling that seemed to be coated with some shimmering varnish that had the same bluish pulse running through it every five seconds as it did out in the alien countryside. Two rows of seats sealed into the concrete floor stretched in a semicircle along the circular wall, facing a platform on which there was a throne of some sort. The backrest and armrests were made of metal, but it looked liquid, like mercury held in shape by magic. Finger-thick cables ran across the floor, connecting the base of the oversized throne to the seats in front of it. On the wall behind them were massive server cabinets with the unmistakable qbit coils he knew from every ship in the Navy, except that here the number was significantly higher than even on the *Amundsen*, his family's former flagship.

As they were led to their seats, Gavin listened to the hiss of the air conditioners, trying to figure out where the strange smell that filled the room was coming from. It reminded him of a mixture of lavender and his childhood, when his mother had roasted ginger to make him a special tea before he slept when he got sick. Gavin didn't know whether to find the recalled memory homey, because of the security he had felt then, or threatening, because it was linked to illness.

Since Dodger, Hellcat and he were at the very end of the column, most of the other inmates were already seated, and there were only eight seats left. Five of them would not be filled, he knew. Automatically, he scanned the armrests for restraining devices or slots from which handcuffs and cuffs might shoot out once he was seated. But except for the fact that the legs were sealed into the floor, they appeared to be ordinary seats. The only distinctive feature was that breathing apparatus dangled from each headboard.

"Sit down," ordered one of the guards, whose voice reached every ear effortlessly despite the size of the room. "Everyone take their breathing apparatus. No restraints, no surgery."

Gavin watched as the total of ten guards retreated to the single door. Attacking them would have been futile as they clogged the one way out with their shock launchers. After they quickly retreated, it was too late anyway.

A hologram appeared on the throne in front of them. It was Varilla Usatami, who sat down on the seat. Except for an occasional flicker, the projection was good enough to think she was real. Gavin always thought she was very tall for a woman, but on the strange seat she looked as small as a child.

"I want to thank you on behalf of the Senate of the

The last Fleet

Future," she said almost solemnly, letting her eyes wander over the faces opposite her. Was it actually a recording? "I'm sure you're wondering what all this is about. Why you've been kidnapped and torn from your lives. Where you came from, whether you were forgotten or deliberately ignored because of the sins of your ancestors, whom you no longer even know. Guilt and punishment had been paid, and yet the Star Empire left you behind after your world was slowly strangled. On behalf of the Senate of the Future, I would like to beg your forgiveness. I apologize for not asking you before we brought you here. Even though I know it is for your own good and for the good of humanity. You are paving the way to a better future, and that future will remember you as bridge builders. As the unlikely heroes of a new age. Please put on your breathing masks now."

After a moment of silence, with only the air conditioners roaring, a rustle, first scattered, then loud, began as breathing masks were removed from headrests and slipped over faces. Hellcat seemed to refuse, but Gavin followed suit with Dodger and put it on.

Usatami continued, though Hellcat was still lacking, so he guessed it was probably a recording after all.

"In a moment it will begin. I thank you and at the same time I envy you. You are creating something here that many would see as the crowning achievement of a lifetime, a real leap into the future and a glimpse into the mysteries of the cosmos."

The holographic image of the Senate President stood up and indicated a bow. Then it disappeared and it became dead silent. Not even the air conditioners could still be heard.

Gavin became very cold all at once, although he

thought the temperature had just jumped. The smell of burnt ginger and lavender increased.

"Hellcat," he whispered without taking his eyes off the throne. "You should put the mask on."

She didn't answer, but he could see movement out of the corner of his eye.

Then something happened above them. A hole opened at the apex of the upward-curving ceiling, and the air flickered between him and the throne. Empty a moment ago, a shimmer spread out there now, as if raindrops were beading off a pane of glass far too complex to reveal a shape.

Before Gavin realized he had held his breath and the echo of his breath had disappeared into the mask, the apparition changed, and before them, not twenty yards away, sat an Orb. He knew and felt it immediately, because he would never forget what he had seen before.

The alien with a large teardrop-shaped head measured almost twice the size of a human. Above the narrow, lipless mouth, six tiny breathing holes opened and closed, three on top of each other. The eyes were huge obsidians that seemed to reflect the infinity of the universe. It was as if they absorbed all the light of space and reflected some of it back. Skin the color of the purest mother-of-pearl shone like polished lacquer on silken jewelry and was covered below the neck by a robe of flexible lamellae on which complex patterns of black ink were in constant motion. A belt of some sort wrapped around his narrow waist, held together by what looked like a display with alien digital symbols on it. Likewise black arms rested on the bacs, ending in seven fingers on each side. Their skin billowed back and forth like the waves of a troubled sea. Pearly legs with taut muscles that stretched beneath the velvety skin

The last Fleet

stood out at unnatural angles, as if the knees were aligned to the wrong side, much like birds of prey.

Gavin felt the cold hand of fear grip the back of his neck as the images of his deployment in the wreck of the *Ushuaia* came flooding back. His mind seemed to have blocked out the traumatic experience against the backdrop of his personal losses and the constant threat of death he had been in ever since. But now it all came back, the terrible, shrill scream in his head, the alien's attempt to impale him with its morphing arms, and his panicked flight through the airlock, always with the feeling that at any moment he would be grabbed and swept away into endless darkness. This time there was no railgun, no Lizzy to save him with a well-aimed shot.

Gavin felt the mixture of tension and paralyzing fascination that held the entire room in its grip. He had felt it himself when he had encountered the Orb on the *Ushuaia*. Something about the alien was beautiful and of an indescribable depth that seemed unfathomable to the human mind. He slid back in his seat as the alien sat motionless, seeming to soak up everything like a sponge. A sideways glance showed him that he was the only one stirring at all. Even Dodger and Hellcat sat there with their mouths open like rabbits in front of snakes, apparently unable to move.

No restraints, he thought. Because it doesn't need any. The hand on the back of his neck grew colder, icy.

Suddenly, there was a hiss, and neural cables shot out from under the seats like thin snakes, burrowing purposefully into the inmates' newly implanted data jacks. The connectors snapped shut as if they were biting, and a sound of terror escaped Gavin as he tried to ward off the bite. He did not succeed, however. The flexible cable was faster than he was, and after a brief moment of pain, it lodged in his temple.

Words formed in his consciousness that were not his own. Thoughts that came from a foreign mind. As if remote-controlled, he had to witness that his mouth opened and he began to speak, simultaneously and in a perfectly synchronized chorus with the other prisoners: "Let's continue. What are the specifications for the reactor's transthermal shielding device?"

Gavin was too irritated by the alien thoughts he was putting into words, too paralyzed by fear to understand what was even going on here. He had - they had - spoken to the Orb, he was aware. But it sounded as if they were in the middle of a conversation whose beginning they had missed. The modified neural cables began to glow as they spoke, pulsing excitedly between their seats and the throne, as if they were feeding the alien with the life energy of the humans.

He wanted to stir, to raise his hands, to scream, but it was as if he were immersed in liquid lead that weighed heavily on every muscle. Panic spread through him, he became a hostage in his own body, used by strange, invisible hands, and the enormity of this attacked the core of his personality. A headaches began to throb between his temples, and somehow he knew they would become more until his brain was nothing more than boiled fat running from his nose and ears, ending his life.

The alien on his throne raised a hand, just a few inches. His answer was imminent, and a single thought fought its way from Gavin's memory through the thickening haze in his mind: the Orb in the airlock, its face lifeless and pale, its frightening beauty faded like wilted leaves, a hole the size of his fist in his chest. Then suddenly he saw Dain Marquandt before him, sitting at the end of the *Mammoth*'s conference table, hours before the battle for Gavin's home system. The stern expression, the lying words from his mouth. Anger burned through the veil, scorching it into flaming cinders.

With all the willpower fed by his greed for revenge, he grabbed his temple and forcibly tore out the neural cable. He felt hot liquid running over his ears, but he didn't care.

All at once his head was clear. He was dazed, but no longer trapped in his own body. Without thinking, he reached for Dodger's neural cable and snatched it from her augment as well, whereupon the mutant shook as if waking from a nightmare.

"Hellcat!" he hissed. "GO!"

It took her an endlessly plodding minute to process his words, then she blinked as if she had to get her bearings in the present, freeing Hellcat as well.

Then the Orb began to 'speak'. A high-pitched whistle sounded, painful to the ears, pricking like a needle. A melody as strange as the light of distant stars sounded, horrifying and fascinating at the same time, driving it to the guts and triggering a cascade of feelings of deep melancholy and loneliness.

The creature's breathing holes began to flutter, and all at once two bluish wings folded out of its back. Like an angel of death, the Orb lowered its gaze, a punishing god before its mortal servants.

The pulsation in the transparent neural cables reversed, and the first prisoners began to scream without restraint. Others babbled obsessively something that sounded like complex mathematical formulas, physical terms that made no sense whenever he could understand individual snatches amid the others' shouting.

He watched as some of the Arcturians slumped lifelessly, blood running from their eyes and noses.

"How does the cross-section of the dew field change under the influence of ..." the half that was still alive began to ask, but Gavin wasn't listening and leaned over to Dodger.

"I'm not waiting until ... Hellcat!" He jumped up at the same time as the mutant as her comrade rushed toward the alien. The Orb's head jerked around, and under its gaze Gavin thought he would burn to ashes.

The flickering that had been seen when the creature appeared began again, and its shape blurred as if under a chameleon suit. The hole in the ceiling opened again, and a bloodcurdling shriek sounded from the alien's tiny mouth before its head also disappeared into the camouflage. Gavin fell to his knees and put his hands over his ears. Dodger tried to grab Hellcat, but she had leapt at the Orb like a cat of prey. A harpy cry, filled with anger and despair, escaped her lips, then she crashed into something invisible and was jerked a yard into the air as a shimmering stream of air shot upward.

When she hit the ground again, she remained dazed. Gavin scrambled to her. She was bleeding from both ears and breathing heavily, her mouth twisted into a bloody grin in which there was no joy, but satisfaction.

"Are you okay?" he asked, but she didn't seem to hear him. Instead of answering, she raised something with her right hand in his direction. It was the mysterious display brooch he had discovered on the alien's belt.

Dodger helped her to her feet while Gavin looked around. He had expected guards to rush in as soon as they left their seats, but nothing happened. Something was different than it should be. From the door he heard muffled sounds that he couldn't place. Perhaps the boots of a hit squad? A glance at the other inmates made him

The last Fleet

swallow hard. They were all dead, bleeding from the eyes and nose, some had white liquid running down their lips.

Only now did he discover something else in the room that he had not been able to see before because he had been sitting on the wrong side: a wide glass panel three yards above the floor, behind which scientists in white coats were sitting at work consoles. They seemed to be in a frenzy, talking wildly to each other. Some pointed toward them, others toward things he couldn't see from his position. They looked terrified and every iota of fear he saw in their gazes made him feel a diabolical satisfaction, even though he knew they were stuck now. Locked up with the corpses of those pitiful Arcturians who had become the lab rats of Dain Marquandt and Varilla Usatami.

"That was... special," Dodger found.

"I think they were trying to communicate with the Orb," he said, not taking his eyes off the scientists behind the glass. They should see him, his anger.

"Doesn't seem so easy."

"Those damn murderers."

"What do we do now?" Dodger pointed upward. "The hole doesn't seem to open for humans."

19

GUNTER

"A transmitter?" asked Masha quietly as they sat back in their cell wing after training.

"Yes." Gunter had considered not telling her, but he would need her help.

"What's it supposed to do?" She eyed the small device that looked tiny in his hand.

"The Lord Captain has a ship nearby. We could get help getting out of here."

As she looked around, he could tell she was struggling. This was certainly better than anything she knew of Arcturus, almost like a spa vacation. After a few weeks, she might have forgotten the strain of her abduction and treatment on Cerberus, but not today.

"They treat us well here because they need us, but as soon as they implant data jacks in us," he tapped his temple, "the stay is over."

"That's what the *lord* said?" asked Masha laconically.

"Yes, and I trust him. He put his life on the line for a passenger liner that had no strategic value whatsoever," he said. "We need to take this transmitter and get to a place where it can transmit its signal."

"We're deep in the ground,"

"But the ship is still docked. The freighter. It will take at least another day to unload. If we could manage to get inside..."

"*We*?" she echoed. "We're not..."

"Fighters?" he broke her off. "I thought *everyone* on Arcturus was a fighter by necessity?"

"Thieves. I said thieves."

"Whatever is going on, it's not going to end well. I know you feel it, too. This transmitter," he held the small tube in front of her eyes, "is our only way out of here, as slim a chance as that is. It's better we try it now than later, when everyone's lulled by the birdsong and the good food."

"I've never heard birds chirping before. There aren't any on Arcturus." Masha looked around sadly and sighed. It was a sound of longing and melancholy in equal measure.

"A last meal might taste good, but it's still the last one."

"What exactly do you have in mind?"

"Cortical disrupter." Gunter tapped his augment blockers.

It took Masha a moment to understand. Then her eyes widened and she looked toward the clusters of people between the cells. Their companions were huddled together, talking in hushed voices. They didn't trust the roast yet, that much was certain. After many days in which their fellow abductees had died and decomposed beside them, they had been locked up and shipped off like cattle, there was no relaxation or relief for them. After a week they might hear birds and appreciate the taste of

The last Fleet

food, but now they were whispering and looking for the hook, the cruelty on which it was all built. What renewed devilry had been done to them with this suddenly much better treatment.

"Talk to your people," Gunter urged her. "After that, I'll take care of the rest."

"You alone?" she asked incredulously.

"No. I won't be alone. A gilded cage might be tempting, but only as long as freedom isn't an option."

"What if they overhear us?"

"Then we're toast. Or we leave them no choice. But," he added as she looked around anxiously, scanning the corners of the wing in search of cameras, "if they housed tens of thousands of us here, they'd need hundreds, if not thousands, of staff just to monitor us. I don't believe that. Maybe they have cameras and have AIs automatically looking for suicides or acts of violence."

"You don't believe it or you don't want to believe it?" she prodded.

"Both. I'm a Marine, I play my cards, and then I ask for the rules of the game."

Masha thought about his words for a few more moments, then she went to the first group of sitters and started talking to them. She spent an hour or more that way, and he saw many heads nodding. That was a good sign. At the same time, the Arcturians looked pitiful. They were haggard and weak, their gazes timid, though he saw fire in their eyes. Barely more than a glimmer, but it was still there. He just had to kindle it.

"You little pissants feel good now, huh?" he shouted loudly so the entire hundred in the wing could hear him. "First you let your fucking mudball kidnap you from a pile of shit like lambs, and now a few birds are chirping and you're feeling fucking great, huh?"

271

The looks the Arcturians gave him grew more and more sinister. He grinned provocatively at them.

"No wonder the Star Empire wants nothing to do with you cowards. What are you afraid of this time, you rust buckets? That the men in the white coats with their clubs and stun guns are going to get mad? Oh, you didn't know their weapons were stun guns, did you? That's because you guys are too pathetic. They were modified Rapier-type shock launchers. They don't want to kill you, they want to control you because they know you're scaredy-cats and can be kept quiet with a little yummy porridge and bird chirping." Gunter spat out and batted his eyes a few times in each direction. "What's the matter? Are you scared of me, you fucking outcasts? You're no better than your mass-murdering ancestors, can't even stand up for yourselves and the filthy families you cowards left behind."

That did the trick, they rushed at him with angry cries. They should know that he was provoking them just for the show, and their kicks and punches were everything but brutal, but at the same time not merely fake, as hoped. Had he possessed a normal body, a meat sack like them, he might have been bruised. More important than the beating, however, was the shouting they were doing. Deafeningly loud and filled with raging anger, for which he was merely the catalyst.

The fire had returned. Through the many legs around him, he looked toward the door, and when it opened, he rose and pretended to beat up the inmates around him. He lashed out in all directions, but always stopped his hands and feet in time - almost always. A few bruises here and there, but nothing serious.

"BREAK IT UP!" someone with a voice amplifier yelled, and the voice reverberated all the way into Gunter's titanium-coated skeleton. He pretended to be caught in a frenzy and not notice them, but out of the corner of his eye he saw them gather by the door until there were ten of them. Five remained standing there with their stun guns drawn, covering the other five, who took their cortical disruptors and began pounding the crowd. Prisoners threw up and staggered away from each other where the clubs touched them. The others scattered, clearing a path to Gunter.

Two guards lunged to hit him on the back, but he saw them coming, was ready, and wheeled around to face them. At the last moment, he jerked his arms up and intercepted the weapons with the smoldering ends using his wrists.

Cortical disruptors met augment blockers and overloaded them for a moment. But that was enough for him. Despite the dizziness that staggered him, he heard the click of the cuffs and ripped the devices from his skin.

For a brief moment, the guards gazed out of their masks in disbelief, then Gunter's reflex boosters and reflex lines activated, sending a shiver through his spinal cord and down into his cyber arms and feet. Neural computers and memory clusters powered up, connecting his brain to the many augments that powered up his largely mechanical body. Adrenaline pump and auto-injector signaled readiness, his artificial muscles vibrated in full action tone, and the Smartnite swarm rushed through his artificial circulatory system again.

"My turn," he growled, and his forearms unfolded, splitting at the elbow into the two weapon sockets. At the top, his augmented hand with monofilament blades extended, the shotgun on the left, the smartgun on the right.

He finished off the two guards with two short blows

to their heads, which slid off their shoulders like jelly. Even before they hit the ground, he sprinted straight ahead and fired from his weapons at the white uniformed men near the door. With his enhanced reflexes, they looked like divers operating underwater, slow and ponderous. The shotgun shells shredded the first two, his smartgun chased tiny arrows down the throats of two others. The three remaining guards with cortical disruptors were cut down by the Arcturians and torn in two with their bare hands. Their furious screams and howls spoke of unbridled anger and hatred fueled by him for the injustice of the universe.

The last guard still managed to shoot at him, but missed by a hand's breadth, and his eyes widened in amazement as Gunter slashed him from crotch to neck. The white chemical suit turned into a red sponge, and it was over.

Covered in blood and with his weapons drawn, he turned toward the open cell wing and stood in the doorway. As the heavy bulkheads were about to close, he spread his arms and held them open effortlessly.

After the weapons were gathered up, some of the Arcturians put on the guards' suits, which were not completely destroyed, and put on their masks.

"On to freedom!" he shouted loudly, smiling grimly as they ran roaring past him, through the door and into the corridors. He stopped the second to last one and told him the way to the ship. The last was Masha, a stun gun in her hand.

"Can you handle this?"

She loaded the rifle with a practiced motion.

"Good, we need backup," he said, letting go of the doors that clicked shut behind them. He motioned for her to follow him and ran to the next wing. With his monofilament blades, he cut a hole in the locked doors and peered

The last Fleet

through. One hundred astonished faces gazed back at him, most of them had poked their heads out of their cells. "You have this one chance to fight and be free. Here and now. Make up your minds."

With that, he left them alone and repeated the procedure down the hallway until he came upon a final door that was much harder to open. By now, a booming loud alarm was howling through the system, creating an oppressive atmosphere of violence, enhanced by distant screams and the din of weapons firing. It was the sound of battle, and it made Gunter's blood boil.

From the other side of the door, he heard an eerie scream that went through his spine. An otherworldly sound like the call of a mythical beast, a nightmare figure from sagas and legends.

"Sergeant!" he heard the Lord Captain shout as he finally forced open the door under Masha's cover. His master's voice sounded close to panic.

"My lord!" He helped the High Lord out and made room for the mutant and the other terrorist to follow. He would have preferred to seize the moment and bring them to their deserved punishment here and now, but that would not only go against his orders, it would hurt their chances of getting out of here.

The captain's gaze fell on his reddened wrists and a smile spread across his lips, but it couldn't mask the horror that was only slowly fading from him and seemed to scream from his eyes.

"There could not have been better timing, Sergeant."

"Ever faithful, my lord."

"Get us out of here."

"Stay behind me." He saw the mutant try to pluck her weapon from Masha's hand, but Gunter intervened and growled warningly, "She earned it."

Dodger looked to him, then to the Arcturian, and finally she nodded to his amazement. That she then looked behind her through the hole in the door and shuddered. He felt a chill move through him. What had happened in there?

"Let's go," Gavin urged him.

20

GAVIN

The master sergeant was a fighting machine. A beast, like something out of a particularly brutal VR movie. He slaughtered his way through the few guards they encountered with an archaic efficiency that Gavin didn't know whether to be fascinated or disgusted. He had never seen the elite Marines fight, as the Navy only released footage of battles that served a news value, and that rarely included the nauseating brutality of ripped bodies and severed limbs. The sergeant turned a dozen guards into corpses that would have left little for forensic scientists.

They hastily distributed the weapons among themselves. Dodger and Hellcat took two of the three shock launchers they found. Gavin took the third. The cortical disruptors were taken by a larger group of Arcturians who had joined the woman who the sergeant seemed to know. He collected more and more breathing equipment, which he tucked into his coveralls.

"Something's wrong here," Gavin said as they arrived at a large doorway with close to a hundred prisoners jammed in front of it, banging ineffectually against the armored steel. "Far too few guards."

"As head of security, I would defend neuralgic points at such a large installation and mass as many forces as possible at them," the Sergeant said. "In here, we're not much of a threat. If it comes to open combat, they'll have to kill a lot of us, which they obviously want to avoid."

"Gas."

The Marine nodded and patted the bulging belly of his coveralls. "Simple and effective. Until it's over, they'll protect the most important places."

"Then why haven't they started piping in the gas yet?"

"I wonder."

"Anyway, standing around won't do us any good. Open that door there."

"With pleasure."

It was not particularly difficult to make their way through the tightly packed Arcturians, as they were respectfully given room. The sergeant and Dodger apparently prevented them from being too brash in their expressions of displeasure.

As soon as the monofilament blades ate through the steel, Gavin realized it wasn't going to be that easy this time. They had to have an important area in front of them because the material was significantly thicker, possibly even molecularly bound. In any case, the sergeant was making obvious effort to get ahead at all.

"You two," Gavin said to two fellow prisoners who had no weapons in their hands but had blood on the hems of their coveralls. "Go back and collect any breathing masks you can find."

"I'll go with them," the Marine's companion said. Her eyes flashed wildly with determination.

Gavin nodded curtly. "Hurry up."

INTERLUDE: MIRAGE

Mirage had no trouble getting into the facility. While all entrances were blocked and her sensors marked hundreds of sensor transmitters along the outer walls of the megastructure, she didn't dwell on it. She had to take out one of them with her ECM launcher before she jumped up the eight-yard-high wall with her chameleon suit on and landed lightly on the plastic concrete roof. It curved slightly upward where, eighty-four yards away, the *Mammoth* freighter was stuck like an overweight meerkat that had gotten stuck in its burrow after a headfirst dive and then died. The house-sized drive funnels stretched a mile above her, aiming up into the cloud-covered sky.

The one sensor she had destroyed hopefully didn't cause too much of a stir. One failure could be a coincidence, two a pattern. Still, she didn't want to bet on it and sprinted up to the hull of the spaceship, towards one of the portholes. From a distance, the indescribable size of the Mammoth had made them look like buttonholes. Up close, they were over a yard in diameter.

With carbotanium spikes extended, she cut a hole just

large enough that she could have pushed a marble through. Then she put her right ear to it and extended one of the acoustic probes, which slipped through the two-centimeter-thick opening as thin as a hair. Noise filters and analysis programs began their work, eventually sending a coherent audio signal to her neural computer. She heard sirens, an alarm, muffled as if it were merely the echo. Whispers, the hiss of water pipes, the whine of secondary engines as the freighter's consumption was far too high for any system to power it.

Mirage pulled back her ear and peered through the hole into a cabin with six bunk beds and a door at the far end. It was empty.

She took a step back and spread her arms while her pulse launcher charged. As she fired it, the Duroglas shattered into thousands of tiny shards that swept into the cabin and dug into the beds and walls. Like a fleeting shadow, she darted through, ran across the crunching glass to the door and into a long corridor that apparently ran along the outside crew cabins once around the long axis of the ship, for its curvature was lost rather quickly.

Red passive lighting barely provided enough light for her residual light amplifiers, so she added ultrasound and ran both visual spectrums in parallel so that her neural computer could make its own live display from them, showing not only contours and shapes but also details such as the colors of door handles and numbers on signs and walls.

Since the corridors and cabins faced the drive section, as on any other starship, she had to work her way down deck by deck. Wasting no time in doing so, she ran through a group of foul-smelling figures in old, damp clothing, looking half-starved, gathered around one of the

The last Fleet

elevator shafts. Their accent was unmistakably from Arcturus.

So these are the abductees, she thought, ignoring the excited shouts as she - invisible in her chameleon suit body pushed aside and pulled open the elevator doors with her hands.

Where she touched others, the ruthenium polymers flared, exposing the respective areas, causing enough horror that most ran away. For Mirage, it didn't matter.

As soon there was enough of a gap, she looked down, ripped the sweater off one of their bodies and wrapped it around one of the ropes suspending the elevator car, then slid downward through the shaft. She counted five seconds until she hit the floor and dented the steel cover. Again, she opened the door and stepped into a large hangar with an open bow ramp that was normally used to load cargo such as aircraft, shuttles, tanks or ships. Now, close to a thousand captives gathered in the two-hundred-by-two-hundred-yard loading and distribution compartment, whispering uneasily. Their fear hung over them like an ethereal haze, heavier even than their physical stench of sour breath and unwashed, sweat-soaked clothing. Cold white light poured into the darkness from the open doorway farther ahead, along with the noise of the alarm, so loud here that her noise filters turned on.

Mirage kept to the left of the wall, walking past hoses that ran openly between steel beams, as in an industrial plant, and bundles of cables held together by arm-thick plastic straps. Once she reached the ramp, she made sure not to touch anyone, which wasn't particularly easy as the captives got closer and closer together the closer she got to the reason things weren't moving forward.

Twenty soldiers in hardened military armor with full-face helmets stood at the foot of the ramp like dangerous insects. In their hands they held Avenger assault rifles of the latest generation. She didn't need to see the Japanese insignia to know they were Red Samurai, Yokatami's elite guardsmen. Heavily augmented, extremely disciplined. Only their nefariousness was more legendary than their loyalty to the corporation.

As they stood motionless, they looked like a wall of rice board that thought it could hold back a storm surge. But Mirage knew that the impression was deceiving and that they could easily slaughter the thousand or so unarmed refugees if they wanted to. Apparently, the willingness to find out was not particularly high among the Arcturians.

That was about to change.

She snaked around a man-sized hydraulic fork at the edge of the ramp and jumped some fifteen yards down, landing lightly on the concrete. With ultrasound turned on, which the samurai undoubtedly had in their helmet sights, they could have detected her even in their sophisticated chameleon prototype, for sound waves were not so easily concealed. But as expected, they had not activated them because they had no reason to.

It was different with acoustic amplifiers. Her impact on the ground had caused noises.

She waited under the ramp until two samurai came around the corner, assault rifles at the ready, searching everywhere. Mirage slipped behind them and had the synthetic skin of her palms pulled back to expose the contact fields underneath. Then she simultaneously placed them on the samurai's helmets. Highly specialized combat software loaded itself into the memory clusters of their armor and shattered the firewalls, taking control of the secondary systems and choosing the most savage yet efficient way to take out the occupants: temperature control.

While the soldiers were being cooked like lobsters in their own tanks and silently slumping to the ground, she grabbed one of the Avenger rifles with a grenade underbarrel and ran to the other side of the one-hundred-yard-wide ramp.

She had just covered half the distance when the first samurai spotted their comrades. While they were still busy trying to figure out what had happened, one of them found the rifle seemingly floating without a guide in the air and got the idea to turn on his ultrasonic vision.

Mirage went into a dive to avoid the well-placed volleys and blindly fired a grenade to buy herself time. Then she peeked over the other side of the ramp and fired two grenades in quick succession at the assembled samurai still at the base of the grooved metal surface. They were lightning fast, springing apart like bees from a stung nest. Still, she shredded a handful and shot another in the chest before having to duck to avoid being hit herself.

With still no one from the Arcturians stirring and no chance against the remaining samurai, she fired the last two grenades at the edges of the upper ramp, causing enough panic and chaos that the captives screeched and poured into the huge concrete cavern like a stampede.

Many of them paid with their lives as the guardsmen opened fire and mowed them down by the dozens. Explosions shredded entire groups and the panic only increased. The herd of frightened lambs turned into a stampede in no time.

Mirage took advantage of the chaos to climb onto the ramp and pull herself behind one of the hydraulic forks further up into the corner. From there, she aimed at the samurai she could see and shot them in the heads with short bursts of fire. For most of them who were still alive, however, she would have had to use grenades, and so far she saw no reason to do so.

Taking advantage of her brief respite, she hid the rifle on her back and took an overview. There was a door with walls leading towards it, forming a kind of funnel. Two more to the left and right that were smaller and had red alarm sirens glowing above them, blaring their warning calls from loudspeakers.

Mirage joined the stream of crowds now sloshing back and forth between the cavern and the cargo bay, not sure which trap they preferred to sit in, since neither offered a way out. On this side, the doors were locked; on the other, the elevators were shut down. She struggled through to one of the dead samurai and took from him the two small grenade magazines stuck in his belt. Then she loaded one into her rifle and lost the other when she was jostled by a group of men. It flew to the ground, was hit by a foot and skidded away before the next shoes came and it changed direction.

No use. She returned to the edge of the ramp, this time on the other side, raised the rifle and fired three shells at the left of the two small doors. The first two dented the armored steel, leaving black soot and chunks of plastic concrete torn from the frame, which came down on the crowd and drove them back. The third blew the first holes in it. Only the fourth and fifth shredded much of the reinforced metal.

She tossed her rifle away and worked her way to the door that soon served as an escape route for the out-of-control Arcturians. They squeezed through the hole and trampled each other trying to get to the only eye of the needle that promised a way out.

Humans were quite stupid at times, she found.

Emotion-driven and devoid of logic once stress hormones took over.

To get ahead, she didn't take a squeamish approach, pushing bodies aside and making sure she didn't get crushed by extending her elbows. Nevertheless, precious minutes passed before she reached the aisle.

That changed when the clatter of automatic weapons was heard from ahead and the tightly packed herd jerked in a different direction. Mirage pressed herself against the wall to offer as little attack surface as possible and waited until it was over.

As soon as silence fell and the last civilians had passed her like horses passing through, she crept further forward and peered to the right, where the corridor ended in a T-junction. On the left, five yards down was a door, on the right six samurai, two of whom were kneeling. They all seemed to be aiming for her, but they could not see her.

After three seconds of silence, they came running in her direction to take new positions. She evaded them by going to the locked door and waited until they lined up so that the destroyed armored steel bulkhead was facing them. Only then did she sneak past them and get to another door that was secured with a control panel. She used her Carbotanium nails to pull off the paneling and identified the data cable, from which she stripped the insulation. She placed the exposed wire on her contact pads in her hands and loaded her sequestration software into the door control system.

Sixty seconds felt like an infinity as the alarm reminded her that time was not her ally. As the bulkhead hissed upward into the ceiling, she darted through and, to her surprise, found herself in a stairwell leading downward. Not stopping to glance over her shoulder, she ran down, taking six steps at a time. In case the samurai were surprised to see the door open as if by magic - if they had noticed it at all - they still faced the dilemma of whether to defend their position or reduce their manpower.

One floor below, there were two doors, one leading to washrooms that appeared to be empty. Another, also unlocked, led into a large circular room. In the center was a dais with a single armchair on it, like that of a fleet commander on the bridge. In it sat Akwa Marquandt, the daughter of the obviously renegade fleet admiral. In front of her was the officially dead Senate President Varilla Usatami.

"What do you mean he's gone?" the politician hissed straight toward the captain.

All around her, staff members in plain black Yokatami uniforms sat at work consoles. With narrow goggles on their noses, they were engrossed in virtual work environments, their movements frantic even though - or perhaps because - it was dead silent, except for the argument of the two women in their midst. Displays ran all around the wall, showing various scenes from the facility: the turmoil and carnage at the central drop-off point for the abductees, where the *Mammoth* freighter was stuck in the roof. Men and women in gray coveralls ran marauding through a maze of white corridors, pouncing like locusts on guards who tried to fight back with stun guns and cortical disruptors. A cursory glance, however, was enough to see that the civilians were unstoppable.

But it was two very specific live shots that piqued Mirage's interest: One showed a large room with a throne in the center, on which sat a creature she saw only for a fraction of a moment before it disappeared into some sort of camouflage field. A woman in a gray jumpsuit tried to attack it, but fell to the floor and was caught by an Invitro. A third person next to them leaned down to the fallen one, and one of the cameras caught his face - briefly only, but enough for Mirage to recognize it: It was Gavin Andal. The other shot was from a hangar that made even the large cavern where the captives were unloaded look puny. Clamped in the middle was a *Triumph*-class frigate with odd modifications that included spikes on top that looked like a forest of sensor spears. The ground was teeming with technicians in white sterile suits with hoods and mouth guards, and workers doing welding work on the hull of the ship above them. Alien machinery was being wheeled in on cargo sleds.

"... He's getting to safety," Akwa Marquandt said just then, looking toward the door. Her cold gaze met Mirage's, but she stared through it, of course.

"What is it?", Usatami wanted to know. Her voice quivered with anger.

"The door..."

"Don't distract me now, Captain!" the politician snapped at her. "If it's gone, then we've got a real problem that's much bigger than a Science Corps ship trying to spy on us."

"There's something else."

"What?"

"The Samurai have reported an attacker with a sophisticated stealth suit in the unloading bay. They're all dead."

"Is it..."

"No." Marquandt shook her head. Her harshly combed-back hair barely moved at that. "A human."

"I don't like this. First this research ship, now this. Go to the *New Dawn*, Captain, and launch. We can't wait any longer," Usatami ordered.

"She's not at full operational capability yet."

"Then you will have to improvise. We're moving up the schedule."

The captain bared her teeth, but turned away and left the command center with springy steps. Her movements reminded Mirage of a predatory cat on the prowl. Behind her, the door slammed shut.

"Ma'am," one of the thirty or so personnel at the consoles spoke up. "What do you want us to do about the High Lord?"

"Initiate the gas. Now that he's gone, there's no reason to delay. We need to restore order, and we need to do it now," Usatami replied from her center chair, about to dial a Quantcom bark on a holodisplay. Mirage didn't even know the system had one.

"Cancel the order,' she said, and let her monofilament blade extend from her right forearm, just under the politician's chin. She widened her eyes and froze. Mirage turned off the camouflage effect of the ruthenium polymer compound that made up the top layer of her suit.

"Who are you?" stammered Usatami.

Mirage extended her left arm and shot one of the Yokatami staff with her implanted smartgun. The targeting optics transmitted the image of his bursting head to her, though she kept her eyes locked on the politician.

"Countermand the order," she repeated.

"Cancel gas feed!" croaked Usatami.

"Open all doors in the facility."

"I can't, if I do that, then..."

Mirage's smartgun fired again, this time two shots in quick succession. The smart three-millimeter rounds picked their way, turning two more heads into red butterflies. A fearful murmur spread among the staff, but no one dared to leave their seats.

"Open all doors!" the former Senate president stam-

The last Fleet

mered, and Mirage checked the displays of comrade data to see if she could be satisfied.

"Since you don't seem to value the lives of your staff very much, I'm raising the stakes. I have little time and certainly none for lies," she said, pressing her left hand to Usatami's left knee. With the blade of her right, she lifted the woman's chin up a bit.

"What are you doing in here? What was that creature?" She already had a guess.

"An Orb. We communicate with it," Usatami stammered in a clenched voice.

"How?"

"It's ... complicated. In their evolution, they've developed a kind of telepathic process that's only partially compatible with our thoughts, based on an organic quantum effect that I don't know the details of. That's up to the scientists."

Mirage looked to the hangar with the modified *Triumph*-class ship and then to the empty throne room where Gavin Andal was locked up with close to a hundred dead people with neural cables hanging out of their temples.

"It's about technology. How many aliens are there here?"

"One. One that we know of."

"You are working with him."

"Yes. We get certain technologies that make us stronger." Alongside the fear in the politician's eyes now came an unmistakable pride. She was convinced she was doing the right thing, that much was certain.

"What is this ship for? What mission did you send the captain on?" Mirage knew she was running out of time. She needed young Andal, and she needed this ship that Marquandt's daughter was targeting.

Usatami was silent, and something in her gaze told Mirage that she was struggling with herself, weighing her survival instincts against her convictions. Mirage could do something about that, because survival instinct was easily triggered when it became something basal instead of something abstract.

She fired her smartgun, shredding the knee under her hand.

The former Senate president began to scream uncontrollably, but still possessed enough composure not to injure herself on the blade under her chin.

"The ... Congress ..." she groaned, saliva spurting from her mouth. Each word sounded clenched and heavy.

"Your funeral service, I take it?" concluded Mirage. "That one is a stealth ship like the one that tried to destroy young Andal's ship." It made sense. "This is the prototype's successor or the prototype under repair. It flies to Sol, undetectable, and destroys the Aurora habitat when the Emperor arrives as the highest guest, along with the assembled elite of the Empire."

Usatami replied nothing, pressing her quivering lips together until they formed a thin line.

Mirage weighed various risks and executed.

"I require the administrator codes of this ship," she announced, even as the fountain of blood splattered to the floor and Usatami's lifeless body slumped in her chair.

This time, she didn't need to extend her arm. From several of the employees in corporate uniform at the same time, her wrist terminal was sent a complex data key. She nodded with satisfaction, turned toward the door, and began running as fast as she could.

21
GAVIN

The door opened. Just like that.

The master sergeant seemed as surprised as he was and withdrew his monofilament blades from the armored bulkhead just in time before it could dislocate his arms. Behind it was a long corridor, not lined with white panels, but built of unadorned plastic concrete with red pipes running along the low ceiling. On the other side of the shaft, a handful of soldiers in dark armor were currently running in the opposite direction through an open passageway. From their position, loud roars and the whine of machinery could be heard, reminding Gavin unmistakably of starship engines.

He exchanged glances with Hellcat and Dodger, who seemed ready to run. Their hesitation, however, was not shared by the many dozens of Arcturians now rushing past them, obeying the adrenaline that spurred them on.

The fact that the soldiers were moving away from them made him suspicious. Especially in a narrow corridor, they could use lethal weapons, not these shock launchers, to hold at bay and kill as many enemies as they carried ammunition, which was not a scarce commodity in the 25th century. At the same time, there was no chance he would return to where he had come from. And as bitter as that thought felt; they had more men and women ahead of them with every passing second who didn't care about tactics and would be the first to run into the knife with nothing he could do to stop them.

"Onward. We know what's behind us, and that's not something that's going to help us. So let's find a way out of here." Hellcat and Dodger nodded grimly and raised their shock launcher, but the master sergeant, of all people, seemed hesitant.

"Any objections, Marine?"

"My lord, Masha, she..."

"Get them back, if no gas has come by now, we won't need the masks."

"I can't leave you alone," the soldier objected. On his usually stony countenance, the discord that was affecting him was evident.

"Go get them, that's an order," Gavin said curtly.

"Thank you, my lord."

"Sergeant." He held the bulky Marine back with a bloodied arm. "If you can find a faster or better way out of here, take it." Seeing an objection threaten, he added, "That's an order, too, now go!"

As the master sergeant ran off, bracing himself against the straggling inmates, Hellcat gave him a look that unnerved him.

"What?"

"Nothing. We should hurry."

Gavin ran, joining the stream of Arcturians. There was little recognition of the lulled, conformist prisoners they had been minutes ago. Now half were armed and their expressions determined.

At the end of the shaft, they entered a huge hangar whose gates formed a kind of dome far above. Where they touched was a dark joint, and just below it a *Triumph*-class frigate was held in place by restraining clamps such as he had seen before. The alien yet familiar sight of her made his blood run cold.

At least she's not cloaked yet, he thought, as something roughly nudged him aside. An object whizzed past his head. Warm liquid splashed his face, and what passed his lips tasted metallic.

Cursing, he wiped his eyes clear and found himself behind a large battery pack on rollers. Dodger released her hand from his collar and fired her shock launcher over the edge of their cover. Hellcat did the same on the other side.

Shots rattled through the hangar with loud echoes, followed by screams and the smacking of shredded flesh. A pool of blood had spread directly in front of the open passageway, where countless corpses lay. Nausea rose in him. More and more Arcturians came running like madmen and split up, but far too many were cut down.

"The gates are opening!" roared Hellcat over the din of battle.

They're trying to get away, whoever they are, he thought, peeking around the corner. In the light of large circular spotlights strung like a string of pearls midway up the circular hangar, soldiers in corporate Yokatami armor, who could only be the Red Samurai, were running around, dashing his hopes of somehow getting to the ship, or at least shooting it down. Prisoners fired from their commandeered shock launchers and swung their clubs, but both had little more effect than cotton balls trying to knock down a house wall.

He pulled his head back as a volley of high-velocity rounds pulverized the battery pack's frame, and he felt a hot pain on his left cheek. With his fingers, he felt for blood - impossible to tell if it was his own - and splinters that had bored into his flesh. Driven by the hope that they had been ricochets, he dared a second look.

Scientists in white and technicians in fleet-standard orange walked among the few soldiers - there could hardly be more than two dozen - and were apparently frantically busy getting the ship ready for launch. Workers on and under the hull, secured with ropes and magnets, stopped their welding and hastily disengaged.

Twenty yards below, explorers rolled away alien equipment that seemed to glow in all spectral colors. Between them, a lone figure in the black and gold uniform of the Imperial Navy walked along to an industrial lift where two workers were just coming down with a loading crane.

He used his neural computer to zoom in on a still image so he could recognize them: Akwa Marquandt, whom he had seen exactly once, at her father's battle plan meeting on the *Mammoth*.

Damn traitor. He looked up at the stealth ship and somehow knew that it was she who had pursued him in Andal and had the two civilian ships on her conscience. Along with the *Demeter* and all her crew.

His anger got the better of him and he left his cover to sprint in their direction.

Two Arcturians, who happened to be flanking him, split up, and one was torn apart. Gavin looked directly down the barrel of an assault rifle as its bearer was hit in the head and slumped to the side. His comrade looked for the threat and swung around, as it had obviously been a live weapon.

Taking advantage of the moment, several prisoners

lunged at the armored man. It would still be their end, but he paid no attention to them, grabbed the rifle from the ground and fired at another guardsman. The first volley hit the breastplate and was deflected, but sent the samurai staggering back. From somewhere nearby, Dodger jumped and grabbed the armored man's arm and brutally yanked him to the ground. But he deftly twisted under her and kicked at her knee.

She grunted - whether in pain or anger he couldn't tell - and caught a right hook. Their fight continued, seemingly even. Gavin tried to shoot, but had no clear line of fire and decided to charge on. On the other side, ten yards away, Hellcat ran and knocked down a technician with the shock launcher who was in the process of moving a rolling container aside. If he wasn't mistaken, it contained nine missiles in containments.

An idea occurred to him. He ran to Hellcat, fired at the back of a samurai he saw shooting at a group of Arcturians as he ran, and hoped they would make the most of it. Arriving at the missiles, he handed her the rifle and began to disengage one from its mount. All he had to do was take off the manual safety clips. The hard part was hacking the maintenance computer. Still, he tried to connect with his neural computer and succeeded. Now the explosive part began. He had to bypass the security systems, which took time he didn't have. But since he could already see Akwa Marquandt riding up on the lift and couldn't connect to the assault rifle's targeting optics, he had no choice.

Shortly thereafter, far above them, the hangar doors opened with a deep rumble of thunder. Dust and raindrops fell down on them, along with blinding daylight and a new alarm that sounded much more urgent and louder than the previous one. Someone began firing at the ship, then more muzzle flashes followed from the carnage around them.

Useless against ship armor, he thought, wishing he could somehow power his attack software. The first firewall succumbed to his high-quality code, which few houses had. So there was a chance.

The stealth ship's engines roared to life, making his legs flap like a primeval force. Beside him, the loud rattle of a weapon sounded.

Hellcat.

He tore away from the display to see a samurai charging at her with katana drawn. She shot him aimed at the chest and neck, but only three rounds cleared, then the magazine was empty. The first two ricocheted, the third seemed to have hit a weak spot between his chest and shoulder, for the guardsman stumbled briefly. When he got to her, moving so fast that he felt like he was in a VR game with a handicap, she was just able to yank the rifle up protectively.

The mono-bound blade cut through it like rice paper and Hellcat staggered back.

Gavin glanced at the display, saw that it was almost done, and at the same time the lift platform with Akwa Marquandt had almost reached the open airlock under the bow.

He had to make a decision, and he did so. He took the missile fuse cover and hurled it at the Samurai. The latter spun out of the flight path far too quickly and stabbed at him as he threw himself with force at the samurai's right leg. The blade penetrated deep into his shoulder, just above the collarbone, shredding muscle and tendon.

It was only due to his kinetic energy that Gavin caused the soldier to stumble as he crashed into the soldier's leg.

Apparently he had been able to surprise his opponent by not dodging.

For that, he would now bleed out.

But he had bought Hellcat time to make an instinctive leap back out of the immediate danger zone.

INTERLUDE: MIRAGE

Marquandt was on the platform and only a few yards separated her from the open airlock, which stood open like the mouth of a predator.

Mirage climbed up the lengthening concertina frame, using all her energy reserves, grabbed the lowest rung and pulled herself onto the platform.

From her right hand she let her monofilament blade extend like a metallic tooth. She was about to lunge when Marquandt wheeled around and looked at her, startled. She was not merely looking in her direction, but directly into her eyes.

"Who..." the captain gasped, and for the first time in a very long time, Mirage was startled. She made the mistake of instinctively looking down at herself, only to find that her cloaking field was no longer working. Her neural computer alerted her with flashing warning symbols that she was in the vicinity of an unknown magnetic field, whose area of effect she should leave as quickly as possible.

Marquandt pulled the pistol from the holster on her thigh with surprisingly quick aim. The gun barked loudly, and the bullet hit her directly in the chest, a hand's breadth below her chin. Since it was a hollow-point bullet, its force sent her rebounding against the railing. She nearly tumbled over backwards and fell into the depths, where out of the corner of her eye she saw a samurai about to slice Gavin Andal in half at his feet, when he was saved at the last second by his Invitro companion, who felled the elite guard like a battering ram from the side.

Grimly, she scrambled to her feet as two more shots kept her down. She was weakening. She raised her right arm and fired after Marquandt, but she had already scrambled up through the airlock, and the projectile hit only her foot, which dissolved into a cloud of blood.

How inconvenient. She assessed the situation and looked at the many warning displays in her field of vision. With some effort, she sprayed sealing wax on the wounds so as not to expire within minutes, and scrambled to her feet, only to be thrown to the ground again as the ship lifted through the nearly fully open roof. The cloak was activated and its contours blurred into a Fata Morgana.

Shortly thereafter, the ship disappeared.

She had lost. At least for today.

22

GUNTER

Gunter found Masha at the end of a corridor, where she and a handful of other Arcturians were engaged in a scuffle with two guards.

He sprinted to them and finished off the two men in their chemical suits.

"Gunter," Masha said in surprise.

"You were late."

"We got held up." She looked with undisguised bitterness at the dead around her. Joylessly, she held up a whole bundle of breathing masks.

"Come on now, we have to go." He motioned for them to follow him and ran back the way he had come until he heard the pounding of heavy boots on concrete before a turn and pressed himself against the wall. Peeking around the corner, he saw half a dozen Red Samurai in black armor with red Japanese symbols running toward where the wide tunnel was through which the High Lord had disappeared.

"What is it?" hissed Masha.

"Bad company," he whispered, peering into the

passage from which the elite guardsmen had come. It was empty and a door was open there, too.

With muffled steps, they turned and found themselves in a new part of the facility. The walls here were also white, but covered with a striking honeycomb pattern. His neural computer reported the influence of a strong magnetic field that could affect the function of most of his augments, which he immediately felt. His artificial limbs lost power and his autoinjector stopped working completely. Most affected, however, was his headware, of which his neural computer still functioned best because it ran in a minimal program of sorts. Still, he had no ambitions to mess with Red Samurai, whose augments were at least as good as his, except that they wore hardened military armor to go with it.

Wherever they had just stumbled into, there was an almost panicked bustle. Through an open door, he saw figures in white coats destroying server cabinets and setting fire to a recycler after throwing data pads into it. Behind a window they passed, he saw operating tables where prisoners had been dissected, primarily their heads. Tiny connectors stuck in the brains connected them to computers, while doctors ran back and forth, also destroying evidence or data - or both.

Part of him would have liked to shoot them all for their crimes against humanity, but he refused to put punishing the guilty ahead of saving the innocent and kept running.

At least until they came around the next bend and nearly collided with a group of scientists trying to push a cargo cart through an open cargo bulkhead into a larger room that contained only one object: a sphere the size of a medicine ball, black and seamless. It wouldn't have been worth a second look if it hadn't been on a pedestal from which countless cables connected to machines that surrounded it like monoliths. Excited gown wearers discussed with each other, pointing at the inconspicuous object again and again.

In an unreal moment of surprise, the researchers with the cargo cart froze in front of him, then raised his monofilament blade and they scrambled for cover.

"Keep going," Masha urged him.

"Yes." He nodded and pointed at the sphere. "I think this is valuable."

23

GAVIN

The traitor's daughter had escaped. All that mattered to Gavin now was getting his crew to safety. Part of him wanted to take out the Red Samurai and help the prisoners, but his rational self knew they wouldn't stand a chance. Not even with Dodger. So far they had been lucky, and because of the sheer mass of the Arcturians, had been able to overpower some of the elite guards, but the balance of power was already shifting.

Akwa Marquandt had escaped with the stealth ship and whatever she was up to, he had to stop her. So he began climbing up the hoist with Hellcat and Dodger. The climb was tough, especially with his injury. With every move and contraction of his muscles, he felt precious blood and Smartnites running from his shoulder wound. The faster his pulse quickened, the more spilled through the gaping wound where the samurai had hit him.

In the last few yards, while the carnage continued below him, gunfire whipping, men and women screaming, and death dancing in the chaos, he nearly crashed twice if Dodger hadn't grabbed him and pressed him back like a limpet to the accordion rack.

When they finally reached the platform, Hellcat, who had arrived before him, had to pull him over the railing like a wet sack.

Staggering, he got to his feet and shielded his eyes from the glare of daylight. The lift was almost level with the open hangar door, which was just beginning to close again, cracking and droning ominously.

"Captain?" asked Dodger, pointing to the floor. There lay the body of a woman, oozing white blood from four wounds at once. She was smaller than him and wore a strange suit that flickered constantly like a malfunctioning display. At times, parts of her seemed to disappear or blur with the metal floor of the platform, then they became a web composed of thousands of tiny platelets like medieval scale armor.

Irritated, he rubbed his eyes. "It certainly doesn't belong to Yokatami."

"What's that white stuff?" wanted to know Hellcat, rubbing some of it between his fingers.

"Nanites," he guessed. "Better not touch those, or you'll provoke an immune reaction from your Smartnites."

"Barely have any left, remember?"

Gavin turned away, his senses seeming to lag behind. "Dodger, can you take her? We need to find out who that is."

"Yep." The mutant lifted the body, and to his surprise, she groaned with exertion. The veins on her arms stood out clearly. Yet she said nothing.

As the gates, each as large as a soccer field, began to close slowly over them, they climbed out by them and lay on their backs, sliding along the curvature immedi-

The last Fleet

ately to the side. The cleared grassland was getting closer, though not very fast. The actually rough plastic concrete beneath them was wet from nighttime rain showers and ensured that their coveralls did not rip, sparing their skin. Still, the impact was hard as they tumbled over the edge of the roof and tumbled over each other.

Gavin lost consciousness briefly, but regained consciousness, jolted awake by the pulling in his shoulder. The pain was well tolerable, but that he felt it at all could only mean that the protozyme lacunae in his adrenal cortices had barely enough drugs and smartnites to maintain all the functions of his neural computer.

Dodger and Hellcat had already hoisted him to his feet before he could get his bearings. They started walking - even though he was stumbling more than running. The sky was still cloudy, but he could hear the unmistakable roar of atmospheric fighters and the low thunder of distant sonic booms whipping overhead. Before they reached the edge of the forest, he tripped over a fallen log that he must have missed.

As he picked himself up, he saw several *Skyhooks* breaking through the clouds. The personnel carriers pushed massive waves of compressed air ahead of them as they slowed their dive with roaring engines and came in for a landing all around the facility. None of the clunky ships had insignia or even identifiers, but he had not the slightest doubt that each carried Red Samurai in its belly.

"No time to rest, Captain," he heard Dodger say before he found himself on his feet and rushing on through the forest. This was getting to be a habit.

Back at the ship, the mutant shuttled her guest to sickbay, where Gavin picked up an IV and had Sphinx pump him full of stimulants to help him think clearly again after roughly spraying the wound on his shoulder with Mediseal.

"Bambam!" he shouted to the mechanic as he ran straight down the corridor. "Come here."

"I have to..."

"Come here!" he repeated impatiently, gesturing to the strange woman lying motionless on one of the hospital couches. "We have a guest. I need you to patch her up and wake her up."

"I thought she was dead and I'm not a...," the mechanic was about to protest again when he glanced past him and saw the stranger. He paled. "Shit, I know her!"

"What?"

"She was here asking about you. Then she took off. Said to get the ship ready to get you out. Like I'm a fucking magician..."

"Patch her up. Somehow!"

"There's something else. She gave me jump coordinates to the outer system."

"She did?"

"I just told you!" grumbled Bambam, rolling his eyes. "But I don't trust her."

"In any case, we've got to get out of here." Gavin left him standing and ran for the bridge. He still felt woozy, but he no longer felt like the world was spinning on three axes at once.

As soon as he slid down through the short tube and dropped into the commander's seat with its gimbal, he noted with satisfaction that Hellcat had already powered up the primary systems.

"We're jumping," he said, already expecting a protest.

"We've got company," Dodger announced over the internal radio. "'Bout a dozen samurai guys."

"Close the airlock!" replied Gavin, making a mental

note to thank Bambam for already charging the jump engines. To everyone he radioed, "Jump in ten seconds! Ten, nine, eight, seven, six, five, four, three, two ..."

"Wait!" shouted Bambam.

"What?"

"The signal booster. I'm getting a signal in."

The master sergeant! Gavin felt a twinge in his guts. Guilt. He hadn't even thought about the Marine anymore.

"Bloody hell!" he cursed, breaking off the jump sequence.

"What are you doing?" asked Hellcat, upset. "Are you crazy?"

"Yes. And we're not leaving our man behind."

She seemed to want to retort something, but remained silent.

"Power up weapons systems."

"We're stuck, in case you forgot."

"Then we'll have to see how strong our armor is and how much juice we can get on the thrusters." Gavin backed up his words with action and slowly increased thrust. The plasma of ultra-hot gas molecules burned into the rock behind them, melting it into hot lava. How far, he couldn't say, since the sensors had no margin, but he took the risk and switched the forward maneuvering thrusters to full power, sending them coursing backward at sixty miles per hour, straight into the hot lava.

"CRAZY!" roared Hellcat. "YOU'RE CRAZY!"

Inwardly, he nodded and sped them up even further. Heat warnings from all hull sections flooded his field of vision as they chased through the lava like a soda can through a hose filled with fire. Gavin didn't have time to worry about the *Lady*, however, because he had to muster all his concentration. The thrusters had to generate enough thrust to melt the rock and tunnel behind them, but only enough to increase the thrust of the maneuvering thrusters from the front so that they could move backward at the same time instead of forward and use the free space.

Then suddenly they were free, shooting out of the mountain as if from a launch shaft, except here there was no vacuum and they plunged immediately downward.

Gavin switched the signal source to the navigation computer and throttled back on the main thrusters. Using the maneuvering thrusters, he stabilized the Lady and blew past the trees toward the *Mammoth* freighter, which jutted a mile out of the forest landscape like a skyscraper dropped out of the sky.

"Four bogeys on radar!" reported Hellcat.

"Shoot anything that moves! I've got to try to land between the *Skyhooks*. Let me have one of the lasers."

"We're down to the maser. The other two have melted away."

Gavin didn't answer and steered them into a brutal right turn, over which he made a wide arc back to the clearing he would have preferred to turn his back on forever. The signal moved from the compound toward the edge of the forest. He tried to aim for the space between them and the first trees, flying close above the treetops so as not to make it too easy for the enemy radar.

Through the windshield he could see the Marine under fire from samurai pursuing him. A total of ten of them jumped from the roof of the facility at that moment with guns flashing. In front of the Master Sergeant, two more figures were running for their lives, one of whom was hit at that moment and went down.

Gavin marked the planned landing point and extended the lower loading ramp. He then took over the maser cannon under the bow and bombarded the guardsmen in the distance with a heavily throttled fifty gigawatts. The microwave beam cut the entire group at waist level, turning ten into twenty.

"Banzai," he growled, radioing Dodger. "We've got company coming in the hold, can you take care of them?"

"Already there."

Gavin was about to thank her when an alarm blared and the *Lady* was shaken violently.

"Hit in the dorsal engine section! Hull breach, damaged..."

"I see it myself!" he snapped at Hellcat more vehemently than intended. On the tactics screen, he saw two of the atmospheric fighters pursuing them had caught up and were swooping down on them like birds of prey. Their machine guns were chasing them with a veritable storm of micro-projectiles that would rip his ship open like a tin can in no time. "DODGER!"

"All in, Captain."

Without checking to see if the ramp was already retracting, he yanked the bow up and switched the thrusters to fifteen percent power, catapulting them skyward with a relentless jolt. Hellcat fired the railguns at their targets, but they were far too maneuverable. It was as if they were trying to shoot flies out of the air with canned jelly.

There was no chance of getting away from them. He was a good pilot, but only in space, which the frigate was made for. Unlike the atmospheric fighters, here the frigate was like a cripple, a diver among sharks.

"Captain?" asked Hellcat warningly.

"I see them." The remaining two fighters had caught up to them and were now engaging them. He increased thrust once more, to the maximum tolerance limits for operations in gravity wells, but it wouldn't be enough. Not even close.

As he was already toying with the idea of triggering the self-destruct mechanism to at least take the bastards with him, a fifth symbol appeared on the tactics screen, moving at ten times the speed of sound and firing at their pursuers. Two immediately went up in fireballs. According to the scanner analyses, the new ship was a *Thetis*-class research vessel. Nevertheless, like a dancing hummingbird, it flew through the air, firing its railgun at the perfect moment as it rolled through a cloud, and punched through the right wing of the last fighter with such speed that it dissolved in a haze of scrap metal and ignited fuel.

"Incoming transmission," said Sphinx.

"Put it through!" he commanded breathlessly.

"Hello, I'm Deus. You have something I'd like to have back."

EPILOGUE

Mirage's eyes snapped open after her neural computer informed her that eighty-four percent of her primary systems and ninety-two percent of her secondary and tertiary systems were back online and functioning properly. Her Smartnite supply had dwindled to less than forty percent.

She was lying on a cot, perhaps on a table, as she appeared to be in a mess hall, which she inferred from the protein synthesizers, coffee maker, and several microwave units.

Around her stood four figures. Gavin Andal, the *Lady Vengeance*'s mechanic, the tall Invitro with the tree-trunk arms and the dull look she apparently cultivated to hide a certain peasant shrewdness, and the Fury on two legs with the shaved temples and digitattoos that snaked across her skin like two-dimensional creatures.

"Illustrious crowd," she remarked, sitting up.

"We saved you," said the young Andal.

"Well done." Seeing him raise his brows, she sighed.

The human condition.

"Thank you," she said, stretching.

His brow smoothed again.

Mirage palpated the bullet wounds on her torso tentatively and had to admit that the silicon patches had been coupled quite expertly with her synthetic skin.

"Where are we?" she asked when no one said anything.

"Still in Yokatami's Seed System, far out, at your coordinates, beyond the outer gas giant. They shouldn't be able to see us," Andal replied, arms folded in front of his chest. "But we are not alone."

Mirage nodded.

"Who is Deus?"

"She's with me," was all she said. "I guess she put a little pressure on you."

"You could say that. We'll let you go, but..."

Mirage wondered if these people really thought they could stop her from doing anything. The Invitro didn't seem to think so, judging by the look on her face.

"... We need some answers that you might be able to give us."

"Akwa Marquandt intends to take the Orb-technology cloaking ship to Sol and destroy the Remus habitat, while the Emperor is addressing Congress on Usatami's alleged death," she explained curtly, standing up and checking the function of her arms and legs. The two women visibly tensed while Andal seemed to struggle with the information.

"How do you know this?"

"Varilla Usatami told me."

"So she's really not dead."

"She is now. Now it's your turn: did you communicate with the Orb?" asked Mirage.

"No, but it was apparently about some reactor technologies. We're going to Sol. Hellcat?"

"On my way."

"Dodger, let the sergeant and Masha know. Bambam? The repairs?" Andal turned back to Mirage after the other two crew members had left the mess hall.

"You helped us." It was more statement than question.

"Yes," she admitted.

"Who are you?" he asked, eyeing her with a penetrating gaze.

"No one." When he followed up, she said, "That's all you want to know. Believe me."

Her words seemed to have the intended effect, for he apparently understood and nodded thoughtfully.

"Meanwhile, we have the same goal."

"Saving the Emperor and Congress."

"Yes." At least indirectly.

"So we're working together?"

"Yes. I'm returning to the *42-QLUE*, then we're leaving for Sol."

"What's your name?"

"Mirage."

"I'm..."

"I know who you are."

"Of course," he said, sounding unsurprised. There was an unmistakable note of unease in his voice.

"Are there many like you? I mean..."

"No." She said it in such a way that he didn't inquire further. "Now we should get to work. We don't have much time. If Akwa Marquandt should beat us to it, the Star Empire will crumble."

TIMELINE

2035: The Ares crew sets foot on Mars for the first time. The international mission by NASA, ESA, SpaceX and a dozen partner countries launches a new space race.
2040: Mining of subcrustal resources on the Moon by a Western space alliance and China begins.
2042: Founding of Luna Mining Corporation, which buys all mining sites and rights from the Western alliance in return for exclusive supply contracts, following a fatal accident involving six NASA astronauts.
2044: First stable nuclear fusion at the LFTR experimental reactor in Virginia using tritium-deuterium fusion.
2045: ESA's Proximity spacecraft, in collaboration with the private space company Deep Space Mining, succeeds in diverting the asteroid '2008 BR-44', popularly known as 'Braun' after its discoverer Justine Braun, from its orbit around the Sun towards Earth.
2050: Braun reaches its target orbit around Earth and Deep Space Mining begins mining its ores and minerals. Beginning of the 'asteroid race' as a result of which more

Timeline

and more resource-rich celestial bodies are directed into high Earth orbit over two decades.

2052: Lighting Gale, a subsidiary of Luna Mining Corporation, unveils its first working fusion reactor on Earth's satellite, based on helium-3 fusion and enabling the construction of more compact small reactors.

2055-2080: Spurred by an enormous economic boom triggered by increasingly efficient fusion reactors, space technologies and massive resource surpluses, exploration of the outer solar system begins with manned missions to Jupiter and its moons, Saturn and Neptune.

2062: After hackers succeed in infiltrating the Pentagon by means of a highly developed AI and in remotely commandeering a B-21 bomber, which can only be intercepted at the last second, the Turing Agreement is signed as a result of a catastrophe that was only narrowly averted. This agreement outlaws the development of strong artificial intelligence and places corresponding start-ups and research projects under strict state supervision. All UN member states are signatories.

2065: Founding of the outer colonies on Jupiter's moons Ganymede and Europa and Saturn's Enceladus. Initially, these are small research outposts of little significance.

2070: The Explorer Incident: In orbit around Jupiter's moon, Io, a conflict between the American ship Explorer and the Chinese Tianlong occurs that remains unexplained to this day, resulting in the Explorer disappearing without a trace. This almost leads to a war between NATO and China on Earth, which is prevented at the last minute by the Napier Treaty. This treaty stipulates that there must be no armaments in the solar system outside of Earth and that inspectors must be granted access to relevant facilities in the course of mutual monitoring.

2073: The People's Republic of China collapses within

months as toxic rain floods vast areas of the impoverished West and the central government in Beijing withholds aid from the military for several days. A national uprising and prolonged consolidation struggles ensue, from which the Central Kingdom will not be able to recover for decades.

2074: The international Martian colonies unite and declare independence from their homelands on Earth. The U.S. sends the USS Nimitz, the just-completed first warship in the solar system, after the Napier Treaty collapses with the collapse of China. The suppression of the colonist revolt fails when the Nimitz breaks up due to a navigational error in the Martian atmosphere. The entire crew, including fifty Marines and a high-ranking government official, are killed. Six months later, President Wilcox and the heads of state of fifty other countries sign the Earth-Mars Pact, which pledges free exchange of science, the supply of vital products from Earth to the red planet, and the independence of the Martian colonies.

2075: The Red Science Consortium (RSC) is founded as the legal successor to the Mars Colonies and signatory to the Earth-Mars Pact.

2078: After decades of natural disasters resulting from an out-of-control climate crisis, eighty nations of Earth join together within the United Nations to form a federal state to deal with the economic damage and accelerate the removal of CO_2 from the atmosphere.

2081: Founding of the Outer Colony Coalition (OCC) as the political representative body of the lunar colonies of Jupiter and Saturn. Conclusion of free trade and alliance treaties with United Nations and RSC.

2084: The deep space probe *Frontier*, tasked with exploring Sol's heliosphere, encounters an extraterrestrial artifact within the heliopause nearly twelve billion miles from the Sun.

Timeline

2086: The *Frontier* artifact is claimed by the UN and placed under military control. As a result, all of Earth's remaining nation-states join the federal alliance.

2086: Establishment of the unified government, Government Central (GovCentral) as the UN's supreme governing body and dominant power in the solar system.

2089: Jupiter Bank established on Jupiter's Remus habitat as an extraterritorial enterprise with participation by all factions: United Nations of Earth, RSC of Mars, and OCC of the outer colonies.

2092: After years of secret research on the alien *Frontier* artifact, GovCentral announces that it is a probe that has a novel propulsion system, but it is inoperable.

2094: UN Defense Department engineers at Armstrong Fleet Base on Luna succeed in deciphering and reverse engineering the *Frontier* probe's propulsion system.

2098: With the help of the Red Science Consortium, construction of a new type of transport medium begins. The hyperspace slingshot is based on the replicated alien technology and is capable of enclosing smaller objects in a normal space bubble and catapulting them through subspace to distant locations without any loss of time.

2100: In the first successful test of the hyperspace slingshot, a twenty-centimeter diameter experimental probe is sent from Luna to Jupiter's Remus habitat and emerges at the destination point without loss of time.

2100-2150: Due to massive research efforts and rekindled interest in interstellar exploration, the first jump engines for larger ships are developed and the possible diameters of so-called 'subspace vacuoles' increase exponentially. Entire fleets of prospectors are sent out to explore and map distant solar systems after the gateway to the stars is opened.

2160: First Colonist Wave: Forty colony ships built over ten years in the orbital shipyards of Earth and Mars leave Sol and jump to neighboring systems with terra-compatible worlds after intensive research and exploration. Founding of the first human colony, New Eden, and thirty-nine others later known as 'Core Worlds'.

2175: Discovery of the Orb. When the prospector ship Rheinland encounters a system on the edge of explored territory that has long puzzled explorers due to physical anomalies, it scans a planet completely covered in metallic structures that emits no radio or gravity waves. During its research flight, the Rheinland is destroyed in an unexplained manner, but is able to send a rescue signal.

2175-2180: Discovery of more systems under the rule of the Orb, the name given by newsfeeds to the mysterious aliens due to unexplained light phenomena reported shortly before their destruction, according to the black box of the Rheinland.

2180-2200: Concerned about a conflict with the Orb, a period of massive armament by the UN, Mars and the outer colonies begins.

2184: Realizing that humanity is apparently not alone and that first contact with the Orb ended violently, the UN, RSC, and OCC join together to form the Solar Union, which all colonies in now over sixty systems join in the following years in hopes of protection and prosperity.

2186-2200: Second Colonist Wave: To address the growing overpopulation on Earth, more colonist ships are sent to colonize terra-compatible planets in the Solar Union frontier. Since GovCentral, as the governing body of Earth, can hardly cope with the growing criminality in the arcologies, it is decided to make far-reaching changes to the penal legislation, so that even minor offenses can result in forced deportation. Thus, the second wave of colonists is colloquially referred to as the 'inmate wave'.

Timeline

After initial unrest, GovCentral makes concessions in the form of paid family relocation for the convicts. Thus, within fourteen years, over one billion colonists leave.

2201: Establishment of the Corporate Council by the five most powerful corporate conglomerates of the Solar Union: Alpha Corporation, Dong Rae, Ruhr Heavy Industries, Yokatami, and Luna Mining Corporation become permanent members of the body, which is granted far-reaching powers by the Solar Union due to its economic power. As veto holders within the council, they are allowed to manage their own corporate sites, maintain their own police forces and enact their own laws in a limited form. A phase of accelerated liberalization of the economic system begins.

2204: When all diplomatic efforts of the Solar Union fail, open war breaks out between the hostile colonies of Arcturus and Kerhal. The Solar Navy, thinly scattered by the just-completed second wave of expansion, arrives too late as ships from the Arcturus colony completely devastate Kerhal with antimatter bombs, rendering it uninhabitable for centuries.

2205: Exclusion of Arcturus from the Solar Union for one hundred years. Complete blockade of the planet.

2206: Law is passed banning antimatter weapons. Ratification by all colonies and the Corporate Council.

2210: Discovery of the Kerrhain system and its asteroid belt with unusual object density. Start of plundering of the system by the Luna Mining Corporation.

2212: Beginning of Union-wide smuggling of Assai, a weed harvested on Kerrhain. The potent hallucinogen is banned that year, and Kerrhain is colonized and controlled by a military administration established by the Solar Union to stop the illegal trade.

2224: The first Seed Vessel is completed at the Lagrange shipyards near Luna and filled with biomass from the largely ravaged Earth. Built by the Corporate Council, it sets course for planet P3X-888.

2225: On P3X-888, christened 'Green Rain' by bloggers and newsfeed moderators, testing of new seed technology begins. By means of dropping huge amounts of biomass, a natural terraforming process is to be set in motion and accelerated by targeted geoengineering.

2229: The Corporate Council buys five more rocky planets in the habitable zones of three systems from the Solar Union and begins to initiate terraforming processes on the acquired worlds with additional Seed Vessels.

2233: Luhan Montgomery develops the first multi-intelligent nanites for human use at the University of New California. The so-called 'Smartnites' trigger a new economic miracle in the still thinly stretched Solar Union, helping previously resource-poor colonies rise through the relocation of Corporate Council production capacity in return for ever-expanding rights and lower local tax rates.

2235: Due to the breakthrough in nanite research and the emerging mass market for Smartnites, a wave of new developments in human and animal implant research follows. Smartnites act as a bridging technology to solve previous problems such as rejection, linkage to the central nervous system, and lack of maintainability of implants.

2238: On the colony of Khorwana, due to a software anomaly that remains unexplained to this day, a genocide of the population occurs at the hands of the local robot workers, known as Servitors. In just one night, which goes down in history as 'The Black Night of Khorwana', all eighty million inhabitants of the agricultural colony are systematically murdered.

2240: After two years of protests, the newly elected Union government institutes a Union-wide ban on autonomous workers, de facto outlawing all robots. In the 'Circuit Genocide', over one billion non-military robots are conscripted and scrapped within five years. The 'Human Empowerment Act' is officially implemented to protect jobs, and the mass murder at Khorwana is seen merely as a political legitimization for a long-struggling reform effort by conservative forces. The Corporate Council lodges an ex officio protest against the new legislation.

2243: When the Solar Union's largest rhodium deposit to date is discovered on the colony of Voria, the planetary Union Government opposes the granting of mining rights to members of the Corporate Council by the central government on Earth. Since this leaves the Union Navy without the means to exert military pressure and still entrusted with the collection of all robotic manpower, a controversial precedent is set: the mercenary corporation Black Nebula, a member of the Corporate Council, is hired to persuade the Voria government to relent after two rounds of negotiations remain fruitless. Voria threatens military countermeasures in case of a blockade, whereupon the 'Two-Hour Battle' takes place in orbit, during which the Black Nebula cruiser Harbinger crashes into the planet. Since the ship had apparently been storing illegal antimatter weapons, a catastrophe ensues, largely sterilizing the main continent of Antarga. Several colonies protest and summon the local representatives of the central government.

2245: Start of the Secession Wars: After Black Nebula is awarded another major contract to patrol the outer colonies despite the Voria disaster, and only management is replaced, twenty worlds band together and pay their own mercenary forces to fight back against the central government. When battle breaks out in the Dagestan system between a fleet of the 'Twenty Worlds Pact' and the Black Nebula Corporation, the Solar Union declares the Pact members renegades and declares a state of war for the first time since its formation.

2248: In a series of unexpected victories, the Pact is able to destroy or repel three Black Nebula fleets. With the new status quo and growing protests within the Union due to the general mobilization, more colonies declare independence.

2250: Formation of the Border Worlds, a loose confederation of a total of eleven colonies on the edge of the human expansion zone, which declare martial law and establish their own armed formations immediately after forming.

2253: The Corporate Council officially declares itself neutral in the conflict and bans Black Nebula from the Council as a non-permanent member, and decides to impose far-reaching sanctions on the mercenary corporation, which subsequently files for bankruptcy.

2254: Battle of Sigma Tiri: A Pact fleet receives unexpected support from the Border Worlds fleet moments before it is destroyed by a Solar Union force under Fleet Admiral Lucas Norton. The Union forces are forced to retreat.

2255: The weakened Pact colonies are attacked by fleet units of the Corporate Council, officially to stabilize a humanitarian emergency. In response, large segments of the Union loyalists declare war on the Corporate Council and launch attacks on the Seed Worlds, which are repelled by Union forces in an attempt to weaken all renegade elements in one fell swoop.

2257: Border Worlds units begin expelling corporate forces from the Pact Worlds and incorporate seven liberated colonies into their confederation.

2258: The widespread stalemate between the various

Timeline

factions of Border Worlds, Solar Union, Corporate Council, and worlds that have declared independence results in the truce of Carvis A, named for the only celestial body in the Carvis system, which is henceforth declared neutral.

2258-2290: In a time of relative peace, a political disintegration of the Solar Union begins. Migration to the independent colonies leads to a population implosion and labor shortages, pushed by the Corporate Council, which is able to take advantage of the situation and negotiate new tax benefits and mining concessions with the fragmented worlds. A period of economic and technological depression begins, in which former trade routes must first be rebuilt.

2290: Outbreak of the Consolidation Wars: After their secession from the Solar Union, many colonies sink into prolonged unrest, civil wars, and political trench warfare, resulting in increasing numbers of autocratic power grabs. Fragile and ever-shifting alliances and unions of convenience emerge between the worlds of humanity. The Solar Union sees in the weakness of its opponents its last chance for reunification under its banner and sends a federation of ten fleets under the command of Admiral Lucius McMaster. He is given the task of keeping order and forcing the renegade planets back into the Union. His campaign, which lasts a total of eight years, finally culminates in a victory over a fleet of sixty worlds, which can only be achieved with the support of the Border Worlds, which are promised far-reaching autonomy rights in return. McMaster becomes a folk hero in the resurgent Solar Union.

2300: Beginning of a tentative economic recovery through massive investment in rebuilding the war-torn Union worlds.

2302: In the Trabantius system, on the frontier with the

Orb worlds, an encounter occurs with three alien ships. During this encounter, several ships disappear without a trace. Calls for retaliation are heard on Earth.

2305: Orb ships are again sighted in the Trabantius system. Union Navy defenders intercept them, whereby their entire fleet is destroyed.

2306: Due to the devastating defeat of Trabantius, Admiral McMaster, hero of the Consolidation Wars, is tasked with building the Wall Worlds: the plan is to turn all of the ten Union systems on the edge of Orb territory into fortresses and establish them as bulwarks against the technologically superior enemy.

2309: After the electoral victory of nationalist parties and driven by a resurgent economy and militarization, calls for a campaign against the Orb increase. Critics see it as an attempt to prevent renewed secessionist wars within humanity. When Admiral McMaster appears publicly and refuses to implement plans to this effect, a warrant is issued for his arrest. This is followed by protests and riots throughout much of the Union Worlds. McMasters returns to Earth with his fleet and, with the support of the Union Admiralty, seizes power. Congress is dissolved, and all members of the government are imprisoned for endangering the Union and corruption. As a result of his seizure of power, McMaster publishes secret government documents purporting to prove that an offensive against the Orb was indeed being planned. He publicly justifies his assumption of power by saying that such a campaign would have meant the end of humanity and that he had taken an oath to protect it.

2310: Lucius McMaster is officially elected President of the Solar Union and begins a stringent restructuring of the political system, resulting in a military council taking over nearly all government functions. The election is

Timeline

considered error-prone and accompanied by irregularities. Beginning of the McMaster dynasty's rule.

2322: Founding of the Saturn Congress: After growing displeasure with McMaster's paternalistic style of leadership, he creates the Saturn Congress, consisting of a lower house, the Senate, and an upper house, the Military Council. Each world of the Union is given a seat in the Senate and thus a say in civilian jurisdiction.

2326: Appearance of the first Never swarm: When a swarm of unknown creatures attacks the colony world Turan-II on the edge of human dominion, there are no survivors. Turan-II disappears without a trace as a result of the invasion. Research stations in neighboring systems register the appearance of strong gravitational waves a few years later.

2328: Appearance of the second Never Swarm: A Union Navy deep space listening station detects a Never swarm heading for the New Berlin system. President McMaster personally leads the defense.

2329: During the Battle of New Berlin, McMaster's fleet is destroyed, but is able to disperse the swarm and prevent an even greater catastrophe.

2330: Lucius McMaster's eldest son, Malfoy, takes power. Contrary to his father, he is a lavish hedonist and unpopular with the people. His confirmation by the Saturn Congress leads to the first protests among the population and their brutal suppression in several Core Worlds.

2333: The Blockade War: When the Border Worlds, which emerged as constitutional monarchies from the Secession Wars, send an incendiary letter to Congress about growing tax burdens and a critical mention of President Malfoy McMaster, the latter imposes a trade blockade on the total of eighteen worlds.

2335: Kong Student Protests: On the Core World of

Kong, second only to Earth as the economic center of the Union, weeks of student protests erupt against the corrupt entanglements and debauched excesses of Malfoy McMaster and other dynasty members in high office, culminating in the July 1st Massacre in which six thousand students lose their lives.

2336: Unknown hackers release internal government documents revealing that McMaster himself ordered the shooting to put down the student protests of 2335. As a result, prolonged protests erupt on all university worlds.

2337: After the Border Worlds again protest to Congress and threaten to leave the Solar Union, McMaster has the heads of the Empire's families arrested and executed after a trial in Earth orbit. As the executions are broadcast live, the condemned turn to the student movement for final expressions of solidarity. Stylized images of the assassinated Border World leaders become a symbol of resistance throughout the Union.

2337-2340: Student Wars: Sparked by the protests and execution of the Eighteen Kings, the McMaster dynasty crumbles just a few decades after its founding. More and more worlds and alliances are turning against the president. The secessionists are led by the Monarchy Movement under King Augustin I of House Hartholm-Harrow, who is considered extremely popular and one of the earliest supporters of the students. He is supported by the Border World Alliance and several influential Core Worlds.

2341: Battle for Terra: King Augustin I arrives in the Sol system with his forces, targeting the center of the Solar Union's power. McMasters defends with the mighty Home Fleet and fleets of the Corporate Council, but they side with Augustin at the last second for reasons that remain unexplained to this day.

Timeline

2342: Augustin of the House Hartholm-Harrow is crowned emperor of the newly founded Terran Star Empire and the accompanying political reorganization of humanity, which has been shattered and fatigued by centuries of civil wars. Establishment of one hundred houses to control newly founded sectors of five inhabited systems each - the beginning of the High Nobility. Establishment of the Council of Nobility, appointment of one hundred Noble Houses and transfer of inhabited worlds to selected Governors from the Nobility.

2343: Dissolution of the Military Council and renaming of the upper chamber of Congress as the House of Lords with one seat for each of the one hundred High Lords.

2345: Establishment of the Corporate Protectorate. The Corporate Council receives its de facto independence by imperial decree. It is granted the five Seed Worlds as a new political entity in exchange for at least five hundred years of neutrality and an unlimited free trade agreement with the Terran Star Empire.

2348: Construction begins on the Imperial Palace in the Swiss Alps and restructuring of the Union Navy into the Imperial Navy.

2351: The first Invitro humans are cloned on Neuenstein and optimized for work on dangerous gas asteroids.

2354: Death of Emperor Augustin. Enthronement of his eldest son, who chooses the reign name Haeron I.

2355: The 'Cloning Decree': to combat a declining population and an impending labor shortage, Haeron I signs a law from the Saturn Congress that diverts large sums of research funding into optimizing cloning processes to provide labor for vacuum mining.

2360: After successful trials with the new clone population, Invitro workers are granted full civil rights.

2364: Star Empire cloning programs are expanded to

accommodate other industries affected by the labor shortage: Invitro workers begin to be used in infrastructure maintenance, construction, cleaning, heavy and vacuum industries.

2367: Ceus-III disaster: An unexplained accident on the mining asteroid Ceus-III in the Castilliana system causes two obsolete nuclear reactors to melt down, contaminating the entire station with radioactivity. One hundred workers are killed. Only eighty Invitro clones used on Ceus-III are saved, which are found in the rescue barges. As a result, racist riots break out across the Star Empire against the disparagingly named 'mutant' clones, who are blamed for the deaths of the victims.

2368: Death of Haeron I. The Emperor dies of unknown causes during a hunting trip on New Eden. Since all other hunt participants are also found dead - without visible violence - the investigation ends without results. Enthronement of his eldest son Haeron II.

2370: After the changes at the top of the Star Empire have provided some distraction, the conflict over the Invitro clones reignites when violent clashes break out in the Akkrulu Sector with militant Invitro groups advocating harsher punishment for racism and exclusion.

2371: When High Lord Gowan Harkin, governor of the colony, is assassinated aboard Neuenstein in the Akkrulu Sector, the Invitro underground claims responsibility, triggering a crisis that soon spreads throughout the Star Empire.

2372-2380: The Invitro Wars: After months of police raids and arrests of countless clones on nearly every world in the Star Empire, attacks and protests by the normal population for a tougher crackdown by Imperial security agencies against the clones become more frequent. After extremist elements in the Invitro movement succeed in blowing up the George Washington in orbit over New California, Haeron II declares martial law and empowers the Admiralty to quell the uprising. As a result of the clashes, millions of Invitros are persecuted and killed or executed. Those who survive are stripped of their civil rights and transferred to the forced service of state agencies, where they are used for dangerous and repetitive work. After a so-called 'trust process' of ten years, they will have the opportunity to apply for naturalization.

2380: Third appearance of the Never: When a Never swarm is detected approaching Rohol, after several months of preparation, an Imperial Navy defense fleet manages to prevent an infestation and the loss of the system. The victory at Rohol generates a renewed wave of public support for the Emperor.

2381: Disappearance of the research vessel Persephone in the Wall System Artemis when it jumps into subspace on course for Orb territory despite warnings from the stronghold forces. It later transpires that, contrary to current fleet doctrine, the Persephone was not fired upon because the Emperor's eldest daughter was on board as senior science officer.

2384: A devastating attack on the Vactram of Caledonia's capital Delize kills over two hundred Imperial Navy sailors who had been transported back to the shuttles from home leave in a special streetcar. A confessional message reveals the existence of a group calling itself the 'Republican Resistance' that rejects authoritarian rule by the Emperor.

2385: As a result of intense intelligence work by the Imperial Intelligence IIA, several Republican cells are rooted out within a few weeks, and their members are arrested and executed. This is followed by a wave of attacks on Core and Frontier Worlds of the Star Empire.

2389: Construction of a second fleet of Seed Vessels by

Timeline

the Corporate Protectorate for the Star Empire. A total of five ships are to be transferred to the Imperial Research Fleet within eight years.

2392: Terraforming of the five Seed Worlds by the Corporate Protectorate is deemed officially complete.

2401: Discovery of three Never swarms moving toward the Border World system of Andal by Imperial Remote Recon deep space listening posts.

GLOSSARY

42-QLUE: Mirage's ship. Originally a research vessel of the Science Corps newest *Thetis* class.
Council of Admiralty: The Council of Admiralty consists of the Navy's twenty-three fleet admirals and their chairman, the only admiral with the title 'Grand Admiral', who also serves as the Emperor's Chief of Staff.
Airjack 222: Old atmospheric plane built at the end of the 21st century, with manual controls.
Akkrulu Sector: Imperial sector consisting of five star systems, each with a colony in the Sigma Quadrant, which includes Newstone, which gained notoriety in the 2370s as the site where the Invitro Wars began with the assassination of Governor Gowan Harkin.
Alabama: An ice tug from the Andal system. Destroyed by unknown ship in 2401.
Alpha Corporation: One of the founding members of the Corporate Council. Permanent member of the Council and veto power. Founding member of the Corporate Protectorate. Specializes in high technology.
Alpha Prime: One of the five terraformed planets in the

Glossary

Corporate Protectorate, named after its founding company Alpha Corporation.

Andal: Border system and seat of the House of Andal. Known for its listening stations and shielding function of the western Seed Traverse.

Antibes Champagne: Expensive champagne from the French-born world of Antibes in the Taarth Quadrant.

Aquarius: Water world in the Taarth Quadrant. Its numerous atolls are also a popular retirement home for the high society of the Star Empire. The largest economic sector besides tourism is the export of fish and seafood.

Arcturus: Colony in the Omega Quadrant. In 2205, due to an attack with antimatter bombs on the hostile neighboring colony Kerhal, Arcturus was excluded from the then ruling Solar Union for one hundred years and subjected to a blockade. Since then an impoverished world, known for its notorious black market on the only space station 'Black Haven' and the high number of pirates in the system.

Arcturusgrad: Capital of the colony Arcturus.

Zurich Arcology: Large megaplex in what used to be Switzerland. Population: 30 million. Considered a relatively safe arcology for Earth and a 'suburb' of the Imperial Palace in and on Mont Blanc.

Assai Grass: A grass harvested exclusively on the colony of Kerrhain that causes hallucinations in humans accompanied by euphoric emotional states. Although its characteristic appearance resembles grass, botanically it is a rock lichen. Its cultivation and processing into (dried) assai as a drug are illegal, as is its sale in any form.

Breathing Pack: Emergency rescue device for spacefarers, consisting of a face mask with breathing tube and attached oxygen pack.

Imperial Navy Marine's Survival Manual: Navy

manual given to each recruit when he or she is sworn in, containing about one hundred pages (some of them illustrated) of information on everyday and unusual situations that a Navy soldier may encounter during his or her tour of duty.

Equalization Caverns: Large gas pressure vessels on rotating asteroids with their own gravity, which ensure that the rotation speed remains the same.

Autoinjector: Augment that can independently inject its user with various substances depending on pre-programmed conditions. Illegal for private users, autoinjectors are mainly intended for special units of the Army and Navy.

Avenger Assault Rifle: Standard Imperial Army assault rifle for combat in gravity wells.

Battlenet: Tactical combat software for networked fleet operations.

Black Haven: Only space station in orbit around the planet Arcturus. Considered a black market paradise and generally one of the most dangerous places in the Star Empire. This is because Arcturus has become economically insignificant after a hundred years of blockade by the Solar Union fleet, and there are no monetary interests there.

Black Nebula: Former mercenary corporation and non-permanent member of the Corporate Council, which had to declare bankruptcy in 2253 after many scandals and its expulsion from the Council. Its role in the Secession War of the 2200s is considered pivotal.

Flash Compensators: protective eye wear that shields its users from overly bright light effects that could otherwise damage the retina or impair vision.

Bone Eaters: Former invitro gang of the world of Kerrhain that saw itself as a rallying point for escaped

Glossary

clones from across the Star Empire. After long hiding in the jungles of Kerrhain and repeatedly committing attacks on the colonial authorities, they were offered exile in the system's asteroid belt, which they accepted. Since then, they have become notorious for smuggling Assai grass.

Botcha: Popular drink made from an herb of the same name, endemic to the core world Grassia and at the same time the only industry. Caffeinated and stimulating with a sweet and bitter note. Since its discovery, the plant which is sold as a powder has now replaced coffee as the most commonly drunk hot beverage.

Bragge: Largest moon of the gas giant Kolsund in the Andal system.

C-555-X: Plundered asteroid in the Kerrhain system.

Caledonia: Colony in the Taarth quadrant. Its capital, Delize, is known in the Star Empire for a serious terrorist attack on naval personnel that killed over 200 sailors in 2384.

Carbotanium: Hardest known composite in the Star Empire, used for starship armor, among other things, and composed largely of Carbin and titanium.

Carvis: Name of a planetless system and its only celestial body, the asteroid Carvis A, where a truce is signed by the Solar Union, Border Worlds and Corporate Council in 2258.

Castilliana: System and planet in the Sigma Quadrant. Famous for its heavy export of high-end cosmetics and smart-tattoo ink. The system gained said notoriety for the Ceus-III disaster.

Cazacone: An organized crime syndicate with presence throughout the Star Empire, commonly and incorrectly called the 'Mafia'. Considered extremely well-connected up to the highest levels of government and infamous for its cruelty.

Glossary

Ceus-III: Former mining asteroid in the Castilliana system, now deserted. In 2367, the Ceus-III catastrophe occurred when a reactor accident leaked radiation and killed the entire human work force, while the eighty Invitro clones who had been deployed were able to escape to safety via escape pods. The tragic event is generally considered the initial spark that later led to the Invitro Wars.

Chemsniffer: Sensor unit used to detect and analyze chemicals in the air and on surfaces. It is available either as an augment or as a handheld.

Com Barque: Communication buoy capable of receiving and transmitting signals at designated jump points within systems and relaying them to drones equipped with jump thrusters, which relay their messages to target system com barques.

Credstick: Personalized data carrier on which all the owner's banking information is stored, including his or her identity data. Central means of payment in the Star Empire.

The Net: Internet analog that works without VR components but with AR support. Unlike the Dataverse, it does not require a neural computer for use.

The Network: Mysterious secret organization. Known members: 'the Voice', 'Mirage'. Former member: 'Zenith', who appears to be Lord Janus Darishma.

Datamotes: Nanocomputers that can form complex neural patterns in the form of nanite swarms in the brain tissue of their users and support neural computers in their work. They are capable of accelerating thought processes and organizing them like a file system.

Dataverse: The Dataverse is a complex virtual network consisting of a pure data plane, accessible via external devices and resembling the Internet of the 21st century,

Glossary

and a virtual plane consisting of the sum of all its users and connected devices, which can be experienced as a parallel reality using neural computers. The third is the AR layer, a kind of virtual overlay of reality by means of which digital elements can be superimposed on the user's field of view.

The Forbidden Planet: Planet on the edge of the Omega Quadrant, discovered in the 22nd century by one of the first prospector ships, and famous for its Saphyra trees, of which only two have been sighted on the jungle world. One was later taken to the Rubov Habitat of Terra as a gift to the Emperor, the other is being cared for on the forbidden planet. Conspiracy theorists believe that secret Science Corps research facilities are located there, studying technologies of the extinct alien civilization that once inhabited the planet. The entire system is a restricted military area and is closely guarded.

The Black Night of Khorwana: A name given to the genocide of the population of the planet of the same name by its robot workers (Servitors) in 2238. The reason was a software anomaly that is still unexplained today. All 80 million colonists were murdered. The Black Night of Khorwana is considered the trigger for the so-called circuit genocide, as a result of which all Servitors and most work bots were banned and destroyed.

Diffundator: Medical device and successor to hypodermic needles. By means of high pressure and active substances atomized to minute particles, the drugs contained therein are 'pushed' through the patient's skin.

Digicolors: Digital dyes that are used to dye clothing, among other things. They can arrange themselves into nanonic circuits and thus change their color or map complex patterns on fabrics.

Glossary

Duroglas: Particularly resistant, mono-bonded polymer glass.

Dust System: Fiefdom of the younger brother of Emperor Haeron II, Jurgan Hartholm-Harrow. His eponymous colony is considered economically insignificant, hosts several training centers of corporate Protectorate mercenary companies due to its remoteness and strict local privacy laws.

E-15 Clearance: Security clearance for enlisted personnel who have completed at least fifteen years of service. Considered the highest security clearance for crew ranks and is relevant for access to sensitive ship areas, such as mechanics.

ECM Launcher: Electronic Counter-Measure Launcher. Augment that emits targeted electronic jamming signals to disrupt hardware and software.

***Einherjar* Orbital Ring:** Orbital ring around the planet Andal, completed in 2350 and used primarily for military and trade purposes.

Evac Bubble: Rescue device for operations in a vacuum. A self-deploying cocoon that protects its occupant from the vacuum for up to forty-eight hours, providing oxygen, heat, and water. Its shell is extremely durable and protects against the impact of debris - up to a certain kinetic force.

Ferret Class: Latest class of Imperial Navy corvettes. Lightly armed and fast.

Flynites: Nanites for spacefarers programmed to line the endothelium of vessels and harden or widen as required, for example to prevent strokes under extreme acceleration forces.

FXTP: One of the two most important exchanges in the Star Empire. The FXTP (Free Exchange Trade Platform) is located on Alpha Prime in the Corporate Protectorate

Glossary

and is considered a counterweight to the mighty JFTSE around Jupiter.

Gagantua Oak: Special species of tree that was originally indigenous to New Eden, but grows on all Core Worlds. Due to the long growth times before it can be harvested, its wood is extremely expensive and sought after.

Gamorah: Colony in the Taarth Quadrant that is a popular vacation destination for guests from throughout the quadrant.

Gleuse: Gas giant in the Kerrhain system.

Grad Forest: Forest area on the colony of Arcturus, north of the capital Arcturusgrad. Adjacent to the spaceport. Considered to be cursed by the local population and used as a hideout by local gangs. There is a road that runs through the forest, dividing it in half.

Grassia: Core World in the Taarth quadrant known for its export of botcha powder.

Grassov: Border World in the Sigma Quadrant, famous for its mines and corruption.

Grid Bike: Electric motorcycle that is Gridlink-compatible and can therefore drive autonomously.

Gridlink: Traffic guidance system for autonomous driving used throughout the Star Empire and controlled by highly sophisticated but weak AIs. Connection to the system is mandatory for every car owner.

Hadron: Homeworld and fiefdom of Lord Janus Darishma, First Secretary of State.

Hain: Gas giant in the Kerrhain system.

Hatzach Deer: Rare antlered deer of the cloven-hoofed genus found only on the colony of Lapiszunt and resembling Terran deer. Named for its discoverer, zoologist Montgomery Hatzach.

Hofzacher Plaza: Luxury hotel in the Zurich arcology.

Caver: Colloquial term for veteran technicians on the

Glossary

Cerberus space station who are tasked with maintaining the equalization caverns.

Imperial State Bank: State bank of the Star Empire, responsible for interest rate policy and budget management, among other things.

Pulse Launcher: Prototype implant weapon of unknown origin.

IIA: Imperial Intelligence Agency, the most important secret service of the Star Empire. Reports directly to the Emperor.

Indirium: Core World in the Sigma Quadrant, known for its exotic flora and consisting largely of protected national parks.

Inferno Rifle: Standard rifle for the Star Empire's space forces. Optimized for use in microgravity, fires ammunition with its own rocket engine, keeping the weapon recoilless.

Invitro Wars: The Invitro Wars are a period between 2372 and 2380 in which brutal purges of the clone population occur as a result of the CEUS-III disaster and preceding mass unrest. Most clones become victims of the police and Navy or the death squads of Emperor Haeron II, whose existence he denies until today.

JFTSE: The *Jupiter Free Trade Stock Exchange* is the Star Empire's most important and largest stock exchange by transactions. It is located on the Jupiter habitat of Remus and is controlled by the Jupiter Bank.

Jupiter Bank: The Jupiter Bank is a powerful institution in the Star Empire that has special status as a separate political and economic entity, similar to the Corporate Protectorate. Formally, it does not report to the Emperor and is independent. Its banking secrecy and the high volume of deposits it manages are considered a kind of shield against any form of interference and threat to its

Glossary

sovereignty. Along with the Imperial State Bank, the Jupiter Bank is the Star Empire's largest lender.

Cacodemon: Attack software that infiltrates and takes over data systems. They are illegal, in that they are based on complex artificial intelligences that are outlawed according to imperial laws.

Karadan: Rural colony in the Omega Quadrant. Famous for its wines and whiskeys.

Karadian Whiskey: Extremely expensive, peated whiskey from the colony of Karadan.

Karpshyn Sector: Border World sector consisting of five systems and three inhabited colonies. Fiefdom of the Andal family. Wealthy and known for its defense industry and wood products.

Kepal: Slang term for a buddy (miner) who works on asteroids. Used synonymously in the Star Empire for a pal/acquaintance. The short form 'ke' is considered a familiar nickname among members of the Navy.

Notched Tooth: Predator at the top of the food chain on Kerrhain Colony. Females engage in sexual cannibalism after mating by eating the respective male.

Kerhal: Kerhal is a former Solar Union colony that is completely devastated in 2204 by ships from the hostile colony Arcturus dropping antimatter bombs. Only a few descendants of the colonists are still alive today.

Kerrhain: Neighboring system of Andal and part of the Border Worlds. Ruled by High Lady Isha Kerrhain.

KH-1: Central star of the Kerrhain system.

Khorwana: Colony in the Sigma quadrant. See also 'The Black Night of Khorwana'.

Kolsund: Gas giant in the Andal system.

Kong: Core World of the Star Empire, where student protests occur in 2335, considered the beginning of the fall of the McMaster dynasty.

Copter: Flying machines with VTOL capability that are among the most widely built vehicles in the Star Empire for private and military end users.

Kushiro: One of the three inhabited worlds in the Corporate Protectorate. Headquarters of the Yokatami corporation.

Lagastia: Frontier World in the Zephyros quadrant, over ninety percent of which is covered by jungle and has no oceans. However, there are huge river systems that criss-cross the forests.

Lapiszunt: Sparsely populated colony in the Sigma Quadrant, considered a paradise for xenobiologists due to its complex and diverse biosphere.

Laprache: Tree species endemic to the colony of Indirium. A single specimen can grow roots and other trees up to several square miles, all of which are one coherent organism.

Light Hauler: Class of light freighters consisting of a connector between the cockpit and the engine section to which standardized cargo containers can be attached. Most common freighter type in the Star Empire, built for over eighty years.

Lugano: System with Frontier World of the same name, bordering the Seed Traverse.

Luna Mining Corporation: Considered humanity's first megacorporation, *Luna Mining Corporation* specializes in mining resources in vacuum and microgravity. Member of the Corporate Council, veto power in the Corporate Protectorate.

Maglock: Magnetic lock. A magnet is embedded in the frame (of doors, for example), which closes the magnetic door or opens it (when the polarity of the magnet is reversed).

Medidoc: Automated medical supply unit.

Glossary

Medicasket: The Medicasket is a closed medical capsule whose interior can be kept sterile and is used for robotic operations or induced stasis states for severely injured patients who require more intensive medical treatments.
Mirage: Code name of an unknown agent.
***Morning Star*:** The *Morning Star* is a former passenger liner. Destroyed by an unknown ship in 2401.
Myelination: Process on Seed Vessels in which minute clumps of biomass are encased by a thin but tough layer of polyp to protect them from atmospheric entry forces on Seed Planets.
Nanocephalon: Prototype of a neural computer extension that massively increases working memory and computing power and is designed to increase the cognitive abilities of its users many times over.
Net Crawlers: Automated programs that search the web for data.
Neuenstein: Core World in the Akrulu Sector. Major colony for Navy research and development, fiefdom of the Crown Princes of House Hartholm-Harrow. Famous for its film industry and the assassination of its governor, Gowan Harkin, whose murder by Invitro extremists in 2371 triggered the Invitro Crisis and ultimately the Invitro Wars.
Neural Accelerator: Augment that greatly accelerates the nerve impulse conduction in the spinal cord of its users.
Neural Computer: Miniature computer implanted on the brain stem that allows its users access to biological monitoring and bodily functions. A necessary interface to control other augments of the human body and nanites such as Flynites or Smartnites.
Neural Shocker: Fingernail-sized projectiles that flood those hit with electrical impulses that overload the

nervous system and can cause everything from twitching to convulsions to epileptic seizures.

Neuroburn: Combat stimulant that makes its users more responsive. Side effects from the drug wearing off lead to depressive moods, dry mouth, and accelerated dehydration.

New California: Core World of the Star Empire in the Omega Quadrant. Famous for its movie industry and orbital shipyards.

New Eden: Humanity's first colony and now a major Core World. In addition to its considerable Science Corps facilities located throughout the system, New Eden is considered a popular vacation destination for high society.

Zero-Humidity Capsule: Stasis capsule for long space flights or preservation of its users indefinitely.

Omega-Zero: Secluded colony in the Taarth Quadrant.

P3X-888: First terraforming world of the Corporate Council, colloquially known as 'Green Rain' after the first Seed Vessel, which was able to turn what was once a rocky world with an atmosphere but no biosphere into an Earth-like planet by jettisoning biomass.

Section 2, paragraph 1 of the Interplanetary Space Traffic Act: Section 2, paragraph 1 of the Interplanetary Space Traffic Act states that any ship is obligated to render assistance to another when it declares an emergency.

Poznan: Polish-ethnic Core World of the Star Empire.

Protein Synthesizer: Automated supply unit on starships that can extract or recombine proteins from all organic source molecules to produce food for its users.

Protozyme Lacuna: Bionic, automatic drug dispenser that must be cloned for the adrenal cortices of its users. Extremely expensive and difficult to obtain, they are largely reserved for nobility.

Psycho-Physiognomics Software: Software that uses

Glossary

artificial intelligence coupled with optic nerve impulses to analyze people's complex facial expressions and draw conclusions about the intentions and feelings of others.

Pulau Weh: World discovered in 2393 in the 777-Goggins system, beyond the Tartarus Void. It is considered biodiverse and habitable, but devoid of usable resources and insignificant due to its distance from the Zephyros Quadrant.

Quantcom: Network of novel com barques that enable faster-than-light communications through non-local quantum effects within star systems.

Queensferry: Main system of Wall Sector Gamma, home of Fleet Admiral Samuel Taggert.

Radendron: Although house-sized, Radendron are classified by botanists as flowers native to the endless oceans of New Eden. Their flowers form a dense cocoon around the ovary and serve as habitat for numerous non-aquatic life forms.

Rapier: Type of shock launcher built by Yokatami that fires neural shockers.

Raptor Engine: Latest generation of compact fusion engines from the Yokatami corporation.

Reaper Suit: Navy's lightweight, vacuum-capable protective suit consisting of an interconnected swarm of programmable nanites with their own oxygen supply, inhaled in liquid form.

Recycler: Waste system that returns all materials deposited to their original molecules and thus recycles them.

Reface Mask: Nanonic face mask that conforms to the shape of its user's face and can alter characteristic features to disguise the wearer's identity.

Rejuvenation: Anti-aging treatment performed with a

Glossary

mix of telomere extension, pluripotent stem cell injection, and NAD+ enhancers.

Rjubel: Local currency not linked to the Imperial Crown on the colony of Arcturus.

***Rubov* Orbital Ring:** Orbital ring around the Earth, and humanity's first orbital ring. Seat of important institutions such as the Council of Nobility and the Council of Admiralty.

Ruthenium Polymer: Special fabric composed of the transition metal ruthenium and several plastics to allow an adherent nanite swarm on its surface to form complex light refraction patterns.

S1-Ruhr: Seed World in the Seed Traverse, which is under the control of Ruhr Heavy Industries.

S2-Yokatami: Seed World in the Seed Traverse, which is under the control of Yokatami. Restricted Area.

***Saphyra*:** Tree species of which only two specimens are known in the entire Star Empire. They come from the forbidden planet and, according to the findings of the Science Corps, are not of natural origin. They are believed to be chimeras of evolved and technological elements. The extremely complex structure of the trees and its internal processes still puzzle researchers today. Little is officially known about their creators or breeders.

***Saratoga* Class:** Class of Imperial Navy destroyers. Medium heavy.

Saturn Parliament: The Saturn Parliament is located on the Aurora habitat in orbit around Saturn and is the seat of the Upper and Lower Houses of Parliament: the House of Lords and the Senate.

Schofield&Brugger: Private bank. Located on New California.

Second Skin Glove: High-tech glove that puts a second artificial skin with fake DNA over the user's hand and is used to trick DNA or fingerprint scanners. Illegal in the Star Empire.

Sensor Dust: Nanites that can be sprayed over large areas on surfaces such as house facades or asphalt and can transmit simple sensor data (for example, pressure, humidity, structural integrity, temperature, etc.).

Sequestration Software: Illegal software designed to make copies of systems it infiltrates that are indistinguishable from the original. After this process, the original system (without its security mechanisms) is replaced and the user is granted full access.

Sigma Tiri: Core system in the Sigma Quadrant, which in 2254 becomes the scene of a major battle between a Pact fleet and the Solar Union, in which the Union forces suffer a major defeat due to the intervention of a Border World fleet.

Skaland: Capital of the Border World Andal and seat of the Andal family.

Skyhook: Heavy transporter used by the Imperial Navy for ground offensives launched from orbit. Produced by Yokatami.

Smartgun: Implant weapon capable of firing programmable high velocity projectiles.

Smartnites: Programmable pluripotent nanites that circulate in the bloodstream of humans, giving them control over important bodily functions.

Sokhol: One of the three inhabited worlds of the Corporate Protectorate. Headquarters of Dong Rae and Luna Mining Corporation.

Somawatcher: Intelligent sensor that can detect the presence of humans and transmit it to a receiver unit. An integrated AI system can interpret the recorded data (ultrasound, infrared, residual light) and distinguish from other living beings.

Southhain: Capital of the Border World of Kerrhain.
Jump Node: Part of the engines of interstellar starships used to generate subspace vacuoles, which are used to enable jumps through subspace.
Stolbova Iron Mines: Extensive mines northeast of Arcturusgrad on Arcturus Colony.
Supervisor: Title of Chairman of the Supervisory Board of the five veto groups in the Group Protectorate.
Taarth Quadrant: Quadrant in interstellar southwest Sol.
Targetlink: Intelligent targeting optics that enable (appropriately equipped) handguns to provide direct eye-target coordination via induction pads in the hands of their users, significantly increasing hit rates.
Tarshan: Capital of the former colony Turan-II in the Turan system. Lost in 2236 in the course of a Never infestation.
Tartarus Void: Empty area in the south of the Zephyros quadrant where there are no star systems.
Tech Aura: Electronic signature of people and objects.
Terra One: Most important and widely watched news feed in the Star Empire.
Thunderbolt Pistol: Standard Imperial Army pistol for combat in gravity wells.
Titan Motorized Armor: Latest generation of motorized armor used by Imperial Navy Marines.
Trabantius: A whale world on the border of Orb territory.
Trafalgar System: Star system, part of Wall Sector Delta. 200 million inhabitants.
Tranit: Colony in the interstellar northwest of Sol, neighboring the Border Worlds and the fiefdom of First Secretary of State Lord Janus Darishma. Economically rather insignificant.

Glossary

Transducer: Augment that allows its users (voice) communication via thought.

Triumph Class: Latest class of Imperial Navy frigates optimized for speed and high mobility.

Tromso Electronics LLC: Major telecommunications company on Andal.

Turan-II: Former colony world in the Turan system that fell victim to the first Never infestation in 2236.

Turing Agreement: 2062 UN agreement outlawing strong AIs, later adopted and ratified by all members of the Solar Union and also became part of Imperial legislation.

Universal Connector: Universal connector in the Star Empire, also used synonymously for universal connectors compatible with the same.

Ushuaia: Former *Light Hauler*-class freighter. Destroyed by the *Glory* in 2401 in the Andal system.

Vactram: High-speed passenger train that travels in frictionless vacuum tubes and is the primary means of public transportation throughout the Star Empire.

Vacuum Forensics: Special forensics area of the Space Police to solve crimes that take place in a vacuum. This includes, among other things, the analysis of radiation, debris, gravitational waves.

Vault Ultras: Elite thugs of the Vaults (see 'Vaults'), recruited from Invitro clones of particular brutality and loyalty.

Vaults: Former gang of the Border World of Kerrhain, which expanded rapidly through the profitable smuggling of Assai grass. Now considered one of the most important criminal conglomerates in the Border Worlds.

VR-Stim: Stimulating VR simulations, which are often pornographic productions, but also violent immersions.

Wall Sector Delta: Sector consisting of five star systems

Glossary

in the wall areas separating the Star Empire from Orb territory. Under the command of Fleet Admiral Dain Marquandt.

Warfield Armored Reconnaissance & Security: Insignificant mercenary group in the corporate protectorate.

Science Corps: The Science Corps is a major institution that coordinates all of the Star Empire's research and development projects. Maintains offices in virtually every university in the human-controlled territory and is the most important scientific institution in the Star Empire.

Zenith: Former alias of Lord Janus Darishma.

Cerberus Station: Secret space station in the asteroid belt of Kerrhain. Seat of the Broker and major transshipment point for Assai grass and other black market goods.

Zulustra crabs: Seafood specialty on New Eden. The native crabs are eaten alive there as a delicacy, usually with an expensive champagne sauce.

CHARACTERS

Adam Goosens: Administrator of the Cerberus Station.
Admiral Giorgidis: Commander of the Ruhr Heavy Industries corporate fleet.
Admiral Heusgen: Fleet Admiral and member of the Council of Admiralty.
Admiral Ramone: Fleet Admiral and new commander of the Wall Fleets in the Epsilon Sector.
Admiral Takahashi: Fleet Admiral and member of the Council of Admiralty.
Afrin Makuba: High-ranking agent of the Imperial Intelligence Agency IIA.
Agent Walker: Agent of the IIA. Specializes in undercover operations.
Akwa Marquandt: Captain of the Imperial Navy and daughter of Fleet Admiral Dain Marquandt.
Artas Andal: Eldest son of High Lord Cornelius Andal.
Broker, the: Mysterious information broker in the Kerrhain system.
Cornelius Andal: High Lord of the House of Andal and Governor of the Karphshyn Sector.

Characters

Dimitri Rogoshin: COO of the Warfield Armored Reconnaissance & Security mercenary group. Former Colonel in the Marines.
Dyke Keko: Captain of the ice tug *Alabama*.
Elayne Hartholm-Harrow: Youngest daughter of Emperor Haeron II. Holds the title of Princess.
Elisa Andal: Daughter of High Lord Cornelius Andal.
Elisabeth Detton: Chairman of the Supervisory Board and Supervisor of Alpha Corporation.
Enrique Fuao: Director of Imperial Intelligence Agency IIA.
Filio Jericho: Fleet Admiral and member of the Council of Admiralty.
Giulio Adams: Courier of the Senate President Varilla Usatami.
Gowan Harkin: Former governor of Neuenstein, assassinated by Invitro extremists in 2371.
Huelga Ferreira: First officer on the *Ushuaia*. Wife of Manuél Ferreira. Physicist.
Ikabot Nurheim: Head of the Seed Vessel *Demeter* with the rank of First Executive at Ruhr Heavy Industries.
Isha Kerrhain: High Lady of the House of Kerrhain.
Janus Darishma: First Secretary of State to Emperor Haeron II. Lord and Governor of Tranit Colony.
Jean Sapin: Mayor of the Arcology Paris.
Jennifer Orlan: Chairman of the Supervisory Board and Supervisor of Luna Mining Corporation.
Johanna Teunen: Captain of the passenger liner *Morning Star*.
Jonathan Haifer: Personal assistant to Ludwig Sorg.
Jurgan Hartholm-Harrow: Younger brother of Emperor Haeron II. Lives in exile on Dust.
Ludwig Sorg: Chairman of the Supervisory Board and Supervisor of Ruhr Heavy Industries.

Characters

Manuél Ferreira: Captain of the *Ushuaia*. Husband of Huelga Ferreira.
Mariella Andal: Daughter of High Lord Cornelius Andal.
Masha Smailski: Arcturian, mother of Artiom and Oleana.
Min Sok Hyun: Chairman of the Supervisory Board and Supervisor of Dong Rae.
Nancy: Secretary of Janus Darishma.
Narun Grassimus: High Lord of the Star Empire.
Nova Ladalle: Fleet Admiral and member of the Council of Admiralty.
Orlon Kerrhain: Former High Lord of Kerrhain Colony and father of Isha Kerrhain.
Pedro Bachelet: Fleet Admiral and member of the Council of Admiralty.
Praia Hartholm-Harrow: Eldest daughter of Emperor Haeron II. Declared missing since the disappearance of the research vessel *Persephone* in 2381. Princess.
Samuel Taggert: Fleet admiral and commander of the Gamma Sector's rampart fleets. His homeworld is Queensferry in the same sector. Considered a fiercely loyal companion of Emperor Haeron II.
Sato Ran: Chairman of the Supervisory Board and Supervisor of Yokatami.
Sophie Andal: Wife of High Lord Cornelius Andal.
Tatjana Schaparowa: Manager of Luna Mining Corporation in the position of First Executive and highest diplomatic representative of her corporation on Luna. Studied mathematics.
Varilla Usatami: President of the Saturn Senate and highest civilian politician of the Star Empire. Former xenobiologist of the Science Corps.
Xavier Bennington: Alias of Gavin Andal.

Characters

Yoshi Ketambe: Member of the management level of Yokatami.
Zara Vance: Chief of the New York Arc Police.

AFTERWORD

Dear Reader,

I hope you also enjoyed this second volume. The first trilogy will be completed with *The Last Fleet 3: Fog of War*. If you'd like to contact me directly, feel free to do so at joshua@joshuatcalvert.com – I still answer every email. As always, I would be very happy to receive a review for this book on Amazon.

If you subscribe to my newsletter, I regularly chat a bit about myself, writing, and the great themes of science fiction. Plus, as a thank you, you'll receive my e-book *Rift: The Transition* exclusively and for free: www.joshuatcalvert.com

Best wishes, Joshua T. Calvert

Printed in Great Britain
by Amazon